MW01519689

Norman Cristofoli began his creative career as a young man writing poetry in the city of Toronto, Canada. In 1984, on top of Mount Snowden in Wales, Great Britain, he made the transition from a person who wrote poetry to a person who is a poet. He has published several chapbooks of poetry and prose and produced two audio compilations of his spoken-word performances accompanied by musicians.

He was the creator and publisher of the Labour of Love literary magazine for twenty-five years, and in 2020, he published his play, *The Pub,* followed by his first major compilation of poetry entitled *Relinquishing the Past.*

Novembers is the first in a series of murder/mystery novels.

For my daughter and grandchildren,
they are my heart
For my family, friends, and lovers,
they are my soul

Norman Cristofoli

NOVEMBERS

For Norm

Life is a mystery -
Fill yours with music
Fill yours with awe!

Norman Cristofoli

AUSTIN MACAULEY PUBLISHERS™

LONDON * CAMBRIDGE * NEW YORK * SHARJAH

Copyright © Norman Cristofoli 2023

All rights reserved. No part of this publication may be reproduced, distributed, or transmitted in any form or by any means, including photocopying, recording, or other electronic or mechanical methods, without the prior written permission of the publisher, except in the case of brief quotations embodied in critical reviews and certain other non-commercial uses permitted by copyright law. For permission requests, write to the publisher.

Any person who commits any unauthorized act in relation to this publication may be liable to criminal prosecution and civil claims for damages.

This is a work of fiction. Names, characters, businesses, places, events, locales, and incidents are either the products of the author's imagination or used in a fictitious manner. Any resemblance to actual persons, living or dead, or actual events is purely coincidental.

Ordering Information
Quantity sales: Special discounts are available on quantity purchases by corporations, associations, and others. For details, contact the publisher at the address below.

Publisher's Cataloging-in-Publication data
Cristofoli, Norman
Novembers

ISBN 9798886937572 (Paperback)
ISBN 9798886937589 (ePub e-book)

Library of Congress Control Number: 2023919480

www.austinmacauley.com/us

First Published 2023
Austin Macauley Publishers LLC
40 Wall Street, 33rd Floor, Suite 3302
New York, NY 10005
USA

mail-usa@austinmacauley.com
+1 (646) 5125767

20231201

A heartfelt thank you to Janet Connors, Chantal Cloutier, Ivy Reiss and Brandon Pitts for reading the raw manuscript and providing insightful comments. Thank you to my family and friends for their integral support throughout the entire creation and publication process, especially Brenda Clewes. A humongous thank you to Richard Mongiat for his wonderful artwork that graces the front cover (richardmongiat.com).

Lastly, an honorary thank you for the writers who inspired me with their works: Herman Hesse, Kurt Vonnegut, Raymond Chandler, Dashiell Hammett, George Orwell, Henry Miller and Simon Occulis.

Chapter One

The sharp hard knock on the front door sounded as if someone was using a hammer on an angry nail.

Ivan looked down at his gold-plated wristwatch and wondered who would be knocking at this hour of the evening. '*It was too early for her,*' he thought to himself, '*unless the sale went well and competing buyers over-bid for a house worth less than its listing.*' He walked to the door, peered through the peephole and saw a man in a dark polyester parka with the bright yellow Delivery Corp insignia on both shoulders. The woven toque on his head also had the Delivery Corp patch sewn on the front.

"Who is it?" he asked gruffly.

"Delivery Corp," said the man. "I have an express envelope for Mister Ivan Malinkov."

Ivan looked at his watch. "Isn't it a bit late for you guys to be making deliveries?" he said, annoyed to be bothered, wanting no interruptions for the evening he had planned.

"I'm just finishing the last delivery on my route," the man pleaded with a tone that indicated he wanted to finish for the day, "I have an envelope for you," which he held up for Ivan to see.

Documents were often sent in the evenings, but it was unusual for delivery companies to bring them. However, as a real estate agent, it was something he had to expect as offers, counter-offers, and lawyers' papers were part of the business. He opened the door with an annoyed sigh.

The baseball bat was thrust forward like a short Roman spear. The blunt end hit him on the bridge of the nose and there was a clear, defined sound of bone cracking. Ivan let out a verbal howl that was part curse and part yell as he staggered backward. Stepping into the doorway, the Delivery Corp man thrust the bat forward once more, hitting Ivan directly in the groin.

The breath escaped Ivan's body as if a pump had sucked it out of him, and he crumpled forward, landing upon his knees, holding his groin, trying to catch his breath, trying to assimilate the pain, the confusion, the terror and the future, all at once.

The Delivery Corp man quickly closed the door behind him and moved toward Ivan. The cathedral ceilings allowed him room to maneuver and he now set about incapacitating his victim. He brought the bat down hard upon Ivan's left ankle.

There was another sound of bone cracking, and this time Ivan screamed. A deep scream that came from somewhere within the hollow of his soul. A scream so deep that you could hear the vocal cords stretch, snap and turn as raw as rusted metal. He tumbled over, laying on the floor, whimpering monosyllable vowels, interspersed between the raw throaty screams.

The Delivery Corp man called him by name, "Hey Ivan," but the man on the floor didn't acknowledge the call for his attention, so the Delivery Corp man forced attention upon him. He raised the bat once more and brought it down upon the back of Ivan's left hand that was reaching for his broken ankle.

This time he couldn't hear any bones crack because of the continuous noise of howling vowels, but he figured something must have broken because the pitch of the howling changed. He raised the bat once more and brought it down with as much force as he could muster on Ivan's other extremity. It was a direct hit on the shin bone of Ivan's right leg, but it was hard to tell if Ivan could even feel the new pain as the intensity of shock had begun to encapsulate his body, and each successive blow of unrequited violence may have been muted.

The Delivery Corp man called his name again, a little louder, and with force, "Hey Ivan!"

Ivan's tear-filled, blurred eyes turned toward his assailant. Bubbling saliva dripping out of his mouth, down his cheek and onto the floor.

"Hey!" he yelled at him again, "are you listening? I'm running out of bones to break."

Ivan just stared at him, or he just stared without any real acknowledgement of anything but the pain. He was falling into that zone when the brain shuts down in a desperate mode of survival. Clinically, it is called severe shock and the mind turns off any comprehension of pain. Nonetheless, the Delivery Corp man wanted to reach him before he shut down completely.

"How does it feel?" he yelled at him. "How does it feel to be the answer to my question, the effect to my cause, the end result to the formulation of my hypothesis? How does it feel to be at the far swing of the pendulum?"

He continued to glare down at Ivan, but after a moment he began to chuckle to himself as he realized the ridiculousness of his absurd questions. He was talking poetic, and Ivan was thinking Paleozoic. He saw that Ivan was losing focus and he bent to one knee so that Ivan could see him.

"I didn't do this for her," he said, "this was purely for me, my satisfaction, my ascendancy."

The Delivery Corp man stood and walked to the kitchen. He removed the phone from its recharging cradle and put it in his pocket. He walked back to what he considered was a mound of wasted humanity, now staring wide-eyed and continuing to make the sound of soft vowels because the brain could no longer construct consonants to go with the vowels.

He looked down at his prey and said, "If I remember correctly, there's a phone upstairs in your bedroom. If you can reach it, maybe you'll survive."

Then the eyes of the Delivery Corp man turned steel, not bright shiny steel, but dark, gritty construction steel that is hard and uncaring. He raised the bat and Ivan could only watch. He had no thoughts in his mind for there was nothing to think about, only pain, and horror, and confusion. The bat slammed down on the elbow of Ivan's right arm. There was no sound but the thud of wood on flesh, and the hand that slapped the wall with an involuntary shudder. The bat was raised again and again, breaking arm, breaking knee, breaking joints.

When he finished what he had set out to do, the Delivery Corp man walked back to the kitchen and rinsed the bat under the tap in the sink. He dried it with the kitchen towel that was hanging on the door of the refrigerator, then wrapped the towel around the phone and put it in the large side pocket of the parka. He walked back to Ivan and dropped the bat on the floor beside him, a gift for Ivan to look at and remember. Just before he opened the door, he stopped and smiled to himself. He turned back and stood above Ivan once more. He squatted down and felt Ivan's pants pockets and retrieved a cellphone. He held it up for Ivan to see, then smiled again.

He put the cellphone in his coat pocket with the kitchen phone and turned toward the door one more time. Before opening it, he reached into his other pocket, pulled out a black ski mask and slipped it over his head, then opened the door and took a quick look outside to see if there were any bystanders who had come to gape at the execution. No one was on the street and no one on the porches of the surrounding houses. He turned and looked back at his accomplishment, relishing in the knowledge that the man on the floor will suffer all the pain that was possible to bear with each attempted movement of his body out of the instinct for survival.

****

The Delivery Corp man stepped onto the front porch and carefully surveyed the general surroundings. No one in sight, but if anybody was looking out their windows, all they would see was a person in a dark heavy coat, a ski mask and toque. He picked up the envelope, folded it and put it into his coat pocket.

He had left the old, cheap bicycle leaned up against the side wall of the house. He had purchased it with cash from a used cycle shop on Queen Street West, which was rumored to be a depot for stolen bikes. He mounted the bike and casually rode up the deserted Kenilworth Avenue. It was one of those Beaches neighborhoods where everybody stayed indoors on cold November nights and watched whatever popular TV show was on.

He cycled up to Queen Street and then turned east toward the Glen Manor ravine and park. There were few pedestrians on the street, and no one took any notice of the cyclist. It was the Beaches and there were always cyclists on Queen Street, even in November. He stopped in front of the park and leaned the bike against the metal frame which held the boxes that offered free copies of Renter's News, Real Estate Monthly and Car and Truck.

He left the bike unchained, knowing someone would probably take it within a few hours, and then proceeded to walk northward up the ravine until he reached Pine Street. On the north side of Pine was the beginning of Glen Stewart Park. He crossed the street into the park where there was a large blue recycle bin and a large gray waste bin. He reached into the blue recycle bin and pulled out an oversized shopping bag that contained a hat, winter coat and a pair of shoes. He stepped behind a clump of bushes and changed out of the Delivery Corp clothes and put on the winter coat and shoes from the shopping bag.

He put the Delivery Corp parka, toque, ski mask and running shoes into the bag and then walked up Pine Street to MacLean Avenue, turned right and walked south to Falkirk. Throughout his whole expedition, he never once heard a single police siren.

Chapter Two

Detective Sergeant Aristotle Boyle had joined a gym near his home because he didn't want to gain weight like some of his fellow officers when they had taken desk jobs. It seemed that alcohol and bad food became a natural way of life for police officers during Boyle's early years. The tension and constant danger often created the need to numb their minds and cope with the experiences of any given day. The deplorable eating and drinking habits became ingrained and they found it difficult to change as they aged. When promoted to a position behind a desk, their activity level dropped, but the quotient of their body fat seemed to grow every year. Boyle had every intention of going to the gym regularly, but his regular turned out to be less than once per week.

He was in his early fifties, and at six foot one he weighed a healthy 185 pounds, which he wanted to maintain. He had a full head of black hair that was generously sprinkled with gray, and on this particular Monday morning, he found time for an early workout. He shaved and showered at the gym and then headed downtown to the Police Headquarters building in the heart of downtown Toronto.

He finished the paperwork on the homicide investigation his team had just completed and quickly filed the report before he headed to the new homicide assigned to his team in the Beaches area of the city. He wasn't in any hurry because Detective Gina Baldoni and the rest of his team were already at the scene, as well as the pathologist and the Forensic Identification Services team, commonly known as FIS.

The morning was filled with a heavy, cold November rain. A hard rain with those uncomfortable big fat drops that bounced off your head and shoulders and splashed into your face. He ran from the back doors of the police station to his car, slammed the door shut and exhaled deeply, as if he had just run a gauntlet. He looked through the front window and the sky was thick with dark, and the rain fell in a malevolent downpour. Each drop crashed upon the windshield like an explosion and the pounding of the droplets sounded like a Morse code message from God lashing out with fury, "Remember Noah. Remember the flood."

The roar of the rain was punctuated by the deafening crack of a lightning bolt. Boyle was a natural cynic, but he respected the power of nature and the potential of a higher force that all humanity needed to answer to, in this life or another.

'God speaks,' he thought to himself, and you could not help but listen and respect the power of the ancient voice. He thought about what his mother would tell him when he was very young and afraid of the storms.

'Positive charges the negative and flashes in a blaze of light. Thunderclouds and lightning are the storms within our souls.'

He was the son of a third-generation English Canadian father and Greek mother who had immigrated to Canada. Boyle's mother raised him in the traditional Greek culture, baptized him in the Greek Orthodox church, and taught him the traditional Gods: Zeus, Apollo, Athena. She taught him that it didn't matter what you called God, or whatever the Omni-present force in the universe was. She taught him how you could use any name as long as you respected the basic teachings and honored the Divine. She taught him that as long as you kept that spirit within you, it didn't matter whether you called him Zeus or Yahweh or Allah or God and Goddess.

He had been in law enforcement for almost all of his adult life, starting as a Constable and going through all the various departments along the way, eventually becoming a Sergeant Detective in the homicide division. He was a 'lifer' in the active force and lacked any ambition to move into the senior positions that demanded dealing with politics, policy, unions and the press.

****

As he drove down Bay Street toward the Gardiner Expressway, he envisioned the streets of downtown Toronto as long, straight ravines at the bottom of deep concrete canyons. He drove east and exited onto Lakeshore Boulevard all the way to the Beaches.

15

"The Beaches" community originally began as small, quaint cottages and grew to become a small, quaint town along the shoreline of Lake Ontario. Even after its amalgamation with Toronto, the Beaches community maintained its picturesque rural atmosphere as almost every house had fully grown, maple, oak or elm trees. In spring and summer, the area looked like a forest from above with the canopy of tree branches hiding most of the houses. In the fall, the Splendora of colored leaves created watercolor paintings of every road and avenue.

It was a middle-to-upper class community filled with a liberal mix of doctors, lawyers, middle management bankers and a scattering of artists and celebrities. It was a section of the city where real estate prices were significantly inflated. You had to have money if you wanted to live there, and having money was always the best way to keep a neighborhood exclusive.

****

He drove along Lakeshore Boulevard past the Ashbridge's Bay Park, turned right on Queen Street and entered the heart of the Beaches, then drove the three blocks to Kenilworth Avenue. The top of the road had been cordoned off, a squad car angled across the street to prevent any traffic. He waved to Constable Jasmine Davis and pulled up over the sidewalk beside the angled squad car, rolled down the window and called to her.

"Morning Jasmine, how you holding up in this rain?"

"Gotta live with it," she said with a frown.

"Is your mother leaving for Jamaica soon?" he asked.

"She goes next week. The weather in Kingston is sunny and over twenty degrees. She can't take the winters up here anymore. It really affects her arthritis," Davis said casually while holding her hand up to indicate the rain.

"Wish I could go with her." Boyle added with a smile.

Constable Davis smiled big as she envisioned the scene of her mother and Boyle strutting amongst her friends like peacocks, "She would take ya," she said laughing, "her walking around the island with a fine handsome Toronto detective. She'd be the talk!"

Boyle laughed a bit and then his demeanor turned into official mode, "What's the scene like?"

Her expression turned sour and the tone of her voice serious, "Brutal," she said, "haven't seen anything as brutal as this."

"Okay, thanks," he said, "keep dry. Try not to catch pneumonia."

Boyle rolled up the window and drove down the street, pulled up on the sidewalk across from the house that contained the crime scene. He pulled his coat up over his head as he got out of the car and fast-walked across the street.

It was a typical Beaches residence, an older home that had been renovated many times over the years. A two-story, red bricked building with a broad front porch that stretched the entire width of the house. The front yard was completely cultivated with flower beds and bushes and small decorative flagstone paths.

The front porch was covered with a solid weather protected roof, an aspect Boyle always noted when looking at any property. The front porch was one of the most important aspects of any home Boyle had lived in. His favorite pastime was to sit on his porch in the evenings and enjoy a Cuban cigar with a glass of brandy and think about the cases he worked on. He was always intrigued by the character of private eye Philip Marlowe, the main protagonist of Raymond Chandler's crime novels, who would sit in his kitchen with a large pot of freshly brewed coffee and smoke cigarette after cigarette while he contemplated the cases he worked on.

Constable William Singleton stood on the front porch, guarding the entrance to ensure only authorized personnel were allowed to enter.

"Morning Bill," Boyle said.

"Morning detective. Nice day for a murder investigation."

"Are we sure it's murder?" Boyle asked.

"Oh yeah, couldn't be anything else."

"Has the FIS or Singh arrived yet?"

"Dr. Singh has been here for about a half hour. He's in there with Gina. He's also been out a couple of times for air," Singleton replied.

"That messy?" Boyle asked.

"No, not messy, very little blood. It's just one of those things that make you cringe, like watching someone getting kicked in the balls. Puts a chill up your back."

"Thanks for the visual. Who else is here?"

"Just Dr. Singh and Gina."

Boyle nodded as he put on the standard latex gloves. He opened the door and was immediately assaulted with the stench of urine and vomit.

"Jesus," he muttered, "hey Singh, don't you have any of those air fresheners you usually carry around with you?"

"Sorry Boyle," Singh laughed, "forgot them this morning."

"I guess that's why you've been out for air."

Boyle could see the prone figure of a body on the floor at the base of the stairs. There was a stain of vomit a few feet from the door and another beside the body.

"Have you determined cause of death?" Boyle asked.

"My preliminary guess would be shock and heart failure brought about by intense trauma."

"What caused the trauma?"

Singh pointed to the baseball bat and said, "I'm pretty sure someone used it to break his arms and legs in several places. His nose is broken as well."

"Where's Gina?" Boyle asked.

"In the kitchen Boss," she called out.

Boyle walked through the dining room, the table covered with estate papers, brochures and other paraphernalia used by real estate agents, and then stepped through the archway that led into the well-lit kitchen.

"What have we got so far?"

"The kitchen phone is missing," she replied, "the re-charging cradle is still on the table, but I can't find the phone anywhere. There's a companion phone in the bedroom upstairs, still in its cradle."

"Is FIS on its way?"

"They should be here shortly."

Boyle looked around the room and then asked her, "What do you think Gina? First thoughts."

"Someone really wanted him to suffer." Baldoni replied, "Singh feels that he was beaten a few feet inside the door and then he somehow crawled to the foot of the stairs. It must have been horrible pain every inch he moved. He threw up a couple of times along the way. Not sure when he pissed himself."

"Didn't he have a cellphone?"

"Can't find it," she answered.

"Do we know when all this happened?"

"Singh figures he's been here for a couple of days."

18

"Who called it in?" asked Boyle.

"He missed an important business meeting yesterday morning. One of his associates was trying to call him all day. Eventually called us."

"Okay, I'm going to talk with Singh."

Doctor Surat Singh had become a pathologist with the Metropolitan Toronto Police Department five years after he had emigrated from India where he had been a pathologist for the Ludhiana Police Department in the Punjab region. He completed the requisite courses that were required to upgrade his medical certificates and spent two years in the Forensic Pathology course at the University of Toronto.

He knew that taking all these courses was redundant to what he had learned in India, but he was fully aware that he would require the proper certificates to practice in his new country.

"What are your preliminary findings Surat?" Boyle asked him.

"It must have taken a while for him to die," Singh stated, "the bruising around the contusions appear to be about 48 hours old. However, the body has not yet reached the preliminary stages of decomposition, so I would guess that he only died sometime late last night or very early this morning. I'll know more when we have him in the morgue."

"My first guess is that someone hit him with that baseball bat as he opened the door," pointing to the murder weapon lying a few feet inside the doorway, "then the murderer used the bat on him over and over again. He fell there (pointing several feet from the doorway) and this is where the beating took place as there are some minor blood stains on the floor. The victim vomited several times as he tried to crawl toward the stairs. However, I can't explain why he would even attempt to go up the stairs. The pain he would have been experiencing is hard to imagine and I'm surprised that he could have even crawled this far."

"Gina," Boyle called out, "I want as many constables as we can spare to question all the neighbors at least five houses in each direction, including across the street and the ones attached to the backyards. We need to find both his cell phone and the kitchen phone and find out about his family members and friends. I want to know what he did for a living and what relationships he had."

Baldoni yelled back from the kitchen, "His business card states that he's a real estate agent and he's affiliated with the Beach Realty Company over by

Queen Street and Lee Avenue. I called their office, and the president of the company is Brian Wicker. I've informed him of the crime and to wait in his office for an interview. I also told him to keep the news to himself for now."

"Thanks Gina," Boyle replied. "I'll go over and talk to him while you continue here."

"What do you think about this Boss?" she asked as she came out of the kitchen and through the dining room.

Boyle stopped for a moment in thought and then replied, "Someone wanted to hurt him bad and cripple him for life, or maybe they left knowing he would die slow. In either case, the killer took a risk, leaving him alive. When we find out why they did it like this, then we might be able find them."

Chapter Three

Boyle stepped out onto the front porch and noted that the rain had let up to a slight drizzle. He turned to Singleton and said, "Stick around the front porch until additional constables come, then Gina is going to need you to search the area and talk to some of the neighbors."

He left the crime scene, crossed the street to his car and stopped where Constable Davis was still re-directing traffic.

"Gina is going to need you later to do some interviews," he told her, "she's going to call in for additional officers as well to manage the scene."

"Yeah right," Davis laughed, "wait until it stops raining and then get me indoors."

Boyle chuckled and turned right onto Queen Street, driving a few blocks east until he reached the Kew Gardens park. He parked just before Lee Avenue and walked to The Beach Realty Company, which was located a few storefronts east of the corner of Queen and Lee.

****

It was a typical real estate office with a receptionist, a number of desks separated by prefab partitions and a couple of glassed-in offices in the back. Carefully positioned on the walls were some mildly original artwork, two forest landscapes and one painting of the Leuty lifeguard station. Boyle estimated that he had probably seen hundreds of paintings and photographs of the lifeguard station. It was one of those iconic structures that artists found to be inspirational.

"I'm here to see Mr. Wicker," Boyle told the receptionist.

"Is he expecting you?" she asked.

"My name is Detective Boyle," he said, "we called earlier today."

"Oh my," the receptionist replied, "we heard that there might be a problem with Ivan. Is he alright?"

"I think it would be best if I spoke with Mr. Wicker."

The receptionist rose and walked to one of the glassed-in offices. A short, heavy set, graying man came back with her to the front desk.

"Hello," the man said, "I'm Brian Wicker. Please come down to my office where we can talk in private. Would you like a coffee or something?"

"Thanks," said Boyle, "I'll take a coffee, double cream, no sugar."

"Janis," Wicker said to the receptionist, "can you grab a coffee for Detective Boyle, double cream and no sugar. And can you grab one for me as well, just black."

They went inside Mr. Wicker's office and Boyle sat in a highly comfortable chair, one Boyle thought, that was cozy enough to help precipitate the transaction of a deal. The office walls were neatly covered with copies of Wicker's diplomas, real estate license, and framed listings that advertised 'Sold Over Asking Price', carefully placed for putting the idea of success in the minds of any potential clients.

"I haven't told anyone in the office about this yet," Wicker started, "they know something is abuzz because the receptionist took the call from a policewoman and put it through to me, however, they don't know that he is dead yet. Can you tell me what happened?"

"We are classifying it as a murder." Boyle replied in a deadpan, monotone so that he could watch the reaction of Wicker to the news, "Usually our first classification is a suspicious death, but in this case, we are certain that he was killed by someone else."

"Jesus," Wicker replied with a soft moan, "how did he die?"

"I'm sorry, but we cannot divulge any information until after we have done all of our preliminary investigations, interviews, forensic evaluation and so on." Boyle answered plainly, "I can only state that it was a violent death and obviously not committed by his own hand."

"Jesus," Wicker moaned once more.

"I need to ask you a number of questions," said Boyle with a firmer voice, "and I know that this may seem a bit cold, but it is important that we find out as much information as soon as we can, so I'm going to need your full cooperation with the answers."

"Yes, of course," Wicker replied as he sat up straight with the realization of the seriousness of the matter.

Boyle retrieved a digital recorder from his pocket and placed it on the desk in front of Wicker. "I will be recording this conversation."

Brian Wicker had a sense of caution on his face, something Boyle was expecting to see in a businessperson who dealt with contracts and sales pitches in which things are sometimes said that could be construed as promises, but might not be kept.

"We prefer it to taking notes," Boyle continued, "I assure you that the recording itself will not be used in any legal proceedings, only the information provided. Someone will transcribe the notes later on for our records."

"I guess," Wicker replied hesitantly, "I guess it's okay."

Boyle turned on the recorder, "This is detective Aristotle Boyle, I am interviewing Mr. Brian Wicker. It is ten-fifteen in the AM on Monday, November 26. We are in Mr. Wicker's office at the Beach Realty company," then in a friendlier tone, he turned to ask his first question, "Mr. Wicker, please tell me as much as you can about Ivan Malinkov."

"Well, Ivan," Wicker said and then stammered, "or should I say Mr. Malinkov?"

"You can call him Ivan if it is more comfortable for you," Boyle answered.

There was a knock on the glass door and Janis brought in two cups of coffee. She placed both cups on the desk in front of each man and then stood for a moment as if waiting for further instructions, or perhaps waiting for information.

"Thank you, Janis," Wicker said, "please close the door behind you."

Wicker took a sip of his coffee and took a deep breath. Then he looked at Boyle and asked, "Where should I begin?"

Boyle's expression took on a look of friendly calmness, "Why don't you tell me about his business. How long he's been with the company, how successful was he, some of his associates who may know more about him, things like that."

"Ivan is one of my top salesmen, or at least he was." Wicker stammered again, "He was very personable but also very aggressive. It's hard to say really. I mean I don't want to speak ill of the dead, but he was a very good real estate salesperson. He knew how convince people to make a commitment, and that's what it's basically all about, committing. When it comes to selling property, he was one of the best and was able to get people to commit on deals that generally benefitted him."

"Does that mean that he wasn't entirely reputable?" Boyle asked.

"Let me explain it this way, in any real estate company there are agents who truly want to serve and take care of their clients, find a property that best fits their needs, ensure they get a fair price and generally care about the people they work with. There are other agents who literally just want to make a quick sale for as high a price as possible in order to maximize their commission. To them a client is just a means toward the commission. I would put Ivan in that later group. He definitely wasn't a saint, and I wouldn't be surprised if he was down in Hell right now selling the Devil his own property."

"How did he get along with the other agents?" Boyle asked.

"The agents often have to work together as one may be the selling agent and another may be the buying agent," replied Wicker. "The company makes more money if both the buying and selling agents are from the same office, so once we have a listing, we encourage the agents to ensure the house is sold to a client who is represented by another of our agents. However, the agents work on commission, so they are often more interested in getting the highest price possible, or in getting the sale done quickly."

"Ivan was not always the most cooperative person when dealing with other agents. He would sometimes use other agents to bring in offers in order to get a bidding war on a property."

"Any conflicts with other agents that could have led to animosity?" Boyle asked.

"For my part no, I never had a problem with Ivan," replied Wicker. "However, it would be best to ask the other agents. Of course, we can provide you with any of the paperwork on any of the properties that Ivan was involved with."

"We'll need to see all of the documents at some point, so if you can have them prepared for us that would be prudent," said Boyle, "by the way, where were you over the weekend?"

Wicker sat up straight, eyes wide, not expecting to be questioned as a potential suspect. "Why, I um, I was," he stuttered, "I was at my cottage up in Haliburton, near Minden."

Boyle enjoyed surprising people with unexpected questions. He found he could discern a great deal about a person from their reaction, their body language, and the tension or calmness of their voice. He also liked to keep conversations off balance so that anyone who was not completely forthright in their answers might slip up. He quickly deduced that if Mr. Wicker ever committed a murder, there would probably be so much evidence left behind as to make it obvious.

"I'm sorry, I didn't mean to startle you," Boyle lied, "but we will need to determine where all of Mr. Malinkov's associates, friends or other parties were at the time of his death."

"Yes, of course, I understand," said Wicker.

"Can you tell me anything you know about Mr. Malinkov's personal life. We are just starting this investigation and we need to find out anything we can about him. His wife, his children, his social life?"

Looking uncomfortable, Wicker started to explain, "Ivan had a wife, her name was Anna, and she died about five years ago. She committed suicide. He also has a son, Anton. He lives up in Alliston. I believe he also has a brother who still lives in Russia; Moscow I think."

"His wife committed suicide?" Boyle asked.

"Yes, it was a pretty tragic case. I remember her as a gentle person, maybe even emotionally fragile you could say, always quiet whenever she attended one of the company parties, would generally only speak when she was with Ivan."

"They were divorced several years ago. However, I always found it odd that he still referred to her as his wife even after the divorce, and that they were still in regular communication with each other, right up until her suicide."

"He continued to have some sort of relationship with her?" Boyle queried.

"I don't know if you could call it a relationship, but it wasn't like any other divorce that I'm aware of. After I divorced my first wife, you couldn't get me to talk with her if you paid me."

"I mean, he loved his wife, that was pretty obvious. How he treated her, well the only thing I can tell you is the gossip that went around. I don't know if you want to hear gossip."

Boyle looked directly at Wicker and said, "I find that gossip usually has a pearl of truth in it. So yes, I want to hear anything you can add."

"Well, his son Anton stopped talking to him years ago, long before his mother committed suicide. At the funeral, the son even punched his father, right there in front of her grave with everybody watching. Ivan was crying and the son just came up to him, called him a bastard and belted him right in the face."

"So Malinkov was a spouse abuser." Boyle made the insinuation.

"Only gossip mind you," said Wicker, "there was never any legal action or official complaints that I'm aware of. You would have those on record I would guess."

"Yes, we'll check that out, thanks. Do you know if he was in any recent relationship with anybody?" asked Boyle.

"Ivan had many relationships, even while he was married," answered Wicker. "The last person I knew about was a woman named Barbara. You can ask Janis for her last name as she had taken messages for Ivan here at the agency."

Boyle thanked Wicker for his cooperation and stated that they will need to speak again as more questions will probably arise as the investigation progressed. He stated he would need to get copies of Ivan's business papers and to have them prepared as quickly as possible. He picked up his digital recorder, switched it off and put the recorder back in his coat pocket.

He stopped at the front desk and asked the receptionist if she remembered the name of the woman Ivan was recently dating. Tears appeared in Janis' eyes and she quickly took a tissue paper to cry into. Boyle politely waited as she tried to compose herself and after a few moments she seemed ready to talk.

"I guess it's as bad as I feared," she said.

Boyle didn't say anything and tried to be sympathetic. To him, being a successful detective was to be a therapist, a psychiatrist, a friend or a cruel inquisitor as the situation required. He made a conscious effort based on the needs of the person he was dealing with.

"The last person Ivan was with, as far as I know, was Barbara Booth." Janis stated.

"Thank you, Janis." Boyle said gently. "Would you happen to have her phone number on file?"

She looked through her e-mails and found one she had sent to Ivan a few months ago. It contained Barbara Booth's phone number and e-mail address. She wrote it down on a notepad and gave it to Boyle. He thanked her once again for the coffee and her cooperation and made a mental note to have her interviewed by Detective Baldoni. It was obvious that Janis had 'feelings' for Ivan, whether she had any relationship with him or not.

He left the office and headed back to the crime scene to see if Baldoni and Singh had any further developments and to speak with the FIS unit if they had arrived.

Chapter Four

Boyle walked over to the Sunset Grill across from Kew Gardens park. The restaurant was a Beaches favorite and known for their excellent breakfast combos.

Some officers' appetites would be affected by what they saw at a crime scene, but Boyle had learned to separate himself from the horrific realities of corpses. Over the years, he learned to develop an alter ego that he could consciously step in and out of as the need required. This self-imposed 'split personality' allowed him to focus completely on the job, disregarding outside distractions, or he could close off his mind from the gruesome details he often saw committed on other people.

Boyle also realized that this ability to switch his personality on and off also made it difficult for any relationship he was in. His partners often found it hard to deal with the cold, callus nature he utilized for his detective mindset, seemingly uncaring about his partner's needs, but later on experience him as completely caring and loving individual. It was difficult for any woman he was with and it was the main reason that led to his divorce. His wife used to call him Jekyll and Hyde, and it caused a lot of friction between them because she never knew which one was going to come home at night. In the end, she had decided that what she wanted was a 'normal' man and she began an affair with the mechanic at the local garage. She eventually left Boyle and settled in with the mechanic.

****

Aaron Silverstein was the Chief Inspector of the Forensic Identification Services unit, which is staffed by specially trained officers of the Toronto Police Force, and by qualified civilians to investigate crime scenes with modern scientific methods and specialized equipment.

Silverstein assigned FIS officers to crime scenes based on the nature of the crime and an estimation of the requirements for gathering evidence. A crime involving gunshots would require different forensic analysis than a case of arson, and he would always try to ensure that an officer with greater experience in the required facet of analysis was present at each scene.

When there were reports of a case that seemed out of the ordinary, or had special sets of circumstances, Silverstein would often take the lead in the forensic investigation himself. He told others that he wanted to maintain his level of experience, but most homicide detectives knew that it was because of his fascination with the bizarre and often malevolent acts humans transpired to commit.

****

Boyle arrived back at the house on Kenilworth and parked further down the street, which was now clogged with an ambulance, the FIS unit van and other official police cars. The rain had stopped, and the air was cold and muggy. His brunch of bacon, eggs, toast and home fries sat heavy in his stomach as he walked up the street. He also carried two take out trays with eight cups of coffee and a bag of milks and sugars.

He lifted the wide, yellow "Do Not Cross" tape, juggling the coffee, and walked up to the front porch and noticed the front windows were open to allow air into the house. He hoped the stench he previously experienced was gone or sufficiently depleted.

As he entered, he saw Silverstein holding the baseball bat and examining it with the headband style magnifying glass he liked to use. It had interchangeable lens for different magnifications and allowed him to flip the lens up and down as needed to inspect evidence or to walk around and communicate with others.

"Does the bat have the killer's initials engraved on it?" Boyle asked with a grin.

"The bat's clean." Silverstein smiled back at him. "We did a quick check for finger and palm prints, can't find any. We'll look again back at the lab, but I don't think it will give us anything. I suspect the killer used gloves the whole time so we'll have to see if we can find any trace material from the type of gloves they used. I'm hoping that we might be able to find something when we pull the tape off the handle."

"The crew is checking the house, but so far we have only identified the fingerprints of the victim on front door, the living room and the kitchen. The house is very clean, and I suspect he had a maid, or a cleaning service come in on a regular basis. I'll have more info for you when we meet in the Argo."

"Thanks Aaron," Boyle replied. He called out to Baldoni to find out where she was in the house. "Upstairs," she yelled down.

He went up the spiral staircase to the second-floor landing and heard her in the bedroom to the left. He entered what apparently was the master bedroom and saw her sorting through the clothes in the walk-in closet.

"This guy had a real taste for suits," she said. "There are several fairly expensive ones and the shirts to go with them. His shoe rack looks like something Imelda Marcos would have been jealous of."

"And what does that tell us?" Boyle asked as if he were tutoring a pupil.

Baldoni thought for a moment and then replied, "He was concerned with his looks, obsessively concerned I would say. That's something I would expect for a real estate agent where you obviously want to be presentable, but with these clothes I'd say he dressed to impress whomever he wanted to be sleeping with."

"You say whomever. Are you just being politically correct, or do you think you know what his sexual persuasion was?"

Baldoni looked at Boyle and smirked, "You don't miss anything Boss."

"Gina," Boyle said, "I wouldn't be surprised if sex had something to do with this murder. Wicker at Beach Realty made allusions to this guy's frequent conquests of the opposite sex. And with this wardrobe, I emphasize the word 'conquest'. What about his personal affects Wolf Runner?"

"Aww, c'mon Boss, don't use that nickname," she implored.

Boyle smiled, "If you're going to call me Boss, then I'm calling you Wolf Runner, or maybe just Wolf."

"Fine, but just between you and me. I don't want that nickname getting around."

Boyle looked at her with the affection he would have if she had been his daughter. "Alright, I won't hang the moniker on you, but when did you start your ritual with the wolves?"

"It's not a ritual. They just follow me around when I run, that's all. I'll explain it sometime when no one else is listening."

"I look forward to it," he said, "now what about his personal affects?"

"His wallet and rings are on the dresser. Money still in the wallet, his watch was still on his wrist. There's some jewelry in one of the dresser drawers; gold cuff links, a couple of more rings, and a string of pearls."

"Let's get photos of everything and then we'll discuss it at tomorrow's meeting," Boyle told her, "but something's not right here. Why did the killer commit this act and leave all the valuables behind? Why are the phones missing? Why didn't anyone hear this guy scream or shout?"

Baldoni watched him and knew not to interrupt. She knew he wasn't asking her any questions, he was free-thinking out loud, as he often did. She had learned very quickly after she started working on his homicide team that when Boyle's mind started to click, it was best to just follow whatever direction it went.

"And most of all," he continued, "why leave him alive?"

Chapter Five

The homicide situation room at police headquarters was nicknamed the 'Argo' after the ship in Greek mythology which carried Jason and his Argonaut sailors in search of the Golden Fleece. A senior detective who had mentored Boyle when he was first promoted, had given the room that nickname because Boyle seemed to treat each case like Homeric quest. It was also a nod to Boyle's Greek heritage, of which he was extremely proud; and lastly, it was the name of the Toronto football club, of which the senior detective and Boyle were ardent fans.

The Argo looked like any regular boardroom in any office building with a central table and chairs around it. The north wall contained two large high-resolution flat screens that could display wireless feeds from any laptop toggled into the system. It was a room that included all the latest in technology, except for an old wooden credenza which was a leftover from the previous headquarters. Over the years, every detective from every homicide team had etched their initials somewhere onto its surface, so this piece of furniture became a treasured history of the homicide division.

Boyle was now one of the senior detectives and was recognized as the leading officer in the division. He was thorough and exacting in his methodology for collecting and analyzing evidence, almost to the point of being obsessive, but he also had the ability for abstract thinking which allowed him to sometimes turn the facts and view them from another perspective.

Through his comprehension of the intricacies of investigations, he learned that when everyone shared their findings on a regular basis, people would start to notice things; similarities, coincidences, links and sometimes even answers to questions others may have had, or that one person's question could raise further questions which hadn't been thought of. He insisted on regular meetings of his homicide team and believed sharing facts, findings, figures, timelines, photos and even gossip were essential when an investigation was in progress.

****

The first meeting of Boyle's homicide team took place the morning after the initial crime scene investigation. The meeting included Detective Gina Baldoni, Dr. Surat Singh, Constables William Singleton and Jasmine Davis, Aaron Silverstein of Forensic Investigation Services, and Donna Chang, the civilian research specialist.

"Listen up," Boyle stated loudly to get every one's attention amid the casual conversations, "let's get started. You all saw the brutality of this murder. A man was beaten with the purpose of incapacitation, and then left to slowly die. This stinks of premeditation, and that's the route we will initially follow. Let's start with the FIS report, Aaron?"

Silverstein opened a blue folder which had print outs of his notes and the different reports of the forensic technicians who had worked the scene with him. "We did not find any fingerprints on the baseball bat. As a matter of fact, it had been wiped clean with ammonia and Pine Sol at one point, so there are no traces of anything; sweat, hair or any other substance that would contain DNA. We could only detect those cleansing agents. We found some very minor traces of skin and blood from the victim. I'm pretty sure that the bat was rinsed in the kitchen sink before the killer left the scene. We'll check the sink today to make sure."

"Yesterday you mentioned something about removing the tape from the bat. Anything come up when you did that?" Boyle asked.

"Nope, nothing." Silverstein replied, "The bat had been soaked in ammonia and washed so clean there wasn't anything we could possibly use."

"And the rest of the house?" Boyle asked.

"We haven't been able to identify all the fingerprints in the house yet, but we know most were from the victim. As there are no fingerprints on the bat, the kitchen sink or the handle on the front door, I'm going to assume the murderer wore gloves of some sort. However, we will need to start the process of finding the corresponding pinkies for the ones we haven't yet identified."

"Anything else you can tell us at this point?" Boyle continued his questions.

"We'll be at the house today and I'll call you if anything important turns up," replied Silverstein. "Also, there is an alarm system in the house, however it doesn't include video, just an entry alarm system."

"Thanks Aaron. Gina, can you get in touch with the alarm company and see what records they keep." Boyle then turned toward Dr. Surat Singh and asked for the pathological report.

"The cause of death was heart failure brought on by extreme shock." Singh stated. "Both arms and legs had bones broken in several places and the murderer seemed to target the areas that would immobilize the victim, including the ankles and knees of the legs and the elbows and wrists of the arms. The bridge of the nose was also broken and the blood on the scene would have mostly come from the nose."

"The blows from the baseball bat happened several feet inside the front door. The victim then tried to crawl toward the stairway. Movement of any kind would have been excruciatingly painful. He eventually succumbed to the pain and his heart failed."

"Do you have a timeline?" asked Boyle.

"From the bruising of the contusions, I would estimate the incident took place on Friday night or very early Saturday morning. My first estimate would be Friday evening. Death would have occurred either late on Sunday or in the early hours of Monday morning."

"If he was potentially beaten on Friday night and died on Sunday, he would have lain there in that state for 48 hours or more." Baldoni speculated.

"Yes, but I hope to have a better estimate of the timeline after I perform the autopsy later today," answered Singh.

Silverstein interrupted, "I would speculate that the nose was broken at the entrance of the front door. There was blood just inside the entrance and some drops of blood leading to the spot where he was beaten. We didn't find any blood leading to the stairway where the body was found."

"The blood from the nose would have coagulated in less than an hour," stated Singh. "I would expect the victim laid in shock for a time before making any attempt to move."

"Thank you, Dr. Singh. Please let me know the exact timelines when you have them. We're going to need them when we start interviewing people." Boyle turned to Detective Baldoni, "Gina, what do the neighbors have to say?"

"Jasmine, Bill and I interviewed all the neighbors in a five-house radius around Malinkov's address. Two of the houses did not have anyone home, the one beside the victim's house and one three doors down on the other side of the road. We have confirmed that they are out of town."

"How far out of town?" asked Boyle.

"One family in India and the other in the States."

"What about the ones that were home?" Boyle continued.

"So far," Baldoni started, "no one reports to have heard or seen anything out of the ordinary. Using Dr. Singh's first estimate that he gave us yesterday, we interviewed the occupants based on the crime occurring on the Friday night. Out of the 26 homes we visited, it was interesting to find out how many people were watching the three-hour premiere of that new Conan the Barbarian series."

"Is it any good?" Silverstein asked.

"Yeah, I watched it," responded Singleton, "lots of graphic violence, full frontal nudity and plenty of soap opera plots."

"Right up your alley, Aaron," snickered Baldoni with a smile.

"Only the violence, Gina, only the violence." Silverstein snickered back.

"Let's get back to business." Boyle interjected, "Go on Gina."

"Some of the neighbors were not home on Friday evening. We haven't confirmed their statements yet, but Bill and I will work on getting those confirmations today. The ones that were home all stated that they did not hear anything. I suspect because it was a cold November evening, and no one would have had their windows open. All the houses in the area have been re-modeled at some point in time, and they all have double-paned windows. They all also seem to have home theatre systems. Any sounds from inside another house would be muted and difficult to hear even if they weren't watching TV."

"And the phones?" Boyle asked.

"We checked through the entire house and the grounds around the house." Singleton stated. "We didn't come up with either the cell phone or the kitchen land line. We checked the garbage cans, the bushes and the surrounding properties."

"The killer could have simply put them in their pocket and disposed of them anywhere in the city." Boyle stated as a conjecture, "They might also want to keep them as souvenirs. However, we need to confirm that they are missing or if they had been disposed. Did we check the sewers in the area?"

"We're planning on doing that today." Baldoni stated, "I've got a call in to the city maintenance department to ask for assistance in the search. I'll probably need some additional manpower to widen the search area. The killer could have simply walked down to the lake and thrown the phones into the water."

"Have you tried calling the numbers?" Boyle asked.

"Yeah, the cell phone went straight to voicemail, so I presume the battery's gone dead or that it's been destroyed or drowned. The home phone went to the second phone located in the bedroom and then to voicemail."

"Alright, let's review," Boyle stated flatly, "the victim opens the door for the killer and his nose is broken immediately, causing him to be temporarily incapacitated. The killer walks in and breaks the victim's arms and legs a few feet inside his doorway. The killer takes the victim's kitchen phone and cell phone and leaves the victim to die. We're certain it was not a robbery because the victim's wallet with a couple of hundred dollars is still on his bedroom dresser along with some jewelry. The victim's watch is still on his wrist. The computer, laptop, stereo, TV and other electronic valuables were not taken."

"One thing to note," Silverstein spoke up, "the wristwatch was smashed and not worth taking. Some of it was actually implanted into the victim's skin from the force of a blow from the baseball bat."

"Thanks Aaron." Boyle continued, "So right now it appears the victim was killed for personal or professional reasons. If this was a professional killing, then the perpetrator would probably not have left the victim alive, and would have finished him off, either crushing his skull with the baseball bat or strangulation to ensure death. Also, the manner in which he was killed may have been done in order to send a message to someone else."

"As of now, I want to treat this as a murder in which someone had something personal against the victim, perhaps some sort of revenge. Unless something else is identified by Dr. Singh or by Aaron's team in the next 24 hours, we'll conduct our inquiries with the suspicion that there is a personal motive."

"Gina," Boyle went on, "I want to expand the investigation and start interviewing people from all of the houses on the street. You can request additional constables to help out with the interviews. Also, have the city maintenance team check all of the sewers going south, all the way to the lake, and north to Queen Street. I also want the phone records for both his cell phone and house line. Donna, contact the phone companies to see which cell provider he used and get the records."

"I also want the staff at the restaurant on the corner, Whitlocks, to be interviewed. There is window seating that faces Kenilworth, so get a record of people who were dining there that night through the credit card receipts and interview them to see if anyone noticed anything."

"Donna, do we have a current list of interested parties to be interviewed?"

Donna Chang responded, "The victim has one child, Anton Malinkov, who lives up in Alliston, Ontario. No parents or other siblings in this country. He has one brother in Moscow, Russia."

"Okay," replied Boyle, "get a line regarding his brother, he will have to be informed of Ivan's death and also find out if he was still in Moscow when it happened. Has the son been informed of his father's death?"

"Yes," stated Baldoni, "an officer of the RCMP visited him last night and broke the news. I spoke with the officer late last night and he said the son seemed very dispassionate about it. He wasn't sure if it was shock or whether the son even cared. He also told him to stay at home and that we would be up to visit him this afternoon."

"Thanks Gina, I want you and I to go." Boyle said, and then continued, "According to Mr. Wicker at the Beach Realtor, I got the impression that the victim was pretty unscrupulous as a real estate agent, so we need to review his sales records for the past couple of years. Wicker is having them pulled for us to pick up, however, I want the recorded timelines of the sales matched to his bank deposits."

"Do you suspect Wicker?" Baldoni asked.

"No," Boyle answered, "but, if this was a case of bad dealings, Wicker would probably know about it and may want to keep the agency's name out of it. They do a lot of business in the Beaches area and any hint of impropriety would have a severe impact on business. Check with the Toronto Real Estate Board to see if there were any complaints made against Malinkov."

"I also want to interview all of the agents who work at the agency, including those who left in the past five years. Let's look into his past real estate deals, find out if there are any agents that he had conflicts with."

"Let's also find out about his relationships. Wicker states he had a number of girlfriends over the years, including while he was still married. He had a wardrobe that was meant to impress, so let's find out if there was a broken heart or two."

"Dr. Singh," Boyle looked over at Singh with a new thought. "I want the toxicology report first, I want to know if there were any traces of recreational drugs in his system."

"I'll call you as soon as I find out," Singh responded.

"Thanks," said Boyle, "anybody got anything else to offer before we close?"

Silverstein looked up from his notes, "I'd like to make an observation. The manner in which this crime was committed definitely points to personal revenge. In all the murders I've investigated, this was one of the most brutal. There have been other murders where people had been beaten to death, but in all those cases, they were beaten until dead, never beaten to such a degree and left alive. Therefore, I don't believe this murder was one of passion or anger. It seems to have been done methodically, as if the killer purposely wanted to incapacitate the victim and directed all their blows to his limbs."

"The evidence, or should I say the lack of some evidence, also suggests the killer had deliberately planned to disable the victim, and then purposely leave him alive. That was a huge risk, but it really emphasizes the amount of planning the killer did ahead of time. We have found no fingerprints or DNA traces on the murder weapon plus the fact the killer took the phones to prevent the victim from being able to call for help. They also took the risk that no one would hear the killing as it happened or come to the victim's aid."

"The killer may have fully expected him to die during the weekend but did not know for certain that he was going to die. This is most unusual for a crime that was planned ahead of time. Also," continued Silverstein, "the victim opened the door for the killer, which means the killer was either expected or was someone the victim knew, or they were disguised."

"I'd also like to add," Baldoni said, "the killer left the house with the two phones but left the phone in the bedroom. Was that on purpose, knowing that Ivan would try to reach it but would not be able to. I think that borders on sadistic."

"And no witnesses when they left the house. They could have gotten into their car and driven away, or they could have walked up the street and gotten onto a streetcar, or maybe even walked down to the beach and rowed across the lake to Hamilton."

"Maybe he's still in the neighborhood." Singleton stated.

Boyle looked his constable, "Don't make the mistake of assuming the killer's gender was male. This crime could have been done by a female or someone that is transgender."

"It's the brutality of the crime that probably makes it masculine," responded Singleton in defense, "It must have been a man who committed this act by the physicality of the way it was done."

"Bill," Boyle looked over with a sardonic smile, "if Gina showed up at my door with a baseball bat, I would bloody well be worried."

"Thanks Boss," Baldoni said, "I'll take that as a compliment."

There was a trickle of laughter and then Boyle ended, "Okay, we've all got lots to do. Gina and I will start the constables on interviewing the neighbors and Gina will talk to city maintenance. In the afternoon, her and I will drive up to Alliston to speak with the son. We'll meet again in the morning. Call me if you find anything new."

Chapter Six

Boyle went straight to Inspector Dylan Stanforth's office, the Officer in Charge of the Specialized Criminal Investigations Unit. Stanforth was only two years older than Boyle and both had worked on many cases together until Stanforth had been promoted. He led the department through a recent series of 'sensationalized' Toronto homicides.

He was a tall man with graying hair and always had a hard, stern look on his face that would make any smile seem like a surprise. Boyle always found Stanforth to be an overly ambitious individual but also one who strived to see a job done well. He was a practical man that wanted results, but to his credit, he didn't expect miracles, and Boyle appreciated this practical sense of logic and reason in his boss.

"Good morning Ari," Stanforth said dourly as Boyle entered his office. "What is the brief on this homicide in the Beaches. We haven't had a murder down there in over ten years."

Boyle gave him a summary of the case by describing the crime scene, a detailed list of the FIS report, Singh's pathological report, plus what he expected the investigation would entail over the next forty-eight hours. Boyle also gave him his personal impression of the case, the brutality of the murder and the startling fact that the murderer left the victim to slowly die.

"That's different," Stanforth said coldly.

"Yeah," Boyle replied, "leaving the victim to potentially call for help, or the outside chance that someone may stumble upon the crime scene was either something the killer did not expect to happen, or simply didn't care if it could happen."

"That's disturbing," Stanforth stated with the coolness still in his voice. "It could mean the killer is either stupid or psychotic. If they're stupid, then we should be able to quickly catch them. If they're psychotic, then we better try hard and ensure we quickly catch them."

"With the forensics we have so far," Boyle carefully measured his answer, "I don't believe the killer was stupid. It appears they were smart enough to prevent or eliminate any traces of fingerprints or DNA, plus they removed the phones from the victim's reach. I fear that we may have a psychotic, or an intelligent person seeking revenge of some sort."

"Well," Stanforth pondered, "I hope this case doesn't become another feeding frenzy for the media. I gave a copy of your brief to Margaret and the press are in the Media Room like a school of piranha waiting for a new carcass. Go talk to Margaret and try to keep this from getting too sensational."

'Thank you for stating the obvious,' Boyle thought to himself. He made his way down the hallway and down one flight of stairs to the Homicide division offices. The Media Liaison officer was in his office waiting to go over the press statement with him.

****

Margaret Hinds was an attractive forty-something officer with fifteen years of experience on the Toronto Police force. Her natural sandy-blonde hair was kept at ear length, which highlighted her artistically oval face and delicately long neck. Her deep green eyes added an acute punctuation to her attractiveness and her make-up was always kept minimal to enhance the naturalness of her look.

She had started work as a civilian dispatch officer and had worked her way through the Corporate Communications division. Her ability to speak publicly, her intelligence, and her keen ability for an accurate perception and quick response on sometimes surprising media questions eventually led her to becoming the main Media Liaison officer.

Three years prior to her taking the position, she and Boyle had a short, passionate fling that quickly fizzled out when the energetic sex had abated, and they actually started talking with one another. The affair ended amicably, and they agreed to keep a strict professional attitude between them and not interfere with their work.

"Good morning Detective Boyle. Stanforth gave me a copy of your initial brief," she immediately started before he could sit, "looks like you have a potential tabloid sensation on your hands. How do you want to handle this press conference?"

Boyle took a moment to sit at his desk and open his laptop before he responded to her question.

Every time he saw her, even when they simply passed each other in the hallway, his primal urges would instinctively arise before he could put them in check. There was always that brief instant where he could envision her lithe, naked body, the skin glistening with moisture, the small beads that formed and slowly trickled between her breasts. She reminded him of the Greek goddess Athena, and could still hear the faintness of her sighs, the measure of her intensity and the sensations she embraced. He could still feel the earthquake of her shudder, and the shiver that went through her body like a divine vibration.

Boyle snapped out of his reverie and responded, "I want to state this crime was a definite murder and I want to start asking for public assistance right away. We need witnesses or information. The killer appears to have been smart enough to plan it to perfection, or they were extremely lucky and left little for us to go on."

"The policy is to classify the crime as being a suspicious death until we know for certain," she reminded him without looking up from the brief she was reading.

He looked at her discernibly, "We already know for certain that this was murder, there is nothing suspicious about it." When she looked up at him after he made this statement, he quickly averted his eyes, trying not to look at her body.

"How much detail do you want to get into?" she asked, ignoring the lustful gaze she had caught. In her mind, she was glad she still had an effect on him, could still bring his blood into a heated passion.

"Basically," he started with a mildly embarrassed voice, "we want to state the name of the victim, which I think has already hit the front page of the papers, and the location of the murder. We want the basic stuff about asking the public to come forward if they have any information on the victim or if they want to report anything they think was suspicious on the night of Friday, November 23, and then all the regular stuff about Crime Stoppers and so on."

"You really want to get a jump on this, don't you Ari," she said as she looked up at him.

"You read the brief. This was one of the most brutal murders I've ever dealt with. I've handled cases where psychotic criminals tortured their victims before they died, but this is the first time that I've seen a killer, or killers, torture their victim and then leave him to probably die. That means we're dealing with a different type of psychosis."

"Alright, let me type up some notes and I'll call you when I'm ready," she said as she got up and began to walk to her own office. "Say about 20 minutes."

"I'll get a coffee and wait for your call," he said as his imagination took him back to that one bead of sweat that trickled down the small of her back.

Chapter Seven

Before heading for the expressway in Boyle's car, he and Baldoni stopped at a deli on Bay Street called 'C'est Nous' where Boyle ordered a Montreal smoked meat sandwich while Baldoni chose a veggie sub.

"Why do you buy the smoked meat from there?" Baldoni asked. "It's not nearly as good as the smoked meat from Montreal."

"I know, but I'm not in Montreal," Boyle smiled the obvious answer.

"My brother always brings me some whenever he comes for a visit," Baldoni began to offer, "he buys it from a butcher on Centre Street in the Point St. Charles area, just south of the canal. I'll ask him to bring me an extra few hundred grams next time."

"Are you trying to bribe me?" Boyle laughed.

"Just saying," Baldoni said at the apparent rejection of her offer.

"You know," Boyle grinned at Baldoni's reaction, "I would like that very much, thank you."

They drove down to the Gardiner Expressway, or as Boyle called it, "The eyesore," and then headed west to Hwy. 427. When they were north of the city and the suburbs, Boyle's mind and body relaxed as the scenery soon turned into farmland and forests. He always enjoyed this divergence away from tall buildings and concrete.

They drove through the town of Kleinburg and past the McMichael Art gallery. His mind went back about fifteen years when he would bring his wife and son Theo for picnics on the park grounds of the gallery, and then explain to Theo the work of the Group of Seven, the primary collection of the gallery.

While Boyle drove with memories in his mind, Baldoni sat in the passenger seat with a laptop open on her knees. Boyle glanced over and jokingly asked, "Are you checking messages from your boyfriends on Facebook?"

Without looking up Baldoni said, "I'm on Anton Malinkov's page. Photos show a nice wife, two young kids and a picture of his mother. Nothing of his father, not even in his friends list."

"Ahhh, the methodology of the modern police force. What will we be coming up with next?" Boyle continued to joke.

"Twitter and Instagram," she replied absentmindedly.

"Explain?" Boyle asked curiously.

"I couldn't find either a Twitter or Instagram account for him and he has less than fifty friends on Facebook. I don't see any links to any other website. He's probably not much into social media. His last posting on Facebook was to say happy birthday to his daughter. That was four months ago."

"So, what do you make of all that?"

"Well, from the few pictures he has on his page, he seems to be a happily married, loving father. His lack of interest in social media would either tell me that he doesn't care about it, or it could mean that he purposely wants to remain private."

"Okay, what does Facebook tell you about the man himself?" Boyle asked.

Baldoni answered the question as if she were giving answers to an oral examination. When she first started working with Boyle, she had a crush on him for about fifteen minutes, but when it soon became apparent that he was more of a father figure, the crush quickly faded. Boyle always treated her in a professional and respectful manner, and she grew to appreciate his fairness, and came to value his experience and willingness to share the intricacies of being a detective.

She saw Boyle as a tutor, and like her own father, he was always ready to answer any of her questions, but also constantly urged her to find the answers herself and this made her very comfortable.

"I would first say that he was a religious individual, but not one of those freaky fanatics. The area where he lives is mostly Christian with a higher percentage of the Protestant faiths. The area also borders on the Mennonite region, but if he was a Mennonite then he definitely wouldn't be on Facebook and probably wouldn't even own a computer."

"I would also say that he is a homebody. He hasn't completed any information on his page regarding where he works, his hobbies, or any other activities. I would guess that he is the type of guy who goes to work and then comes home and nestles with his family."

"If we consider him to be a potential suspect, then finding out as much as we can about him, before we interview him, would be beneficial. That's something you taught me," she looked over at Boyle and smiled.

They turned off on Country Road 89 and traveled west, passing through the little village of Cookstown and then through a stretch of farmland that always seemed eerily deserted during winter, a scenery of grey skies, furrowed fields and bare trees.

In Alliston, they quickly found Paris street which was lined with Victorian style homes. Anton Malinkov's home was red bricked with beige corner bricks and a turret style window on the second floor. The front porch had been enclosed with white panel siding, something Boyle had noticed right away. *'You could never smoke a Cuban in one of those,'* he thought.

They turned into the long driveway that had recently been cleared with a riding snow blower.

Boyle stopped the car at the end of the drive and glanced over at Baldoni. "You take this one," he said in reference to the interview.

****

They walked along the wide stone path to the old but solid wooden steps at the front of the house.

Inside the enclosed porch, the front door opened before they had a chance to knock.

A man in his late thirties stood in the doorway, dressed in jeans and an old, dark burgundy knitted sweater. He wore moccasin style slippers, had a two-day stubble on his face and a hard look of expectation. His short, dark brown hair showed the beginnings of a rising forehead but the tuft of hair in the middle expressed a strong resistance to the receding hairline. Overall, he had a look of sturdiness, not hard, but strong in purpose.

"Are you the police detectives from Toronto?" he quickly demanded.

"Yes, I am Detective Baldoni and this is Sergeant Detective Boyle," she said in a curt, authoritative fashion. She wanted to deliver a sense of importance. "Are you Anton Malinkov?"

"Yes, you better come in before all the heat goes out of the house," he replied just as curtly as she had given.

They stepped in the front door and closed it behind them. "Is your father Ivan Malinkov, who lived on Kenilworth Avenue in the Beaches area of Toronto?" Baldoni asked her first preliminary question.

"Not anymore," Anton said with a snarl.

There was a long, strong pause in which Baldoni and Boyle both noted the inappropriate cold irony of his answer.

"How do you mean?" she eventually asked.

Anton's eyes had an impassioned, almost disgusted look to them, "I disowned that bastard years ago. I had extracted him from my life and discarded our relationship like a diseased organ."

Baldoni was slightly taken aback by the blunt, harsh response, "We understand that you have been informed that he has died."

"Good for him," Anton brusquely stated.

"Mr. Malinkov," Baldoni spoke in tone that took offense to his reaction, "we are required to ask you some questions? We can ask you the questions here, or you can accompany us to the RCMP station in Newmarket."

It was Anton's turn to be taken aback by the detective's serious demeanor. He raised his right hand to his face and rubbed his eyes. He took a breath and then said, "We can talk here. My wife is at her parent's house with the kids for the rest of the afternoon. How long will this take?"

Baldoni's distaste of Anton's reaction to his father's death was obvious, and something Boyle took note of to discuss with her another time. What Boyle didn't know was that his junior detective had difficulty relating to people who did not like their parents, or that some parents did not like their children.

Her own relationship with her parents and siblings was always one of love and respect, and even though she had dealt with many cases in which there were ill feelings within the family, it always strongly bothered her.

"Mr. Malinkov," Baldoni started, "I need to remind you of the seriousness of this situation. Your father has been killed, murdered, and we need to investigate who may have committed the crime and why. I am going to need quite a bit of information from you, plus some DNA and fingerprint samples."

"Wait a minute, are you arresting me or something?" Anton said startled.

Boyle took one step forward and calmly stated, "Mr. Malinkov, we are just here to ask some questions for now. Your cooperation would be appreciated. If you need a moment to compose, then feel free to take the time. If you wish to have someone present, like a lawyer, then we will wait before we start asking any questions."

Anton took a deeper breath, exhaled and then stated, "Yes, you're right, I'm sorry, it's just that this is all so upsetting for my wife. Please come in, we can talk in the kitchen."

"We would prefer to talk in the living or dining room." Boyle stated. He never liked interviews in kitchens where knifes and other sharp objects were always present.

Anton led them toward a chair and sofa in the living room. The television was on and he switched it off as he sat in a reclining chair. Baldoni took a seat on the sofa opposite him while Boyle remained standing.

Baldoni took out her digital recorder and put it on the coffee table, switched on the recorder and stated, "This is detective Gina Baldoni. I am interviewing Anton Malinkov. Detective Aristotle Boyle is also present. It is four-twenty in the PM on Tuesday, November 27. We are in the living room of Mr. Malinkov's home."

She had a distinct edge to her voice and started the interview, "Mr. Malinkov, I know this is a difficult time for you and we'll be as patient as needed. Please tell me about the relationship between you and your father."

"My father and I did not get along very well, as a matter of fact, I couldn't tolerate the fucking bastard." Anton disclosed, "I haven't had any contact with him for the last few years."

"Since your mother's funeral?" Boyle asked.

Anton looked up surprised, "Yeah, that was the last time that I saw or spoke with him."

"Why did you assault him?" Boyle asked.

"Because it was my father who killed my mother." Anton replied.

"Our records show that your mother committed suicide." Baldoni stated as she picked up the interview.

"Yeah, well, people commit suicide for a reason. He was the reason." Anton said sharply.

"How so?" Baldoni asked.

"He was abusive." Anton continued with a sharp tone, "I saw it all as I was growing up. He was always yelling at her and sometimes hit her. I think my mother cried almost every day, at least that's what I remember. Even after they got divorced, he still abused her. He stole from her, swindled her out of money, even tried to take me from her, tried to get custody. When I was sixteen, I punched him in the stomach and told him if he ever came near me or my mother again that I would punch the shit out of him. But he still kept at her, and she never once confronted him with anything, never called the cops, never called him out."

"I eventually got sick of the whole thing and left, I left both of them behind, started my own life without all that shit. It was a fucked-up family and I wanted to be well rid of it. He could never see what he was doing to her, kept telling her that he loved her, and then the next minute he would be berating her for not cooking the steak the way he liked."

Anton stopped and took another deep breath, then he thought for a moment and said, "You know, he even cried at her funeral. That's when I punched him."

Baldoni waited for a few moments to let Anton compose himself before continuing with the questioning. "Can you tell us where you were this past weekend, particularly on Friday night."

"I was here with my family. I got off work and came home, had dinner and played with the kids until about eight o'clock. Around nine o'clock Julie and Richard came over from next door and the four of us played Euchre until eleven."

"Your wife and the next-door neighbors will verify this statement?" Boyle asked.

"Yes, of course, but you will need to ask them. I believe Richard and Julie are home right now if you want to go over and check." Anton became less agitated and started to focus on the situation. He wanted to express his feelings and fumbled some words, "Listen, I know that you have to check everything out and I suppose that you think I'm a likely suspect. However, even though I couldn't stand the bastard, I didn't kill him. So please, take whatever samples you need so that you can take me off your list."

When Anton said this, Baldoni felt less tense and took the interview into the normal measure of gathering basic information. She asked Anton what he did for a living and where he worked. He replied that he was a carpenter and worked for a company called Custom Cabinets Unlimited in Barrie. She asked about his personal and social life, to which he replied that he spent most of his free time with his family, but that they had some good friends in Alliston. Their friends were other married couples with young children. He also mentioned that he and his wife were active members of the local Roman Catholic church, St. Paul's, where a great deal of their social life was generated.

Boyle and Baldoni stayed for another hour, going through a series of formal questions in which they got the names of Anton's boss, the priest at the church, and the names of his wife and children.

Baldoni went back to the car and retrieved the SOCO kit, a black plastic briefcase that contained the forensic equipment required for Anton's fingerprints and swabs of his saliva. Boyle thanked Anton for his cooperation and expressed sympathy for the death of his father. Baldoni, still miffed at the reaction to his father's death, was not as generous. Her only parting words were to let him know that they would return for further information as the investigation progressed.

Boyle and Baldoni proceeded next door to speak with Richard and Julie Morgan. They were a retired couple, in their late sixties, and they both acknowledged that they had played Euchre with the Malinkovs on Friday night. They stated this was a common occurrence between the two families.

It was early evening when Boyle and Baldoni left, and the highways were congested with northbound traffic as people were leaving Toronto on their way home. Southbound traffic was only a bit lighter as the detectives headed toward the city.

"Maybe he hired somebody." Baldoni suddenly blurted out.

"Let's check his bank records for an extended period of time just to see if there are any expenditures unaccounted for," said Boyle. "The hatred for his father is an obvious motive, and there is the potential for revenge as he believed that his father was responsible for his mother's suicide."

"Also, since he is the only child," Baldoni noted, "he would stand to inherit all of his father's estate, including that house in the Beaches. With the current real estate market, that house would probably go for over a mil. When we get back, I'll check if Donna has received the bank records for Ivan and we'll see what his estate is worth, plus I'll get her to check on his transactions over the past couple of years."

"Find out if there is a will and who inherits the estate," Boyle said. He then decided to broach the subject of her interview. "Gina, I want to discuss your interview. Whatever the feelings or relationship between any two parties are, we have to be as objective as possible and our only concern should be with regards to solving the case."

"Yeah, I know Boss," she said with a little awkwardness, "I was just taken aback by the negative feelings that he had for his father. It's not something that I've ever experienced to that degree. I mean, I've dealt with other kids who had abusive fathers and the anger or fear in those children was apparent and even expected. But this guy was just so callous in speaking about his father's death."

They drove in silence for a while, both of them thinking different thoughts. Baldoni then expressed another potential angle, "The neighbors left around eleven o'clock," she started to speculate, "Singh has stated the murder happened during the evening on Friday night. What if Anton left after the neighbors, drove down to his father's place and committed the murder, then drove back home to Alliston."

"It's a possibility we'll have to consider, but I don't think that's what happened," Boyle said, "remember, if Anton left after eleven, maybe even eleven-thirty so the neighbors wouldn't hear him go, it would take him an hour and a half to get all the way down to his father's place in the Beaches. That would put him there about one o'clock. Now the father was fully dressed, expensive shirt and dress pants. He wasn't dressed for bed, so I don't think Ivan would have been so fashionably dressed at that time."

"It's possible," she said defensively.

"Yeah, it's possible, so let's look into Anton's alibi with his wife and check to see if Malinkov had any appointments or dates listed in his electronic calendar."

Chapter Eight

They returned to Police Headquarters and dropped off the digital recorder for one of the civilian employees to transcribe. Boyle was tired and checked out at the front desk then headed for the one place he knew where he could eat and drink, sit and talk, or simply listen to something other than police business. It was a cold but clear late November evening, and he wanted the warmth of friendship, food and liquor to pacify his mixed emotions about murder.

He was soon in the heart of 'Greek Town' on Danforth Avenue just east of the Don Valley.

From the beginning of the twentieth century, people had immigrated to Canada from almost every other country and created their own cultural communities in Toronto. Every summer, Greek Town had a festival called 'The Taste of the Danforth' which attracted thousands of people to the culture and music, but mostly for the food as Greek restaurants put up outdoor sidewalk kitchens.

Boyle's childhood friend owned a restaurant-tavern in Greek Town, and he often visited with Orestes to talk about anything, or nothing at all, or simply just drink and eat. Orestes Panikos and Boyle had first met at the Greek cultural school their parents had enrolled them in. They quickly became fast friends, and this friendship remained a solid, lifelong union between the two men.

Orestes had inherited the Parthenon Tavern from his father who had established the business in the sixties after his immigration from Greece. Orestes had basically grown up in the tavern and knew almost every Greek family that lived in the area.

"Ari," Orestes yelled when he saw Boyle come in the front door. "Come my friend, sit with me and share an Ouzo."

Boyle's heart and mind would always settle into a comfort zone whenever he heard the booming voice of his friend. He sat at the end of the long bar on the high stool. "Today I will need three or four so that my brain stops thinking about murders and victims and anything else."

"I heard about that one in the Beaches," Orestes said, "are you working on that one?"

"Yeah," said Boyle with a partial groan, "it's different, a puzzler, and one that will make your teeth clench with disgust."

"Fine, sit here and drink as much as you need to close the night lights in your brain. If you drink too much, you can sleep upstairs, I'll have Kostas help me to carry you up." Orestes said with a grin.

"You're too good to me, my friend."

Orestes pulled down two liqueur glasses from the overhead rack and sat them on the bar. He turned and reached behind for a bottle of Ouzo of Plomari, then poured both glasses to the brim with the clear anise flavored liquid.

"To your health Ari, may the Gods bless you with patience and insight."

"I would be happy if they just sent me a couple of clues that I could use," replied Boyle.

"You always think too much Ari, trying to figure answers, who killed who and why. You don't give yourself time to relax, time to just be Ari and not Detective Boyle. Why don't you come to the Ritual for Apollo on Saturday? There will be a bunch of friends attending and dinner will be served afterward. However, I even think there will be some new women there as well, some nice Greek women who write poetry and love to have sex with important policemen."

Boyle gave a small laugh and downed the Ouzo in one gulp. "Orestes, you always know how to cheer me up. Pour me another and tell me about these women."

The two men sat at the bar and talked with an honesty that can only be found between good friends who have shared the same experiences from childhood, growing up together with a bond of trust and love. Orestes had to get up every so often to deal with business or to greet long-time customers, leaving the bottle of Ouzo on the bar for Boyle to help himself.

****

The Parthenon Tavern had a very Mediterranean décor, the ivory-cream-colored walls had burnt orange trim and edges. They were decorated with large black and white murals that depicted various Greek mythological scenes and were framed with ornate edges painted an aqua-marine blue. Orestes' father had wanted to recreate a part of his homeland and taught his son that creating the ambience of the Greek Mediterranean somehow managed to make the traditional dishes taste better.

The main doorway consisted of massive, blue-gray double doors surrounded by Ionic columns on either side. Once a patron passed through the foyer, they couldn't help but think they were in Greece.

Boyle sat at the bar nursing his Ouzo when a woman entered the foyer from Danforth and sat at the opposite end. She was in her mid-forties, Boyle guessed, and had long jet-black hair with beige streaks on either side. She wore leather pants and a leather jacket that had a fur collar. Beneath the jacket, she wore a loose-fitting white shirt with a long shoestring style cord to fasten the front. The cord was quite loose, and the top was opened well enough to exhibit her small perky breasts.

She ordered a drink and looked along the bar at Boyle, and then past him, around the bar, then back to her drink. Boyle was feeling the effects of the Ouzo and was in a gently intoxicated, relaxed mood. He looked at the woman and studied her manners, demeanor, expressions and body language.

Very early in his career, Boyle became a student of human nature, watching people wherever he went, seeing how they reacted under different circumstances, whether in normal settings or under pressure situations. He listened to what people were saying and how they said it. He watched how people reacted to violence, to joy, to desire and to power, and he learned how to determine the way someone would react in almost any situation. All he needed was to determine what their nature was. It had become his habit, and everyone, except those closest to him, became a case study in behavior.

When asked, Boyle liked to say that he had his BA in human nature. If the person asked if human nature was an actual graduate course, he would simply reply that the BA stood for Behavioral Analysis.

He studied the woman at the end of the bar. He could see she once had a natural beauty, but that it had been wasted by the years of indulgent abuse. He perceived she was at that point in time when the beauty of youth had begun to lose to the years of booze, late nights, junk food and even junkier men.

Boyle guessed that she now went from bar to bar looking for Mr. Right, even though he had probably come and gone years ago. It was obvious that she

54

had already had a few drinks before she had come into the Parthenon, but as Boyle thought, the drinking probably helped to make all the men seem like Mr. Right.

Her eyes gave Boyle a second appraisal and then she delicately smiled, indicating that he should come over and talk. She hadn't thought much of him at first, but after a couple of drinks, her view had changed. *'Now,'* Boyle thought to himself, *'she thinks I'm Mr. Right.'*

Orestes returned and poured two more shots of Ouzo. He saw Boyle looking at the woman and said, "Not you're type Ari. She's been here a couple of nights each week for the past month. I think she must have moved into the area recently."

Boyle replied in a soft tone, "You're being a bit judgmental Orestes. Maybe she's just lonely. Maybe she has a story that goes all the way back to Mount Olympus."

"Maybe she's just a slut," snickered Orestes.

"Everyone loves a fallen woman." Boyle said with a smile, "Saints inspire. Saints are guides to your soul. Saints are revered. But everyone loves promiscuity."

"Slow down on that Ouzo my friend. You're going all philosophical on me again. Why don't you get yourself a nice Greek woman to take care of you? There always one girl after another, and they always leave, or you leave them. If you found a nice Greek woman and got married once again, then you would have a solid home, good meals, plenty of sex, and I would have someplace to go and get drunk myself once in a while."

"Orestes," Boyle's voice had a slight slur, "this woman wants me. She wants me to be her prince, her savior, her long lost dream. And I could probably be that for her, at least until the morning. Then there would be disappointed. She would have that look in her eye that says she had settled for second best again. She would even worry that maybe I'd start thinking that I was the one."

Boyle looked down to the end of the bar, smiled, and softly said, "Don't worry lady, it ain't me."

"Eh, what are you talking about Ari. What happened to that last woman I saw you with a couple of weeks ago, what's her name…Miranda, or something like that?"

"Yup, that's her name."

"Are you still seeing her?"

"You know, I guess you could say that we have an open relationship," Boyle smirked, "whenever she opens her legs, we're in a relationship."

Orestes let out a hearty laugh and then poured two more drinks. At the other end of the bar, a tall, good looking man walked up and stood beside the woman with the black hair and leather. He ordered a drink and offered to buy her one as well. She smiled a thank you. The man looked down at her and said, "You're very beautiful and I'm very rich. How can we make this work?"

The woman laughed and entwined her arm around his. They talked in soft whispers and in a short while, put on their coats and walked out the door together.

"Jesus," said Orestes, "that was a good line. I'll have to remember that one."

Boyle laughed and said, "She goes to the bar and gets drunk every night, then goes home with whoever buys her that last drink, whoever asks her what she thinks, whoever's left at the end of the bar, whoever's got a fancy car."

"Whoever's feeling really tight. Whoever's feeling alone tonight. Whoever leads her by the nose, whoever smells her stagnant rose."

"You're a fucking Greek poet, Ari, always have been." Orestes pronounced, "I don't care if your father descended from the King of England, you're a Greek on your mother's side and you're a Greek in your heart. Now let's get drunk, Kostas can close up the place."

Chapter Nine

The next morning Boyle started with a double espresso to match his double hangover. He made it to headquarters with another espresso and met detective Baldoni in the Argo with Aaron Silverstein, Dr. Surat Singh and Donna Chang, who did the clerical requirements that were required for warrants of bank records, phone records and other information. She was also the department's computer expert and was able to unlock computers with little technical help from the manufacturers.

Silverstein began his report by stating further inspection of the baseball bat did not reveal any more evidence than what was already reported. He also affirmed that the traces of blood and skin on the bat belonged to Malinkov. He had spoken with Dr. Singh before the meeting and both had agreed the baseball bat was the official murder weapon. He would continue to examine the bat to determine if any other evidence might be found.

He then plugged the wireless toggle into his laptop and connected directly to the two high-resolution screens. He opened a file labeled 'Plan Drawing Malinkov' which displayed a two-dimensional drawing of the crime scene. The drawing showed the layout of the main floor; the location of all the furniture, doorways and windows; the location where the body was found at the base of the stairs; and the location where it was suspected the beating took place. The drawing also indicated the location of the phone cradle in the kitchen and the location of where the baseball bat was found.

Using the cursor on his computer, Silverstein pointed to where a partial footprint had been found near the area where the beating occurred. There was some blood on the floor, possibly from the bleeding nose, and the front part of a running shoe had stepped on the blood. He stressed that it was only the top quarter of the shoe, a heavy impression from the right forefoot, as if someone had gotten into a squatting position in front of the victim to either look down or to speak to him.

He went on to state they were still attempting to verify all the fingerprints found in the house but had concluded that most belonged to the victim.

Baldoni announced the cleaning lady, Mrs. Maria Carmen, and the gardener, Mr. Philip Chin, would be in later that day for interviews and to have fingerprint and DNA samples taken for analysis.

After Silverstein had finished, Dr. Singh gave his report and confirmed the cause of death was heart failure due to severe shock. He plugged a second toggle switch into his computer and took over the digital projection from Silverstein and opened a file labelled 'Malinkov, Ivan'. The file was a black and white medical drawing of the human body and skeletal system with notations of all the injuries. Dr. Singh went on to explain each injury:

- A break of the radius bone of the left arm and three carpals of the left wrist.
- A dislocated joint of the right elbow and a fracture of the humerus bone of the right arm.
- A severe dislocation of the Lateral and Medial malleolus in the left ankle, plus a fracture of the Tibia in the middle of the left leg.
- A broken Patella on the knee of the right leg, and a dislocation of the knee itself.
- A break of both the Lacrimal and Nasal bones of the nose.
- Severe bruise on the penis and testicles, with a rupture of one of the testes.
- Severe bruising of the skin in the location of each skeletal injury.
- Minor internal hemorrhaging in the areas of all injuries.

Dr. Singh confirmed the time of death to have occurred between 6:00 and 8:00 pm on Sunday night. He also confirmed his previous estimate of the beating to have taken place between 8:00 pm and midnight on the Friday night.

Boyle asked about the toxicology report and Dr. Singh stated there were no recreational drugs in the victim's system. There were only traces of standard medications for high blood pressure and cholesterol control. He also stated that there were traces of alcohol but nothing that could be considered as a potentially problematic.

Boyle asked Baldoni for her update and she stated that Constable Singleton and a team of three other constables had begun interviewing all the houses on the rest of Kenilworth Avenue and the adjoining street with nothing new to report. She also stated the city maintenance team is searching all the sewer grates in a five-block radius in the search for the missing phones.

Baldoni then presented her report on the interview with Anton Malinkov. She began by saying it appeared the son had an extreme dislike of his father and that his reaction to his father's death was very dispassionate and uncaring. She noted that she detected a lack of motivation to cooperate, not in an obtrusive way, but as if the death of his father was a finality to an ongoing problem. She also reported that samples of the DNA and fingerprints had been given to Aaron's team for analysis. She stated Anton had an alibi for Friday evening at the time of the murder and that she will confirm the alibi later today when another officer will be interviewing Mrs. Malinkov.

Boyle asked Donna Chang if she had been able to open Malinkov's computer. Donna smiled and stated that Malinkov had saved the passcode in an automated mode so that there were no authentication requirements. She briefly searched through the hard drive and found a day timer, contacts list, expense reports including tax forms for the previous ten years, a photo album, an I-Tunes playlist, and a number of other programs and games. She was planning to start a detailed search of the contents as soon as the meeting was finished.

Boyle requested that she focus on obtaining the requisite permissions for Malinkov's bank records, the current business he was doing as a real estate agent and the contacts in both real estate and other affairs of interest. He wanted a printout of the contacts list to go into the case files.

He also asked if Mr. Wicker had provided a list of all the other real estate agents at Beach Realty.

When she responded that she had received the list, Boyle asked her to set up meetings at 55 division with the agents for mid-morning of the next day, and to remind them that the interviews were mandatory unless there was a reasonable excuse.

At this point, one of the civilian clerical employees knocked on the door of the Argo and informed Boyle that Mrs. Maria Carmen had arrived for her interview and was in the waiting room. Boyle thanked the group for their work and that they would reconvene the next morning to review any new information that may come up.

As everyone left the room, Boyle turned to Baldoni and said, "The house cleaner was employed on a weekly schedule. Mrs. Carmen will probably know more about Ivan than almost anyone else we interview. I will take the lead in this interview."

Chapter Ten

Maria Carmen was a heavy-set, middle-aged woman who was originally from Argentina. She had migrated to Canada before the turn of the century with her family and had started her own business as a professional cleaner when her children had all grown and left home for school, marriage or work. She had first met Ivan Malinkov through the Beach Realty agency, which hired her periodically to professionally clean homes prior to an open house.

She was sitting in one of the smaller interview rooms when Boyle and Baldoni entered. "Good morning Mrs. Carmen," Boyle started. "Were you offered a coffee when you first arrived?"

"Si, gracias, but I did not take any," she replied, "I have my espresso in the morning but then I try to remove coffee for rest of day. It upsets my stomach when I have too much."

"Yes, I also have an espresso to start my day," Boyle said in a friendly manner, trying to make the woman feel less nervous, "Mrs. Carmen, do you know why you are here?"

"Si, it has to do with Mr. Malinkov."

Boyle put the digital recorder on the interview room table. Mrs. Carmen had a look of bewilderment at the recorder and visibly tensed up.

"It's alright Mrs. Carmen." Boyle said, "We record our interviews to ensure we do not misquote anyone. This is common procedure now, so that we don't have to write notes on a pad of paper."

When she seemed to relax at Boyle's re-assurance, he turned on the recorder and continued, "Now, please tell me, how long did you work for Mr. Malinkov."

"I clean his home for about four years."

"How often did you clean his home?" he asked.

"Once a week, usually on Wednesday unless he ask me to come another day sometime."

"Why would he ask you to come another day?"

"Sometime he have business meeting, or sometime he has party and want me to come the day after party," she spoke as she started to feel more comfortable.

"Was Mr. Malinkov ever home when you were cleaning his house?"

"Sometimes," she replied, "he was mostly not home but sometimes he come to get papers or change clothes."

"How did Mr. Malinkov treat you?" Boyle asked.

"How he treat me? How do you mean?" she responded with another question.

"Well, was he nice to you?"

"He was okay. I mean he strictly professional. Sometimes he ask for me to do things extra like clean windows and things like that," she replied.

"Did he ever mistreat you?"

"No, no, he never make pass at me," she quickly responded.

"I'm sorry Mrs. Carmen, ah, would you mind if I called you Maria?"

"Si, please, go ahead," she responded with even less tension.

"What I wanted to ask was if he was ever mean to you? Did he criticize the way you cleaned the house or was he ever angry at the work you do?"

"No, I always do good job, so he never say anything bad to me."

"During all the time that you worked for him, did you notice anything out of the ordinary?" Boyle asked.

The change on Maria Carmen's face went from plain to a look of suspicious worry. "What do you mean?" she asked, "what is ordinary?"

Boyle changed his tone to a manner he called his 'personal-friendship' style. He used it when he wanted the person he was interviewing to relax and to feel comfortable about answering questions, as if they were a friend. It was something that he learned from observing salespeople, how they often acted as if they were best friends with the client, and how this seemed to work in putting clients at ease with whatever the sales pitch was. "What I meant to ask you Maria was if you noticed anything or anyone in the house that didn't seem to be proper as far as you were concerned? We value your opinion as you were someone who was often there."

"Well," she started with a more relaxed tone, "Mr. Malinkov was a nice man and he always gave me good tip for Christmas. I didn't notice anything bad, but sometimes he would have women come to house and the next morning when I come, the house was very messy. Especially his bedroom."

"How so?" asked Boyle.

"It was like party, with wine bottles on floor and sometimes stains on bed."

"What kind of stains?"

"You know, wine stains and sexy stains. Sometimes I have to wash sheets two three times before they clean."

"Were these women his girlfriends?"

"I don't know about these things. Always gone when I come to clean."

"Thank you, Mrs. Carmen." Boyle calmly spoke, "You have been very helpful. Detective Baldoni will take you to another office where we will need to get your fingerprints and DNA sample."

"Why you need my fingerprints?" Mrs. Carmen stated with a fright.

Sticking with his 'friendship' tone, Boyle explained to her that in all crime scenes, the investigators take fingerprints from all over the house. There are usually many fingerprints, most of them from the person or people who live in the house, and as she was the cleaning lady, there were probably many of her fingerprints. The investigators need a sample of her prints so they could eliminate her prints from their investigation. In this way, once they have eliminated her prints and Mr. Malinkov's prints, they might end up with some fingerprints that were unidentified or perhaps fingerprints of people who said they were not in the house.

He explained all this to her in great detail. In his experience, he found that taking the extra time to explain the procedures to people would make them feel at ease and often helped ensure their cooperation when more questions were needed to be asked later on.

Mrs. Carmen nodded and smiled and then followed Baldoni.

****

Boyle stepped out of the interview room and went to the waiting area where a thin, balding, fifty-something man of oriental descent was seated. Boyle walked over to him and asked if he was Mr. Chin, the gardener for Ivan Malinkov.

"Yes," replied Mr. Chin.

Boyle introduced himself and asked Mr. Chin to follow him to the same room where Mrs. Carmen had been interviewed. As they passed another room, Mr. Chin looked into the open doorway and saw Mrs. Carmen in the process of having her fingerprints taken.

"You think she did it?" Chin stated as they sat down.

"I beg your pardon" said Boyle.

"The cleaning lady. Do you think she's the one who killed Mr. Malinkov?"

"Why would you think that?" asked Boyle.

"I dunno, do you think I did it?" Chin said excitedly.

"Mr. Chin," Boyle responded, "we don't know who did it. The investigation is still in its early stages and we are currently interviewing people who knew Mr. Malinkov in order to get a perspective on the man and to see if any potential leads arise from the interviews."

Boyle switched the digital recorder on and stated, "Now Mr. Chin, let's just start with the basics. Can you tell me what your relationship was with Mr. Malinkov."

"I'm his gardener." Chin replied.

"How often did you work on his garden?" Boyle asked.

"I worked every Friday. I start at ten o'clock in the morning and work until finished."

"Did you work on Friday, November 23 at Mr. Malinkov's residence."

"No, on that week I worked on Thursday, raking leaves for the pickup on Friday by the city."

"What other kind of work did you do for him?"

"I did garden work." Chin responded quizzically.

"I'm sorry Mr. Chin, I mean was there other types of gardening work that you did for Mr. Malinkov."

"I did a number of basic things like cutting grass, control the weeds, plant flowers and maintain the plants, clearing rubbish from the flower beds, rake the leaves, you know stuff like that." Chin stated.

"What was Mr. Malinkov like as an employer?" Boyle asked.

"He was an asshole." Chin said in a deadpanned statement.

"That's a rather strong statement. Can you explain what prompts you to make such a condemnation of him?" Boyle requested.

"Sure," Chin started, "he expects you to work hard and he doesn't like to pay. I'm sorry I ever agreed to take on his property."

"Can you be more specific?" Boyle asked.

"He had a professional landscape designer come and do a complete plan for the front and back yard." Chin explained, "The designer made plans and maps, plotted everything, how it was supposed to look. Then the designer brought in a landscape crew who laid the flagstones for the path and dug the flower beds and planted the bushes. Once it was all completed, he expected me to take care of the landscaping as if it was my responsibility."

"He just paid me to be the gardener," he continued, "I'm not a landscaper. I planted the flowers, watered them, snipped the bushes, cut the grass, pulled out the weeds. Just the basic stuff like I said. But he criticized my work all the time, and sometimes when there was something that the landscaper did and it needed to be fixed, he expected me to do it. Like this one time when the flagstone path started to get uneven, he expected me to dig them up and fix them, and he refused to pay me until the problem was fixed."

"However, he didn't pay me any extra for fixing the flagstones, he insisted that it was part of my weekly duties. Also, there was this one time, an expensive rose bush had died, and he tried to tell me it was my fault. I told him, this is the Beaches, the soil is too sandy and I'm only here once a week. If he wanted the rose bush to thrive, then he should have looked after it himself."

"So, you had grievances with him." Boyle commented.

"Sure, I had grievances," said Chin with an assertive response, "I have grievances with assholes in general, but I don't go around killing them if that's what you are insinuating."

"No, I'm not making any insinuations," replied Boyle, "I'm just trying to get a clear understanding of what the man was like, what his business dealings were like, how he treated other people and so forth. I need to build a personality profile of the victim. It's a crime investigation technique in order to determine what could have been the motivation for the crime, and who may have had the motivation to commit it. By the way, were you ever in his house?"

"Sometimes, when I needed to use the bathroom."

"Does that mean you had a key for the house?" Boyle asked.

"No, there is a lockbox on the back door that has a key in it. As long as you have the code to the lockbox, then you can get into the house." Chin replied. "He was a real estate agent so having the lockbox was something that he was used to. Didn't the house cleaner tell you about the lockbox?"

"No, she didn't." Boyle answered. "Did she use it as well?"

"Sure," replied Chin, "the asshole wouldn't trust anybody, probably not even his own family."

"Okay, thank you for your time Mr. Chin. That's all we will need for now." Boyle said. "However I will also need to get your fingerprints and DNA samples."

"No problem," said Chin, "I understand these things must be done."

Boyle rose and opened the door to the interview room and led Chin down the hall. The Identification Officer was waiting until Mr. Chin arrived.

Chapter Eleven

Boyle walked down the hallway toward the cafeteria. He wanted a coffee to help offset the lingering hangover that seemed to have set up a roadblock between his logic and reality. Baldoni was in the cafeteria, the ear plugs of her phone an appurtenance of her age. She saw Boyle and waved him over, motioning with her finger and mouthing the word 'Singleton' indicating that she was listening to Constable Singleton's report.

Boyle sat down and waited for her to finish. He heard her ask Singleton a couple of questions, waited for the answers and then hung up the phone.

"We've interviewed everyone within a two-block radius of the home," she reported, "no one heard a thing. No one noticed anything unusual. We checked all the grounds, the backyards, the parks along the beach; everywhere, and we didn't find anything that could be related to the case. We've checked all the sewers in the neighborhood, the municipal trash and recycling containers. Singleton says everything has been checked and there isn't a witness or thread of evidence."

"As for the phones," she continued, "we've tried calling the numbers but all we get is the answering machine on the house phone and dead air on the cell phone. The murderer might be keeping the phones as mementoes, but they're not re-charging the cell phone."

"Maybe, but I don't think they're mementoes," replied Boyle, "I think they took the phones away because they meant for the victim to die slowly. They took the phones knowing that his only chance for survival was to crawl upstairs, and the attempt to do so would cause so much pain that the victim would suffer greatly."

"It must take a really sick person to go that extent to murder someone." Baldoni stated incredulously, thinking back to her youth when she had suffered a broken arm.

Boyle continued, "Just the act of killing another human being is something that most people would not be able to bring themselves to do. And yes, I know I'm discounting things like war, revolts and other violent killings, but those are societal events and death happens. However, people in general are not prone to killing. There are cases where people will kill in self-defense, and I've seen situations where someone loses a loved one and they go temporarily insane to take revenge. But those cases are usually not planned to this degree, hence the temporary insanity classification."

"But to murder this way, there had to be some sort of motivation, like cold blooded revenge, and we have to figure what that particular motivation was, otherwise we might never understand how any person could commit such a gruesome crime. We have to know why there was such a revenge factor involved, why they wanted this person to suffer so much pain, and why it appears they took so much cold calculated pleasure in doing it."

"So, you're basically talking about a Sadist." Baldoni said.

"Yes, a Sadist but not the modern use of the word. No, this is far deeper than your basic run-of-the-mill Sadism where people use whips and spankings while looking for a bit of wicked fun. This is way more psychotic. Something more cruel like the inquisitors of the Spanish Inquisition who took pleasure in the torture and torment of their victims."

"Are we talking about a potential serial killer?" she asked.

"Let's not go down that road unless we have to. However, it wouldn't be a bad idea to check the database for anything similar. I'll speak with Donna about researching if there are other cases with a similar MO. Let's finish up and go over to Whitlock's."

****

Whitlock's was a family restaurant that had been in the Beaches for over forty years. The interior was all stained dark oak, with a large fireplace located near the entrance that added both décor and warmth during winter months. The pine-wood tables and chairs were stained in a dark walnut and along with the ebony stained hardwood oak floors, the restaurant had an early colonial ambiance. The tall windows along the east wall looked out on Kenilworth Avenue.

The owner's name was Edi Patel, whose family had taken over the restaurant two years ago. Keeping the original name of Whitlock's was part of the requirement for the new owners because the name had a certain amount of goodwill and was a known establishment in the Beaches community.

Boyle and Baldoni entered and looked for an employee to direct them to Mr. Patel. A waitress approached and asked them, "Will this be a table for two?"

Baldoni smiled and said in a hushed tone, "We are here to see Mr. Patel, he is expecting us. We are detectives with the Toronto Police force."

The waitress looked alarmed for a brief second, and then regained her composure and led Baldoni and Boyle to the office in the back, behind the kitchen. She knocked on the open door and said, "Edi, the police are here to see you."

Edi Patel was a short, slender man with a clean-shaven face and a full head of neatly trimmed wavy hair. He wore a tweed suit jacket and faded blue jeans. He immediately rose and came to the doorway with his hand extended. "Hello, hello," he said, "how my I help you? Can we get you some coffee or tea, or perhaps something from the bar?"

"No thank you," Boyle replied, "I've already had too many coffees today. How about you Gina?"

Baldoni looked at Boyle and wondered if he was seriously asking her if she wanted something or if it was his sardonic sense of humor in play. "No thank you, I'm fine as well." She then pulled the digital recorder from her coat and placed it on Mr. Patel's desk.

"This is detective Gina Baldoni. We are interviewing Edi Patel, owner and manager of Whitlock's restaurant in his office. Detective Aristotle Boyle is also present. It is four-fifteen in the PM."

"Mr. Patel," Boyle spoke up and asked, "are you aware of the crime that was committed on Friday night, November 23, just down the street from this restaurant?"

"Of course, it's been the biggest news in the Beaches since my family acquired this business."

"We are seeking witnesses to the event or even someone who may have seen something peculiar that may help in our investigation. You have large windows overlooking Kenilworth Avenue. We want to find out if any of your staff or patrons may have seen something or someone on Kenilworth that

Friday evening, after eight o'clock pm. Can you give us a list of your staff who were working during that time?"

"Yes, of course. There were two cooks, three waitresses and the bar manager. I was not here at that time. As for the patrons, I could check the receipts of those who paid with debit or credit cards. However, if they had paid with cash, I probably won't be able to provide you with any information."

"Is the restaurant equipped with security cameras?" Baldoni asked.

"No, I'm afraid we decided the expense was not worth it." Edi spoke frankly, "This area is the heart of the Beaches and there is very little cause to worry about crime or even problems with customers. I don't believe we have ever had any issues since I've been here. Not even someone skipping out on the bill, so we decided to save the money instead."

"The names and contact information for the employees will be a good start, we'll have one of our constables contact them," Baldoni stated. "As for the patrons, we will need copies of all the receipts for Friday evening. Would there be any way of knowing where they sat in the restaurant."

"Sorry, no, not from the receipts." Edi replied, "We don't identify the table positions on the receipt. However, the waitresses are identified for tip dispersals and they generally are assigned sections of the restaurant so we could ask them if they can remember."

"I will have all of the contact information of the employees for you in about fifteen minutes. I can have the receipts pulled for you in about an hour. If you would like to wait, you are welcome to be a guest in my restaurant. I have great respect for the police force and would be most happy to have you dine with us." Edi seemed to be quite sincere in his offer.

Baldoni was prepared to thank him and refuse the offer, but Boyle quickly spoke up and stated that he was hungry and would be glad to enjoy a small meal in his establishment. However, he also insisted to Edi that they pay for the meal. Edi protested at first and then understood the police were under great scrutiny in these times, and even a simple free meal could be considered as corruption. He apologized, showed the detectives to a large table, and then went to tell the cook that he was to ensure the meal was superb, with generous quantities.

Chapter Twelve

Thursday morning, six days after the night of the murder. Boyle knew that witnesses would soon begin to forget, and evidence would start to dissipate as per the theory of erosion. A blood stain would turn into a clump of dirt. A fingerprint would smudge until it was unrecognizable. Footprints would wash away with the rain and snow. Winter was just one cold breeze around the corner and Boyle didn't have any real suspects, except for the son who had an impeccable alibi.

He met Baldoni, Donna Chang and Aaron Silverstein in the Argo. Donna confirmed that all of the real estate agents would be present at 55 Division, except for one woman who was on maternity leave. Donna had set up the interviews to start at 9:30 am. Boyle knew it would be a full day of asking people if they had any dealings or relationships with the victim, where they were on Friday night, and if they knew of any reason someone would want to kill him.

He expected to come away with nothing. No cold-blooded killer walks into an interview, breaks down and confesses after a few simple questions. If this had been a marital dispute where one spouse killed the other, he could use his psychological know-how to trick the still living spouse into a trap of logic, lies and lines of reason, and eventual confession. However, this case was a well-planned act of revenge. No witnesses and little, if any, evidence. Winter was coming and this case was already getting cold.

Aaron Silverstein reported there was no further information regarding the murder weapon. It was completely clean apart from a trace of the victim's skin and blood, and the faint residue of both ammonia and Pine Sol.

With regards to fingerprints, the FIS team had completed checking the main rooms and all the door fixtures in the house. The only prints they could identify were of the victim and the contracted house cleaner, Mrs. Carmen. He even joked that he could provide Mrs. Carmen with a great business reference as the home was so well cleaned that there were few prints to be found anywhere.

Silverstein also reported that he could not identify the shoe from the print left in the blood stain.

It was only the front third of the shoe and the print was smudged as the killer would have turned and moved while squatting and then standing up. He was also unable to determine the shoe size from the partial print. Lastly, he could not determine if it was a man's or woman's shoe.

He then gave details about the home alarm system. He stated that it was a 'basic' system and did not include central monitoring or surveillance. It was a simple, cost-effective (or cheap as he would put it) system that would be turned on when the homeowner left the premises and turned off when they returned. Once turned off, there would be no alarm function. He stated that according to the data within the system, it hadn't been turned on for a month prior to the assault. Malinkov obviously did not put much stock in having an alarm system and it was probably simply there for 'show' so that any potential thief might believe there was a system in place.

Donna Chang presented Boyle with a printout of the contact's list from Malinkov's computer and stated the list was also on the network server in the case file folder. She stated she had managed to get into Malinkov's e-mail account. She mildly giggled when she said that he had a separate file on his computer called 'Wine List'. In the file, he listed all of the passwords for his Facebook page, LinkedIn page, e-mail, dating sites, I-Tunes, and, she said with a surprised voice, his banking passwords. Anyone hacking into his computer could have found everything they wanted once they opened that one file.

"Anything of interest within the e-mails?" Boyle asked.

"Most had to do with business," Donna replied, "however, there were a number of e-mails that went back and forth between him and a woman named Barbara Booth. The e-mails he sent to her sounded like pleas for forgiveness and that they needed to talk. Other e-mails stated how much he loved her, a few with some really schmaltzy love poems and more requests for meetings and dinners. Her replies to him were to stop bothering her and to basically go jump in the lake, but not in such a courteous manner."

"Can you set up a meeting with her for later in the day, and an interview with Anton Malinkov's boss." Boyle requested, "I'll talk with the Booth woman and Gina will go up north to speak with the owner of the cabinet making company…what's it called again?"

Baldoni looked over at Boyle with a sly look and said with sarcasm, "It's called Custom Cabinets Unlimited. And sure Boss, make me travel up to Barrie through rush hour traffic while you interview the love interest in a nice cozy downtown apartment."

Boyle and Donna Chang both laughed, and Donna said, "You said it yourself Gina, he is the Boss."

"Thanks Donna," Boyle said, "you better get started, you've got a few phone calls to make and a lot of research to get done by tomorrow. Gina, I want to talk for a moment before we leave."

Donna Chang folded her laptop and left the room along with Aaron Silverstein. Boyle waited for the door to close and then turned to Baldoni, "I don't like the way this case is shaping up. We have a killer, or more than one, and it seems they are intelligent enough to have planned this crime to the last detail. Now, I've dealt with intelligent murderers before, in which they did incredible feats to cover their tracks and leave little or next to no evidence behind. But this one is different, and I am starting to wonder about the mind of the person, or persons who set this up."

"What's got you so concerned?" Gina asked.

"It's the crime scene, what happened at it, the way the murder was committed, left him there to die slowly in the heart of the Beaches community. If this had happened in the middle of the desert or deep in the forest, I can see where they could safely assume the victim wouldn't be found, but this was in the middle of a family-oriented community, with people next door and potentially walking on the street."

"Maybe they're not as intelligent as you think Boss. Maybe the lack of evidence was pure luck on their part. Maybe the killer didn't know any better than to leave the victim alive."

Boyle looked up at the ceiling in thought, "The killer didn't even try to make it look like a robbery. They could have taken his watch, his wallet, his jewelry just to give an appearance of a robbery but didn't. I don't think the killer was stupid or lucky. As a matter of fact, I think whoever did this is quite intelligent, and what they did, the way they did it, was something that had a great deal of forethought and preparation."

"Why?" she asked.

"Look at the whole of this crime scene, I almost think the killer wanted us, and the rest of the world to know that this was personal. At least, they wanted someone to know this was personal. Maybe they wanted their personal Gods to know this was personal. This killing appears to be a vendetta, and I think there was a purpose in leaving him alive."

Baldoni looked hard at Boyle, "This is really bugging you, isn't it?"

"Yeah," he replied, "this one isn't just about catching a killer. This is one I need to understand, where the motive is almost as important as the deed."

He stopped talking and looked down at his laptop for a few moments. Then he quickly closed it and said, "Okay, let's go. We've got a lot of interviews ahead of us, but first Stanforth wants to see me."

****

"From your reports I can see you're not getting anywhere." Stanforth said with a touch of admonishment.

"I admit this case is different." Boyle responded defensively. "FIS can't find any evidence that we can use, and so far, there are no witnesses that heard or saw anything. I'm starting to believe the invisible man is our only suspect."

"Ari, get your ass in gear and get this done." Stanforth's voice was hard. "Margaret says the press are asking a lot of questions, and we don't have any answers for them, I mean nothing. It's the Beaches for God's sake. It's supposed to be one of the places where everyone wants to live."

"What about the footprint?" Stanforth's voice pushed for an explanation.

"It's the front third of a well-worn running shoe with indeterminate treads and with no way to indicate brand or size." Boyle response to the question showed his frustration with Stanforth's attitude, "We can't even tell if it's a male or female shoe."

"What about the son? It seems like he had motive, hated his father and is due to inherit a shit-load of cash and property."

"The son has an alibi. I'm not saying that it couldn't be him, but until we find any evidence that would connect him to the crime scene, we can't touch him."

"Find something." Stanforth remained inflexible. "And find it fast. I've taken too much shit over the past couple of years for this department's inability to resolve some sensational crimes, and believe me, that shit is going to start flowing downhill from now on."

"Yes, sir," Boyle responded with the irritation of a child that's been unjustly scolded.

Chapter Thirteen

Boyle and Baldoni arrived at 55 Division station where Donna Chang had made arrangements for all the real estate agents to meet. It was the station that encompassed all of the Beaches area as part of its zone. She had set the interviews at staggered times so the seven agents could all be interviewed in one day.

The first agent they interviewed had little contact with Malinkov and could provide no information toward the investigation. The second agent was Melinda Bailey, who had a couple of professional associations with him as either buyer or seller of a property but had also met him at company gatherings. She stated she purposely avoided Ivan because at one company gathering, Ivan had put his hand on her bum and squeezed it, repeatedly. She had been totally offended by the action and told Ivan to never bother her again. She told him she was a happily married woman and wanted nothing to do with him, in business or personally.

The next agent they interviewed was Laura Cahill, who walked into the interview room as if she were a model walking the runway at a fashion show. Laura was an attractive woman in her mid-thirties. Her sandy brown hair had been dyed blonde and a tinge of the natural brown was carefully left to suggest highlights. Her high, well-shaped cheekbones, blue eyes and full lips accentuated the beauty of her face. Many people actually mistook her for an actress or a model. She was slender in figure with deep, full breasts and curves throughout her body that most men would call perfect.

Baldoni was generally unimpressed with women who used their sexual appeal to get what they wanted. She worked hard, using her brain and brawn to achieve her goals and felt animosity toward women who used a stylish pout or revealing cleavage to their advantage. She placed the digital recorder on the table and switched it on. "Ms. Cahill," she started right away, "how long have you been working with the Beach Realty company?"

"I started working with them several years ago." Laura replied while leaning back and crossing her legs to give Boyle a full view of her shapely body.

Noticing the display that Laura was obviously providing for Boyle, Baldoni went into the questions with a hard tone, "Have you ever had a working relationship with Ivan Malinkov, real estate dealings that you both worked on?"

"Yes, Ivan and I had worked on a number of properties together."

"How did you get along with him?"

"Professionally, we worked together well," she replied.

"And personally?" Baldoni asked with a sense of knowing.

"I detested the man." Laura stated as she glanced up at the ceiling.

"Why?" Baldoni asked.

"He was a misogynist bastard who took advantage of women. He was unscrupulous in getting what he wanted, and he would just as easily fuck you or throw you aside." Laura stated with flushed cheeks.

Baldoni noted that the top three buttons of Laura's blouse were open, providing sufficient view of her well-shaped breasts. Baldoni suspected that Laura Cahill may talk harshly about misogynist men, but had no problem using her looks to finalize sales with them.

"Can you give me an example in regard to what you just stated?" Boyle interjected.

"Well, when I was just starting out, he kinda took me under his wing, brought me in on a couple of sales that he was working on. I met him at his house one evening on the pretext that we were going to be working on the closure of a sale. He offered me a glass of wine and the documents were on the coffee table for two different properties. We started talking about them, the wine went quick and he offered me another glass. Next thing I know, his hand was on my thigh and his fingers were stroking my leg. I didn't know what to do, I was new, I was scared and said that I couldn't do this. He looked at me and smiled and told me to calm down, and then he told me, 'This is all part of the business baby'. Those were the exact words that he used, 'This is all part of the business baby', I remember them like it was yesterday."

"He went on to tell me a load of bullshit about how it would be bad for my career if I established a bad reputation within the real estate community. He said that agents have to work with each other and they have to present an aura of trust and confidence to the clients. He told me that working with him would build my reputation in the community, and that he could include me in his contracts, split commissions and so forth."

"So, you slept with him." Baldoni said with hardened disapproval in her voice.

"Yeah, I slept with him a few times. Didn't particularly like it, but I didn't know what else to do, because the implication was clear that if I worked with him, I would be successful, and if I didn't, then my career would suffer." Laura said looking defiantly at Baldoni. "I was determined to make this my career and I didn't want some asshole ruining it for me before I could really get it off the ground. So yeah, we had sex for a few months."

"And how did this professional relationship eventually end?" Boyle asked.

"We worked on a large condo project a few years ago. I was assisting Ivan and when the sale was finalized, my name wasn't even on the papers. I wasn't entitled to any of the commission. When I confronted him, he just smiled and said if I were to come over to his house, he would give me a cheque. He said something along the lines that this was all part of my training, and I had just learned from the best."

"And how did you react?" Baldoni asked, her mouth set in a hard line.

"I was mortified, I didn't know what to do. He made me feel like I was just a cheap whore. I went and talked with the head of the agency, Mr. Brian Wicker, but he basically told me to put it behind me and that I shouldn't deal with Ivan anymore. Brian told me these things must be kept quiet, and any complaints or bad publicity would hurt all the agents in the company. He told me that he would have a 'word' with Ivan"

"And did he speak with Ivan about your complaint?"

"I believe they went out for drinks and laughed about it." Laura said without emotion, "I had to put it behind me. I did not want to start a war, I needed to work. That was a few years ago, and ever since I've barely spoken a word to either of them."

"On Friday, November 23, can you tell us where you were that evening." Baldoni asked.

"I was at 593 Willow Avenue, from seven-thirty until after ten o'clock. I was the listing agent for the property and there were multiple bids on the home, so I was with the homeowners fielding calls from the other agents who were bidding. Around ten thirty, I left the home and went to the realty office where I completed the paperwork on the final bid."

"What time did you get home?" Boyle asked.

"It was after midnight by the time all parties signed off on the paperwork." Laura stated with confidence.

"Thank you, Ms. Cahill," Baldoni said with a tight-lipped smile. "We will need to see the paperwork on the sale, and I will confirm with the home-owners that you were present throughout the evening."

"I'll have Janis send a copy of the paperwork to you. She's the secretary at Beach Realty." Laura stated with a sarcastic smile aimed at Baldoni.

"Yes, I've met Janis," Boyle said, "she seems like a very nice woman."

"Yes, she is." Laura's smile changed to an allure as she replied to Boyle. "If there is nothing more, then I would like to leave now as I have some appointments."

"Detective Boyle will take you to the next office." Baldoni stated with the cold smile of the final word. "We would like to take your fingerprints and a sample of your DNA."

****

Boyle decided to split up the last four interviews in order to get through them more quickly. He wanted to ensure that both he and Gina would be able to make the afternoon appointments with Malinkov's ex-girlfriend and with Anton's employer.

The two interviews that Boyle held did not provide any useful information. Both agents only dealt with Ivan on a professional basis, however, one man seemed to think Ivan was a 'nice guy'. The same lack of information was given by the first agent Baldoni interviewed but the last agent was the very interesting Awesome Gandhi.

Awesome Gandhi had a jolly appeal to his round face and thick moustache. He wore thick, black framed glasses which accentuated his deep dark eyes and very high forehead. It was the type of face that seemed to always have a hearty smile, even when he wasn't smiling.

"That is a very interesting name you have," Baldoni commented at the start of the interview.

"Thank you, my mother was very creative," replied Mr. Gandhi.

"May I call you Awesome?" Baldoni asked as she switched on the digital recorder. "Pardon my forwardness, but I just like saying your name."

"Yes, by all means. That is my name," he said with a smile.

"What was your relationship with Ivan Malinkov," she asked in a tranquil, composed manner.

"We didn't have a relationship, we just worked at the same company." Awesome replied with the perpetual smile.

"Did you ever have any business dealings with him?"

"I tried not to, but in this business, it is sometimes unavoidable. If he is representing one of the parties on the sale of a property, you don't have much choice."

"Why didn't you want to have any dealings with him?"

"I didn't like him. I didn't like him as a person."

"Why?" she asked inquisitively.

"I found him to be a very callus man. He was the selfish type of individual that only cared about what could benefit him. He wasn't very caring about his own clients, never mind anyone else's. Or shall I say, he used what I call the 'Sales Deception' with his clients."

"What is the Sales Deception?"

"It is when a salesperson acts as if they were your best friend, even goes so far as to make promises to baby sit your kids. They act this way to gain your trust and then just as quickly ignore you once the sale is complete. I saw Ivan do this a few times, but that's just the way some sales agents go about their business."

"Did his behavior ever cause any problems?" she further asked.

"Well," he thought for a moment, "I actually once heard him tell his own client a lie. I didn't say anything at the time because we were in the middle of negotiations over a property his client owned, but the things he told his client were despicable as far as I was concerned. He lied to them in order to get the sale done quickly, not to ensure they got the best price or what they needed."

"What was the lie?"

"He withheld information that there was a second offer on their property."

"Why would he do that? Wouldn't that boost the sale price and garner him more commission?"

"Yes, that would be so, however he wanted to make sure that my client would successfully purchase the home. I cannot verify this, but I believe he had some sort of deal with Beach Realty where he would try to ensure the property was sold to an agent from the same agency. This would increase the profit for the agency itself, as the commissions from the buying and selling agent would both go to the agency. I'm not sure what the deal was, but when he told his clients that there was no other offer, he pressured them into selling the property for the offer that my clients had made."

"How did you know that there was another offer?"

"The agent representing the second offer was a friend of mine. He told me about it afterward. He told me that he had tried to call and had left messages stating his clients wanted to make the second offer. Ivan never took the calls or returned the messages until after our deal was accepted and signed. He told my friend that his calls had come too late. A couple of days later, I asked my friend what time he had called, and that's when I knew Ivan was scamming his clients."

"Did you report it?" Baldoni asked.

"I didn't know it was happening at the time, and later, I couldn't say anything because I had represented the party that bought the house. I found myself in a complicated situation. How could I go back to my clients and inform them there had legally been another offer? They had legally purchased the house and would not have any interest in rescinding the sale in order to ensure the other people had a fair chance of bidding on the house."

"Yes, I can see where that would leave you vulnerable." Baldoni said with a sympathetic voice. "Did you confront Mr. Malinkov with the knowledge?"

"I mentioned it to Mr. Wicker," Awesome now chose his words carefully, "because I didn't want the Real Estate Board or other agencies intervening in future business if this was ever to be reported."

"This is what I do for a living and stirring the waters will only give you a bad reputation. In this business, reputations are very important, especially for people of ethnic backgrounds."

"That is a dilemma." Baldoni noted, "However, it's still bad practice, also unethical, I believe it should have been reported."

"But who's going to report it?" Awesome pointed out, "our industry is supposed to be self-regulating. Things are often swept under the carpet in order to prevent any negative publicity. This happens with many organizations, there are always bad apples who sometimes remain unblemished."

Baldoni looked at him with a wary eye and wondered if this was a slight toward the police department, but Awesome quickly smiled and said, "Of course this happens in any industry, be it manufacturing or distribution, and if you look thoroughly at any organization, whether it is political, social or charitable, you'll always find something. So, do I put my job in jeopardy because of some obnoxious individual whose motivations are for selfish gain."

Baldoni looked again at Mister Gandhi and thought about the intelligence and wisdom behind that jolly face and pleasant demeanor, and she thought about what Boyle had instructed her on not letting the initial impressions or feelings toward someone deceive your perceptions.

"Mr. Gandhi," Baldoni sounded concerned, "these are serious allegations that you are making. The information from these interviews will most likely be brought up at other interviews, including further interviews with Mr. Wicker."

"That's fine by me," Gandhi continued to smile, "Wicker needs me as his connection into the ethnic community. All the other agents at Beach Realty are lily white, so if he wanted to get rid of me, that would be his loss. I would just bring my clients with me to another agency. Plus, there is also the fact that I have all the documentation supporting my claim, so I would sue his ass."

Baldoni smiled broadly, "One last question Mr. Gandhi, can you tell me where you were last Friday evening, November 23?"

"Yes, my family and I were at the Vishnu Mandir temple on Yonge Street, up in Richmond Hill. You know the one that has the giant sixty-foot statue of Hanuman in the back-parking lot and the life-size statue of Mahatma Gandhi in the small park beside Yonge."

"You're namesake." Baldoni said with a twinkling eye.

Awesome puts his hand together as if in prayer and said, "I only wish I could be as dedicated and holy as that man."

"Thank you, Mr. Gandhi," she said with respect, "if you would now follow me into the next interview room, we would like to take your fingerprints and a sample of your DNA."

"You're most welcome," he replied, still smiling.

Chapter Fourteen

When the interviews were completed, the two detectives met in the division cafeteria to discuss what they had learned. Boyle looked at his drab ham sandwich and wished he was sitting at the Parthenon in front of a fresh Horiatiki salad. He ate half of the 'forensic specimen', the nickname given to sandwiches at the cafeteria, while Baldoni gave a complete account of Awesome Gandhi's interview, focusing on the 'shady' sales antics of Ivan Malinkov, and the implication of Mr. Wicker in the unethical practices. Boyle agreed that another interview with Wicker was imperative.

They both left 55 Division, Gina making her way to Hwy. 400 to drive north and Boyle heading to the Yonge Street and Eglinton Avenue area to meet with Barbara Booth, the last known female relationship of Ivan Malinkov.

****

Boyle always like to conduct interviews of a personal nature in the person's home. His experience taught him that you could tell a lot about a person from the way they lived, their taste for furnishings, the books they read, whether they were neat and tidy or whether they were slobs. A person's home could give you a great deal of information about their character; religious symbols that were present, the art they displayed, and quite often, their cultural heritage.

The home of Barbara Booth told him that she was a non-descript person who lacked imagination, creativity, and flair. The few books on her shelves were pulp romance fiction; and the only pieces of art were a couple of framed posters from the Art Gallery of Ontario and some Inuit statue reproductions.

The furniture was a mix of Ikea and local discount shops. The most telling feature of the furnishings was the home entertainment system that dominated the living room.

Barbara Booth was of medium build, about five foot six inches tall, long dark brown hair that fell below her shoulder, but with a friendly face. She lived on the seventeenth floor of one of the many condo buildings that had sprung up in the Yonge/Eglington area over the past decade. Her real estate agent had been Ivan Malinkov, with whom she was attracted to, and eventually had a relationship with.

Boyle took out his digital recorder and explained about the latest policies of using recordings instead of taking notes. Her expression to this explanation seemed to indicate that she was oblivious about her rights or any other implication this may have. Her reaction was to simply smile and wait for Boyle to begin.

He began by asking her all the standard questions about where she worked, what her relationship with Ivan had been, where she had met him and when it had ended. She responded that she was a professional cosmetician, had met Ivan when she purchased her condo and how they had dated for about six months. She had decided to leave him back in September when she had found out about the other women he was seeing while he was supposedly in an exclusive relationship with her.

"Can you give me a better understanding of who the man was and what he was like?" Boyle asked.

"Oh sure, he was a real romantic, and yes I'm being sarcastic," she snickered, "I mean, who takes their girlfriend out for dinner and saves the receipt in order to claim it as an expense. I know this is done by lots of salespeople, but he did it every time. I'm surprised he didn't try to claim the condoms he bought as an expense as well."

Boyle chuckled at this remark and then continued. "Was that one of the reasons you decided to end the relationship?"

"No, there were a number of things that caused me to leave," she replied, "he sometimes cancelled our dates with the excuse that he was closing a sale, and later on I would find out he was with some other woman in a bar instead."

"How did you find out?" Boyle asked.

"Once, I was invited by him to a party at the real estate company. Some people didn't know I was his girlfriend and they told stories about him, which I believe they always did because of his reputation as a womanizer. They liked to gossip about his antics."

"Later, when I confronted him with the gossip I had heard, he was cool and calm and started talking his way out of it. That's when I realized how good of a liar he was, which is probably why he was so successful selling real estate."

"And that's when you left him?" he asked.

"It was about a month later," she responded, "he was good in bed and I was enjoying the sex, but after a while, I decided that I didn't want to put up with his bullshit, so I asked him to make a commitment to our relationship and stop seeing other women. He told me he felt the same, and I could see that lie covering his face like a Mardi Gras mask. The next day I sent him an e-mail telling him that it was over."

"And that was the last time you saw him?"

"Oh, no. He would show up at my work and wait for me wanting to talk. He would send me e-mails telling me that I was the one woman that was meant for him. And then one night, I went down to one of the pubs around the corner and he was there with another younger, blonde woman. I went up to him, called him a bastard and to never contact me again."

"That must have impressed the other woman." Boyle said with a smirk.

"I'm not sure," she said, "she didn't seem to respond in a negative way, except to give me a look that made me feel like I was an annoyance."

Boyle thanked her for her candid remarks and stated he may need to interview her again if anything else came up in the investigation. He left her apartment with a feeling of ambivalence. She seemed to be an example of the shallowness within society. In the elevator, he fought against his ego and reminded himself he needed to accept people for who they are, and to accept them without this superiority feeling that often crept up on him like a Trojan horse.

This had always been a struggle within him. His study of various religions and philosophies accentuated his own practices in his Greek heritage. He generally classified himself as a humanitarian with a deep respect for most spiritual ideologies, but he always found it hard to keep his ego in check when he met people that just seemed to float through life, without any true convictions or even a sense of the divineness that was inherent in human beings. He even had a deep respect for atheists and agnostics who had chosen their paths based on their own personal discoveries and intellectual explorations.

He decided to drive down to the Parthenon for dinner and meet with Orestes. Whenever his ego began to flare up in a contentious manner, he knew that an evening with his friend would always cure whatever ill feelings he had.

****

Detective Gina Baldoni was one of the youngest officers to ever become a detective in the Specialized Criminal Investigations-Homicide unit. She joined the Metropolitan Toronto Police force after graduating from the two-year Police Foundation program at Georgian College and then completed the Toronto and Ontario Police College programs.

Gina had been raised in a loving, Italian family. Both her parents were very liberal and raised all four of their children, two older and one younger brother, with the idea that love and support were the most important qualities in life. Religion always came a poor second to education, and traditions were respected as long as they did not place illogical restrictions on the development of either the males or females of the family.

Sexist axioms like 'a woman's place was in the home' were derided by both of her parents and she was taught her place was as an equal to all the other members of the family. As she grew, she was often surprised at the way some of her female Italian friends were treated in their own homes, and her sense of independence had caused a few rifts between the parents of her friends and herself. There were a few occasions where her friends were forced to abandon their friendship with Gina because she was deemed a 'bad influence'.

Now in her mid-thirties, Gina was an attractive woman, not a great beauty by Hollywood standards, but she had an appealing look about her. At five-foot, ten inches, she easily passed all the physical tests and psychological requirements. Her shoulder length, sandy brown hair was usually tied behind her head in a bun or ponytail and this accentuated the bangs that ended just above her eyebrows. Her almond shaped brown eyes sat well above her distinct cheekbones. Her lips were a touch above thin and her neck was a touch short of long.

She was of medium build, but she was pure athlete from her neck down. Her body was toned and muscular, and she methodically went to the gym as often as she could. Working out was an addiction for her, and she often thought that a good workout was better than sex. Whenever the work schedule allowed, she was up early and ran for miles, often at the Metropolitan Toronto Zoo.

She joined the police force because she wanted to be an independent person. The police force, although it had its own gender bias among individual members, still allowed women to take control of situations, and this enabled them with a sense of equality and even superiority compared to the general population. She supported equal rights for everyone but was not a true 'women's rights' activist because she never saw herself as being less than anyone else.

She liked being a cop and she had started working with Boyle when she was first promoted to the homicide division. She liked Boyle because he was fair. He was in charge because he was a senior detective, but he never seemed to look down upon anyone on his team. He expected from her the same quality of work that he would expect from any detective.

****

Lawrence Mulroney was the owner of Custom Cabinets Unlimited in Barrie, Ontario. With the rush hour traffic, Baldoni knew she would be late and asked if he could remain at his place of business until she arrived. Mr. Mulroney said he would grab an early dinner at the diner next door and to call him when she got there.

Custom Cabinets Unlimited was the large corner unit in an industrial park that housed a variety of business. It was six-thirty in the evening when she arrived and the parking lot was nearly deserted, except for three pick-up trucks. The pick-up in front of Custom Cabinets had the name of the business stenciled on the side doors and she rightly guessed this vehicle belonged to Mr. Mulroney.

He was waiting just inside the front door and opened it for her. As she stepped inside, the aroma of freshly cut pine filled her nostrils with a pleasant scent. The front office was a small room with two desks, one for the secretary-accountant and one for Mr. Mulroney. Before they started the interview, he took her on a short tour of the shop and gave a brief history of the company which his father had started, and which Mulroney had greatly expanded.

They went through the front office door and into the carpentry shop which had several large workbenches for the carpenters to produce the custom-made cabinets. Throughout the shop were several stand-alone machines, including table saws, routers and lathes, plus finishing and laminating machines. On each wall was a shelf system where smaller equipment was kept and plastic drawers for fasteners, handles, nails, screws and glues.

"Quite an operation you have here," she stated with sincerity, "my father would be impressed."

"Yes, we have a number of customized styles that we create for our catalogue, but generally we do custom work based on the individual tastes of the homeowners." He spoke with an obvious amount of pride.

"What's that large machine in the corner," she asked with real interest.

"That's our industrial dust collector. It works like an air filter and sucks in most of the smaller sawdust particles that float in the air. The unit filters the air, and the dust is pumped through the vent into a collection tank on the outside of the building. The men still wear masks because no unit is going to give you one hundred percent protection, but that baby is one of the best on the market and was well worth the investment."

"However, you can still see sprinkles of sawdust on the floor which are the heavier particles that are too big to be airborne, things like the shavings and excess slivers of wood. They get swept up on a regular basis, but as we say in our business: 'no matter how well you sweep, a good shop will always have something on the floor'."

Throughout the short tour, Baldoni quickly came to the conclusion that Mr. Mulroney was a talker, and she knew she would have to regulate the interview to prevent him from going off in tangents about unrelated subjects. When the tour ended, they went back into the small office and sat at Mr. Mulroney's desk. Baldoni extracted the digital recorder from her bag and explained its use, then switched it on.

"Any relations to the former Prime Minister?" she began the interview with a humorous casual comment to keep the conversation light.

"No, thank God," Mr. Mulroney replied. "I'm a dedicated member of the New Democratic Party. Those were eight years of hell as far as I was concerned. Every time I went to a party conference, I was the butt of many jokes. People kept asking me if I could do anything about my right-wing cousin."

"I know it's late so I don't want to take up too much of your time," she stated, "as we discussed briefly on the phone, I would like to ask you about

Anton Malinkov, anything that might give me a better understanding of the man and his relationship with his father. How long has he worked here?"

"Anton has been working here for about ten years. In my personal opinion, he is a dedicated family man, has pictures of his wife and kids all over his workspace. I've been to their home on a number of occasions for a barbeque or other church socials. He's a very hard and meticulous worker and his cabinets are real craftsmanship."

"What's he like as a person?" Baldoni asked.

"Well, he can be a real intense guy at times, not crazy intense, but whatever he's doing, he gets real focused. It doesn't matter if he's working or praying or whether he's in a conversation, he takes things very seriously."

"When his mother died," Mulroney continued without Baldoni asking any further questions, "he took it pretty hard, and he was off work for a couple of weeks in order to come to terms with it. He spent the time with his family, and he took some counselling with Father MacGregor over at St. Paul the Apostle church. When he came back to work, he didn't talk about it with any of us. He thanked everyone for their support and the cards and flowers, and then he didn't ever mention it again."

"We were all aware of the fractured relationship with his father, not that he spoke much about it, but every so often when we were in the lunchroom and the other guys talked about their relationships with fathers, Anton rarely said anything. When he did, it was always something negative. I remember one time when he responded to John's insistence…oh sorry, John is one of the other cabinetmakers, and he was asking Anton if his father ever took him hunting. After a while, Anton just looked at John and said with a cold stare 'the only thing my father hunts is other humans, mostly women'. Well, we all just sat there for a moment, none of us knew what to say. Then Anton said, 'Sorry guys, I really don't want to talk about that asshole, so please don't ask me about him or bring him up in any conversations.' I think that was the last time anyone ever mentioned it again. After that, we mostly talked about sports, the Maple Leafs, the Blue Jays, Raptors, and the soccer club. Every summer we do a day trip with our families to an Argo game. We rent a bus and have a picnic in the parking lot, just like they do at the NFL games. Even Father MacGregor comes. He says the Argos are his penance for past sins." Mulroney laughed.

Baldoni realized that Mulroney was more than just a talker. He was a rambler that loved to expound on any subject and if she didn't take better control the interview, then he would probably keep talking until the next day.

"That's cute," she said in order to keep the mood friendly, "but you mentioned this Father MacGregor and that Anton went to him for counselling. Is Anton a religious man?"

"Yes, when he met Beth, that's Elizabeth, his wife, she grew up in Alliston where they now live, Anton was introduced to the church through her. I don't know if he had any religious upbringing as a child, but once he was with Beth, he took to it with a gusto. Went to study classes and attended church every week. However, I have to honestly say that it wasn't at Beth's insistence, she's not like that, no…I think it was one of those things where someone without direction finds something that makes sense to the confusion in their life. I have a cousin who went through a lot of crap and then one day—"

Baldoni quickly cut him off, "Are you also a member of the same church?"

"Yes, I also live in Alliston. I keep the shop in Barrie because of the availability of the working space and because it's central to a lot of the cottage country where many of my customers come from. Plus, with all the new housing that is going up everywhere, it's a convenient location for people who want better quality cabinets than the prefab crap the developers put into their homes."

"So, Anton has been a religious person for a few years now," Baldoni said as she brought the conversation back to the subject.

"Yes, when he met Beth, he fell for her completely. I guess she was the foundation he had been looking for, and he embraced her religion. They got married, had children and now he's a fixture in our community. However, the one thing I can tell you for sure is that he loves his family. You can see that joy in him whenever you see them together, with his wife and kids, he just loves being with them. You know, if he ever won the lottery, I bet he'd quit his job just so he could spend more time with them, maybe even open up a pie shop. Beth makes wonderful pies. Every so often Anton will bring one in for the lunchroom. My favorite is her apple pie with the crisscross crust."

At this point, Baldoni figured she had gotten as much pertinent information she was going to get and decided to respectfully end the interview. "Thank you for your time Mr. Mulroney. I will need to get back to Toronto and write up my report, and it's getting late."

"If you're hungry, the diner around the corner is very good. Their meatloaf is excellent, and the gravy is home-made, none of that canned stuff."

She turned off the digital recorder and placed it in her bag. "Thank you, but my boyfriend is taking me to an expensive restaurant as soon as I get back," she lied, "if I need to return for any questions I may have missed, perhaps I'll check it out."

"Sure," Mulroney said, "just let me know if you need anything."

She left the industrial park and made her way to the highway. She wondered to herself how Boyle would have handled the interview with Mulroney. Would he have been abrupt with him or would he have let him go on. She knew the interviewing process was a delicate but integral part of any investigation and that you always want the person being interviewed to open up and present accurate information to your inquiries. The last thing you wanted was to cause the person being interviewed to feel threatened or uncomfortable with the process in which they might close up and not be willing to offer information that might be vital to the investigation.

She decided to get Boyle's advice when they met in the Argo tomorrow.

Chapter Fifteen

Early Friday morning, Boyle sat in the empty Argo conference room with a coffee and bagel, reviewing Baldoni's interview with Mr. Mulroney on his laptop.

All detective's notes and interviews are kept in a central database on a protected electronic server system. All homicide teams have access for 'Read Only' privileges once the information is entered onto the server. Files on the protected server could only be edited by one of the Information Technology specialists and all edits had to be accompanied with written consent from the team leader.

This digital system allowed for easy access to all reports, interviews, forensic information, crime scene maps, videos and photographs, and it prevented any 'accidental' altering of information that may be required for the prosecution of a crime and other court proceedings. Any official edits were saved as electronic requests for an audit trail if required.

Boyle read over the contents of Baldoni's interview and the personal notes she had added, describing Anton's boss, and his predilection for extended conversation. The thought of the 'direct-and-to-the-point' Gina sitting with a man who loved to hear his own voice brought a smile to his face.

As he read over the report, he was keenly interested in Mulroney's description of Anton. It seemed the son had become the exact opposite of his childhood experiences. Throughout his years on the force, Boyle had seen too many instances where the abused child became an abusing adult, plus the lingering effects a dysfunctional childhood would have on some individuals throughout their lives. It was one of the 'human condition' observations he recorded in one of his many personal journals, that children often inherit more than personal property from the parents. They often also inherited their parent's fears, prejudices, ignorance, and morality.

He kept reading Gina's report while other members of the team reported in, greeting them with a casual 'good morning' while his eyes were still focused on the laptop screen. No one interrupted him as they had all learned that when Boyle was focused, only something important or pertinent would be allowed to break his concentration, and if someone did so with some casual, inane interruption, the annoyed stare he directed at you was like an angry lion.

He started the meeting by reviewing the reports of Constable Davis and Singleton, which stated all houses in a two-block radius had been questioned and no one had heard or seen anything out of the ordinary.

Donna Chang spoke up and said she had found additional information that affected the constable's reports. Donna was a forty-something woman whose parents had originally come from Taiwan. She had long black hair that was parted in the middle and hung straight down almost to her waist. The length of her hair amplified her thin body frame and long thin face. She was the longest serving member of Boyle's team, and he had come to depend on her precisely detailed research abilities for information on any investigation.

She stated that Ivan Malinkov had installed sound-proof installation blankets when the house was last renovated several years ago. She noted that this was in his tax records and that he had received an excellent deal from the insulation company as the price he paid for the installation was well below market value. She suspected he received the deal with the company on agreement that Malinkov would send business their way by recommending the company to his clients.

However, the point she wanted to emphasize was that the house had been fully sound-proofed, which could be a factor as to why no one heard anything on the weekend of the murder. If Malinkov had tried to call out for help, there was little chance of anyone hearing.

Boyle stared at Donna for a moment and thanked the gods he had her talents on his team. He thanked her and asked Donna Chang to continue with any information she had derived.

She stated that at the time of his death, Ivan Malinkov was representing three properties that were up for sale, two in the Beaches and one in the newly developed Regent Park region of downtown Toronto. An open house had been scheduled for one of the Beaches properties on Sunday, November 25 and there were a number of voicemail messages from the client on his home phone when he didn't show up, and a complaint that his cell phone was not responding.

There were also two messages from Mr. Wicker demanding to know where the hell he was. Apparently, Mr. Wicker had received an angry call on Sunday evening from the client whose home was supposed to have had the open house.

"Have we managed to get the records from his cell phone? Voicemail, texts, etcetera?" Boyle asked.

"I had to create a warrant to open the cell phone account." Donna replied, "The phone companies are being quite diligent about revealing personal information ever since the latest scandals about breach of security and private information. I'm hoping to have it soon."

She continued with her report and disclosed the contents of his computerized Day Planner. All entries in November were mostly for real estate business purposes, a consultation meeting with a personal trainer, and a dental appointment. She had called the dentist and it was for a check-up and cleaning. She stated that the name and contact info for the personal trainer was in her report.

His banking records showed monthly payments to the Supreme Workout gym, on-line payments for all of his utility, phone and internet bills, various withdrawals of cash almost every other day, and credit card payments through the same bank that issued his credit card. Lastly, there were automated mortgage payments on the house. He currently had thirty-seven thousand dollars in his savings account and eighteen thousand in his checking account.

He had a twenty-thousand-dollar line-of-credit with the bank and the balance was currently two-hundred dollars. She went on to state that there were several RSP's, all invested in Guaranteed Income Certificates worth over three hundred and fifty thousand dollars, plus a Direct Investment account in which there were mostly blue-chip stocks worth another eighty thousand dollars.

"We have not yet retrieved a copy of his Will," she concluded, "but someone stands to gain a good inheritance once the value of the house is taken into consideration."

Boyle thanked Donna once again for her efficiency in getting all the information so quickly. He asked Baldoni to update everyone on the interviews with the real estate agents and Anton Malinkov's boss.

Baldoni stated the consensus was generally negative regarding Malinkov's business practices with one statement of actual unethical practices that might constitute an illegal act.

She also stated three of the female agents reported that Malinkov had made sexual advances toward them and one agent had consummated the advance. Laura Cahill had reported that Malinkov had convinced her into having sex under the pretense of business reasons, but that he had also potentially defrauded her from one of the deals. Baldoni stated she believed this would make her a suspect with clear motivation, however, she also stated that Cahill had a solid alibi for the entire evening of Friday, November 23.

Baldoni continued with a review of her interview with Anton's boss at the Custom Cabinet company. She noted how Mr. Mulroney saw Anton change after the marriage and having children. He apparently became a very religious man and an active member of the church community.

"Having children will often have that effect on people." Jasmine Davis stated, "You end up with a new perspective on life when you are suddenly responsible for another human being, one that is of your own blood. I've seen that type of change in myself and in many of my friends and family."

Boyle spoke up at this point, "I want to interview some of his friends and his priest at their church, what was the name, St. Paul's?"

"St. Paul the Apostle." Baldoni corrected him.

Boyle continued, "For now, Anton is our main suspect. He has an alibi for that night, but I want his bank records checked to determine if there were any unusual amounts being withdrawn at any time. Also check the bank records of the wife. Check for a second or third mortgage, a lottery win, or anything that would present them with a sudden influx of cash."

"You think this might be a murder-for-hire crime?" Singleton asked.

"Currently we are in the dark about what happened, who wanted it to happen and who actually did it." Boyle stated with a grim face. "If it was done by a paid killer, he wouldn't have been left alive. Then again, if this was supposed to be a warning of some sort, maybe he wasn't supposed to die, but the killer, or killers, got carried away and went too far. It could have been about drugs or gambling debts. Donna, I want you to check Malinkov's files for any indication of potential debts, payouts or other nefarious activities."

"Also, set up the interview with Elizabeth Malinkov, the priest and his friends as quickly as possible. See if some of them are available tonight. We'll meet again in the morning with whatever new information we have."

"Gina, I want confirmation of Laura Cahill's whereabouts on that Friday night. If she was in the middle of a real estate deal, then I want witness statements, and the paperwork that went with the sale. I don't think she has the physical capabilities to have committed this crime, but she definitely has the motive."

Boyle looked around the room and saw downcast looks and he spoke tersely, "I know tomorrow is Saturday, but this homicide is the focus of media attention and Superintendent Stanforth, and the Chief of Police. Eyes are focused on us and we need results."

****

Boyle left police headquarters in a hurry on his way to 55 Division to meet with Mr. Wicker once more. He decided to meet Wicker at 55 Division for the interview instead of Wicker's office, because he wanted that imposition of authoritative formality to take precedence over the mood of the interview. He wanted Wicker to feel the presence of the police station all around him.

He arrived at the station and was informed that Brian Wicker was waiting in Interview Room A. He had been there for about twenty minutes, which suited Boyle fine. He walked in and humbly apologized for his tardiness, purposely putting Wicker into a frame of mind that would seem to make him feel important.

"That's alright," Wicker replied trying to sound graceful. "I'm a busy man so if you could ask me whatever you need to know, we can wrap this up and I can be on my way."

Boyle sat down without saying anything and placed the digital recorder on the desk. He then went straight into hard and fast questioning, catching Wicker a little off guard. "To your knowledge, was Ivan Malinkov a participant in any gambling activities?"

Wicker's back straightened and his eyes expressed a surprise at the directness of the opening question, "Well, um, yes," he said hesitantly, "he liked to go to Casino Rama up in Orillia on occasion."

"How often?" Boyle quickly asked.

"I don't know, about every couple of months, I think."

"Did you ever go with him?" Boyle accelerated the speed of the questions, asking the next question as soon as Wicker answered the previous one.

"A few times."

"And what was the nature of the gambling? Roulette? Black-Jack? Dice? Slots?"

"A little of everything. At least, that's what he did when I was there."

"How long did you stay?"

"Oh at least four or five hours."

"Win or lose?"

"C'mon Detective, you know you always lose at those places."

"How much did he lose?"

"Look Detective," Wicker said a little overwhelmed, "I don't know where this is going, but Ivan was not a gambling addict if that's what you want to know. It wasn't a problem it was just some fun."

"And you are sure of this. How?" Boyle snapped back.

Wicker turned his neck from side to side as if he was relaxing the muscles. He looked up at Boyle and then said, "Ivan was a frugal spender. He was very good with his money. People around the office often joked about how miserly he was. Ivan would go to a casino and set a limit for himself, and as far as I know he always stayed within that limit."

"How much was his limit?"

"When I was with him, it was a thousand dollars."

"So, he would go and lose a thousand dollars every two months." Boyle said, "That's a lot of money to some people."

"I didn't say he lost," Wicker quickly responded, "I said he would set a limit of one thousand. Sometimes he came back with winnings. Ivan was a very cautious gambler, he didn't take wild risks, he'd only take a big chance if the situation was right, like having an Ace as your first card in Black-Jack. However, being cautious also meant he didn't win big either, but he sometimes came home with a few extra bucks."

"So, you wouldn't consider him to have had a gambling problem?" Boyle wanted to clarify.

"No, he enjoyed himself when he played, but it wasn't anything that I would call a problem."

"What about women?" Boyle asked.

"What do you mean? Did he gamble with them?" Wicker asked wondering.

"No, I am now asking if there were any problems with women."

"Well," Wicker stated with a sly smile, "Ivan never had any problems with women. He was quite a romancer."

"Did any of his romances turn into problems?"

"What do you mean by problems? You mean like that movie 'Fatal Attraction' where the girlfriend becomes a homicidal killer." Wicker stopped as soon as he made that statement and his eyes grew wide with the knowledge of where this questioning was going, and then said incredulously, "You think that someone killed Ivan because of a bad love affair?"

Boyle sat back, relaxed his voice and slowed the tempo of the interview. "It's been known to happen."

****

Wicker sat back in his chair with a pensive look on his face. He now knew this interview was meant to identify potential suspects and that anything he said could put the focus of suspicion on any number of people. He took a deep breath, and his face took on a more guarded expression, "From what I know personally, I believe all of his romantic interludes were very casual. He once told me that the only person he ever wanted to marry was his wife, Anna. She was the only real commitment he wanted to make, and probably the only person he truly loved. All the other women I saw him with, well, if he had been with any of them more than six months, that would have been a surprise to me."

"Do you know if he ever engaged prostitutes, or escorts." Boyle now asked the questions in a calmer manner. He could tell that Wicker had realized the serious implications of his answers and so he gave him time to deliberate the thoughts in his head before he offered any commentary or opinion.

"I would have to say…" Wicker thought about his answer for a moment, "I would have to say probably not. I mean I can't be entirely sure, but like I said earlier, he was frugal with his money, and I can't see him paying for sex, especially since he was such a schmoozer. He knew how to talk to women and they often thought he was a catch." He stopped and looked up at the ceiling while in thought, "No, he enjoyed the whole game of seducing a woman, paying for sex would not have been the kind of thing he would do."

"We heard from a number of the female real estate agents who all claimed Ivan had made sexual advances, made a 'pass at them' as they put it."

"Ivan wasn't a saint, Detective Boyle. Like I said he was a romantic and sometimes he tried to mix work with pleasure. He was wrong to do so, and I had to speak to him once or twice to emphasize the needs of the business."

"In one case," Boyle went on without acknowledging Wicker's feigned attempt at being a responsible owner, "there was a claim that Ivan used his position to lure a junior sales rep into an affair."

"Oh, you're probably talking about Laura." Wicker said with a touch of contempt, "She's what I would call a gold digger. Tried to use her feminine persuasion to get Ivan to include her on a number of deals. She made one complaint and I spoke with Ivan and her separately and everything was sorted. Since then, she's learned to become a good real estate agent and I would give credit to Ivan for helping her along the way."

Boyle looked at Wicker and tried to remove any expression from his face. He wanted Wicker to be at ease as he now wanted to enter into the part of the interview that he knew would be contentious. "What about his business practices. Were there ever any irregularities as far as real estate dealings?"

"Irregularities?" Wicker's back straightened again, "What do you mean?"

"We heard from some of the other agents we interviewed that Ivan wasn't always completely ethical in his practices."

"Who said that!" Wicker exclaimed.

"Mr. Wicker," Boyle said in an explanatory style, "all witness interviews go into the case file and remain confidential unless they are required by the prosecution as testimony for legal proceedings or a court case."

Wicker took a defensive tone and said, "Well people can't just say whatever they want without proof. That would be slander."

"One of the agents claimed there was an impropriety in which Ivan kept additional offers on a property secret from the owners, and that this was for the purpose of ensuring Beach Realty would get both the selling and buying commissions."

"If you are referring to the complaint made by Mr. Gandhi, I can tell you there was no improprieties involved." Wicker was now defiant in his tone.

Boyle looked directly at Wicker and with a new serious tone in his voice said, "So, you are officially stating that there was no verbal agreement between you and Ivan about ensuring those types of transactions."

"I take personal offence to that." Wicker raised his voice, "Beach Realty is well known for servicing their clients with business integrity. Whether it's getting the best deal on a house for the listings or ensuring that when a client is buying a property, they only pay for what the value of that property is."

The anger rose in Wicker and he continued to defend himself, "I take very deep personal offence to you making these allegations, toward me and my company."

"Mr. Wicker," Boyle forcibly furrowed his forehead to intone his most serious look, "I am not making any allegations. I am investigating the brutal murder of one of your business associates. Any allegations of impropriety are statements made in interviews by other associates of your company," and now Boyle raised his voice just enough to add strength to his statement, "any potential business irregularities could also be potential motivations for murder."

"There were no improprieties." Wicker steadfastly insisted, "We run an honest legitimate business. If you have any proof of any improprieties, then I suggest that you provide me with this proof and also bring it to the Toronto Real Estate Board for investigation."

Boyle reverted back to a calmer but still serious tone, "I will not be providing anything to the Toronto Real Estate Board. If we determine there is any evidence that indicates a Conspiracy to Commit an Offence, the case files would be turned over to the Financial Crimes Unit of the Toronto Police force and dealt with through our Fraud Squad. However, at the moment, I have no intention of proceeding along this path."

"Thank you," Wicker said with a sigh of relief in his voice, "if there are no further questions, then I would like to leave…if that's alright."

"Mr. Wicker, this is just an interview. You are free to leave at any time."

Wicker rose and was about to leave when Boyle spoke up again, "Brian, just so you know, our investigation has raised a number of questions regarding Ivan's personal life and his business dealings. We're probably going to be talking again in the near future."

Wicker glared down at Boyle who was still seated in his chair, and then said with a distinct chill, "Detective Boyle, whenever you need any more information, I will gladly provide it. The Toronto Police department is one of the world's best police forces and I am always happy to cooperate with them." He then turned and walked stiffly from the room.

Chapter Sixteen

It had been week since the murder of Ivan Malinkov. Silverstein's FIS team had been unable to discover any material evidence to determine the identity of the perpetrator, or perpetrators, if there had been more than one. His team was also unable to find any evidence that could be used to link the killer to the crime scene.

Boyle was perplexed. There was always something left behind, always. A patch of moisture from the sweat of the killer, a hair from the killer's body, fingerprints, palm prints, even prints from the bottom of the feet and toes had been used in the past to identify a murderer. In this case, there was absolutely nothing, and this forced Boyle to think about the killer in another light.

The conference table in the Argo had several cups of coffee, a plate of muffins and croissants and a small plate of strawberries, grapes and melon slices. The breakfast snacks were courtesy of Donna Chang. She had stopped at a health food grocery on her way to headquarters and picked a selection for the group; Boyle, whom she knew would have only had a small bowl of cereal for his breakfast; Baldoni who had probably come straight from her run at the zoo; and Singleton; who would have snuck out of his home quietly so that he didn't awaken his wife. Jasmine Davis, Donna suspected, was the only one who ate healthy.

Donna took great pains to know the people she worked with. She was a conscientious co-worker who wanted to elevate the mood of the people around her. Her parents were adherents to the teachings of Confucius who professed the golden rule of 'treating others as you would like to be treated yourself'. She believed that creating a warm, friendly environment around you would nurture positive feelings within her own daily experiences.

Once everyone was present, Boyle thanked Donna for the food she had provided and then went straight into discussion. "It's Saturday," he said, "so I don't want this to drag on longer than we need to be here." He then looked down at his computer and spoke while reading, "Bill, I read your report about the patrons at Whitlock's. Can you expand on this for us?"

Singleton put down the muffin that he had just taken a big bite of, took a sip of his coffee, swallowed and spoke, "We interviewed several people who had been at Whitlock's restaurant on the night of the murder and we found one person who thinks they might have seen something peculiar. A Mr. Raymond Chow was just finishing dinner with his wife. They were sitting by one of the windows that faced out onto Kenilworth and he stated he saw someone on a bicycle riding north on Kenilworth and then turn right onto Queen Street. He thought it was odd that someone was riding their bike in late November, but he also remembers they were wearing a Delivery Corp uniform. His company uses Delivery Corp, and he recognized the uniform. He didn't think Delivery Corp had bicycle couriers. He couldn't give any description as to what the person looked like as it was dark and the person was well covered in coat and hat, he just noticed the Delivery Corp uniform and thought it funny."

"He was sure that it was someone in a Delivery Corp uniform?" Boyle questioned.

"Yes, I had him repeat his story a couple of times to make sure he was accurate." Singleton replied.

"Okay," Boyle said, "let's check with Delivery Corp to see if they have any offices nearby, and if so, do they have any employees that ride a bicycle to and from work, or if they have extended their business to include bicycle couriers. Jasmine, I want to start that first thing Monday, this might be the only lead we have."

He turned his attention to Donna Chang and asked if she had managed to come up with anything on Elizabeth Malinkov's finances.

"I have not obtained anything on the bank statements yet as the warrant is still pending until Monday. However, I was in touch with the lottery corporation and they have confirmed that there have been no prize payouts to either Elizabeth or Anton or anyone from Elizabeth's family."

Boyle turned to Baldoni, "Gina, you and I need to go back up to Alliston and talk with Mrs. Malinkov and with the priest. Donna, make the arrangements for late Monday morning."

He then made a quick review of the case, the brutality of the murder, the lack of any evidence that would either identify the killer or be used in court proceedings, the potential motives of both Anton, Laura Cahill, other real estate agents and ex-girlfriends. Now Boyle began to think out loud as much as he was talking to the group.

"How did the perpetrator know that Ivan was at home on Friday evening? How did they know there was an alarm system that did not have video surveillance? How did they know that no one would be able to hear Ivan if he called out for help? How did they know someone wasn't going to be coming to Ivan's home at some point during the weekend? How did they know all of that…or did they just not care? Or was it simply a lucky guess?"

"The actual killing was well thought out in advance," he went on, "so I have to believe that the killer wasn't guessing about everything else. They must have known in great detail everything about Ivan's home, which meant that Ivan probably knew his assailant. But, if he knew them, why would they dress up as a Delivery Corp person, if that was the case? Was Ivan expecting someone to come by? He was dressed in fashionable clothing as if he was expecting a woman, but we know that his last girlfriend Barbara Booth wanted nothing more to do with him. Was this a new girlfriend?"

He stopped for a moment and then said with an angered sigh, "There's just too many questions and nothing makes sense. Jasmine, I want that Delivery Corp information first thing. Press them for it. Gina, you and I are going to meet here on Monday and then we're heading straight for Alliston. We need to dig."

Chapter Seventeen

On Sunday, the first big snowfall of the year hit the greater Toronto region. Traffic would be slow and fender benders would be plentiful. Others would be driving cautiously, sometimes too cautiously, and impatient drivers would swerve around them, or into them, or into another vehicle.

Boyle arrived at headquarters on Monday morning at seven. The streets of Toronto are usually bad after a big snowfall, so he didn't bother going to the gym. He had his coffee and sat at his desk, reviewing the case files on his laptop, while waiting for Baldoni to arrive.

She arrived at eight-fifteen, her jaw clenched, her eyebrows furrowed, and she scowled, "You'd think people would fucking know from experience! One snowflake and they turn into fucking monsters or zombies!"

"Traffic?" Boyle knowingly asked.

"Duh!" she replied with snarky sarcasm.

Boyle smiled at her. He liked her youthful enthusiasm, and he liked her untainted emotional outbursts, which were both expected and sometimes surprising. She was ambitious, but she was also conscientious and, like him, she always wanted to succeed. She wanted cases to be solved properly and not quickly for the sake of looking good. She wanted to make sure the right person was arrested.

He liked that she was not lazy in doing all the little things that were required of investigation. He liked that she didn't assume the obvious suspect and not bother to dig further. He had seen other cases where the investigation was stalled or went 'cold' because the detectives focused on one suspect and ignored the evidence that may have pointed to someone else, and a different motive. When their initial arrest turned out to be wrong, vital evidence that should have been detected was now unavailable or gone.

Boyle looked at his own past and knew it took him a while to reach those conclusions and learn those lessons, and he respected that she had reached it so quickly. He never thought for a moment that it was his influence on her, he just thought she was very good. He liked Gina, because she was like him, only a younger version of him.

They took Baldoni's car and headed north to Alliston. Donna Chang had contacted the priest, Father MacGregor on Saturday afternoon and made arrangements to meet him at one o'clock on Monday. Elizabeth Malinkov agreed to take Monday morning off work and wait for Boyle and Baldoni at her home.

They took the Gardiner Expressway to Highway 427 and made their way north. As they passed Steeles Avenue, the northern border of the city, the flakes of white started once more, and the further north they drove, the heavier the snowfall became. Traffic going southbound into the city was at a near standstill. Travelling north was only slightly better.

The snow came down like a white blanket pulled over a corpse. As Baldoni drove, her hands gripped the steering wheel with tense muscles, and whenever she saw flashing red lights on the road ahead, it brought back memories of the days when she was a constable, having to attend traffic accidents. There were some memories that she didn't want to keep, some that she worked hard to bury. Every time she saw those red lights on the road, some of those memories would come back to her, and the nerves throughout her body would shiver with a sense of unease and her hands would grip the wheel even tighter.

The flashing red lights that she now passed was just a minivan in the ditch, no ambulance required, just a tow truck. A police car was staying by to ensure that no one else joined the minivan. Drivers of passing cars often took their eyes off the treacherous road for extended gazes…they had to look because it was their potential future they were seeing.

The two detectives had mostly been silent on the long drive, made longer by the snow accumulating on the windshield and the wipers creating ever-increasing ridges on both sides of the window. Whenever there was a stoppage in traffic, Boyle would quickly get out and wipe the ridges away, then quickly get back in the car with white flakes on his head and shoulders.

They passed through a pine forest, and the boughs of the trees laden with the fresh snow expressed a sense of purity. The starkness of the deep green and brilliant white cried out the beauty of the natural world, and this inspired Boyle to whisper to himself, "Thank the Gods."

Baldoni heard the whisper but didn't quite make out what he said. She wanted conversation to alleviate the thoughts in her mind. As they passed the town of Schomberg, the traffic dissipated to just a few passing cars on the road ahead. Snow drifted across the road in thin wisps of wind and the landscape blurred into the distance.

****

"What are you thinking about Boss?" she asked.

Boyle turned his head to look at her and carefully measured his answer, "Quantum physics and God."

"Me too," she said with a giggle. "I often think about mortality in this kind of weather. Are you ruminating in a general sense or is it anything in particular?"

Boyle had never entered into any serious discussions about his Hellenic practices with her. He was sure that her Roman Catholic upbringing had not included any of the teachings of other religions, especially the Pagan theologies, even though many of the Christian holidays were based on ancient Pagan rituals. He wondered now how deeply he should open up to her, not fully knowing her bias toward abstract thought.

"I was thinking about the beauty of the natural world around us," he offered, "how the snow and the trees are a collection of molecules, and yet they come together to form a stunning pageant that is only temporal. I was thinking how this collection of molecules has such an effect on our thoughts and feelings."

"I feel that way sometimes when I'm running at the zoo," she answered back.

"When did you start this practice of being the Wolf Runner?" he asked a little shyly.

"It started two years ago in the spring. I had taught a four-week seminar to some of the security staff and they offered me an employee's pass that would allow me entrance during the off hours. I think some of them wanted to establish an association with a member of the police force on a personal level, and some wanted to date me, so they let me come in the early mornings, before the zoo opens to the general public."

Boyle's thoughts sparked with new questions, "And while you run, you think about the spiritual aspects of the natural world: the animals and the birds, the trees, the rocks and the water? You think about what this means to a solitary runner as the sun breaks the horizon."

Baldoni was caught off guard by his comment. She was astonished that he was able to paint in words her exact experiences when she ran amongst the animal enclosures. She paused while these thoughts went through her mind, and then she replied, "Sounds like someone else has been watching the sun rise on the world."

He smiled and decided it was time to get to know his partner better, to reveal a little about himself, and hopefully, find the conscience of the detective he worked so closely with, "I used to bike to work in the mornings, back when I was a gym teacher," he said, and then quickly added before she could say anything, "Yeah, I was a gym teacher before I became a cop."

She smiled at the thought of him teaching young students about health and physical fitness. "Did you coach the football team?" she asked teasingly.

"Both the football and basketball teams," he said, "but after a year I knew it wasn't what I really wanted to do in my life. That's when I joined the police force."

"Tell me about your bike rides," she requested.

"I lived in the Beaches and I worked in Etobicoke. It was a long ride each way, but in the morning, I would often stop and watch the sun come up over the lake, watch that first spear of light break the horizon above the lake. It was at those times that I probably felt as you do when you run in the early mornings at the zoo."

"And you thought about God and nature?" she asked.

"Yes, I thought about the spiritual world and the connection between humans and everything else," and then he spoke of a memory, "I used to save old slices of bread so I could sometimes feed the birds on my way to work. One morning I stopped down by Sunnyside beach and I parked my bike and stood at the shoreline."

"The first birds to come were the seagulls with their harsh shrieking calls. Then a few mallards came by to partake in breakfast and they were followed by some geese, honking their way into the fray and gobbling everything in sight. And then came the one bird I was hoping for, one of nature's truly magnificent creations. Seven swans floated gracefully toward the shore."

"They came up on shore and approached me, cautiously at first and after a moment of making sure I meant no harm, they took the bread directly from my hand. I fed the swans, speaking to them as I held out my hand. They spoke back, in their low, guttural honks and snorts. It was then that I realized the swans were like people, once you gained their trust, then they willingly let you into their confidence."

"One swan stood beside me the whole time and would even try to take the bread from my hand while I was trying to break it into pieces. I asked it to be patient and oh what a look it gave me. It was a brave one with no fear, confident in its own will."

"When the bread was all gone, I sat on a bench, and the swans stayed with me. I continued to speak with them, as if I was talking to friends. I asked them about love and the meaning of life. The brave one looked at me and stared, and that's when I realized they didn't understand what my concern was. It was in his look, and it said we are swans…we mate for life…whether times are good or bad."

"I sat quiet and watched them. After a while, when they realized there would be no more bread, they waddled back into the water and gracefully swam down the shoreline. They left with such tender grace and I had an insight to my own questions."

"I realized that science cannot explain the soul, and often doubts its existence, because the soul cannot be dissected or quantified. It was the swans that taught me the soul is something tangible, but unmeasurable, something you can feel deep inside, and connect with everything else in the universe. It is that single variable that speaks for God. It's difficult to put into words, however, that morning I felt something profound, like touching the divine."

Baldoni drove and listened with fascination to this man whom she had come to respect as a teacher. Now he was opening up his idiosyncratic uniqueness to her, and the sincerity of his revelations made her want to pull into the next coffee shop to just sit and talk with him.

"Other emotions such as hate and fear are instinctive," he continued to extoll, "all animals have a protective nature, even plants. The mother bird will put herself at risk to protect her young. She will give up her own life without hesitation, but will she mourn their deaths? Will she regret or fear when it is time for them to leave the nest?"

"No, she will push them out and refuse to let them return, ever! Once she has completed her instinctive assignment to rear her young, she has no other thoughts or feelings for them. She will even consider them competitors for the food."

"Wait Boss, wait." Baldoni said as her head still considered this sudden, candid disclosure of his personal self. "We've crossed over topics and I'm a little confused while at the same time trying not to drive off the road."

"Sorry Gina, you're right. I tend to ramble a little when I mix philosophy, religion and science. We're approaching Cookstown, so let's grab a coffee somewhere and take a break from all this snow."

She looked over at him again and wondered if he was psychic. Did he sense her impulse to get a coffee somewhere? Her sense of wonder grew as they pulled into Molly's dinner.

****

They pulled into the long driveway of the Malinkov home and saw Elizabeth Malinkov looking out of the turret style window on the second floor. There was only a thin layer of snow on the driveway and both suspected that Elizabeth Malinkov was just as adept at managing the riding snow blower as her husband. They proceeded up the stone path and into the enclosed porch. Like her husband, Elizabeth Malinkov opened the door before they had a chance to knock.

Elizabeth had a country freshness, and her looks could have been the textbook definition of rural.

She was attractive in a plain way, wore very little make-up and had long blonde hair that was parted in the middle. She was of medium build, but you could see the strength within her frame.

She had been a rural woman her whole life, born and raised in Alliston, seldom travelled and was a devout Roman Catholic, but moderate in her stances toward many of the social issues the church frowned upon. She worked part time at the local country market, tailoring her schedule to the needs of her children, which along with her husband, were the most important aspects to her life.

She had met Anton at one of the country fairs. She was selling homemade pies and he loved pies. He quickly fell in love and courted her with respect to her family, asked her father for her hand in marriage and was welcomed into the community. Even though she asked him many times, he absolutely refused to allow his father to come to the wedding.

"Good morning officers," Elizabeth said, "please come in, would you like a coffee, I just made a pot?"

"Thank you, not for me," Baldoni replied.

"Thank you, Mrs. Malinkov," Boyle said, "however if you don't mind, we would like to get straight into the interview as we have a couple of other people to see today, and then make our way back to Toronto in this blizzard."

"You can call me Beth," Elizabeth said in a friendly voice, but Boyle saw that her body language expressed tension. Her muscles visibly tightened, and her arms were crossed with her hands under her armpits in a form of self-hugging. "Quite a storm over the past couple of days. I've had to plough the driveway a few times to make room for the cars." She was obviously nervous, and Boyle wondered if she worried about revealing something of consequence, or if this was the anxiousness he frequently encountered with people when talking to someone in authority.

Boyle decided to take the initiative and asked Beth if they could go into the living room to talk.

They removed their coats and boots and she invited them into her home, which was quite warm. An electric fireplace had been installed within the original mantel of the old wood-burning fireplace, with curved columns on both sides and a mantel shelf that had pictures of the children, a vase with flowers, and an antiquated ship in a bottle.

Boyle asked Baldoni to set up her digital recorder and he explained to Beth the interview would be recorded. This seemed to make Beth even more tense, which was the affect Boyle wanted. He wanted her to be nervous because he perceived that if she was going to lie, then her nervousness would make any lies easier to detect. As Anton was currently the main suspect, Boyle wanted to ensure any testimony his wife would provide was either incriminatory evidence pointing to Anton's guilt or exculpatory evidence that would prove him innocent.

It had been more than a week since the murder, and Boyle knew the lack of any compelling physical evidence at the crime scene, and the lack of witnesses would mean there was little or no corroborative evidence that would be required to lay charges or be used in the prosecution of an accused suspect.

Under the Canadian Charter of Rights and Freedoms, Beth could not be compelled to testify any communication between her and her husband, but she could be compelled to provide circumstantial evidence such as his location at the time of the murder or if he had owned a baseball bat.

"Mrs. Malinkov," he stated, purposely using the formal term of her married name, "how long have you and Anton been married?"

"We've been married for eight years."

"How old are your children?"

"Sarah is six and Jessica is four."

"How well did you know your husband's father, Ivan Malinkov?"

"I only ever saw him twice, but I can't say that I actually met him."

"How well did your husband get along with his father?"

Beth took a deep breath and let it out with a long sigh. She looked up at Boyle and then over to Baldoni and then back at Boyle. With a nervous voice, she asked something that was more of a statement than a question, "Detective, may I speak plainly."

When he heard this, Boyle expected the usual negative reaction to the police many people spout when they are being questioned. It had become part of the public consciousness that the police were self-serving and sometimes dishonest. It was the result of too much publicity on a few bad cops, and the entertainment industry's need for extravagant storytelling. He braced himself for another anti-police tirade that he would have to endure for a short time and then use his authority to end the diatribe, which only led to the person thinking their opinion had just been proved.

"Yes, please go ahead," he said hesitantly.

"My husband is a good man," she said, "he is a wonderful father and a good, good husband. When we were first married, I knew that he had a troubled childhood, and this had some effect on his character. It became truly evident when he refused to let his own father come to our wedding. He broke down and told me everything at that time."

"However," she continued, "he took some counselling to resolve those feelings. He spent a great deal of time with Father MacGregor and he became an active member of the church community. It's no secret how he felt about his father, and he has discussed this in different open group sessions at our church. When his mother committed suicide, it affected him greatly and he went into a depression because he felt it was partly his fault for not protecting her more."

"Our community embraced him, my family was there for him, and I was there for him. He became more involved in the spiritual teachings of the church, and he found some solace in the love of those around him. When the RCMP came to tell him about the murder of his father, I was afraid that he might fall back into depression…but he didn't."

"I know that you are recording this, and I know that there are laws about a spouse not having to testify against her husband, but I'm telling you this now because I want you to understand. My husband did not recede back into a depression because he had resolved all of those feelings, and they were now in the past. He has his children, and he has me, and he has the support and love of my family, and he has the church, and many, many friends, and he even has the support of the people where he works. He didn't go into depression again because he has so much to live for."

"Yes, he was shocked and confused when his father was murdered, and yes, he was somewhat un-compassionate, but that was because he had distanced himself from him. He was so far removed from his father it was as if he had been told a stranger had died. And in essence, his father was a stranger to him."

"Now this is the part I really want you to understand. My husband did not kill his father. As far as he was concerned, his father was gone a long time ago. But it happened, and I know that you have to find who did it. I know that you checked with the neighbors next door and that they verified they were here playing cards with us, so what I really want to say is please ask me anything you want, because I want Anton to be cleared as quickly as possible. The longer this hangs over him, the more whispers will start, and it will affect the kids in school, and the last thing he wants is to cause any problems or suffering for his family."

"I want you to check anything you need to," she now spoke with strength and determination, "ask me anything that will be required so you can make the decision that my husband is innocent of any part of this crime. And once you have come to that conclusion, then you can go about the business of finding the real culprits."

Boyle sat in silence and wasn't sure what to say. He had been totally wrong in his judgement of her character, which was something he was seldom mistaken. This woman impressed him with her strength and resolve and he was sure that she was probably the main force behind Anton's recovery and development of standing in the community.

Baldoni witnessed the silence of her partner and quickly stepped into the interview, "Mrs. Malinkov, just for our records, can you state where you were on Friday evening, November 23."

Beth confirmed Anton's original statement about playing cards with their neighbors until eleven o'clock, then washed the dishes and went to bed. Baldoni asked a few more questions regarding her relationship with Ivan Malinkov. Beth stated she knew very little about the man apart from what her husband had told her, and that she felt sorry for him in the sense that he missed out on his grandchildren.

Baldoni thanked her and turned off the digital recorder. Boyle rose and was almost embarrassed when he thanked her for her cooperation. Beth just looked at him with a sincere look and said, "Detective, I know you have a hard job, and that it's not easy to be dealing with murder and suffering. You probably have to deal with many unsavory people. I understand, so please believe me when I say God bless you and keep you safe."

Boyle looked her in the eyes and saw real compassion. He smiled and said thank you once again, this time with a sincerity that came with deep respect.

****

They left the Malinkov home and it took longer to clean the snow that had accumulated on the car windows than it did to drive the two blocks to St. Paul the Apostle's church parking lot. They walked past the entrance of the church to the rectory and rang the doorbell. The housemaid-secretary greeted them.

"Father MacGregor is in his study," she explained, "let me take your coats and I have some disposable slippers for you." She handed Baldoni and Boyle a pair of powder blue slip-on foot covers. She led them down a short hallway to the study room.

Father MacGregor was a robust older man with a head of silver-gray hair. His face beamed with a sunlit smile and the thick lenses within the wire-framed glasses made his eyes look twice as large. He quickly got up from his desk and offered his hand to shake and thanked them for coming out in this weather. He offered them the two chairs that sat opposite his desk.

"Just working on my sermon for next Sunday," he said, "can I offer either of you some refreshment. Martha makes iced tea the old-fashioned way and it is quite addictive."

Both accepted the offer for iced tea and Father MacGregor called out to Martha and asked her to bring in a pitcher with three glasses. When Martha brought the refreshments, it included a plate of home-made chocolate chip cookies. She left closing the door to the study behind her.

Baldoni pulled out her digital recorder and asked Father MacGregor if he minded that the interview would be recorded. Father MacGregor said he had no objections and then joked that he might want to get one for his confessional. "Too many people making the same mistakes twice," he laughed.

Boyle explained the reason for their visit was regarding the murder of Ivan Malinkov and his relationship with his son Anton.

"I guess that you have him pegged as your prime suspect." Father MacGregor smiled.

"Currently, we do not have any suspects in the case." Boyle answered, "We are still interviewing people of interest and obviously Anton would be one of them. He was estranged from his father and had a great deal of resentment toward the man. It was reported that he even assaulted him at his mother's funeral."

"Yes, that was a difficult time for him." Father MacGregor said with a somber tone.

"We've been told that Anton has often come to you for advice and that you have counselled him in times when he was depressed." Baldoni stated, "We want to get some background information regarding his character."

"I'll be glad to give you my opinions," Father MacGregor said, "of course, I'm sure I don't need to remind you that I cannot convey any information that was told to me during confession. Those are sacred vows a priest cannot break. However, I would be glad to talk generally about Anton as a man and as an active member of this parish."

"When did you first meet Anton?" Baldoni asked.

"I met Anton when he started dating Beth, um, I should say Elizabeth Morton, which was her maiden name. He was living in Barrie working as a carpenter. When he and Beth decided to marry, they came to the marriage classes we offer through the church, and that's when I first met him. When

114

they decided to live in Alliston, he started to attend the Sunday services here at St. Paul's."

"When did he start coming to you for advice?"

"After he married Beth and started coming to church with her. About the time that Sarah was born, he came to me for advice, he just wanted to talk. He was…well, I guess what you would call a lost soul, someone with a lot of internal confusion and questions about life and God and what it all meant in the greater reality. With the birth of his first child, a sudden new type of vibrancy came into him and the need to find a direction became an important aspect that he felt was missing. Having the child meant so much to him, and he suddenly realized the extreme power of love and responsibility."

"I felt the same way with the birth of my own son." Boyle stated, both as an admission and to engender respectful relationship with the priest.

"I think having a child made him revisit his own childhood where…well, let's just say there were problems." Father MacGregor added. "I counselled him, we talked about life, we talked about God, and we talked about what it meant to be a good man, a good religious man, a father and a husband. I guess he must have found some answers in our discussions because it wasn't long afterward that Anton embraced the church in a very meaningful way. I believe he found value in the structure of faith and the basic precepts of love, charity and compassion that the church adheres to."

"When his mother died, it was a tragedy for him, and he went into a deep depression. However, he had Beth, and she took care of him with what I would call 'a love for the ages'. She's quite a woman."

Boyle gave Father MacGregor a knowing look and Father MacGregor acknowledged the look with one of his own. "She is his rock," he went on, "everyone should be so blessed to have as strong a marriage as those two."

Chapter Eighteen

The next day, Boyle and Baldoni were reviewing the notes on the case file server in the Argo. Also present were Donna Chang, Jasmine Davis and William Singleton. Mei Liu, one of the FIS team specialists attended in place of Aaron Silverstein.

"I have checked all the financial statements for Elizabeth Malinkov." Donna Chang stated, "There are no irregular withdrawals on her personal account or in the joint account where most of their money is kept. They are also in good standing with the bank with regards to mortgage payments. There is a Line-of-Credit account associated with the joint account, but the records for the Line-of-Credit do not show any large sums withdrawn over the past three years, mostly small sums every few months. I suspect that they are using the Line-of-Credit account for small loans when needed."

"The bank accounts only show monetary deposits from their places of employment and the odd cash deposit for up to three hundred dollars during the summer months."

"That would probably be from Beth working at county fairs." Baldoni added, "She apparently makes very good pies."

"Thank you, Donna," Boyle said, "Gina, can you brief the group on our meetings yesterday with Elizabeth Malinkov and Father MacGregor?"

Baldoni spoke at length about how Elizabeth was very strong in character and supportive of her husband and how she was careful not to relate any communications that would incriminate her husband. However, she added as an opinion, this could also be detrimental in the investigation, because if Anton had committed the crime, Elizabeth would probably aid her husband in a cover up. She was a family-oriented woman and would want to keep the family core safe and secure.

Baldoni then related Father MacGregor's statements about Anton's depression after his mother's suicide, and how Anton had taken solace in the teachings and practices of the church. By all accounts, he was now a very religious man and an active member of the church community.

When she finished, Boyle asked Mei Liu if there were any further developments on the forensic investigations. Mei Liu stated the team had completed the forensic investigation at the Ivan Malinkov home. The team had found a small fiber in the kitchen sink that matched the tape on the handle of the baseball bat. The assumption was made that the perpetrator rinsed the bat in the sink when they were finished, probably to doubly ensure there was no DNA evidence that could be retrieved.

Mie Liu also stated there were fingerprints of the gardener, Philip Chin, on the flush handle of the guest toilet on the main floor. The FIS also found a small fragment of a maple leaf on the kitchen floor beside the back door. She suspects this may have been brought into the house by the gardener when he used the washroom. She concluded by stating there were no other items to report.

Boyle asked Jasmine Davis what she had learned from Delivery Corp.

"The local Delivery Corp office is on Lakeshore near Carlaw Avenue." Davis began, "They stated that they do not use bicycle couriers, but were unaware if any of the other offices had taken up that style of business. The downtown head office would be the place to ask those questions. They checked their employment files and do not have any employees that live in the Beaches area."

"I also inquired about their uniforms and they stated these were issued to an employee after their training had been completed. This included winter clothing, parka and hats. If an employee needed additional clothing, they were expected to purchase the required article. When an employee leaves the company, they did not expect the clothing to be returned."

Boyle took a deep breath, grunted, then spoke, "Alright, let's re-cap what we know about our main suspect, Anton Malinkov. He has an alibi for the Friday evening when his father was killed. His wife and two neighbors vouch for his location at that time. There are no exceptional monies that were garnered to pay for a hired killer. No withdrawals, no extra income of any sort."

"However," Boyle said with emphasis, "this does not mean it's not possible. He could have borrowed money from an unknown source, a friend, or a loan shark, something that's not traceable. He could have put aside twenty dollars a week for the past five years or something crazy like that. Let's not disregard any possibility because we know this was a well-planned murder."

Boyle stopped for a moment to gather his thoughts, then calmly went on, "We also know that he has become a deeply religious man, goes to church every Sunday and is active in his religious community. His priest, his boss at work, his neighbors and others all vouch for his character. If he had reacted murderously toward his father immediately after his mother's suicide, then I think we would have no doubt and would focus on him. Remember that he struck his father at his mother's funeral. But it's been four years since his mother's death, and he has gone to counselling to help him through his issues."

"If he had been planning this for four years...well, I find it hard to believe he is that kind of a mastermind who could set this up so perfectly."

"But if you wanted to be perfect," Donna Chang spoke up, "this would be the way you would plan it. Put everything in place as far as witnesses, counselling, finances, and so on."

"True," replied Boyle, "but if he personally committed the crime, it would have been in conspiracy with the neighbors who are his main alibi. And if he paid someone else to do the crime, then two things don't fit; First, and this is crucial, a contract killer would not leave the victim alive; and second, there would have to be an exchange of a large sum of money of which we have no record."

"Jasmine, keep going on the Delivery Corp angle, see what you can find out from their head office. Gina, you and I are going to check with the Financial Crimes Unit and get a list of known loan sharks, one of them may want to cooperate when politely asked about this murder. Also, Bill, I want you to check with the Gang Task Force to see if they have any information that might include Anton."

"You think he might have been a member of a gang?" he asked incredulously.

"No, but he could have hired one to kill his father."

Boyle and Baldoni spent the rest of the morning and afternoon with the different crime units to see if Anton's name had surfaced in any of their investigations. It was one dead end after another, and the frustration was beginning to get to Boyle.

"Let's go for dinner and talk," he suggested to Baldoni, "my friend Orestes will make us a fine Greek meal."

****

Later that night in the Parthenon Tavern, they were sitting with Orestes having a traditional meal which consisted of a large bowl of Greek salad, a plate of Dolmades, grape leaves stuffed with ground lamb, and another plate of deep fried, breaded Calamari with Tzatziki sauce. A bottle of Metaxa sat on the table between them.

"I'm telling you Ari," Orestes said as the discussion between the two friends got very serious, "people can be horrible creatures. Throughout history there's been massacres, murder and slaughter. Our ability for genocide is what mankind has become experts in."

"Orestes," Boyle said as he finished chewing another Dolmades, "in my job I've seen more blood and death than most people could even imagine, and yet, I've also dealt with a lot of good people who want to help."

"Sure," Orestes continued, "there's good people as well, but look what happens to supposedly good people when they are given the opportunity to do horrible things, just because they could get away with it. Once these so-called, well-intentioned good people are given a measure of power, however small, and the immunity to commit atrocities, they succumb to the evil that lurks within. Look at all those recorded cases of concentration camp guards during World War Two. Regular guys who were your neighborhood barber, bartender or shopkeeper. Some were even university students, and the atrocities they committed were unfathomable. All because they were permitted, and encouraged, to do so."

"And this has happened throughout history," he continued, "the Roman Empire used slaughter and terror as its weapon. The Spanish massacred the South American natives, the Arabs wiped out the Egyptian races, the British, French and the Spanish almost killed off the native North American Indians. Hell, even Alexander slaughtered entire civilizations as he marched his troops throughout the Mediterranean."

"Orestes, Orestes, you can't point to specific times in history and state this proves the entire human race is evil." Boyle became passionate, "History generally only records times of war, strife, and the lives of kings, and tyrants and conquerors. History doesn't care for times of peace and prosperity. There's probably more history written about the life of Alexander than there is about the lives of Socrates, Plato and Zoroaster put together."

"I have found that most people are good." Baldoni tried to get in between the two friends, "Most people are loving, kind and generous. Maybe not always toward strangers, but usually toward family and friends."

"People make mistakes," she went on, "and people are forgiving. People will help other people. Most people are religious and the ones who don't have religion are often the ones who lead exemplary lives. People don't want to hurt other people, but then people do make mistakes. People are willing to work hard and honestly to fulfill their needs."

"And people hate," Orestes interjected as he dipped a piece of Calamari into the white Tzatziki sauce.

"Hate does not come naturally to people," Boyle said as he sipped another glass of Metaxa, "it usually has to be instilled by an exterior force. People don't join the KKK or white supremacist groups because they have independently thought that this should be the right thing to do. No, in almost all those cases, they were taught by their parents or their peers or by some form of propaganda."

"There are over seven billion people in the world." Boyle added, "Maybe ten percent, about 700 million of them may be hateful, evil, naturally cruel and mean. That's a lot of people, but that's only ten percent of the total population. Six and a half billion people are generally good people."

"How do you know?" Orestes demanded.

"How do I know? It's proportional." Boyle answered, "Think of all the people that you know personally. Think of your family, your aunts and uncles and cousins. Think of your friends and all the people in the Greek community associations that you belong to. Think of all the customers that come here on a regular basis. Are they generally good or bad?"

Orestes admitted hesitantly. "Generally, they are good."

"That's right," Boyle stated, "and like Gina said, they are all going to make mistakes. All seven billion of the people in this world are going to make mistakes. Some will make really big mistakes and they will seem to be the bad people."

"Wait a minute Ari," Orestes stopped him, "you're off on one of your philosophical lectures with too much Metaxa on your brain. What's your point?"

"It's as simple as this," Boyle said, "forgive people for their mistakes and give them a little understanding. The people I know can be kind and charitable and they can be brave and humane. They can be intellectual and logical, industrious and determined, but far too often, the true evil of humankind gets all the publicity."

"Given the power, many will abuse." Baldoni said, her speech quite slurred, "Given the immunity, many would plunder, rape and kill. Given the opportunity of distraction, the ease of privilege and the lure of ignorance, most would simply follow the herd as Nietzsche described."

"I guess that's the cop in both of you," Orestes said with a sigh, "all you see are good people doing bad things. Ari, you're messed up. This real estate murder case is turning your sense of reason into fragments. You want to be intelligent, logical and humane, but deep down inside, you think this fucking real estate agent bloody well got what he deserved."

Boyle looked at his friend with the hard eyes of someone who had been exposed, and he hated the fact that someone else knew the truth about him. "Yes, Orestes, you're right. That bloody real estate agent was a terrible human being and he probably got what he deserved. But I'm a cop, and I can't think that way, because if I do, then I start to sympathize with the murderer, and that's something I can never let myself do, otherwise I might start missing things, important things."

Baldoni sat back and took a sip of Metaxa and thoughts went through her head like a rampaging bulldozer. She had learned more about Boyle in the past two days than in the entire two years she had been on his team. First the discussion in the car ride to Alliston, and now in this discussion with Orestes.

Orestes sighed and then spoke in a comforting tone to his friend, "Ari, you're a man, just like the rest of us. You're allowed to make mistakes too you know. You're allowed to have feelings and sometimes you're allowed to have awful feelings, but you can't let those feelings blind your conscience."

"It's hard." Boyle admitted. "I'm a cop and I'm supposed to uphold the law. Laws that were created by a consensus of a supposedly just society. It's what I chose to do, the path I decided my life was meant to follow…but sometimes this path goes through darkness, and this darkness touches me, and I cannot always see clearly."

"Ari…" Orestes spoke with a sense of sympathy, "people do irrational things. You can never know what to expect and there is no way you can pre-determine your own actions."

Then Orestes sat back and picked up the bottle of Metaxa and refilled all three of their glasses. He took a long sip, took a deep breath and spoke with a warm tone, "Do you remember that one time when we were driving up the east coast of New Brunswick on a dreary, wet day, when suddenly a flock of geese flew right in front of our car. Remember that one goose that ended up flying just ahead of the front window. It was about two feet above the hood of the car and a couple of feet in front of the window, flying as hard as he could to keep ahead of us."

"The expression on the gooses' face was one of the funniest things I ever saw. It was as if he were in a panic after realizing what he had gotten himself into. It was as if he was yelling to himself, 'Oh fuck, oh fuck! oh fuck'. And then suddenly, he flew up just high enough to move away from the car, safe and sound."

Baldoni laughed and Boyle smiled at the memory, "I'll never forget that goose."

"Well," Orestes said, "that was five seconds of unpredictability. Sure, it's funny to look back at that incident and funny to see the reaction of that huge bird, but at the same time, it could have smashed through the window and caused an accident, or it could have bounced off the window and ended up as more roadkill. Either way, it wasn't something that was intended to happen. It just did and thank the gods neither us nor the bird were harmed."

"What's your point?" Boyle asked with tiredness in his voice.

"What can anyone really do?" Orestes asked him, "What can any one person do to change the world and fix what we all know is wrong." Then he looked at Boyle with a firmness that implied, "You know I'm right."

"I donna know, what one person can do," the slur in Baldoni's speech made her less and less intelligible as her brain began to turn cloudy.

Boyle looked down and gazed into his glass of Metaxa. "Nothing," he said, "really and truly, there's probably nothing you can do to make a real difference in this world."

"That's exactly the point I'm trying to make." Orestes replied, "There's nothing we can do, so why bother? The only thing we can ever hope to accomplish is to survive, to take care of our families and friends and to try and improve ourselves in the process."

Boyle sat with the glass in his hand, looked down at the tab spoke to his friend as if he was giving confession, "There's nothir can do Orestes, because you really don't want to."

Orestes looked at his friend with a question mark in his eyes, b held up his finger to his lips and gave the *shhhh* sound, and then pointed to Baldoni who had leaned back in her seat and fallen asleep. He spoke in a whisper, "You read about the carnage and destruction around the world, the horrific slaughter of innocent people, the starving refugee children, and you are disgusted by what goes on. You sit back and disdainfully watch as political leaders lie and cheat and follow their corporate religion of corruption. You are repulsed by the knowledge that our environment is slowly changing from something we once called 'nature' into something that we now call unnatural."

Orestes made to interrupt but Boyle cut him off. "No, my friend, I don't mean you in particular. I say the word 'you' as a general statement and I think I really mean 'me'. I can see and feel all of this happening around me, but I am complacent to survive in this secure, consolidated existence that I have fallen into."

"Me, you, we cannot effect change because we truly don't want to upset that sense of security that has become our lives. We do not want to give up this life, which we placidly endure because we are not willing to make the sacrifices necessary for change. Our interests lie in the minimal comforts of our existence, the one that was handed to us by the very people we revile."

"And what's so bad with this life?" Orestes asked with a softly defiant look. "What's so wrong about being with good people, with having family and loved ones, with celebrating the festivals and worshipping the gods, with having friends that you would die for."

Boyle picked up the bottle of Metaxa and poured himself another drink, then he reached over the table and poured Orestes' glass full.

"You're right," he said, "the argument has turned around. First you were complaining about people while I defended them. Now I complain about the dark side of humanity and you bring the light to them. It's this fucking case Orestes, this fucking real estate bastard. It's in my mind all the time. There's something that I don't understand, or at least I cannot fathom. Not yet, but I know it's there."

"C'mon," Orestes said as he put his hand on Boyle's shoulder, "let's get Gina up to the couch in my office where she can sleep, then you and I can come ck down and get drunk, really, really drunk, so that you don't think about anything when you sleep tonight."

Chapter Nineteen

The mood in the Argo meeting room was somber on the last day of the year. Donna Chang and William Singleton spoke in low voices about their plans to celebrate New Year's Eve. Donna Chang would be having dinner with her family. The official New Year for her family was not until the end of January as it was based on the lunar cycle. Singleton and his wife were going to Griffith's restaurant in the Beaches where many members of the homicide teams were planning to meet. The homicide division had made reservations for the whole restaurant.

Baldoni sat across the table and listened to their conversation. She sat beside Aaron Silverstein who was buried deep in his computer, typing notes on a variety of cases that his FIS team was working on. Boyle walked into the room looking sour and grumpy. "It's the last day of the year," he spouted, "more than a month since the Malinkov murder."

He stood in front of the digital screens. "I don't like perfect murders," he grunted, "I don't believe in perfect murders. I've never seen a perfect murder. There are cold cases because we didn't have enough information or because the suspect has fled and is still on the loose. We've had cases in which the body has never been found, and yet even in some of those we still managed to gather enough evidence to get a conviction."

He sat down and looked over the group gathered in the room and repeated, "I don't believe in perfect murders. Aaron, have you anything new to report?"

Silverstein raised his eyes from the computer. "Have I sent you anything new?" Boyle was not in the mood for sarcasm. "If I haven't sent you anything, then I don't have anything." Silverstein said and just stared back at Boyle for a moment and then looked back down at his computer.

Boyle turned to Davis and said in a tone that sounded like wood, "What further information do we have regarding Delivery Corp?"

Davis had spent many hours during the past month at the Delivery Corp offices, interviewing employees and reporting all information back to Boyle, and then going back with more questions that Boyle wanted answered.

"It was confirmed that none of their offices provide bicycle courier services." Davis started, "We have obtained a list of all employees for Delivery Corp including their distribution centers, offices and delivery personnel. Only one employee lived in the Beaches and she worked at the head office in the accounting department. She was never provided with a parka or a toque as it is not a requirement for the office staff to wear the company uniform."

"However, the company does require all of their delivery staff to wear the official Delivery Corp uniforms and they do not keep track of the uniforms when an employee leaves the company. This could mean that someone who used to work for Delivery Corp was on the bicycle the evening of the murder."

"That's great, now we've got a couple of hundred more interviews." Boyle's mood turned a little dour for a moment, but then he took a breath and decided not to transmit his edginess to everyone else, "You've brought up a good point. Make a request to Delivery Corp for a list of past employees and then start the process of checking each one of them. It's going to take time, but this seems to be the only lead we have at the moment." He turned to Baldoni, "Gina, bring everybody up to date."

Baldoni looked down at the notes on her laptop and read them without looking up at the group. "We interviewed a number of people who know the Malinkovs in Alliston. This included neighbors, members of the parish community, Anton's co-workers and a couple of his childhood friends. All testimony was in corroboration with what we learned previously about Anton and Elizabeth's character."

"I checked with the Financial Crimes unit and the Fraud Squad and they do not have anything on record for either Ivan Malinkov or Anton and his family. There are two main loan sharks working out of pawn shops in Barrie and a few more who work the Casino Rama circuit. The Barrie loan sharks both claim to have no knowledge of the Malinkov family, and as far as we can tell, Anton has never been to Casino Rama."

"Bill, anything on the stuff you looked into?" Boyle asked.

"I checked with Assistant Inspector Wilson of the Integrated Gun and Gang Task Force. Anton Malinkov does not show up in their database, but that does not mean he didn't hire a street gang to kill his father, there's just no record of him in the database." Singleton looked up from his computer at a series of blank faces staring back at him, except one.

Boyle did not want to end the year on a sour note. His team had worked hard over the past month, digging what little evidence they could find. His team had also dealt with a parental homicide in which a father had left his child in the back seat of his car. The father had supposedly gone into a bar for a quick meeting with a friend, and then forgot about the nine-month-old child. It had been snowing that day and the snow covered the front and back windshields of the car, therefore the interior was not visible to pedestrians walking by. The child fell asleep in the back seat and died of hypothermia. When the autopsy had been completed, there were indications of bruising and scars from previous injuries, and child abuse of a physical nature was suspected. The father was charged with criminal negligence causing death. When the father was officially arrested, both Singleton and Davis had to physically hold Baldoni back from assaulting him.

Boyle looked around the table at the faces watching him and he said once again, "I don't believe in a perfect murder. Try not to think about that while you're celebrating the New Year tonight."

****

New Year's Eve was usually a joyous occasion for Boyle in which he would gather at the Parthenon for dinner with Orestes, other friends and members of the Greek Cultural Association. Orestes prepared a new year's fare of Orzo soup followed by a Greek cabbage salad, and then the main course of a Greek beef stew.

The highlight of the meal was the Vasilopita cake, in which a small coin is hidden in the mixture during the baking process. The one who finds the coin is destined to have good fortune in the new year.

Boyle didn't find the coin in his piece of cake and the sense of grimness he had been feeling grew the more.

Orestes always closed the Parthenon early on New Year's Eve because he would rather spend time in celebration with the friends he loved instead of dealing with the drunks and revelers who often caused damage. He and Boyle also wanted to enjoy the ritual celebration for St. Basil of Caesarea with their friend Phedra, and after the meal, Boyle and Orestes drove up Pape Avenue to

O'Connor Drive. Phedra lived in an older home that had an exceptionally large backyard in the East York area of Toronto.

A small fire was ablaze within a steel ring in the middle of the backyard, and a number of prayers and stories were read in Greek. This was followed by the ritual of writing something on a piece of paper that you wished to discard or leave behind, such as negative feelings, a sickness, or even a weakness in one's personality, and burn it in the fire.

Boyle had a number of negative feelings he wanted to incinerate. The Malinkov case had settled into his mind like a demon from one of the Greek myths. He looked to the stars and prayed to lift his negative thoughts about the victim from his heart. He prayed to the Gods for wisdom and insight on the human nature of the killer, on why any one person would commit such a crime. After the ritual, Boyle excused himself and headed back down to the Beaches where the homicide teams had planned to meet at Griffith's restaurant.

Griffith's restaurant was a deceptive place in which there was a small storefront that sold deli products, but as you went through the small store, it opened up into a large restaurant with three floors. The top two floors were dining areas and the bottom floor was a lounge with a massive traditional fireplace. The center of the top two floors were open and circled by a heavy oaken railing so that you could looked down to the lounge.

When Boyle arrived, the fireplace was burning high and the food was plentiful. The liqueur and whiskey bottles had been opened and nearly drained, and his fellow officers and many of the civilian members of the Force were well on their way to toward complete inebriation.

Boyle rarely drank alcohol in front of his co-workers and never lost his composure by getting drunk with them. He only drank heavily when he was alone or when he was with Orestes, because he knew Orestes could be trusted and would respect Boyle's need for privacy.

Boyle poured himself a glass of carbonated mineral water and wandered through the restaurant greeting his co-workers and exchanging well wishes for the new year. As he went down one of the large hallways toward the restrooms, he saw Gina in one of the dark corners with one of the bartenders who worked at the 'Lion on the Beach' pub. He watched the two of them in a passionate embrace and wondered if this was an on-going fling or if the alcohol influenced their decision to make a public display of their enamored pursuits.

He left them to their privacy, went to the bar and ordered a Drambuie for himself. He sat on a bar stool and began to think about his own relationships, and why so many of them had been highly passionate and then ultimately failed. There were a number of romances since the end of his marriage, but none were ever serious enough to warrant a significant commitment.

Boyle pondered about the lifestyle of being a detective and how it often led to problems in relationships. He knew of very few detectives, male or female, whose marriages lasted for any extended period of time. The 'on-call' nature of the job meant that dinners, movies, theatre and whatever other social activity their partner wanted to share, were often cancelled or postponed, or sometimes just simply forgotten.

As he sat there and reflected, he began to visualize Margaret Hinds and wondered if she had come for the end of year celebrations. He decided to walk around the three floors to search for her, but as he was about to stand up, he noticed one of the waitresses standing in a small hallway that led from the bar to the kitchen. She was preparing a dessert tray for one of the tables that had ordered pastries and a container of coffee. She had caught Boyle's eye because she was a young, beautiful blonde with a Marilyn Monroe body.

Boyle watched as she picked up one dessert plate and noticed that it had not been completely cleaned through the dishwasher. He guessed there were water spots on the plate. The waitress quickly looked around and then she wiped the plate on the ass of her pants in order to remove the spots. She picked up more plates and did not inspect them, she just instinctively wiped each of them on the ass of her pants.

Boyle smiled at first, and then started to chuckle, sitting there by himself, and watched her deliver the dessert tray to the table of Sergeant Detective Joanna Johnson's team. Boyle and Johnson had an amicable professional relationship, but they had often quarreled over procedure and their interpretive intent of the law. He continued to chuckle to himself as he watched the people at Johnson's table fill their 'ass' plates, oblivious to the secret that he knew. He was almost tempted to go and tell them, just so he could see the look on their faces.

Instead, he waited for the waitress to return and then smiled and told her that he knew her secret. She returned his smile with a glint of mysterious delight in her eye. Boyle wondered if she knew that he had seen her with the plates or whether she thought he was talking about something else. He sipped his Drambuie and wondered what secrets she might really have, and let his imagination run wild.

Chapter Twenty

It was the last week of March and Boyle called for a meeting in the Argo to discuss the progression of the various investigations assigned to his team. It was four months since the murder of Ivan Malinkov and it seemed this investigation had run up against more dead ends than potential leads. Donna Chang had completed digging through all of the information on Ivan's computer and his financial records, plus determining the value of his estate.

Constable Davis had been in frequent contact with the Toronto head office of Delivery Corp and they had compiled records of all previous employees. She and Constable Singleton had sorted through the records to determine which employees could be suspect and may have been in the Beaches on the night of the murder. It was another long process of eliminating employees who were obviously too elderly or dead, and then researching where the potential suspects were on the night of the murder.

Boyle had advised them to compile a list of all potential suspects with Donna Chang in an Excel file so it could be used for future reference. If the killer was as intelligent as Boyle suspected, they would probably have an alibi, and he wanted all alibis listed on the file.

Boyle's cell phone began to buzz. He looked down at the number and saw it was from his own home and he answered, "This is Boyle."

"Hello, Dad, how's the hunt for criminals going?"

A smile spread across Boyle's face as he heard the voice of his son. "Theo, how are you?" He looked at the members of his team and excused himself and then walked into the hallway. "Are you calling for money, ha, ha? Why are you at home? How's school?"

"I'm fine Dad. I'm at the house. Wanted to drop my bags off before I called to let you know I'm in town. I called from the home phone because my cell is almost dead and needed charging." Theo said all this knowing his father was probably already deducing this fact.

"It's not the end of the semester yet, is it?" Boyle asked with a little suspicion.

"I'm on a break right now, but I wanted to come into town an spend some time with you and talk." Theo said.

"What about?"

"Later, let's eat first and then we'll talk."

"Okay, meet me at the Parthenon at seven. Orestes will be happy to see you." Boyle said without being able to hide the joy in his voice.

"I'll get there a little earlier so that I can chill." Theo said and then asked with a little trepidation, "Uncle O isn't going to try and kiss me again, is he?"

"Probably," Boyle said, "but then, he loves you as if you were his own son. You know that if anything ever to happened to me he would probably adopt you."

"Dad, I'm twenty-two." Theo said with a sarcastic reminder to his father.

"Doesn't matter, he would want to take care of you anyway. I wouldn't be surprised if you were in his will. You'll probably get the bar."

"Okay Dad, I'll see you when you get there." Theo said as he hung up, wondering how he was going to break the news to his father.

****

Theo showered and shaved and then put on a fresh pair of jeans and shirt from his closet and then turned and looked round the room. He looked at all the things his father saved from his childhood, the school pictures, the Greek laurel wreath he wore from the play he performed at the cultural center, the album covers that used to decorate the walls above the closet. He smiled as he thought about his father, the cop, the detective, the man he wanted to be when he grew up, the man he has to talk to about his life.

He left the house after a few minutes and walked up Main Street, past the Ted Reeve arena, where he played little league hockey while his father watched from the stands. He walked over the bridge that spanned the railway tracks for the commuter trains, then up to Danforth Avenue to the Main subway station.

He took the subway to the Chester station and walked to the Parthenon Tavern. He did not see Orestes anywhere. Maria, one of the waitresses, nodded her head toward the kitchen and Theo walked down the hallway. Orestes was at one of the stoves stirring a pot of sauce. "Hi Uncle O, how's everything with you?" Theo called from the doorway.

Orestes turned, and when he saw Theo in the doorway, a surprised beaming smile spread across his face, "Theo my boy, when did you come into town, your father never mentioned that you were coming. If I knew, I would have made my special Moussaka."

"I just got into town this morning Uncle O. Dad didn't know that I was coming. I thought I would keep it a surprise."

Orestes put the stove element on a low heat, then he took off the highly stained apron and hung it on a hook that bore his name. He walked over to Theo and gave him a bear hug that Theo believed would one day break his spine. Orestes then grabbed Theo by the head with the palms of his hands and planted a huge kiss on each of his cheeks.

"You look wonderful my boy. School is treating you well?"

"School is fine Uncle O, I'm on a break right now and I've come home to visit with Dad. He's going to meet me here when he gets off work."

They went into the main part of the restaurant and sat by a table near the window with cups of coffee, a plate of pita cut into triangles and a bowl of Taramasalata. Orestes called to Maria and told her that he and Theo were not to be disturbed. Maria gave a knowing smile to indicate she knew that this meant only to call Orestes if it was a regular customer, a member from the Greek cultural center or an attractive woman.

The two men talked as if they were truly uncle and nephew. It didn't matter if they were not of the same blood, it only mattered if there was love and respect. They talked about Theo's school and his courses, and they talked about the restaurant and how business was doing. They talked about their dalliances with women and they talked about the events that are happening in the Greek community. After an hour of catching up, Theo told him that he wanted to go for a walk along Danforth Avenue and see how the neighborhood had changed.

"Too many chain restaurants taking over the old places," Orestes complained. "I think there's more Sushi bars than there are Greek restaurants now. It's not the same anymore, too much gentrification for the young, hip millennials who only care for fashion and style. The quality of traditional food isn't important to them, at least that's my opinion."

"Uncle O," replied Theo, "I'm one of those millennials you are talking about."

"Yes, but you're different. You were brought up to respect the traditional values."

"Give the millennials a chance Uncle O." Theo replied with warmth as this was a man he respected more than almost any other, "You might be surprised at how traditional many of them are. You can't judge everyone under 30 by what you read in a magazine. A lot of young people are searching for their own way in life. They look around and they are trying to find a way to live without creating the same shit their parents made."

"Theo," Orestes said with a touch of pride, "You're going to be a philosopher like your father. Do me a favor and stop in at the Akropolis bakery when you walk past Pape Avenue. I want to get some of their special spinach swirls for desert after we have dinner. Here, take forty bucks and get enough for the three of us."

"Uncle O," Theo said in protest, "they're not going to cost that much."

"That's okay, pick up something else you can take home with you for breakfast tomorrow." Orestes said with a wide grin on his face.

Theo accepted the money with a smile and a little shake of his head, knowing that Orestes would probably give him everything in his wallet and whatever was in the cash till if he asked for it. He put on his coat and walked out the door of the Parthenon, turning east along Danforth. He looked across the street and saw a Sushi Bar where the small Aegean restaurant used to be, and just down the street to where a Lobster King franchise had taken over the building where the Mykonos restaurant once operated.

Yes, the area was changing, just like everything else in this world. Just like his own thoughts and feelings about life.

****

Just after 7:00 pm, Boyle walked into the Parthenon to meet his son, whom he hadn't seen since last Christmas. The two embraced with a bear hug that was filled to the brim with love.

"Take it easy Dad. Between you and Uncle O I'm going to end up with a broken back."

"It's good to see you," said Boyle ignoring his complaint. "Toronto has become a hollow city since you moved to London for school."

Orestes pointed to the back corner, near the kitchen, to a table with a booth that provided privacy and comfort. "You two sit there," said Orestes, "I'll bring some wine and bread and a plate of olive oil and balsamic vinegar."

"How many hearts have you broken?" Boyle asked his son in a playful manner.

"Well, I have one for each course," Theo boasted playfully, "so that makes six. The only problem I have is the English Lit class because all six of them are in that same class. I have to walk on eggs shells between Shakespeare and Homer and avoid sitting with any of them."

"As long as it doesn't interfere with your studies." Boyle laughed.

Theo only smiled at his father's last remark. He tried to keep the smile on his face, but it was forced, and Boyle could see this, but didn't not want to rush the conversation.

"How far along are you with that case of the murdered real estate agent?" Theo asked.

"Dead ends, nothing but dead ends." Boyle said.

"No suspects?"

"Hell, I got lots of suspects," replied Boyle, "half the people we interviewed seem to be glad this guy is dead. And from what I've learned about him, I couldn't blame any one of them if they did it. I've had cases that have gone cold before, but this one is really frustrating. There's too many people with motives and yet they all have concrete alibis for the time the murder occurred."

Orestes came back to the table with a bottle of Greek wine, a basket of bread and a plate of oil and balsamic vinegar. The three men talked and drank wine, taking pieces the bread and dipping it into the oil-vinegar combination. The two older men continued asking Theo about school, his classes, friends he had made, and Orestes kept plugging questions about the young women.

"Tell me," Orestes said jovially, "how many?" and then he held up his forearm, made a tight fist and sang is a low deep voice, "Ooga Chacka Ooga Ooga, Ooga Chacka Ooga Ooga."

Theo winced and said, "What's that, a Greek fertility chant?"

Boyle laughed, "That's from one of his favorite songs in the seventies."

"Hooked on a Feeling," Orestes said with a sardonic smile, "Blue Suede."

Theo smiled at Orestes and asked him to pass the menu. Orestes told him not to bother, he had already ordered their meal. Ten minutes later, Maria brought a large plate of traditional Greek salad, a plate with skewers of lamb and vegetables, a plate of large meatballs in a creamy sauce and a large side plate of rice and potatoes.

The conversation continued throughout the meal with Orestes eventually re-telling Greek mythological stories and joking how Theo's father was created by the Gods as a mixture of Dionysus, the god of wine and theatre, and Glaucus, the fisherman who became immortal when he ate magical herbs. Boyle grinned and shook his head, stating that Orestes was actually describing himself.

"Maria!" Orestes called over to the waitress, "bring us another bottle of wine, and bring the spinach twirls that are on the counter."

"Orestes, you're too generous." Boyle remarked.

"Nonsense amigo. The gods would send lightning bolts at me if I didn't take care of the people I loved." Orestes put his arms out and clasped the hands of both father and son.

"I think Uncle O only lets you come back here because of all the money you spend." Theo said with a laugh and a wink to Orestes.

"Ha!" Orestes pronounced, "I could buy a boat with all the money he doesn't spend here!"

"Yeah but look at all the protection I give you." Boyle said smiling.

"Protection? What do you mean protection?" Orestes quizzically smiled.

"Everybody knows that if someone were to harm you, I would go to the ends of the world to hunt them down and bring them to justice."

"Now that's a very good point," said Orestes, "Theo, your father is worth every penny I spend on food and drink for him."

"A toast!" cried Boyle, they each raised their glasses and stated together, "to the Gods."

"Orestes, my friend," Boyle finally said, "I think my son wants to talk to me, so I'm going to have to say goodnight. Theo, let us depart this fine establishment and let the owner schmooze with his customers and the pretty ladies at the bar."

****

136

They drove along Danforth talking about the changes in the area. Boyle pointed to the beautiful new mosque that was built on Danforth near Donlands Avenue, and two blocks later the new Ethiopian Cultural center.

"Have you ever had Ethiopian cuisine?" Boyle asked his son.

Theo shook his head no and Boyle said, "I'll have to take you to one of the restaurants in this area. The food is wonderful." After a few moments, he added, "But don't tell Orestes."

When they arrived home, Boyle went to the liquor cabinet and asked his son what he would like for a nightcap. Theo stated that he would like a beer and went to the kitchen. Boyle poured himself a double shot of Ouzo and they settled into the kitchen for what Boyle hoped was nothing too serious.

They sat for a moment without saying anything and in that moment, Boyle realized that his son was deeply troubled, a suspicion that had lingered with him ever since he had called on the phone earlier in the day.

"What is it Theo?"

Theo was hesitant in his reply, "Dad, when did you know that you wanted to be a cop?"

"I think when I was a couple of years older than you are now." Boyle answered.

"How did you know," Theo said, "I mean, how did you know that this was what you wanted to be for the rest of your life. Was it like a little voice in your head telling you what to do?"

"I'm not sure what to tell you," Boyle said, "I was working as a teacher after I graduated university and realized that I really didn't like it. Dealing with a bunch of young kids just wasn't what I was cut out to do."

"What did you do?" Theo asked.

"Well, I remember talking to Orestes about it. He suggested I go into the army for a couple of years and get experience in a number of things. I thought about it and decided the army wasn't for me, but the idea came to me that the police force was something I might want to do."

"So you joined the force because it might be something you would want to do?"

"No, it wasn't as thoughtless as that." Boyle stated sourly.

"I didn't mean it like that," Theo said apologetically, "I just meant…well I mean, was it that simple or obvious to you, that this was what you wanted."

"I spent a great deal of time thinking about it, really thinking. I talked it over with your grandparents and my mother suggested I take the orientation course the police department offered. So, I did, and then I really had to think about it, I mean I had to think about everything that it could entail. In my mind, I had to imagine seeing dead mangled bodies in car accidents, I had to imagine being a member of crowd control during a riot, even if it was a protest that I believed in. I had to imagine the potential of shooting someone, and whether or not I could do it."

"I had to think about all the bad things that I would be involved in. Logically I knew there could be a lot of dead bodies, whether they were natural deaths, accidents or overdoses. I had to decide if I could handle that. I had to think about how some people would hate me because they just hated cops, and some people would be afraid of me, and that there would probably be more hatred and fear than what most other people would have to deal with."

"So no, it was not an easy decision," and then he took his glass and gulped the Ouzo down. Boyle got up and went back to the liquor cabinet, grabbed the bottle of Ouzo and brought it into the kitchen. He poured himself another shot and set the bottle on the table. He sat down, prepared for a long night of discussion, prepared himself for argument, prepared himself for the patience he would need, prepared himself for tears, but most of all he prepared himself for remaining strong for whatever his son needed.

Theo looked at his father, the cop, the detective, the authority figure that was always strong, but always loving, always playful and was always there when he needed him. He took a deep breath and then said, "Dad, I want to quit school."

Boyle waited a moment and then asked, "Why?"

"I don't think it's what I want to do."

"Do you know what you want to do?" Boyle asked with sympathy in his voice.

"No." Theo said with resignation.

"Then why quit school?"

"I don't know. I figure why bother going to school and end up doing something I don't want to do." Theo answered with confusion.

"What does your mother have to say?" Boyle questioned.

"Aw, you know Mom. She wants me to be successful and to stay in school. She wants me to be a doctor, a lawyer, an astronaut and be rich."

"Oh, so you talked to her first."

"Aw Jesus Dad, let's not make a case out of this okay."

"Alright, have you given any thought about what you want?" Boyle asked.

"I thought about becoming a cop like you, but I don't know if that's what I really want or whether that's just another way to not make a real decision."

"You know," said Boyle, "a lot of fathers would be honored if their sons followed in their footsteps. But that's not me, I would rather you find your purpose and that you were happy. That's what I would want, for you to be happy. That's why I wanted to name you Theo, because Theo means to be happy."

"No, it doesn't," said Theo, "it means a gift from the Gods."

"Same thing in a way, but the point is I want for you to be happy."

"Happy," Theo said with a sigh, "how can anybody know what they need to be happy?" He stopped and the two of them, father and son, sat in silence as they both pondered what needed to be said and how to say it.

"I was sitting in a bar one night in downtown London," Theo tried to start an explanation of his feelings, "it was a dive that local drunks would hang out at. The beer was cheap, so a lot of students liked to go there to watch the hockey games."

"There was a middle-aged couple who often sat at the video slot machines. I had seen them on numerous occasions, playing the slots," he continued, "and they just kept playing, every night, hardly ever winning, probably didn't even expect to win, just watching the slots spin. I watched them and thought to myself, *'That's what their life has become, watching the slots spin.'* At the other end of the bar was an animated conversation between two older guys that seemed important, but all they were talking about was what happened in the hockey game from the previous week, not even the one that was taking place on the TV, but one that happened last week."

"I sat at the bar and asked myself 'is this life?' this monotonous spin of an unlikely games of chance and the inane arguments of drunkards. I knew at that point I was just not happy, and I didn't know what my life was supposed to be about. It made me angry and it made me sad, and all I could feel was this frustration I couldn't find any answers for."

Boyle sat and looked at his son and yearned to reach out and hug him. He wanted to comfort him, to guide him, to protect him, to lift the confusion of life off his shoulders and burden himself with all of Theo's problems and worries and frustrations, like Atlas carrying the world.

All he could say was, "It's not easy. I wish I could tell you all the answers and solve your dilemma, but I can't, I don't have an answer for what your life is about."

"Maybe I should just go to work for a while and think about it." Theo said.

"What kind of job?" Boyles asked.

"I don't know," Theo blurted out with obvious frustration, "maybe something that will let me experience life. A job on a merchant marine ship or a long-haul trucker."

Boyle poured another glass of Ouzo, took a sip and let a calmness settle over him. He let the pressure of the situation dissipate and he let a clearness enter his mind. He looked across the table and he thought to himself, '*This is my son. This is my blood. He wants my advice. He wants me to guide him with the wisdom of the Gods. He wants the ultimate answer that I cannot give.*' And in that moment of clarity, Boyle realized what he had to say, no matter how hard it would be to say, he must tell his son the only answer that he could give.

And then he spoke softly, "So, you're fed up with school and want to go to work for a living. You want to find yourself a job that presents daily challenges and provides personal self-fulfillment. Why don't you join the Salvation Army?"

"You're not serious, right?" Theo asked with a touch of frustration.

"Of course I'm not serious about the Sally Ann, but Theo, I don't think a job is what you're looking for," he continued, "you're looking for something that's going to pick up your life and inject a boost of adrenaline. You're looking for something that's going to make life interesting and adventurous. Maybe, just maybe, you're looking for a reason to live."

"Maybe you're right." Theo slowly admitted.

"Well then, let your father tell you something I learned many years ago." Boyle said with calm reflection, "There's only one thing in this whole world that is going to give you a reason to live, that will make your life worthwhile."

"And what's that?" Theo asked.

"It is something," Boyle hesitated, gathered his thoughts and then continued, "well, once you've got it, then it won't matter what job you have, what you do or whom you meet. Once you have it, then every breathing moment you experience becomes an adventure; and everything you see between the blink of your eyes becomes fresh and alive; and everything you hear will sound as if it has never been heard before."

Theo looked at his father as if he was seeing a different person. Someone in the same shape and form and with the same voice, but with words that he had never heard before, words that made him think of the philosophers that he studied in school and could never imagine them as real people. He sat there in silence and waited for his father to speak again.

Boyle picked up his glass and took a deep sip of the Ouzo. He sat for another moment to think, and then he continued, "What do you think this wondrous, magical thing that could make your life worth living is?"

Theo didn't respond, he just sat and pondered this man who was different from what he remembered his father to be and then asked, "I don't know. What is it?"

Boyle shrugged his shoulders and answered after a moment, "Sorry, I can't tell you. Not because I don't want to, but because it cannot be passed from one human being to another. It is impossible to communicate its essence."

"The only thing I can tell you is where to find it. And the only thing I can promise you, is that it will be the most difficult search you will ever make. It is deep inside of you, like at the bottom of a dark pit."

"All those Greek myths that I read to you as a boy," he went on as Theo sat in a silent trance, "all of those stories about the quests, the adventurous travels, the wars, the monsters…they were all about finding yourself, about finding your own purpose in life."

"This pit inside you is filled with one-eyed Cyclops, snake-headed Medusas and a savage Minotaur. It is filled with beautiful goddesses and angels, and sometimes you will not be able to differentiate between the two."

"The answer to the meaning of your life can only be discovered by you. No one else can find that answer for you. You can listen to the guides, the philosophers, the clerics, crazy drunkards and even to your own father, but you are the only one that can truly answer the questions you have, you are the only one that can find a purpose to your life."

****

"Dad," said Theo, "why didn't we have this type of conversation when I was younger?"

"We did," said Boyle, "every time I read you one of the stories, I told you about the wonders of life and how you must go on your own quest. But you were young, and you only saw the adventures, and that's what boys do, they rarely see the truth behind the adventure."

"I'm twenty-two years old," Theo spoke through his melancholy, "and I don't know what to do. I look around me, at all the shit in this world, and I don't know where I fit in. I look at my friends, and most of them are just doing what they think they are supposed to do, what is expected of them, and they seem to think they are happy. But I'm not."

"Well, why don't you go and find out who you are." Boyle told him.

"And how do I do that?" Theo asked.

"Go on a quest." Boyle answered.

"A quest? A quest for what?"

"A quest to find out who Theo Boyle is. A quest to find the soul of the man that is inside of you."

Theo went to the cupboard and chose a glass. He picked up the bottle of Ouzo and took a big gulp. He felt like he was on the verge of a precipice, looking down into a deep canyon and he felt a sense of vertigo.

"Dad," Theo began in a soft voice and then stopped because he couldn't think of what else to say.

"Why don't you travel?" Boyle suggested. "Go to Greece and start with your roots. Visit with your grandmother's family. Start there and then let the wind take you."

"What about school?" Theo asked with trepidation.

"Don't worry about school, they will wait for you, or another school, once you find what it is you truly want to be."

"What about Mom?" Theo asked with a sarcastic smile.

"Your mother will understand. She'll have to, and if you want me to be there when you talk to her, then I will."

The voice of Orestes came softly from the doorway of the kitchen, "He's a fucking Greek poet. To know the story of the gods and the heroes is one thing, but to truly know the truth and meaning behind the stories is a poet."

"How long have you been listening?" Boyle asked with a touch of annoyance.

"I figured something was up, so I brought over a couple of bottles of Plomari." Orestes smiled, "You can never have enough Ouzo when you start a quest."

Chapter Twenty-One

For three months, Boyle's homicide team had experienced periods of hectic activity and times that were sluggishly slow. The paternal homicide case had been completed and the father charged.

Everything was now in the hands of the prosecutors. Boyle's team was also involved in a gang related slaying which was quickly turned over to the Integrated Gun and Gang Task Force.

The team also worked on an arson-homicide case. This case was quickly solved as the boyfriend of the murdered woman confessed within two days of committing the crime. His team spent most of the month gathering evidence and witness statements for the prosecution.

However, it had been four months since the Malinkov murder, and the investigation was no farther ahead than it was in December. They were no closer to charging a suspect than they had been on that first Monday morning when the body was discovered, and this aggravated Boyle in every respect.

Under Boyle's direction, the homicide team had re-interviewed the occupants of all the surrounding homes and no further information was produced. Mrs. Carmen the house cleaner and Mr. Chin the gardener, were also re-interviewed. Their statements were consistent with their original interviews.

Boyle called for a team meeting in early April to review the investigation in hopes that something would spark a new idea or root out a nondescript fact that would engender a potential lead. In the back of his mind, he knew there was something they had missed, and he wanted to flesh out his thoughts to the group.

It was a short meeting.

Donna Chang confirmed there were no irregularities in the financial statements for Ivan Malinkov, his son Anton or Anton's wife Elizabeth. She added that Anton was the sole inheritor of Ivan's estate, which included the house on Kenilworth Avenue. However, none of the monies had been dispersed as there was a freeze on all assets pending completion of the investigation.

She also stated she had completed reviewing all of the electronic calendars, phone books, journals and other digital information from Ivan's computer and apart from some porn that was downloaded and a series of exclamation marks beside the names of some women in his phone book, she did not find anything peculiar.

Constable Singleton reported that all of the documents provided from Beach Realtor Company regarding the property transactions Ivan was involved in, seemed to be in order. There were no disputes apart from the one instance reported to Detective Baldoni by Awesome Gandhi. Singleton then stated that he purposely used the phrase 'seemed to be in order' as all documents were strictly for the offers, counter offers and final sales. If there had been anything un-ethical in the transactions, the improprieties would not be visible on any document.

Constable Davis updated the investigation of employees who had worked for Delivery Corp. She explained the list was extensive as the turnover for employees was higher than most other industries. "It's the type of job you take until you can find a better one," she smirked. She explained that many of the past employees were either retired or dead. Four were currently locked up in the Ontario penal system, and the rest were spread out all over the province.

Only three previous employees lived in the Beaches area of Toronto and all three were interviewed. She could not make any connection between them and Ivan Malinkov. None of them had worked with the Beach Realty Company for any type of business and none of them owned bicycles. All three had valid alibis for the night of November 23.

Boyle took a sip from his coffee and paused before saying anything. "We're four months in on this case and apart from the Delivery Corp info Jasmine just gave us, we seem to have exhausted our investigations. This case is going sub-zero cold, and I really hate having cold cases associated with my team's investigations. If anybody has any ideas or thoughts or suggestions, bring them forward to the team or to me personally."

The meeting ended and Boyle asked Baldoni if she could stay behind for a moment. "Are you working on anything important right now?" he asked.

"I was just planning to complete some paperwork, but nothing that couldn't wait," she answered.

"I need to get out of here and think, maybe go for a walk along the boardwalk in the Beaches. I want the wind and the waves to tell me something. I want the trees to point to the answers. You want to join me?"

She agreed because she knew that he wanted to have a conversation away from the office and away from any other member of the force, official or civilian. She had taken 'walks' with him before and they often turned into abstract discussions about potential possibilities of a case, or sometimes about the mundane, routine aspects of an investigation, but she always found the walks to be stimulating.

Boyle's mind was thought provoking, and the walks were one way of sifting through his instinct and intelligence. She also knew that he liked to walk close to the crime scene, as if there was some mystical frame of reference he might tap into.

****

They took Boyle's car and drove down to the public parking lot near the boardwalk. They walked to the coffee shop and each ordered a coffee. March had been a warm month and April seemed to follow the trend. Today, the temperature was well above average. The sky was overcast, and medium gusts of wind blew in off the beach as they made their way down to the wooden planked boardwalk.

The boardwalk is three kilometers long and they walked in silence westward toward the Ashbridge's Bay park and boating docks. There were always people strolling along the boardwalk when the weather was good and Baldoni waited until they had some space between the seniors, the mothers with baby strollers and the dog walkers.

"What did you want to discuss?" she asked.

"The Malinkov case," Boyle said. "It's gone cold." She remained silent and listened.

"I don't like being frustrated by evidence that goes nowhere," he said, "and I don't like to think that someone, or maybe even a group of people, have been able to commit a murder that can't be resolved. I have never believed that there could be a perfect murder. The murderer always misses something, and if

146

there's more than one murderer involved, then the chances are greater that one of them left something behind, or a trail that can be followed, or a lie that can be uncovered."

They walked on and Boyle looked out over the water. The overcast sky had a melancholy feel, and the wind began to pick up strength. The branches of the trees swayed back and forth like hands waving an ominous warning. The clouds raced away from the horizon and the rustling leaves that had remained on the ground from the previous autumn mumbled their consent. Neither one of them spoke for a short time and when they approached the end of the boardwalk where it curved back in on Kew beach, they made their way onto the paved path that took them into the park.

The wind began to quiet down and grow softer. Nature became silent until only a seagull's choir could be heard, singing a rustic, yet reverent Hallelujah. A distant flash of light in the south and a slow, rumbling thunder rolled across the lake.

Boyle looked up and watched Pegasus gallop low among the clouds. His faded, ivory mane dulled against the higher overcast blanket of white. He briefly looked away to the north, but only for a few seconds. When he turned back, Pegasus was gone, gently dissipated into the mists of the approaching night.

"I don't think we've missed anything." Baldoni said.

"No, we haven't, and that's what troubles me the most." Boyle responded with the frustration mounting in his voice. "There's nothing at the crime scene to provide any leads and only one potential eye-witness who saw a person in a Delivery Corp parka on a bicycle, and for all we know, even that lead may not have anything to do with the case."

"We've got a couple of potential suspects who may have revenge as a motive," he continued, "but they all have verifiable alibis. If we arrested any one of them, we would have absolutely no case to bring against them."

"You want to start from the beginning and go back over it again?" Baldoni hesitantly suggested.

"We may have to." Boyle said with a sigh, "C'mon, let's go back to the boardwalk, I want to get some water at that little snack bar just south of the skating rink."

They turned and walked back through the park to where the boardwalk began. The look of concern on Boyle's face caused Baldoni to inquire about what was troubling him, "You've got other things on your mind Boss. More than just this case."

"Yeah," Boyle said but didn't expand on his personal life.

"I hear Theo's back in town. Is everything alright?" she asked.

Boyle looked over at Baldoni with a touch of fatherly affection for his partner, and then said with a touch of sarcasm. "He wants to quit school because he doesn't know what he wants to do with his life. He believes that until he knows what he really wants, then school is just a waste of time."

"People can go years without actually knowing what they really want from their life," she said matter-of-factly. "Not everybody is as lucky as you and I."

Boyle peeked over after her remark and asked, "When did you know that you wanted to be a cop?"

"Ever since I was about fifteen."

"How did you know at that age?"

Baldoni thought for a moment and then answered, "I wanted the respect that the uniform commands. I wanted that authority, and maybe even a little bit of that sense of power. I never liked that many women are forced to endure second-class citizenship in a male dominated society. I just wanted to be me, and when I thought about cops, I knew that the authoritative power would automatically put me a step ahead of the majority of males in our civilization when it came to recognition and equality, and if they didn't like it, then I could run them in," she said with a smile.

****

They kept walking and as they talked, the wind turned into a gentle off-shore breeze, and the late afternoon sun darted between the billowing clouds that still filled the sky with shapes and dreams. They walked all the way to the other end of the boardwalk, to the Water Treatment plant, and then turned back until they returned to Kew Gardens park where the ice rink sat empty with the milder weather. The snack bar was still open.

Boyle stopped for a moment and looked around. A gentle smile grew on his face as an old memory came to his mind. "Have you ever come down to the Beaches for the fireworks display on the Victoria Day weekend?" Boyle asked, changing the conversation.

"Nope, never have. Are they any good?" Baldoni asked.

"I used to come here with my ex-wife and Theo when he was much younger." Boyle's smile grew considerably as he began to relate his memories. "Just down there," he said pointing east along the beach, "see where that promontory of sand juts out into the lake. That's where we would set up our beach chairs and blankets."

"I remember we always began the night with the lighting of the 'Burning Schoolhouse' which Theo would label with magic markers with the name of his school. We drove home with the fireworks still in our mind. Sometimes I had to carry Theo into the house and gently put him to bed." Boyle stopped at that point and just stared into the sky as he let the memory linger in his mind.

"You're really concerned about him." Baldoni said with a compassionate voice.

"Yeah…" his voice dropped off as he checked his emotions, "I'm going to head up to the Parthenon. Why don't you come with me and we can have dinner. Tomorrow I want you to set up interviews with everyone on the list once more. You're right, we have to go back to the beginning and re-investigate everything."

"Okay Boss," she said respectfully.

Boyle stopped and then turned to face her and spoke with a touch of irony in his voice, "You've been calling me Boss ever since your first couple of months on the team. You do know that I'm not your real boss."

"I know," Baldoni replied, "it's just feels more comfortable than saying Detective Boyle."

"What about Ari?" he suggested.

"Nah, that's too familiar for me. I need structure, so I call you Boss out of respect."

He stood and looked at her for a moment and could only smile in response. They crossed the park once more to the parking lot. The exit went straight up Coxwell Avenue. As they passed 55 Division station Boyle inquisitively asked, "Are you still jogging at the zoo?"

"Whenever I can," answered Baldoni.

"Why do you go all the way there to jog?"

"Have you ever run with the wolves?" she asked.

"No, but I saw the movie." Boyle snickered.

"Funny," she smirked in light of his humor, "that was Dances with Wolves. Sometimes they run along with me on the other side of the fence. It's a very unique and sometimes transcendental feeling."

"Maybe I'll join you one day." Boyle thought aloud.

****

The next morning Baldoni awoke at five and drove over to the employee's entrance of the Metropolitan Toronto Zoo. She had been given an admission pass card when she had presented seminars for the zoo security team on law enforcement and emergency situations. She became friends with a few members of the security team, some of whom had high hopes of entering into a relationship with her, and they allowed her access to the facility when the zoo was closed to the general public.

She entered through the restricted entrance near the compound where the Chinese Panda bears were housed. Standing before the heavy Plexiglas viewing windows, she went through a series of warm-up stretches, smiling as she watched these giant teddy-bears sitting upright, munching on the fresh bamboo stalks and then tumbling about with each other in playful antics.

She began her run along the main path toward the area that housed animals from the Canadian tundra. She headed for her favorite path which circled the large, open spaced compound of the Artic Wolves.

The wolves noticed her right away as they heard the rhythmic steps of her running shoes approaching, and their heads raised as they caught the familiar scent of the morning runner. One wolf, then two raised themselves from the structured assembly of the pack and began to run along the edge of the trench that separated the wolves and the security fence.

Baldoni was focused on the rhythm of the movement and the wolves ran in unison, keeping pace with a sense of mystical human-animal ambiguity that created a connection between them.

After the first circuit around the path, other wolves joined the first two and that sense of mysticism heightened to a point where the polar bears in the next enclosure began to voice their identification within this anima of feeling. When she completed four full circuits of the wolves' ground, she stopped at the bridge that looked upon a small hill in the west end of the compound. The wolves formed in a group, and as they watched her, she wondered if this connection between them formed a communion of instinct.

She quietly said goodbye to the wolves and headed northwest along a path that led the African Savannah. It was a wide expanse of open grounds with separate enclosures for the cheetahs, zebras, baboons, rhinoceros, impalas and lions. She ran the empty pathways, bereft of other people, and glanced into each enclosure as the sun of the morning dawn began to illuminate the grounds, the animals shaking off the night-time cold and celebrating the warmth of the great light in the sky.

Once she had completed the circuitous route of the African Savannah, she headed back down to the main employee entrance where she was greeted by the arrival of the daytime security team. She exchanged a few greetings, and delicately fended off a few advances. She drove home and had a shower, all the time with thoughts in her head about the paradoxes between the human and animal zoos.

As she dried her hair, she thought back to that time when she was in the Museum of Natural History, looking at all those stuffed animals and thinking how they looked exactly like the living animals, but realizing they missed that internal essence of being alive, that life energy emission, or telepathy of being.

She stopped and looked into the mirror and began to think about the significance of our consciousness. "If we were just biological mistakes," she said to her reflection, "then our life and death would be the same…meaningless. But when we die, there is a definite change. Our life energy force leaves our bodies, leaving the atomic structure and chemicals to decompose."

She stood staring into the mirror for a few moments more. "Fuck it," she finally said aloud and put on a minimal amount of makeup, then went into the bedroom to dress for the day.

Chapter Twenty-Two

The leafless branches of the elm tree created an assortment of geometric shapes in the night sky. The wind chime that hung on the front porch made no sound in the stillness of the twilight. Down the street, the whirl of a roller blade's wheels rumbled on the pavement and faded with a Doppler effect as they skated down the street.

The smoke from Boyle's Cohiba Cuban cigar draped lazily in the open air, then faded into the open firmament of the front yard. A distant siren announced a far-off emergency outside of the close-knit world that Boyle had created on his porch.

Sometimes Boyle needed to withdraw from the intensity of his job and briefly live outside of its reality. He needed to just sit and contemplate within the metaphysical sphere. He picked up his tumbler of brandy and held it to his lips, but stopped and thought in reflection and then spoke, "To the Gods," he toasted and then took a sip.

Whenever he had the opportunity, Boyle would sit on his front porch in the evenings by himself, turn his phone to silent mode, bring a glass of brandy, smoke a Cuban cigar, and just think. It was meditation for him, letting the brain soak in the moment of what is 'now', not what was before or what will be. He would watch the sunset until the starlight began to appear and then sit in the darkness of the night with only his own ruminations to keep him company. A thunderstorm would always call him to the covered porch of his home, and he would watch the dazzling display the Gods would perform for his benefit, cigar in hand, watching the messages from above, listening to the voice of the natural spirits roll across the sky like the echo of Divine importance.

The nights were mild enough now, the heavy cold of winter departed from the city like a lover who sneaks out of the bedroom while you sleep. He sat on the front porch with a warm spring coat and enjoyed his cigar. In winter, it was too cold to waste a fine Cohiba. You do not extinguish a partly smoked Cuban because of the weather. That was sacrileges in his mind, and one reason he did not share his Cubans with those who didn't understand.

Boyle was a man of habit, bordering on obsessive compulsive, but not the disabling type of disorder. He didn't have to check the lock on the front door over and over, he only needed to check it once, but he had to check. Everything had to be in its place, the dishes stacked just right, everything within the fridge in its proper place, cupboards organized according to his needs.

His mild obsessive-compulsive nature was one of the reasons he was a good detective, always making sure nothing was left unturned, all the information was presented and available for review, and further review. He always told his junior detectives that you can't truly analyze a final outcome until all the facts have been found and all the questions answered.

He always followed procedure, and did everything according to departmental policy, but he never let the procedures dictate his course of action or minimize his efforts. He was able to think in the abstract, outside of rules and regulations, and it was in those moments of abstract thinking that allowed him to gain insight into motive or method.

In most of the cases, the answers usually came quite easily when you collected all the facts and examined them as a whole. The murderers always left something that pointed directly to them, always had a motive no matter how obscure it was, and that if you dug deep enough, you would find it.

That's where his hypothetical insights allowed him to put each piece of information, every shred of evidence, and the character of every individual in its right place. Like putting together a jigsaw puzzle without having the picture on the front of the box. He would put the pieces together slowly, logically and precisely, until the puzzle became apparent as to the exact reality of the crime. Sitting on the front porch with his cigar, he could see the pieces and he would start putting them together, one with the other, how did they fit: who, where, when, how, and then finally, the why.

When he thought in the abstract, something that wasn't apparent would show up, and it would spawn a question, or it allowed him to see something, attain an insight on the unexpected, and then a whole different line of reasoning would come to him.

As he smoked his cigar, he considered the nature of the crime; Why did the killer leave the Malinkov scene to be obvious that it was of a personal nature, that the motivation for killing was revenge, and that the killer either didn't care or maybe even wanted it to look like revenge. Who wanted revenge, or who wanted it to look like revenge? And then the abstract thought came to him; *'They wanted revenge for an ulterior motivation, a revenge that would be used for another purpose, something that could linger and be recalled, or something that could be used as proof of an action.'*

It wasn't a robbery, there was no apparent ransacking of the house looking for valuables, and all of the obvious valuables were left. *'Perhaps,'* he thought, *'there were papers or photos taken, something scandalous or worthy of blackmail.'* But if that was the case, then the killer must have known where they were kept, meaning the victim would have known the killer.

He took a deep puff of the Cohiba, blew the smoke out slowly, and watched it drift through the air. He picked up the tumbler and took a deep sip of the brandy and let the strong taste of the liquor sit in his mouth for a moment before he swallowed.

He looked up into the tree and continued with his thoughts; If the killing had something to do with business, it would have been quick. The killer would have bashed him on the head and that would have been the end of it. The killer would ensure that Malinkov was truly dead. And then another abstract thought slid into his mind like a passing cloud; We're assuming that the killer didn't know for sure that he was going to die. We're assuming the killer suspected that he would, but that they didn't know for sure…or did they?

Anything could have happened. Somebody could have come to visit at some point over the course of the weekend. Did the killer know the victim was going to be alone all weekend, or was the killer taking a chance? Perhaps they just didn't care. But if it was true that the killer didn't care, or was taking a chance, this would mean the killer was probably NOT known to the victim. The killer may have worn a disguise, but not such a disguise as to change his looks, just to obscure them, so had the victim lived, whatever description he gave to the police would not have been enough for a proper identification.

Then Boyle thought, *'That's why the first blow to the nose was so important, as it would have made the eyes blurry.'*

But to gain entry, to get Ivan to open the door, unsuspecting of what was to happen, and then it struck him…the Delivery Corp courier!

Ivan didn't know the killer, but the killer knew that Ivan received deliveries by courier. Another real estate agent would know that, but it wouldn't be an agent that Ivan knew. *'No,'* he thought, *'this was not a professional killing because a professional killer would never leave the victim alive.'* No, this was personal in some way, very personal and for a very different reason than what they suspected.

He puffed his cigar and then spoke softly to himself, "It's not what am I missing, its who am I missing? Who wanted revenge enough to confidently leave the victim alive and know that there was a great probability he would die? Who wanted revenge and didn't care if he survived?"

Ivan was an unethical bastard, a misogynist womanizer with no compassion for his partners. That much he could deduce from all of the testimony and statements they had collected. Who wanted a brutal, savage revenge and who wanted revenge for a motivation that Boyle could so far only try to imagine?

Chapter Twenty-Three

Boyle texted everyone on his homicide team to meet in the Argo the following morning. Baldoni, Singleton and Davis, Aaron Silverstein of FIS, Dr. Surat Singh, and Donna Chang were all waiting for him when he arrived.

"I've been re-thinking this Malinkov investigation," he pronounced to the group, "and I want to take us in another direction, somewhere where the facts are not so black and white."

"You've been smoking those cigars again?" Silverstein jokingly commented.

"With the change in weather, we change our habits." Boyle replied with a flair of the dramatic, "And when we change our habits, our motivations for what we do also change."

"Okay, now hear me out before you ask any questions. I believe we are approaching the Ivan Malinkov murder case with too much focus on the obvious motives, but with little evidence or testimony to back it up. We're fairly sure that revenge was probably the main motive, but we are only looking at the obvious people for revenge, and each one of those obvious people have secure alibis. However, I don't believe that the killer even cares if we know the true motive, because the killer thinks they are smarter, and the killer believes that they have outwitted a bunch of dumb cops."

Boyle paused for a moment before he spoke once again, just to make sure he could verbalize what he was thinking, "I almost think the killer wanted us to know that this was personal," and he emphasized the word 'wanted', "I think the killer wanted the whole world to know that this was personal, or maybe they wanted the Gods to know that this act was a personal commitment to something we currently don't understand. The killer wanted Malinkov's death to be slow and painful, and they knew that Malinkov was surely going to die, having broken every limb in his body, taken his only means of communication, and knowing the only way he could survive was to painfully attempt to get up the stairs to the second phone, which the killer knew would be impossible to do with the injuries that they had inflicted."

"The killer wanted this slow agonizing death for a personal reason, and the killer didn't care if Malinkov survived by some miracle. Lastly, and most important, the killer doesn't care about the police investigation. The killer is confident all of their tracks were covered, that we would end up with a dead end with what little evidence we have. The killer was sure there would be no witnesses that could tie them to the crime. This killer is one intelligent, methodical psychopath."

He looked around the room and everyone waited for him to give them their orders. They all knew that when Boyle had his 'insights' there would be new angles they would all have to delve into, and they waited for his commands.

With their complete attention, Boyle started right away, "Donna, I want you to go deeper and further back into Malinkov's bank accounts, his e-mails, his calendars and any other information we have. Go back as far as the electronic files go and look for anything that might be out of the ordinary for what we know about this man. Also, call the Beach Realty company and I want records for every business transaction Malinkov had, plus see what you can find about other side businesses he may have been involved in, something like that business with the sound proofing company. There may be more of those types of deals."

"Lastly Donna, you stated that there was an electronic phone book and that some of the female names had stars attached to their names. I want a list of all the women he spent any amount of time with, relationships and even single dates if need be. Get their contact information and arrange interviews for Baldoni and me."

"Gina, you and I are going interview Anton Malinkov once again. I want him to tell us of all his mother's relationships with other people and I want a list of her family. We are going to check into that possibility for revenge motives."

"I'll call him at work right after the meeting and have something set up for tomorrow." Baldoni quickly replied.

"Bill and Jasmine," Boyle continued, "I'm giving you two the toughest part," and they both looked skyward knowing what was coming, "I want every interview, every statement, every shred of documentation re-examined. I want you to look for anything, and I mean anything that might hint at some ulterior motive or even some item that just doesn't fit with what we know. Look at the all the evidence with what I said earlier about the killer, that this crime was a personal vendetta, and the motive is something other than the obvious."

He then turned to Silverstein, "Aaron, I want your team to re-examine all the forensic evidence. What I'm looking for is any hint that would take us into the mind of this killer. Look at all the evidence individually and as a whole. What pattern is there, or maybe, what evidence don't we have that we think should have been there."

Silverstein held up his hand and commented, "The other homicide teams have got a number of investigations that we're dealing with right now. I'll have to take someone off one of the other crime scenes. Are you going to authorize the overtime?"

"I'll talk to Stanforth," Boyle affirmed, "we need the resources."

"Do you have any idea what it is you want us to find?" Silverstein asked.

"I want to find whatever doesn't fit. The baseball bat for example. It had been thoroughly cleaned prior to the murder, and the killer probably wore gloves. So why did they rinse it in the kitchen sink after the beating? Did they think that there may have been new DNA that might have stained the bat during the beating, like sweat, or blood, or something else? And after they rinsed the bat, why did they leave it at the crime scene?"

"If we think the killer may have been the Delivery Corp courier that was seen on a bicycle, then they could have left the bat behind because they were riding a bicycle." Singleton offered as a reason.

"Good point," Boyle stated, "but then they would have ridden to Malinkov's house with the baseball bat in one hand or across the handlebars of the bike. Re-check with that witness from Whitlock's who saw the person on the bicycle riding up Kenilworth. Did he see someone going down the street earlier on? Also check with the other dinners to see if they noticed anyone riding a bicycle with a baseball bat."

"The baseball bat could have been planted, hidden near the house or in the garden prior to the night of the murder. The killer could have ridden the bicycle to and from the house without being encumbered by the bat." Davis suggested.

"Excellent point Jasmine," Boyle said with a sense of excitement, "you and Bill can check with the diners about a cyclist going to and from the house and check with the neighbors if they noticed anyone walking around the neighborhood with a baseball bat."

"You want us to check the diners and re-review all the others?" Singleton asked with a sigh of facing repetitive work.

"Both." Boyle gave him a sardonic smile. "Do what you can when you can."

Lastly, he turned to Dr. Singh, "Surat, you've pretty much given us all the information that you can, but there's one thing I would like to know, or even if it is possible to know."

"If I can help, then yes. However, the body has been interned for a few months now, so I don't know if there is anything that I could provide."

"I would like something speculative from you." Boyle said, "Could you determine the best way to commit a crime like this so that the killer would have no problem completing what they set out to do? For example, I'm pretty sure the very first blow would have been the one to the nose because that would have stunned Malinkov, but it also would have filled his eyes with tears and made them blurry. This would have prevented any definite identification in case he had lived. Would the next blow have been the one to the groin area in order to incapacitate him so that all the other blows to the limbs would be easier to accomplish?"

"Yes, I see what you're getting at." Singh replied. "Let me re-examine all of my notes and see what I can find for you."

"I want to be able to determine the mind of this killer." Boyle spoke to his team, "I want to determine if the killer is truly that intelligent to have planned this to perfection." He turned to Silverstein and spoke again, "Hell, I want to know if this person has a severe obsessive-compulsive disorder which would explain how they were able to ensure there was no physical evidence left behind." Then he turned once again to Singh, "I want to know if this person has a medical background that would give them an insight on what to strike first, second, third and so forth, so that this crime would progress as they had planned."

He turned to Davis and Singleton, "If this person really is that intelligent, then I want everything re-checked for any possible pattern in their thinking or any slip up they may have made." His last turn was toward Baldoni, "If there is a greater motive than revenge, then we need to get more detail about his family, the ex-wife's family, older relationships. We're going to start with Anton tomorrow."

Chapter Twenty-Four

The weather was vastly different when Boyle and Baldoni drove north to interview Anton Malinkov once again. The spring season was upon them and the forests were fresh with budding leaves. Pine trees were a lush dark green and the fields were the deep brown of freshly turned earth. The morning sun reflected on the landscape like a fresh coat of shellac.

Boyle drove with ease and Baldoni sat calmly with her laptop, the uneasy edge of driving in the snow was a remote memory and forgotten every spring. She asked Boyle questions about his theories on the crime and how he had come to their projected hypothesis.

"I meditate." He said plainly, "I sit back and wonder, let my mind go in any direction without placing any mental restrictions on what I think. If it goes in a direction that is absurd or ludicrous, I still let it go there, just to get that thought pattern out of the way. When I keep my mind open to whatever it wants to think, eventually it will find an insight, a perception of something abstract that could lead to a potential truth, or maybe even just the possibility of a truth."

"You sound like one of those characters from TV, Boss. You know, like Sherlock Holmes or one of those other fictional detectives that seem to be able to pull answers out of thin air."

"I rarely watch TV Gina and I'm not a fictional superhero. I'm just a man who takes the time to study and learn. Everyone has the capability to elevate themselves in whatever field or practice they desire. You've heard the stories about the aesthetic monks who walk through fire. They've trained their minds and their bodies to accept the concept that everything is just molecules, both the fire and their feet, and that the molecules intermingle and exchange, allowing them to focus their mind to control the metaphysical reaction of those molecules."

Baldoni sat in silence with thoughts about his exceptional mind that seemed to be light years from where she existed. Boyle noticed the quietness of the moment and then gave a small laugh. "Gina, none of this is mumbo-jumbo. There is documentation for all sorts of psychological phenomenon and mystical experience. You simply have to put your beliefs and pre-conceived notions on hold and allow the possibility of something abstract to open your eyes."

She continued to look fixedly at him for a moment longer, then she turned her gaze toward the forests that lined either side of the highway. "I understand what you're saying Boss, I just never thought that way about murder. To me, it's always been black and white, determining the truth from the lie, fact from fiction. But to actually get down to the manipulation of molecular structure…well, I can understand where that may be important in chemical analysis in forensics, but in determining motive?"

"What I've learned in the hundreds of criminal investigations I've been a part of," Boyle answered, "is that you can never see anything as black and white. It's like that old saying, one man's garbage is another man's treasure. What motivates one person to commit a crime may be a meaningless objective to someone else. However, crime, especially murder, is always more complicated than we think. It's never just one thing like jealousy or greed, or in this case, revenge. There are always multiple aspects to any motivation and what we need to do as detectives is to determine that intricate web of stimulus or impulse that would provoke someone to plan AND carry out a murder like this."

"Instead of calling you Boss, would you mind if I called you Guru instead?" she said with an affectionate smile.

Boyles winced at the thought, "No. I'd rather stick with Boss."

They arrived at the parking lot of the Custom Cabinets workshop and walked into the front office. Mr. Mulroney was all smiles and welcomed both detectives with what Boyle thought was a bit too much grandeur. He summoned Anton Malinkov from the workshop, who was expecting the detectives to arrive.

"I knew you were coming so I didn't start any new projects, just spent the morning cleaning out the filters on the dust vacuum and putting the tool shelves in order." Anton said in what seemed to be a more confident, friendlier manner than either detective had seen before.

"Mr. Malinkov," Boyle started to say as they left the Custom Cabinet building toward the diner around the corner. "We are at an impasse in the investigation into your father's death. We want to ask you some questions regarding your father's family and your mother's family and friends."

They entered the diner and sat at the corner booth that was farthest from the front. There were a couple of other customers enjoying a late breakfast when they entered.

"Hey Anton," the waitress said, "don't see you in here too often at this time of the day."

"Hi Marge. We're here to speak about some private business matters regarding my dad. Can we just get some coffees all round." He glanced over at Boyle and Baldoni who both nodded.

They sat down and put a digital recorder on the table. However, they wanted to speak in subtler tones, which might not be picked up by the recorder, so both Boyle and Baldoni took out pens and notepads and also wrote down information in the traditional way.

"As I was saying," Boyle started, "we are running out of leads and options in the investigation to your father's murder. We need to start looking into his older affairs with women and we also want to find out about your mother's friends and/or relationships with other men."

"I don't know anything about my father's associations with other women," he said bluntly, "when I was younger, I would only see the arguments between my mother and him. After they split up, I preferred not to see him at all, and I definitely didn't see him with any other women. I didn't care, really, he was part of a past I wanted to forget. After the funeral, I refused to have any contact with him, so I can't really help you in that regard."

"What about his family?" Boyle asked, "We know that most of them are back in Russia but have you had any contact with them?"

"No, I barely knew any of them. The only one I ever met was his brother Yakov, and I was only a young teenager when I met him. I've never been in contact with him so I couldn't give you any information."

"We feel the murder of your father was for some sort of revenge." Baldoni stated, "Can you think of anyone in any situation that would want revenge on your father?"

Anton remained calm and did not let the remark affect his manner. "Let me explain something," he began, "and I'm not trying to be obtuse or anything, I just want to make it clear. I had already achieved revenge on my father by simply cutting him out of my life. He had tried to make contact with me over the years, e-mail, phone calls, text messages, even mailed a letter once. I've blocked his number each time he got a new one. Every couple of months he would send me a friendship request on Facebook and I simply deleted them, so I know that I had hurt him to some degree, just by ignoring him. But the worst hurt that I did to him," he paused for second and then stated, "I never allowed him to meet his grandchildren."

Baldoni replied in an embarrassed tone, "I wasn't referring to you. I was asking if you could think of anyone else who may have had issues with your father."

"That's okay," Anton said, "it's good that you asked so that I could get it all out, so you could understand the divide that there was between me and my father. Yes, I hated the man, but I didn't kill him."

"How about your mother?" Boyle asked.

"What do you want to know?" Anton replied.

"After her divorce, did she have any close friends or relationships with other people that we should talk to? We know that her sister lives in London, England and the British authorities have confirmed she hasn't been out of the country since your mother's funeral. Basically, we're looking for someone who may have had some resentment toward your father."

"There was one man whom my mother grew exceptionally close to." Anton said, "About a year or so after she divorced my father, she met someone, and they were quite inseparable for a while. I think she met him through some on-line dating site. They seemed to have a pretty good relationship and were together for just over a year. I remember he came here two or three of times with her. We all had dinner together and he seemed like a nice fellow, a very intelligent guy."

"Do you remember his name?"

"His name was Michael, and he had an operatic last name like Baritone or something like that. He and my mother eventually parted ways, I'm really not sure why, but I thought they were good together. He came to her funeral and was very sincere and respectful."

"Would you by chance have any contact information for him?"

"I still have my mother's old phone book. I kept it in case I needed to contact people after she was gone. If we go back to my house, I can let you have it. Just let me go tell Larry that I'll be gone for the rest of the day."

Chapter Twenty-Five

The house of Michael Barratino was over one hundred years old and had been built when the Beaches community had become the preferred location for the affluent upper middle class. Not rich enough to live in the exclusive Forrest Hills or Rosedale areas, they developed their own elitist society in the Beaches.

The light brown brick exterior walls and the ochre-colored pillars gave the house a rural flavor that would not be out of place in any of the farming communities outside of Toronto. The front lawn was bordered with a short stone wall and a large elm tree in the middle of the yard. Boyle looked at the covered front porch that faced north with an overhang of branches from the elm and determined that this was would be a perfect 'cigar' porch.

They took one of the vacant parking spots on Crown Park Road and Boyle was immediately impressed with the quiet street that ended a few houses west at the entrance to Glen Manor park. He and Baldoni walked up the stone path to the front porch and rang the doorbell.

A slender, six-foot man with short chestnut brown hair opened the door. He looked out at the two detectives and politely asked what they wanted.

"Hello Mr. Barratino, my name is Detective Baldoni," Gina answered, "and this is Sergeant Detective Boyle. We are with the homicide unit of the Toronto Police and we want to ask you some of questions regarding a case we are working on."

Michael stood in the doorway, looked directly at Gina and asked, "Do you have any identification?"

Baldoni pulled out her police issued leather wallet that contained her documentation. "Yes, here."

Michael reached out for the wallet and then stated, "Hold on for one moment while I get this verified."

Baldoni looked up at Michael with mild surprise and then looked over to Boyle. Boyle nodded his head with a look that said Michael had every right to check. Baldoni then responded to Michael's request, "Yeah, sure, we'll wait here on the porch. Do you want Detective Boyle's ID as well?"

"No, just yours." Michael stated as he closed the door and locked it. He picked up his cell phone from the small table and called the general inquiry number of the Toronto Police Department. He stated the situation about two people claiming to be police detectives at his front door and recited Baldoni's identification number from her wallet. After a moment of waiting, he received an authorization code for his inquiry about the identification of an officer.

While Michael was inside making the call, Boyle tapped Baldoni on the shoulder and spoke in a low voice, "He has a superiority complex against women. We can use that."

Michael opened the door and handed Baldoni's wallet back to her. "Thank you, but you can't be too careful these days. Please come in, what can I do for you? This isn't anything serious I hope, about anybody I know?"

Baldoni entered and replied, "We're just asking some routine questions with regards to a homicide that happened a few months ago in the Beaches."

The open door led directly into the living room and both Baldoni and Boyle waited for Michael to indicate for them to enter. "Please sit anywhere," Michael offered, "your shoes aren't dirty I hope."

Boyle took a quick glance down at his feet and then immediately realized that he was being led instead of him doing the leading. "We have been in an office and in the car all day," he said, "I think our footwear is fine."

"Okay then," Michael said as he sat in a tuft, high-back, velvet accent chair. "Who died?"

Boyle sat on the couch while Baldoni remained standing, "This is regarding the investigation into the death of Ivan Malinkov." Boyle said as he took out his digital recorder and placed it beside him on the arm of the sofa. He explained the use of the digital recorder and stated all the information required to identify the interview.

"Oh," Michael looked surprised, "why are you asking me anything?"

"Did you know Anna Malinkov?" Boyles asked mildly.

"Yes, I knew her."

"How well did you know her?"

Michael looked up with a frown on his face, "What is this all about?"

"We are investigating the murder of Ivan Malinkov." Boyle said calmly, "We are making inquiries with anyone who may have been associated with either Ivan, his son Anton or Anna."

Baldoni now entered the conversation. "How did you meet Anna?"

"We met through an on-line dating site," Michael answered, "she was my girlfriend for a about a year and a half."

"Was she your girlfriend when she died?" Baldoni asked.

"No, we went our separate ways before that."

"Did you know that she committed suicide?" Boyle asked.

"Yes, I was aware of that."

"Did you attend the funeral?"

"Yes. Anton's wife Elizabeth called me and told me about her death."

"Do you have any idea why she committed suicide?" Boyle continued.

"She was always fighting with depression while we were together, so I imagine you should get that information from her analyst. Also, I would assume a lot of that depression was a direct result of her ex-husband, Ivan Malinkov."

"Why do you say that?" Baldoni jumped in.

"The guy was abusive. I mean, even after they were divorced, he still abused her. At least, that's what she kept telling me."

"So, you felt some animosity toward him." Baldoni suggested.

"Sure, who wouldn't?" Michael said with a look on his face as if he'd been asked a dumb question. "Any moral human being would feel something toward that guy. That's one of the reasons Anna and I ended up parting ways. I offered to help, get a lawyer, document stuff, whatever, but she kept insisting she didn't want me getting involved, so we ended up parting ways. It was just too frustrating for me."

"Can you tell us where you were on the night of November 23?" Boyle asked as he took over the interview. He had spoken with Baldoni about how he wanted to conduct the interview when they were driving to Michael's home. He told her he wanted her to jump in on the questioning to keep Michael off balance, never knowing who was going to ask the next question. When she asked him why he wanted to do it this way, Boyle simply replied that he had a hunch.

"God, how should I know, that was over four months ago. What night was that?"

"It was a Friday evening." Baldoni replied.

"Okay, if it was a Friday evening then I'm sure I was with my girlfriend. We're together every Friday evening." Michael responded. Then with a degree of concern in his voice he asked, "Are you accusing me of anything here?"

"No," Boyle's voice returned to a friendly manner, "we are just asking some questions to fill in the background information of this investigation. We have to ask everybody that had any connection, even remote, with the victim. It's a homicide investigation and we have to rule out all possibilities."

"Look, what is going on here?" Michael spoke with a touch of imposed anger, "that was five years ago. She's dead and I've moved on."

"How was your relationship with Anna?" Baldoni asked. "She was older than you, wasn't she?"

Michael looked back and forth at the two detectives and realized the approach they were taking with him. He remained quiet for a moment and collected his thoughts and then replied calmly after taking a breath, "I felt great affection toward her. We were close. We had a lot of things in common, socially and sexually."

"Had you ever met Ivan Malinkov?" Boyle picked up the questioning again.

"I only ever met the man once," Michael started to explain, "and before you ask, yes, it was somewhat confrontational."

"What happened?" asked Baldoni.

Michael sat back and looked at Baldoni. He paused long enough to let her know that he would answer when he felt like it. "One night I was at Anna's apartment and we were having dinner when there was a sudden pounding on her door, and I mean a real pounding. I saw the look in her eyes, one of fear and embarrassment. I started to say something, but she assured me that it was okay, she would take care of it."

"She went to the door and opened it and all I could hear was this guy yelling at her. I couldn't understand exactly what they were saying, I guess it was in Russian or something. Anyway, he's standing in the hallway outside the door, yelling at her, so I came over and said something to the effect of what the fuck's going on. He looked at me surprised, as if he expected Anna to be alone, and then he said it was none of my business. I turned to Anna and asked if she wanted me to get rid of him or if I should call the cops. She didn't say anything, like she was frozen in fear or something, and while trembling, she told me that it was her ex-husband. I stood between her and him and told the guy to fuck off or I was going to call the police."

"Then he said something in Russian I think, probably an insult by the way it sounded, and I told him if he wanted anything to do with Anna he should go to his lawyers and communicate through them. They were officially divorced, and she wanted nothing more to do with him. He swore at me and I swore at him and after a couple of minutes he backed down and went away."

"I never saw him again after that, and she never brought up the subject. I asked her about it, but she didn't want to talk. It wasn't very long afterward that we separated."

"The girlfriend that you mentioned," Boyle asked, "the one you think you were with on the Friday evening that Ivan was murdered. How do you know you were with her?"

"It's in our contract." Michael stated plainly.

"Your contract?" Baldoni asked quizzically.

Michael stared at Gina with a look that seemed to dismiss her presence. He made her wait for an answer. "Are you aware of the BDSM community?"

"Is this a standard Dominant-Submissive contract?" Boyle asked without any sense of surprise.

"Yeah," Michael replied, looking at Boyle a little more respectfully.

"And you meet every Friday night as part of the contract." Boyle stated.

"Yes," Michael answered.

"We would like to speak with your girlfriend. We are going to need collaborating testimony that you were with her that night," Boyle requested as if giving a command.

"Listen," Michael said with a sense of unease. "We have a relationship that is quite private, especially for her. She has a child, and we don't want the secrets of our relationship to become public knowledge."

"Mr. Barratino," Boyle's voice raised with authority. "We are investigating the brutal murder of an individual. Your private life is of no concern to me. All information will go into our case files, which are classified and will only be referenced if and when it may be needed for the prosecution of whomever is arrested and brought to trial. If the information does not have any bearing on the case, then it will remain in the classified file. No one," he said with complete authority, "will publicly disclose any information unless required.

We will need to speak with your play partner and verify your location for that particular evening."

Michael sat with a blank stare on his face. He had been confronted and put in his place, and he did not like it. His reaction to Boyle's sudden confrontation of power threw him off balance, just as Boyle anticipated.

Michael sat up straight and took a moment to compose himself, to bring his sense of dominance back into his will. He looked at Boyle and then at Baldoni and wondered if the two of them had the same dominant-submissive nature that he so often enjoyed. With that thought in his head, he carefully responded in an attempt to reclaim his own authority, "I understand fully. I will instruct my submissive to be open to your queries. I will explain to her that it is our duty to cooperate with the police in these matters."

"All you need to do," said Baldoni with a touch of contempt in her voice, "is to give us her name and contact information. We'll take care of the rest."

"I believe that you are not privileged to demand this information unless you have a warrant." Michael stared directly into Baldoni's eyes. "However, if you want to ask again and say pretty please, I might just cooperate."

Baldoni's reaction to this affront was interrupted by Boyle. "Mr. Barratino, we would appreciate any cooperation you are prepared to offer. It would save us the time of having to file a warrant and forcibly bring you to the nearest police station for official questioning."

Michael saw that Boyle was a man of comparable sagacity. He rose and retrieved his cell phone and purposely did not look at Baldoni as he answered, "Here is her number Detective Boyle. Are you restricting me from calling her as soon as you leave?"

"No," Boyle replied in a calmer tone, "I would expect you to do so."

Boyle stood at the same time as Michael, for neither wanted to be in a seated position with the other standing over him. Boyle thanked him for his cooperation and turned toward the door. Baldoni purposely walked slowly toward the door, giving Michael a hard glare with every step.

Boyle abruptly stopped and turned, "Did you have a similar type of relationship with Anna Malinkov? Was she also your submissive?"

"I would prefer not to answer as she is no longer with us, and I wouldn't want to bring any more grief to Anton and his family with any knowledge of his mother's intimacies."

"I understand," said Boyle, "it will be our secret unless we need to delve deeper into your behaviors."

Michael stood at the doorway and watched the two detectives get in the car and drive off. He picked up his cellphone and immediately punched Linda's number.

****

"Wow." Baldoni said as they got into the car. "That was like watching two lions compete for the head of the pride. Glad you won."

Boyle sat in the car staring straight ahead, managing his thoughts and assessing Michael as an individual, "He's controlling, in a physical sense but more in terms of psychological control. When you questioned him, he controlled the timing of his answers. Even though you tried to control the interview, he purposely made you wait until he was ready to answer. He just stared you down and then gave an answer when he felt like it."

"It made you a little frustrated," Boyle continued to think as he spoke, "and it made you annoyed, but he kept holding back on purpose, controlling the interview process and thereby controlling you. That's what he does, he's a control freak, and that's what gives him his sense of power."

****

Baldoni contacted Linda Santiago, Michael's girlfriend and arranged for her to come to the 31 Division station the following morning for the interview. She arrived at the appointed time and walked through the front doors of the station, was stopped at the security desk where she was asked by one officer to put her purse, phone and any other metallic items into a plastic tray bin. Another officer electronically scanned her with a detection rod.

This security check seemed to visibly upset her, and the officer told her these were the standard precautions used by many institutions to ensure visitors to the premises were not bearing any harmful devises or weapons. She was directed to the Duty Desk and reported that she had been requested for an interview. The Duty Desk officer noted that she seemed under duress and tried to assure her these procedures were in place to ensure her safety.

Boyle and Baldoni were in the interview room when Linda Santiago was brought in by one of the civilian clerks. Boyle immediately stood up and pulled a chair out for Linda to sit. Linda was a very attractive woman with a classical Spanish look. She had dark hair that fell below her shoulders, a very long, thin face with wire frame glasses that seemed too big, but they amplified the beautiful almond brown eyes.

Boyle offered her a coffee and when she didn't accept, he asked if she would like some water. She looked at him still in distress, and then put her hands to her face and began to cry. Baldoni reached behind her for a box of tissue paper and placed it on the table in front of Linda. From behind her tears, Linda started to apologize, "I'm sorry," she said, "I'm not sure why I am here and I'm so frightened."

Boyle calmly told her there was nothing to fear and they only needed to ask her some questions in order to verify a statement someone else had made. He explained that she was not in any trouble and only needed her cooperation.

Linda slowly re-gained her composure and Baldoni brought a paper cup of water from the office cooler. Linda thanked her for the water and dabbed at her eyes with a tissue. "I'm very sorry," she repeated, "but I've never been in a police station before."

"I understand Ms. Santiago." Boyle said with a total measure of reassurance, "The security checks at the front have become a necessary procedure for most law enforcement agencies these days. They can be somewhat unnerving when you experience it the first time." He kept talking to allow her to calm down. "It seems the world has come to this point where even the police are required to safeguard any visitors from potential harm."

"I'm sorry," she repeated once more and then took a deep breath. She folded her hands in her lap and looked toward Baldoni and then to Boyle. "How may I help?"

Baldoni placed her digital recorder in the middle of the office table. She explained to Linda that they would be recording the interview to have on file. She switched on the recorder and stated, "This is detective Gina Baldoni. I am interviewing Linda Santiago in interview room B at the 31 Division station. Detective Aristotle Boyle is present as well. It is eleven-fifteen in the AM."

Linda began to tear up once more and took another tissue from the box on the table. "Is this recording going to get me in trouble?" she asked with her voice breaking in trembles.

"These recordings are simply for us to use instead of taking notes." Boyle kept his voice calm and soothing. "They are completely confidential, however, if you would feel more comfortable without the digital recorder, Detective Baldoni will take notes instead."

Linda peeked up at Boyle and dabbed her eyes once more. "If everything is going to be confidential…it's just that Michael told me you would be questioning me about our relationship, and I've never spoken to anyone about it except for Michael."

"Thank you, Miss Santiago," Boyle's voice remained as smooth as velvet.

They started the interview with the regular basic information. Linda was a single mother with a nine-year old child. She shared custody with her husband, and he took the child every other weekend. Boyle then explained to her the purpose of the interview, that they were investigating the murder of Ivan Malinkov on Friday, November 23. He slowly explained to her that all investigations included interviews with everyone who ever had any dealings with the murder victim, either personally or through business.

"One of the people we have spoken with recently is Mr. Barratino." Boyle watched for her reaction and saw her eyes dip and move sideways in a nervous tension. "He once had a relationship with Anna Malinkov, the victim's ex-wife. She committed suicide four years ago and the purpose of our interview with Michael was to ask if he had any information about Mr. Malinkov that could help our investigation." Boyle did not reveal the information they had obtained from Michael in order to keep the composure of Linda at an even balance.

"Could you please tell us if you were with Michael on that Friday night in November?"

"I'm sure that I was. I'm with Michael every Friday evening." Linda said nervously.

"What about your child?" Boyle asked, "if it was one of the weekends in which you have custody, who takes care of your child?"

Linda wondered if this question was a slight on her ability to be a good mother. "On the weekends that I have custody, I arrange for a babysitter on the Friday night. Michael knows that those must be early nights and I am always home before eleven o'clock."

"And that particular Friday, November 23?"

Linda reached down to her purse and retrieved her phone and checked the electronic calendar. "On that particular Friday," she said with a measure of resolve, feeling that the police had insinuated negativity toward her as a mother, "my husband had my son that weekend. This means that I spent the entire evening with Michael until the next morning."

"You're absolutely sure you were with him on that night, all night?"

"Yes, like I stated, I'm with him every Friday evening and sometimes all night."

"So, it's like a planned date that you have with him?" Baldoni questioned her.

"It is part of our relationship, that's how it works." Linda now seemed a bit more confident.

"I'm not sure what you mean by 'part of your relationship', can you explain that to me." Baldoni continued to question.

"I would really prefer not to get into that because it is very personal."

"Ms. Santiago," Baldoni said, "this is a homicide investigation. We need you to get very personal."

"Is this really necessary," Linda complained while looking toward Boyle, "isn't it sufficient to just tell you that I was with Michael."

Boyle returned to the calm demeanor that he used when he wanted to gain a person's trust. "When we are investigating a murder Ms. Santiago, the evidence that we obtain has to be clear and concise, whether it is physical evidence or testimony from witnesses."

Linda listened to Boyle and accepted his explanation. "Would anything I tell you go on public records or something like that?"

"No, anything you tell us will just be in our classified case files."

Linda again took a deep breath and let it out with a long slow exhale. She thought about what Boyle had told her and what it might mean for Michael. "Well," she started very slowly, "we have a dominant, submissive relationship. I am his submissive."

"Is it S&M?" Boyle asked, "Sadism and Masochism?"

"No, there's no S&M. I'm not a masochist, and he's definitely not a sadist."

"Why do you say that?" Baldoni asked.

"Michael is very gentle and loving. He is dominant, but not cruel. What we have is very cerebral. Michael takes the role of controlling our play, so that makes him the dominant."

"And you have done this every Friday night?"

"Yes, it's part of the contract we made. We agreed that we would both keep Fridays open and strictly for ourselves. Sometimes we'll go places, like Fetish parties, or sometimes we'll go away to Michael's cottage for the weekend." And then she quickly added, "Only on the weekends that my ex-husband has custody of our son."

At this point, Boyle saw no reason to go any further with the questioning. "Thank you, Miss Santiago. You have been very cooperative. We appreciate your help. Detective Baldoni will see you to the front door."

Linda reacted with surprise to Boyle's dismissal. "You mean that's it?" she asked.

"Yes, Miss Santiago," he responded with a mildly dominant tone in his voice, "you are free to leave."

Chapter Twenty-Six

Dylan Stanforth looked across his desk with a grimace that made his usual surliness appear to be tame. He had reviewed the latest report on the Malinkov case with a series of grunts and mumbled swear words, and then with an even deeper grimace he looked up at Boyle.

"I'm disappointed Ari, fucking disappointed. After this many months, we're no closer to solving this case than we were on that first week of investigation."

"Dylan," Boyle said, using Stanforth's first name in an attempt to remind him they once worked together, "what little evidence we have, we've gone over a hundred times. Everyone hated the guy, and every potential suspect has a credible alibi. What we've done so far is to eliminate suspects and stop spending resources on dead ends."

"Then it must have been professional," Stanforth insisted for what seemed like the hundredth time.

"No, I'm positive that it isn't." Boyle said with repeated determination, "This murder was totally different than all other experiences we've had with professional killers. If someone is hired to kill, they don't leave their victim alive, they make sure the job is done."

"Unless the victim wasn't supposed to die," Stanforth repeated his argument, "maybe this was supposed to be a message."

Boyle sighed in frustration. It always irked him when he had to repeat his arguments to a brick wall, "We checked all through Malinkov's background, his business dealings, his love affairs, everything. There are no drug connections or gambling debts. If this was a message, then I couldn't even begin to guess who it was for, unless some new terrorist organization is targeting the real estate market."

"Maybe the killer wasn't as smart as we think they are. Maybe they screwed up." Stanforth posited.

"This killer planned everything to perfection. No forensic evidence, no video surveillance, no witnesses. They knew when Ivan was at home and that he would be alone. Ivan even opened the door for them, so we can only believe that it was the Delivery Corp person, or someone who was dressed as a courier. This killer was intelligent, patient and methodical."

Stanforth sat back in his chair with a humph. "I don't want this to be one of those cases where the press continue to question our capabilities and our budget!"

"So, what do you want me to do?" Boyle asked out of frustration.

Stanforth now made the suggestion he had planned well before the meeting. "Ari, your frustration is beginning to block your investigative view. Maybe we should get another set of eyes to look into it."

"You want to take me off the case!" Boyle asked with defiance.

"No, of course not, you're still the best fucking detective we have." Stanforth hoped to placate Boyle's anger, "I want Johanna to look over the case files on the server. Maybe a different set of eyes might spot something, a different perspective."

Boyle sighed loudly, looked down at his shoes for a moment and then looked up at Stanforth with a sly grin, "I somehow don't think the killer was a vegan," he said referring to Johnson's lifestyle.

"Fuck you Boyle, bring your pride down a notch. You're not fucking perfect. You've had other cases that have gone cold you know."

"One," Boyle snapped back, "and it was the case of a homeless man who was murdered in an alleyway. Anyone could have done that," and then he paused for a moment to let his exasperation dissipate. He spoke in a calmer, rational tone, "We've all had cold cases Dylan. Most of the time because the suspect has fled or gone into deep hiding. But I've never had a case where there was no empirical evidence or suspect."

"Just the same." Danforth said indifferently, "Just the same."

"No, it's not. Malinkov's killer literally disappeared into thin air," and as he was saying those words, a thought crossed Boyle's mind and he stopped suddenly. He looked out the window, thinking for another moment then turned back to Stanforth as he spoke his thought aloud. "Disappeared! Malinkov's killer didn't disappear, they made sure they were never there to begin with."

"What the hell are you talking about?" Stanforth said.

"The killer planned this out in such a way that their alibi was perfect," he thought for another few seconds and then said, "Anton could have hired somebody, even though we found no traces of monetary discrepancies. However, he stands to gain a fair sum from the inheritance. Maybe we need to look at the financial expenditures after he gets the money."

"Huh?" Stanforth grunted, "a layaway plan for a hired killer. Get serious Boyle."

Boyle continued with his thoughts, "Then again, maybe there was no monetary exchange, maybe it was something else, a family heirloom, or jewelry. Maybe he inherited something from his mother."

"Ivan Malinkov possessed some pretty expensive jewelry. Perhaps he had bought his wife expensive jewelry. Spousal abusers often try to make up for their misdeeds with expensive gifts. We need to find the executor of Anna Malinkov's will and determine what Anton inherited."

"Good, now you've got another lead. I'm glad I could be some help," Stanforth said with a haughtiness that exaggerated his own self-importance.

"Yeah, thanks for your insights," Boyle's voice was purposely sarcastic. Stanforth grimaced once again as Boyle quickly left the Chief Inspector's office.

****

One week later, Donna Chang had a copy of Anna Malinkov's will, and the executor's report from the lawyer who handled her estate. Included in the estate was a 2.4 carat, round diamond ring, valued at twenty-three thousand dollars.

When questioned, Anton stated he had given the ring to his wife, and Beth had put the ring in their safety deposit box at the local Queen's Bank of Canada branch. They were keeping the ring as a present for their daughter when it was time for her to marry. Baldoni checked and confirmed the ring was still in the safety deposit box.

Sergeant Detective Johanna Johnson spent three weeks reviewing all the case files and forensic evidence. She was unable to discern any new information, suggest any new direction for the investigation, or determine any other motivation for the murder. She concluded that all avenues of investigation had been properly exhausted.

After reviewing Johanna's report, Chief Inspector Dylan Stanforth declared the case to be put on hold for the present and re-assigned Boyle's homicide team to other cases. A few months later, Stanforth ordered all information files and evidence to be put into cold case folders on the police server and evidence warehouses.

Chapter Twenty-Seven

The Umbergo retirement home was located on the corner of Caledonia Road and St. Clair Avenue West, an area where Italian immigrants lived and raised their families. It was a neighborhood rich with Italian culture, reflected in the stores, community clubs, coffee shops and churches.

The retirement home was built in the 1980s to house the older grandparents who had come with their families during the mass wave of migration after the second world war. Over the years, the retirement home had expanded several times to accommodate the aging population, and the significant increase of older people with Alzheimer's or Dementia. Many Italian families wanted their parents to be housed in a facility that had respect for their heritage, language, and culture.

Michael Barratino stopped at the front door and punched in the security code on the keypad that would allow visitors to enter, but more to prevent older and sometimes senile residents from escaping. He walked through the reception area to the elevators and entered the security code once more for the elevator to activate.

At the seventh floor, the doors opened into another protected area and he entered the security code once more to gain access to the hallway. The smell always hit him like a wet mop and made him wince. There were receptacles comprised of oversized plastic bags within a metal framework that contained dirty diapers and stained sheets. They were not emptied as often as they should have been, and the smell accumulated in layers.

He made his way to his uncle Pino's room, down a long hallway where vacant eyes sat in wheelchairs, oblivious to anyone walking past. He entered into his uncle's room and walked over to the bed, bent down and gave his uncle a short kiss on his forehead.

From the room next door, he could hear the familiar shout of 'Tony! Tony!' at intermittent times. He imagined that Tony was a relative, maybe a son that he was calling. In all his years coming to the retirement home, Michael had never seen anyone ever visit the man.

The woman in the room across the hall laughed and sang, then rambled on incessantly to someone that only existed in her head. The woman on the other side of Uncle Pino's room sporadically made a wailing noise that sounded part mechanic, part animal, as if it were a bad recording of an angry cat.

Uncle Pino's eyes were open and staring at the wall. That was the way he would always be now, that's what had become of his life, immobilized in bed and staring at a blank wall, unable to think, which was probably best, for who would want to have mental comprehension in a place like this.

"Tony! Tony!" the voice next door got louder as he began to sound desperate in the search for his mysterious son. The cat in the other room droned on, and the one across the hall sang another childhood Italian favorite.

Suddenly, Michael heard a new sound, someone singing opera. A baritone down the hall sang passages from La Traviata. The voice was strong, and Michael wondered if this man was new to the ward. He thought about visiting the man and asking him if he knew passages from Carmen, or The Barber of Seville, or if this one opera was all the man could remember.

He closed the door to reduce the noise from the 'Fellini Film Festival', a nickname he had given to the seventh floor. He reached into his pocket and pulled out the key for the large bottom drawer of the bedside cabinet. He had padlocked it about a year ago after different things had gone missing. There was no way to determine if the staff or the wandering residents had removed whatever was inside.

He kept a little portable stereo that he had bought at a discount shop, lifted it from the drawer and plugged it in, then reached into the plastic shopping bag he had brought with him.

"Guess what I finally found?" he said to his uncle with the joy of a discovery, "the 'Greatest Country Hits of Jim Travis'. Found it at the recycle shop around the corner from me. Remember how you used to play that album over and over and sing along with it."

He paused for a second as if listening and then said, "You're welcome. I knew you would like it."

He inserted the CD and hit the play button. The quality of the cheap stereo sounded like a tube radio from the Forties, but that cheapness brought back memories of when he and Uncle Pino would sit in his uncle's kitchen, drinking coffee and smoking cigarettes, listening to Uncle Pino's old cheap record player. They would sit for hours on end and talk about any subject that young Michael wanted to know about.

He let the music play for a time as he sat in the guest chair beside his uncle's bed and then told him about the events of the week, how the Toronto sports teams were doing, and what he had heard from Pino's daughter Maria.

"She and Carlo are both doing well and have been thinking about leaving Villanova and moving into Rome. Their practice was well established and there was no shortage of patients. Your granddaughter Cinzia was expecting her first child, and their boy Michael was in his second year at medical school." He stopped and waited a few moments, then went on, "Yes, I agree, I think it will be a boy as well. Another male heir to the throne of Garabaldi."

He laughed for a short moment at the 'in' joke between him and his uncle and then continued to discuss the news from Pino's daughter and her children. He mentioned that the payments for the retirement home were all up to date so his uncle wouldn't have to worry. He told him that she would come to visit in the near future once the baby was born and when she found time to leave Italy. Her husband would arrange for another doctor to come in on a temporary basis to help out with the practice.

Michael sat back and remained quiet for a while as he listened to the smooth velvety voice of Jim Travis, and he reflected on the song that was playing, feeling it was somewhat appropriate to his uncle's situation.

"My life is now a prison. They will not let me out. My life is now a prison. No one hears my shout."

He listened to the song and watched his uncle to see if there was any hint of recognition to the music. He couldn't detect any and his thoughts drifted on to questions about quality of life, death and euthanasia.

He remembered how his uncle had become a father figure for him when his own father had passed away when he was a young teenager. He remembered how they would talk about women, politics, sports, how the rich white Anglo-Saxon protestants were all money-grubbing bastards, and they talked about the need to place your trust only in your family.

At the end of the song, Michael turned to his uncle and said softly, "It all went as planned. I made the bastard pay for his sins."

He waited a moment and answered, "Yeah, that's right, the asshole who was the ex-husband of the woman I was dating. He's dead now." Michael then started to describe the entire incident, from the first knock on the door to the last look before he left.

"You needn't worry, they will never be able to figure out who the killer was. I planned it perfectly, made sure not to leave any traces of fingerprints or DNA for comparisons. I wore surgical gloves under the other gloves and wrapped my arms in saran wrap to prevent any bodily hairs escaping. There's no pictures or street-cams that caught any identifiable images and if anyone heard anything, nobody called the cops, because none came."

He paused again for a few moments then said, "No, no, don't worry, I've got the perfect alibi for that whole night. My girlfriend Linda truly believed I was with her the whole time. Honest, I'm not kidding. You remember how I told you about that special relationship we have, the bondage relationship, where we have kinky sex and other things. Well, several months ago we made a pact to meet every Friday night. Sometimes we meet on other nights as well when the mood is there, but definitely every Friday. I purposely set it up that way, I wanted every Friday so that I could develop this pattern, and she agreed. We even put it into a written contract."

"Well, on this Friday, Linda was instructed arrive at the exact time I dictated. We did the customary salutations that she would perform for her Master. Then I instructed her to go into the bedroom and to get dressed in the leather Basque I had chosen for her to wear."

"We had a light dinner, and at my command, she stood against the dining room wall while I took each wrist and fastened the leather restraints. I also put a leather restraint on each of her ankles. Lastly, I pulled a black leather mask over her head, a full mask that covered her entire head. There are no openings for the eyes or ears but there's one for the mouth. It has leather hinges that can be pulled over to cover mouth."

Michael paused again listening and then responded, "Yes of course, there's two small openings for where the nose is, the submissive has to be able to breathe. It's what's known as a sensory deprivation mask that restricts the ability of the submissive to see, hear or talk."

"I guided her to the bedroom then I laid her down on the bed, on her back. I stretched each of her limbs to the metal eyelets at each corner of the bed and used a connector to fasten the iron rings of the restraints to the eyelets, leaving her immobile. I sat beside her and gently moved my fingers lightly over the skin of her neck and shoulders, then down between her breasts."

"She moaned softly as her anticipation for a long night of pleasure began to play with her mind. I got up from the bed and went to the stereo, putting in the USB stick with the music I had prepared for the experience. I played the music at a volume that would drown out any other noise but not too loud as I wanted her to remain in the 'mood'."

"I sat down beside her again and slowly moved my fingers up and down her body. I opened the box of sex toys that I keep in the closet and I laid them out on the bed, touching her with each one as I did. I left her restrained on the bed and then texted my friend Henry, telling him it was time to join us. I taped a little button vibrator to her clitoris and turned it on to a very low setting. She was softly moaning through the mask when I went to the front door and let Henry in. The look on his face showed he was anxious to participate."

"He's an old friend of mine from New York. He comes to Toronto a couple of times each year for business and he sometimes stays with me. One time, when he was here, I disclosed my relationship with Linda and asked him if he wanted to enjoy a unique sexual experience in which he would pretend to be me. His enthusiasm for the idea bordered on fanatical."

"However, I explicitly stated that if he wanted to have this experience, then it would have to be strictly done my way. I told him it was imperative that he not to say anything during the experience, not even a moan or groan. I told him that if Linda suspected it wasn't me, her reaction would be unpredictable and she might freak out and go into a panic, which might cause her harm in her restrained position. This could mean the police getting involved. It could get very ugly and she could claim that it was rape or something. The consequences would be bad for both of us. I emphasized the importance of ensuring that Linda never suspect that it wasn't me with her."

Michael took a drink from the bottle of water he had brought. "As an incentive, I let him think that if everything went okay, then I would let him do it again."

"I even made Henry put on the same aftershave I was wearing so that the sense of the aroma would enhance Linda's belief it was me. Henry went into the bedroom, and I left. The bicycle and baseball bat were inside the shed beside the garage. I also had a large shopping bag with the Delivery Corp toque and coat. No one saw me leave and no one was on the street. I cycled over to the asshole's house and killed him."

****

He paused once more as Pino continued to stare at the far wall, oblivious to the world.

"No, it didn't take that long," Michael responded, "I got back to my house in less than an hour. I went upstairs and found Henry on top of Linda, pumping away like a possessed sex fiend. I waited for him to finish. Underneath the mask I could hear Linda's muffled moans and shouts of orgasms. Henry got off her and I motioned for him to bring his clothes and follow me to the living room. I indicated for him to hold his voice and that he could tell me everything that he wanted the next day when we met for coffee." Michael paused for a moment, "Yeah, you should have seen the smile on his face when he left.

"I went into the bedroom and sat beside Linda and slowly traced the beaded trickles of sweat with my finger along her body. She had so many orgasms that she didn't notice a thing, and with that hood on, she was totally clueless that it wasn't me. She moaned sweetly, and then I leaned in and spoke close to her ear so that she could hear me, 'one more orgasm my dear, I want one more from you', then using the vibrating wand, I slowly forced her to another orgasm."

"Afterward, once I had removed the restraints and taken the hood off, we cuddled on the bed and talked about the experience. I'm convinced she believed it was me the whole time. She even praised my ability to make each Friday night's experience so different from the others. I laid back and started to think about what I had done that night. I felt so powerful, so ultimate, I was as hard as a rock, and then I turned Linda on her back and mounted her for my own pleasure."

Pino stared at the wall as the Jim Travis CD came to an end.

"Yeah, you guessed it, she stayed the night. In the morning, I made her breakfast in bed, and then I drove her home. I picked up the Saturday paper and a double espresso, then went home and sat in the kitchen to read the paper. I put on the radio for the news and I didn't read or hear any news about that asshole. That's when I knew I was clear."

184

Michael looked at his uncle, got up and started the CD once more. "In the afternoon," he continued, "I drove up to the cottage and had a midnight bonfire. The coat and running shoes smelled of burning rubber and they gave off a thick black smoke, but no one could see the black smoke at midnight, and no one was around to smell it. None of the neighbors were up that weekend." Then he gave a little chuckle as he spoke, "You know something, a midnight bonfire at the edge of a forest is a lonely place to be in November." He sat quiet for another moment then said, "Yes, I burned all the planning material as well; maps, drawings, notebooks, everything."

He stopped suddenly and turned toward his uncle as if he had been insulted, "What do you think, I did this for nothing. I was handsomely paid. I have my jewel that I intend to keep safely hidden."

After another pause, he continued, "Don't worry Uncle, I'm a professional. I made it look like it was a vengeful killing. No one will ever know."

There was a short knock on the door to Uncle Pino's room and one of the retirement home attendants walked in. She saw Michael and said, "It's really wonderful that you come here to sit and talk with him. I don't know how much he's actually able to take in, but I'm sure there must be some comfort to have a familiar voice speak to him of family and loved ones."

"Well," Michael responded, "my cousin, his daughter, lives near Rome, Italy. She's married to a doctor and they have a couple of children, one with a baby on the way. They have a busy practice so it's difficult for them to come over for any extended time. My uncle and I were always close, especially after my father died. We used to be able to talk about anything, and I guess I still do."

"That's very commendable of you," said the attendant, "some of the patients in here are all alone and rarely get visitors. It's nice that you care for your uncle."

"Thank you," replied Michael, "in a way, he's my confident. Always has been. I can confess all of my sins and get wonderful advice in return."

The attendant gave him a polite, quizzical smile. "Well, I'm sure he's comforted all the same," she stated as she picked up the laundry bag and dumped it into the wheeled bin, then turned toward the door.

"Yes," said Michael, "I'm sure he is. Have a nice day."

Chapter Twenty-Eight

It was a cool Tuesday morning in the middle of November, one year after the murder of Ivan Malinkov. The 10:15 bell rang throughout the hallways. Students sauntered out of their classrooms on their way to the next class or stop in the hallway to check their cellphones for messages and other social media updates.

The teacher sat at his desk, opened the top left drawer and retrieved his own cellphone. He quickly texted his girlfriend and asked if she wanted to see the latest 'Galaxy Battle' movie at the Beach Cinemas on Wednesday night. He wanted to go to the nine-fifteen show as he would be working late to grade papers. His girlfriend, Christine, was also a movie buff and they often went to the cinema for a date.

The teacher met Christine through an on-line dating site and their mutual love of the cinema experience, as opposed to staying home and watching movies on large screen home theatres, was the common trait that brought them together.

As the students from his next scheduled class began to file into the room, his phone blinked a return message from Christine stating that she can't wait to see the latest instalment of this science fiction franchise. She suggested that they meet 8:00 pm for a quick supper at the Tulip Diner, a place where they usually met prior to the movie.

****

A few hours later on Tuesday evening, the teacher parked his car in the cinema parking lot, purchased a ticket from the auto-payment machine and went into the Beach Cinemas. He wore a dark brown winter coat he had purchased from Value Village and a dark brown Fedora hat that he pulled low over his forehead. At eight forty-five, he purchased two tickets for the 'Galaxy

Battle' movie with his credit card to ensure there was a record of him being at the theatre. He entered the cinema and casually sat at one of the tables in the refreshment area, keeping the Fedora low to mask as much of his face as possible.

As the crowd from the seven o'clock showing began to exit the theatre, he stood and showed his ticket to the young teen collecting tickets for the next showing. The interior structure of the theatre was badly designed so that the crowd exiting the movie theatre was usually mixed together with patrons who were coming into the hallway for the later shows. The teacher timed his entry so that he blended with the people who were leaving the theatre through the side exit. He walked back to his car, put the parking ticket stub into his glove compartment with about two-dozen other stubs from the same theatre, left the parking lot and drove downtown to the King and Bathurst Streets area of the city.

Driving north on Bathurst, he turned right onto the one-way, eastbound Adelaide Street and parked in front of the construction site of a new condominium. He got out of his car and went to the automated parking meter, put in sufficient change for overnight parking.

He returned to his car, put the parking ticket on the dashboard of the driver's side window, ensuring that any parking control officer would see the ticket and simply proceed without taking any records. He reached into the back seat for the large blue duffle bag. There was a short dark alley next to the construction site, which he entered and put on oversized black sweatpants over his jeans and a heavy black leather jacket. Once properly attired, he went back to his car and sat in the driver's seat.

He began the mental preparations for what he needed to do, rehearsing the plan, remembering the timing, thinking about the precautions and internal warnings to himself if the situation was not ideal once more. He looked through the windows to the sidewalks on both sides of the street. The Factory Theatre at the corner of Adelaide and Bathurst was dark and empty as there were no shows scheduled for the weekday evenings in November. The few remaining factories and office buildings were closed and the condominiums that were being constructed had no workers this late into the evening.

Most of the windows of the condominium on the south side of Adelaide were dark or had their curtains drawn. There was little chance that anyone was looking out into the grim darkness of the street on this November evening, and even if they were, they would not be able to see into the car parked on the north side.

The sidewalks were deserted, and the teacher took another moment to close his eyes and focus. In his mind, he thought about the power he was about to extract from the universe, the power that will augment his strength of purpose and give him the potency of dominion over the feeble-minded ennui of all others. The teacher bent his head forward and clenched his hands into tight fists. His nerves twitched with anticipation and his muscles were taut with the mixed sense of fear and excitement. His eyes snapped open and the transformation was complete.

The teacher had metamorphosed into the hunter.

Chapter Twenty-Nine

The hunter stood in the darkened shadow of the alleyway beside the Sly Fox Pub on the northeast corner of King and Bathurst Streets. He knew his prey was in the pub, just as he had known the other nights he had waited. He had staked out his prey numerous times over the past few months, following him to this pub, timing when he left, who left with him, which way he would walk, how much he usually drank, what he would be wearing.

The front portion of the alleyway was in complete shadow as there was one streetlight on the intersection corner and the next light eighty feet east. The next building beside the alleyway was a restaurant with a sidewalk patio that was closed for the season. A permanent awning covered the patio and also blocked the light from the second streetlamp. In the alleyway, there was only one light near the rear exit of the pub where staff would take out the garbage.

The hunter had stood there many nights and watched people walk by, completely hidden in the shadows. Some had even glanced down the alleyway, but none had noticed him standing there as their eyes were not accustomed to seeing through the darkness.

During his planning, he had also completed a survey of the area, where each alleyway and street led, how many streetlights there were, how light or dark the kill zone was at any time during the night, how busy the traffic was, how many pedestrians were walking in either direction on all the sidewalks at different times of the evening. He estimated how many security cameras there could potentially be in the stores and business in the area of the kill zone and in the areas where he wanted to escape. He logically estimated what view each of these cameras would have, figuring most would cover the doorways of the nearby establishments, but he also estimated what peripheral range of vision they might also capture.

On the south side of King, three buildings east of Bathurst, there was a ten-story condo tower that rose above the retail units at street level. Whenever the hunter surveyed the area, he noted that almost all of the condo windows were covered with closed curtains. However, to ensure his invisibility, the hunter would approach King Street through the alleyway and remain in the shadows with only brief glimpses into the street.

The westbound King streetcar stop was at the northeast corner of the intersection, in front of the Pub. A bus shelter with the clear polycarbonate sides stood on the sidewalk. At that time of night, the streetcar was scheduled to arrive every 12 minutes, however the hunter could clearly see a half-mile down the road and know if one was coming. A quick glance around the corner would let him know if there were any bystanders waiting at the stop.

As all good hunters knew, it was necessary to have the patience to wait for the best time, and he had spent more than a few nights in which he let the prey pass by without consummating the plan, because the timing wasn't right or the situation had too much potential for witnesses, or even a bystander who might interfere. No, he wanted it to be perfect, and so the benighted prey had walked by a number of times unaware that his life was spared by sheer circumstances.

Tonight, the prey stayed in the pub later than usual. The hunter checked his phone and the circumstances seemed right. It was a cold November night and within this hour of darkness there was almost no traffic on the road and no hapless souls walking the sidewalks. The hunter quickly glanced and saw no one waiting for the westbound King streetcar, which was so far away that its distinctive lights were barely visible. The eastbound King streetcar on the south side of the street was several blocks to the west of Bathurst and would take at least another five minutes to journey through the many traffic lights. He looked up at the condo tower and noted that most windows were dark, and not a single lighted window had open curtains.

The prey left the Sly Fox and stopped in front of its doors on King Street to get his bearings, then he turned and walked east. He drank more than usual that night as he had been celebrating a new success at work. He walked very close to the wall by natural instinct to keep his bearings.

As the prey passed the corner of the building to the opening of the alleyway, he heard his name being called. He stopped and looked up with a casual curiosity at hearing the words 'Kyle Wilson' come out of the darkness.

The crowbar smashed the prey's kneecap, and he could hear the bone crack like a scream pumping through his veins. He crumpled to the ground and the torment was so great that he could not cry out. His mouth opened but no sound emerged, only the gulping intake of breath after breath. His eyes watered but there were no tears.

All the impulses from his brain to his body were put on hold while his mind tried to comprehend the sudden excruciating nightmare in his knee. The knife in the hand of the man dressed in black added to the confusion that was in his head. Shock had him in a deep state of paralysis and he was unable to understand the reality of what was happening as the edge of steel slid across his throat.

The hunter had dropped the crowbar on the sidewalk, knelt down on the left side of the prey and put his hand over the prey's forehead, turning it up and toward him so that the right side of the throat was exposed. A quick thrust went deep and the slash upon exit of the knife cut both the carotid artery and the jugular vein on the prey's right side. The spray of blood spewed mostly out in that direction, away from the killer.

The hunter immediately rose and turned into the alleyway, leaving the crowbar on the sidewalk, and ran into the shadows. When he turned the corner at the end of the alleyway, he dropped the knife and did a quick walk to the other end that came out onto Bathurst Street. Now he quickly walked up the street and turned into the next alleyway, one building north of the pub, went to the end, put his hands on the top of the four-foot chain-linked fence and vaulted over to the other side.

He grabbed the duffle bag that he had left behind the garbage can, reached into the bag and pulled out the clothing that was stored. He changed his coat and hat, removed the black sweatpants and ski mask and put the murder clothes into the bag, then walked through the adjoining parking lot to Adelaide Street and down to his car. He had previously determined that if he saw anyone on the street, he would walk past his car, turn at the next street and wait until the street was clear. However, there was no one walking on the street, so he safely went directly to his car.

He opened the passenger's side door and threw the bag onto the floor of the front seat. He walked to the driver's side and quickly got in the car, turned the ignition and casually drove eastward along Adelaide all the way to Spadina Avenue. Just before making the right turn at Spadina, he removed his hat and drove south to Lakeshore Boulevard.

****

The late-night coffee shop on the corner of Queen Street east and Kingston Road was cozy and warm with only a few patrons sitting at the tables. They were mostly men who had come from the Off-Track betting facility beside the Beach Cinemas, which had replaced the Greenwood Race Track many years ago.

The coffee was dark, and the aroma was infinitely better than the death he had left behind. He warmed his hands by wrapping them around the cup, hands that were cold from the long run outside.

From the kill zone, he had driven along Lakeshore Boulevard to the Don Valley Road, a short roadway that acted as the on ramp of the Parkway. He pulled into the entrance of the parking lot that was once the old soap and detergent manufacturing plant. The sign stated the area was now called 'The East Harbor' and was scheduled for re-development, but the lot was empty except for a couple of construction tractors that waited for the development to begin.

He parked the car beside the entrance to the lot and then walked the few yards south to the paved bicycle path. He crossed the Don Valley Road and followed the path to the steel bridge that crossed the Don River. The narrow bridge had iron railings that ran waist high and a steel arch that reached up to fifteen feet at its crown.

The hunter stopped at the mid-point of the bridge where the arch was highest and looked down into the murky waters of the polluted river. He took the cell phone from his pocket and threw the phone as far as he could into the middle of the river. No one was within hearing distance of the small 'plop' as the cell phone hit the water and sank to the bottom. He stood for a moment, looking into the dark water, and thought to himself, '*How many other items had been disposed of from this very spot.*'

He crossed the bridge to its other side where the bicycle trail came to the fork in the path, where one trail continued its westward direction and another trail ran north, adjacent to the river. On the west side of the bridge, he picked up a few rocks that were strewn around each side of the path. He put the rocks into his pocket and headed up the path for about two-hundred yards, until he reached the railway bridge that crossed the river.

There were no cyclists or pedestrians at this time of year, especially at this time of night. He left the path and walked down to the embankment of the river to a secluded spot where he knew he would not be seen. He removed his gloves and reached into his pocket for the rocks and put them inside the gloves. When they were sufficiently weighted, he threw one glove as close as he could to the center of the river. He knew that he could destroy the gloves, but there was a sense of adventure, the potential danger of being caught that thrilled him. He knew it was unlikely the gloves would ever be found, and the fact that he had worn blue nitrile medical gloves underneath the leather gloves would mean that there was little chance of finding any DNA evidence. It was the fact that the gloves were in the river, potentially drifting up on some shore one day, or being fished out by an unknowing sportsman, added to his sense of power. It would be a secret that only he and the devil would know.

Holding the second glove in his hands, he stood and watched the black waters of the river acclaim his dominance. He held the glove above his head and looked to the sky. Without voicing a sound, he proclaimed his mastery over the universe, and then threw the second glove into the river. He made his way back up to the unlit bicycle path and ran back to his car under the midnight stars. His hands were cold. His nerves were ice. His heart was frozen.

The coffee was good, easy to swallow, and the bitter taste of the bile faded down his throat with every sip. He had to hold in the bile and vomit until he was far away from the spot where the gloves and phone were drowned. He didn't want to leave any clues as to where to drag the river. He was sure that no one saw him, and even if they did, the only thing they would be able to report was a man dressed in black, in the middle of the night, not wearing gloves.

The second cup tasted better than the first. The rest of the night would be wide-eyed caffeine, but that would be okay, because he wouldn't sleep anyway.

Chapter Thirty

Detective Sergeant Randal Curtis arrived at the crime scene in the early dawn of Wednesday morning, parking on the wide Bathurst Street sidewalk just north of the pub. Constables Owen Garrison and Katherine Evanko had been on the scene for most of the night and Detective Pierre Archambault had arrived two hours previously. The body had been removed but the chalk outline on the sidewalk was highlighted by the stain of blood in both directions.

Curtis knew that traffic would be at a standstill for the morning rush hour, and the westbound King streetcar would have to be held. The Toronto Transit Commission would implement a temporary bus route that would be diverted around the intersection. He greeted Garrison and Evanko with short waves of his finger and went directly to Detective Archambault for information.

"Morning Pierre, give me the details."

"It's pretty messy," Pierre started, "the victim came out of the Sly Fox pub and was attacked on the sidewalk in front of this alleyway. It appears that he was hit in the kneecap with a crowbar and then had his throat slashed. All took place just after midnight."

"Robbery?" Curtis asked.

"Victim still had his wallet, cell phone and rings when he was found."

"Any witnesses?"

"None that saw the actual crime itself. Some people in the pub knew him and they came out afterward. The westbound streetcar driver saw the victim lying on the sidewalk and assumed it was a drunk. He didn't see anyone running away from the scene. We haven't checked the condos across the street yet, but nobody has reported anything from that building."

"Who called it in?"

"There were two 911 calls; one from a patron in the pub who left a few minutes after the victim, and a man who had left the Wheat Sheaf tavern and was crossing the street to the where his car was parked just east on King.

Neither saw the crime nor anyone leaving it, however we found a knife around the corner in the alleyway, and it is stained with blood. The crowbar was found a few feet from the victim's body."

"What do you think, the murderer was in the pub or someone just walking down the street?"

"I think they came from inside the alleyway." Pierre postulated. "Like they were waiting for them, or something like that."

"What makes you think that?"

"Well, according to the witnesses in the pub, there weren't any fights or arguments, so I don't think anyone would be in the pub with a knife and crowbar in their coat pocket just waiting for someone to leave. And if this was random, then some psycho was walking around on a cold November night with a crowbar. The victim could have seen it coming and tried to run or struggle. The streetcar driver said that he didn't see anyone running away, so the killer probably went down the alley very fast, no thinking involved, which means it probably wasn't a random psycho who probably wouldn't have known that the alley turns at the corner of the building and comes out on Bathurst."

"Maybe," Curtis offered, "we'll have to get the input from forensics. How's your leg doing in this weather?"

"The cold creeps into the area where I broke the bone. I think I'm going to end up like one of those old guys who can tell when a storm is coming by the aches in their bodies."

"Yeah, spilling the bike on a mountain road does have its small measure of benefits." Curtis grinned at Archambault and pointed down the alley. "Is FIS down there?"

"Yeah, it's Mei Liu." Archambault smirked at the comment about the motorcycle accident. "You ever gonna let up on that?"

"Only when it stops being funny." Curtis smiled.

They went down the alleyway where they found Mie Lui and another member of the FIS team bent over, sorting through three large gray trash containers, two large blue recyclable containers and the two large green compost bins. When Mie Liu saw Curtis, she stopped her sorting and stood up to answer any of his questions.

"Find anything useful in all that?" he asked her.

"We found the knife." She responded in the formal official way she always did. "It was on the ground beside the garbage container. I'm surprised they didn't toss it into the trash. It would have been harder to find at night, but perhaps they just didn't think about it in their rush to leave the scene. So far, there's only stuff from the restaurant in the containers. There are a few more members of my team on their way to help us sort through it all."

"Okay, let me know if you get anything." Curtis requested and then added, "I don't want to pressure you, but there's going to be one massive traffic jam in about an hour, so try to clear it up as soon as possible."

"And," he continued, "can you finish up what you need to do as quickly as possible at the front of the pub. There is a lot of blood on the sidewalk and I want to have it cleaned up before pedestrians start walking by it this morning. It's not the kind of thing we want to have on display for the general public during business hours."

"I'll get the extra FIS personnel to work on that right away," she agreed.

Curtis and Archambault walked the rest of the alleyway and came out on Bathurst, just north of King street. They walked back down to the intersection and turned left toward the crime scene once more. Curtis turned back to Archambault, "Anything from pathology?"

"Singh was here early. Owen told me that he only lives a couple of blocks from here. According to Owen, Singh established the cause of death as the stab and slash into the neck, along with the broken kneecap. He estimates the time of death to be just minutes before the 911 calls, but he'll confirm everything when he does the autopsy."

"Have we got a list of the people in the pub and how many have made statements?"

"We got statements from about a dozen people who were milling around the crime scene when the constables first arrived. We have statements from people who were in the pub and the names of others not yet questioned. This includes the Sly Fox pub staff. We have the name of the streetcar driver and we'll have to get the security tapes from the TTC to determine if there could have been any witnesses on the streetcar as it passed the King-Bathurst intersection."

"And the condo?" Curtis said as he looked up at the ten-story building across the street.

"Some of the residents came out during the night when they noticed all the flashing lights. We got some of their names. Owen and Katherine will request help in order to knock on every door."

"Okay Pierre." Curtis said with a restless sigh, "I'll call headquarters for additional back up to control the scene. Send Owen and Katherine home to get a couple of hours sleep. I want a full meeting in the Argo around noon. I'll stick around to manage things here. You get some sleep as well."

"It's okay Randal, I'm fine."

"It's your leg I'm worried about, not your head." Randal said jokingly, "You're going to be my future weatherman."

"I was going to check the local businesses about the security cameras they may have facing out onto the street." Archambault said as an afterthought.

"When the other constables get here, I'll take one of them with me and start the process of getting any video that's available. Now go home."

Chapter Thirty-One

It was well past noon when the meeting was held in the Argo later that day. Sergeant Detective Curtis had a short nap in the 'Rest Room' on the tenth floor of the police headquarters building. The Rest Room had been set up to accommodate officers and civilian staff who have worked extended hours during emergency situations or investigations. The room contained a number of full-length sofas and some retractable lounge chairs and it was the accepted custom that people would walk softly and speak in whispers anywhere near that room.

Detective Sergeant Randal Curtis was an African Canadian whose ancestors originally came to Toronto in the 1860s through the famous 'underground railroad'. They found life to be equally as hard in Canada, as the population consisted of mostly British Loyalists and an increasing mix of European immigrants. What they mostly found was varying degrees of the same racism they thought they had left behind. His great-grandparents lived for a number of years in 'The Ward', a dense slum that is currently the location of Toronto's City Hall, and they survived by working as laborers in odd jobs. His grandparents eventually scraped enough money together and bought a small farm in the Niagara region, near St. Catherines, Ontario.

His father moved to Toronto when he began to study at the Faculty of Law in the University of Toronto. He decided to settle in Toronto to 'article' with an established law firm and married his mother, who had immigrated from the Virgin Islands in the Caribbean.

Randal's father was a strong human rights advocate and his mother never became a full Canadian citizen because she refused to take an oath of allegiance to the Queen of England. They had four children of which Randal was the youngest. When he was a teenager, Randal's eldest brother was wounded by a police officer during a brawl at a downtown bar. Randal's anger toward the police never changed, even when his brother confessed to him that he had started the fight.

In university, he began to research the statistics of police violence and even went so far as to interview a number of police officials at police headquarters. His dissertation on the subject showed flaws in the system but there was no condemnation of the police force in general. Instead, his focus was on the need to improve training for individual officers on human social issues, and the need to improve societal standards. The dissertation earned him a high mark but alienated him from a number of his friends.

Randal Curtis joined the Toronto Police Force in his early twenties and had risen to the rank of Sergeant Detective of a homicide unit. During his time as a Constable, he received several Commendations for courage and exceptional performance, plus an award for dedicated service to the community.

****

Curtis entered the Argo and found Mie Liu, Surat Singh, Detective Pierre Archambault, constables Katherine Evanko and Owen Garrison and the civilian research specialist Amal Mirwani already present and discussing the case.

"Sorry I'm late everyone," Curtis said as he took a seat at the head of the table. "Bring me up to date on what you've discussed while I was resting."

The map of the crime scene was projected onto one of the digital screens and Mei Liu told Curtis that she had been discussing the geography of the area with the rest of the team.

"The murder took place right on the sidewalk," she continued, "in front of the alleyway beside the Sly Fox building. The killer used a crowbar to disable the victim and then a knife to cut into his throat. The knife was a sturdy steak knife, the kind you would get at really good restaurants, with a thick handle and a strong, thick blade. However, the blade had been keenly sharpened, probably on a grinding wheel so that the serrated edges had been filed away and only the sharp flat steel remained. If the serrated edges had remained on the knife, then the slash across the throat would not have been easy and would have caused more ripping than slicing. Dr. Singh will explain that in greater detail."

"The knife was found around the corner in the alleyway," as she pointed to the crime scene map showing the Sly Fox building that faced King Street. The alleyway ran north and south on the east side of the building, and the adjoining alleyway ran east and west at the back of the building, "The knife was found on the ground beside the large grey trash containers. We believe the killer ran down the alleyway after the murder, turned the corner and went down the adjoining alleyway and simply dropped the knife near the trash cans."

She continued without any pauses for questions, "The crowbar was found four feet from the body. It's your basic steel crowbar with a hook at one end that has forked fissure for removing nails and a slight curve at the other end that flattens out for prying apart objects. It's a standard brand that can be purchased from almost any hardware store."

"We believe the killer used the crowbar to incapacitate the victim by hitting him on the kneecap, and then dropped the crowbar immediately and switched to the knife as the murder weapon."

At this point, Detective Archambault raised his voice for a question, "Are we able to determine where the killer came from? Was he walking on the street facing the victim, did he come up from behind the victim? Did he come from across the street, or did he come from inside the alleyway?"

"We are not yet able to tell how the attack occurred from the positioning of the body. We can only assume that the killer exited through the alleyway by the location of the knife." She stopped at this point and left the crime scene map up on the screen.

"I'm surprised you didn't join me in the Rest Room." Curtis light-heartedly commented.

"We have our own rest room at the forensics facility," Mei Lui stated without humor.

"I know," Curtis replied and wondered if she ever broke from her serious demeanor. "Dr. Singh, what have you been able to determine. Have you completed the autopsy?"

"I've only done a preliminary examination so far," Singh said, "I will be doing a complete autopsy later on this afternoon."

"Okay, so what have you learned from the preliminary?"

"Just as Mie Lui stated, the crowbar was used against the kneecap with a significant enough force that it crushed the Patella and literally separated the lower Tibia from the upper Femur bones. The victim fell to the ground and the killer stabbed the victim in the right side of his throat and slid the knife across the throat as far as they could manage. You can see from Mei Lui's crime scene map that the blood spray mostly went to the right of the victim, but a great deal bled onto the sidewalk all around the body. The victim was probably unconscious within five to ten seconds and death would have occurred after another thirty seconds. The initial stab to the throat cut the carotid artery and the slash across the throat cut the jugular vein."

"The only time I've ever seen anyone killed with a slashed throat is in the movies," Constable Evanko mentioned, "I don't think it's a common MO in real life."

"It's not an MO that is commonly used because it's hard to perform accurately." Archambault explained, "If you miss, then the intended victim has the ability to defend themselves."

"Is that all you have for now Singh?" Curtis asked wanting to move forward on what he knew was going to be a long meeting.

"Yes, I'll have more later today or this evening when I've completed the full autopsy."

"I'll join you at the morgue later today to get the full report." Curtis said and then moved to the next subject, "Okay, we haven't mentioned anything about the victim yet. What's his name, where is he from, why was he there at that time, and why was he the victim?"

"The victim's name is Kyle Wilson." Archambault quickly added, "He works at the Queen's Bank of Canada, Financial Services division, just down the street, about two blocks away from the Sly Fox. The pub staff stated that he was a regular customer, often coming to the pub after work. Apparently, a number of employees at the Queen's Bank frequent the Sly Fox. It's their after-work hangout."

"What do we have in the way of witnesses?"

"Basically, the same as I mentioned this morning, some people from the pub who saw the victim leave, the two 911 callers who both found the body on the sidewalk, but neither of them witnessed the crime or anyone leaving the crime scene. Then there's the driver of the eastbound King streetcar who saw the body as he passed the crime scene. However, he says that he just saw a glimpse of someone lying on the sidewalk and thought it was a drunk or homeless person."

"Why didn't he stop the streetcar and find out, or at least call it in to his supervisor?" Curtis asked.

"He stated that it's not unusual for him to see someone on the sidewalk on King Street." Archambault responded as he had already inquired, "He stated that if he called every time he saw someone on the sidewalk on King Street, then he'd spend half of his nights making calls."

"Yeah, I see his point," Curtis said bemused, "let's start with all the people in the pub, the staff and whatever customers that we can identify. I want a list of his family and the people where he worked."

He turned to Garrison and Evanko, "There should be security video from inside the pub. See if there are any security cameras in the alleyways behind the building. Begin interviewing the pub staff and the people who congregated around the body after it was found."

"Pierre, you and I are going to visit Kyle's boss when the meeting is over. Amal, call the Queen's Bank and set up the interview. Make it for 30 minutes after we leave here." Curtis took a short pause while he was thinking of anything he might have missed, "Alright everyone, we've got work to do. We'll meet again in the morning. Call me if anything pertinent comes up."

Chapter Thirty-Two

The Queen's Bank of Canada branch was located two hundred yards east of the Sly Fox pub. It was late afternoon when Curtis and Archambault entered the financial management offices of the bank to meet George Martinique, the managing director. They were greeted at the reception desk and were asked to wait as Mr. Martinique was finishing up with another customer.

Curtis never liked waiting, and only did so because he knew the police force was under heavy scrutiny for their actions and relationships with the general public. However, he also knew that the courtesies expected of him would quickly change to desperation if a person was in need of a cop.

After several minutes, Curtis rose and walked to the receptionist and asked how much longer Mr. Martinique would be. The receptionist replied that she did not know and to please wait until he was free.

Curtis looked sternly at the receptionist, "We are going to be leaving now. Please tell Mr. Martinique that he is expected to be at 52 Division station in the next sixty minutes. If he is not there by that time, we will send a constable to officially escort him."

The receptionist sat straight up with the wide eyes of surprise. "Please, let me ring him once more and let him know that you wish to see him immediately."

Curtis sat down and smiled at Archambault who was grinning from ear to ear. They heard the receptionist speak in a low excited voice through her hands-free headpiece. She turned to them and said Mr. Martinique is now available and that she would take them back to his office. They rose and followed her down a corridor of glass offices to the end corner unit. She lightly knocked on the door and opened it for the detectives.

Mr. Martinique was sitting behind his glass desk and rose when Curtis and Archambault were shown into his office. He was a tall, slim man in his early sixties. His white hair was neatly trimmed, and it highlighted a face that was tanned from his devotion to golf games in the southern states and the Caribbean islands.

He came around his desk and reached out to shake Archambault's hand and said, "My apologies Sergeant Detective, I was dealing with a contentious client and lost track of time. Would you and your assistant like to have a seat?"

Archambault shook Martinique's hand and smiled saying, "I'm Detective Archambault," and then nodding his head toward Curtis, "this is Sergeant Detective Randal Curtis, who is heading up the investigation into Kyle Wilson's death."

Martinique paused for a moment while his brain performed the quick analysis of realizing how he may have offended Curtis by automatically assuming Archambault was in charge. He quickly set about to correct this potential affront and establish a parity with the superior officer. He extended his hand to Curtis, which was left hanging in the air for an awkward moment as Curtis did not offer his own. Feeling a little perturbed at the slight, he motioned for Curtis to take the chair in front of his desk and offered Archambault a seat on the couch that was against the far wall.

Curtis motioned for Archambault to sit in the chair while he remained standing. Archambault sat down and retrieved his digital recorder, which he placed on the glass table. He switched it on and completed the required identification information, without giving any explanation to Mr. Martinique about the usage of the recorder.

"Mr. Martinique," Archambault started the questioning right away, "as you were informed this morning by Constable Owen Garrison, Kyle Wilson was killed just after midnight. We want to act fast on this investigation and we are going to need a great deal of information from you and your company."

"Yes, of course." Martinique replied, "Anything I can do to help will be made available to you."

"Can we first start with a little information about Kyle. Your employment papers should list the next of kin and we will need to interview people he worked closely with in the office." Archambault requested. "However, can you personally give us some information about Kyle?"

Mr. Martinique sat back in his chair and started arranging his thoughts, "Well, Kyle was very good at his job." He took another moment, wanting to ensure that he did not reveal any information that could be negative toward the bank, or to himself. "He was very knowledgeable about banking and the financial industry, and he was very amiable with all the clients. He dealt with many of the local businesses, and they all enjoyed dealing with him."

"Mr. Martinique," Curtis spoke up, "this is a murder inquiry. We are not looking for recommendations or platitudes about the victim. If you need to take a few moments to think about the information we require, then please have a cup of that fancy tea you keep on the counter behind you, and then we will continue the interview."

Martinique leaned forward and looked up at Curtis and realized he was going to have to deal with this situation as if it was one of his more complex negotiations. He had risen to his position within the bank because of his subtlety and charm, which camouflaged his ruthless, cold-blooded business sense.

"I've already had my tea, thank you." His frigid voice calmly answered Curtis, "If you have particular questions that you require to ask, then please do so."

"We would like to know more about Kyle as a person, especially in business?" Archambault continued the questioning while Curtis watched.

Mr. Martinique sat back in his chair once more and took a more expressionless demeanor, "Kyle was a very aggressive individual in his business dealings. He took great pride in his work and was very competitive. In his years with the Queen's Bank of Canada, he always wanted his branch to be number one in transactions and earnings."

"He held a position in the Beaches for a number of years and he raised the financial assistance accounts of that office to be one of the top branches in the country. I encouraged him to come to our King-Bathurst office because of all the new developments and condos that are being built in this area. We brought him in here to oversee a lot of the financial planning, mortgages, new clients, business loans and other services, and he did an excellent job."

Martinique paused for a moment and then continued, "I can't say he was much of a family man. I don't believe he ever married. He was an enthusiast about hockey, playing and watching it. He would even set up a TV in the lunchroom during the Winter Olympics. I'm not sure what more I could tell you about him."

"Are you aware of his social activities? Did he have a girlfriend or was he in any sort of relationship?" Archambault asked.

Martinique looked skeptical at the question and then decided to answer, "He dated quite a few women. He often had a different partner every time we had a company function. Nobody looked down on him for that. We don't insist or expect our people to be family orientated, we just expect people to do their jobs."

"So, he liked women and he played hockey." Curtis said with touch of his own cold steel.

"Kyle played in a number of hockey leagues across the city. He loved the game and it kept him in shape. During the off-season, he liked to travel. He went to a number of Caribbean island resorts, and he always brought me back cigars whenever he went to Cuba."

****

Curtis felt the buzz of his cell phone in his breast pocket. He had informed the main desk at headquarters to hold all of his calls unless it was something of significance.

"Excuse me," Curtis stated to both men, "I have to take this call." He looked at Martinique, "Is there somewhere private where I can talk?"

"There is a boardroom next door, to the left as you leave my office. It should be empty."

"Thank you," Curtis replied with a friendlier tone toward Martinique, "Pierre, please continue with the interview."

He answered the phone as he stepped outside the office door and walked into the empty boardroom, "Detective Curtis."

"Hi Randal, this is Mie Liu from FIS."

"What have you found?" he asked knowing that there would be something of interest.

"When we were inspecting the knife where the shaft of the blade is inserted into the handle, we detected traces of Pine Sol and ammonia. It appears the weapon had been cleaned prior to the murder. We haven't found any traces of either solvent on the crowbar because it is a smooth steel which can easily be wiped clean, but we're going to keep checking on that."

"What's the significance?"

"I'm reporting this because of the similar usage of these solvents with the murder weapon used in the Ivan Malinkov murder case last year. The baseball bat had also been cleaned with Pine Sol and ammonia." Mei Liu's words drawled as she yawned while he spoke, "Sorry about that, I was up most of the night going over the scene and then back in the lab."

"You think there's a connection?" Curtis quickly asked.

"Yes. We've checked the knife for fingerprints and there are none to be found. It is the same MO as the Malinkov case, where no fingerprints were found, plus these same cleaning compounds were also identified on the baseball bat that was used to beat the victim. I don't believe the use of ammonia and Pine Sol is a coincidence. I don't have any other records on file in which both these chemicals were used in combination with each other."

"Is this absolutely definite?" Curtis tightened his jaw as he contemplated the implications.

"Yes," replied Mei Liu, "I worked on the Malinkov crime scene with Aaron Silverstein and we were both surprised at the lack of evidence on the bat because it had been so meticulously cleaned with these solvents. I think we have the potential of this being the same killer."

"What about the crowbar?" Curtis asked.

"We found one set of prints on the crowbar however it was found lying on the street amidst a number of people who were gathered at the scene. We'll need to ensure no one tampered with the weapon before we can confirm the prints as evidence."

"Thanks Mei Lui. Keep me posted if anything else comes up." He ended the call and then pressed the quick dial key for the main homicide number at police headquarters. When the receptionist answered, he spoke with some urgency, "Hi Marge, is Gina Baldoni still in the building?" and after a moment, "can you put me through to her."

"Detective Baldoni," she stated as she answered her phone.

"Hi Gina, this is Randal. I just got a call from Mei Liu pertaining to a murder that happened last night. A banker named Kyle Wilson. Does the name ring any bells with you in the Malinkov investigation?"

"Nope, the name never arose during our investigation. Why do you ask?"

"Mei Liu reported that the weapons used in the Wilson murder had been pre-cleaned with Pine Sol and ammonia."

The phone went quiet on both ends of the line for several seconds and then Curtis spoke again, "Hi Gina, are you still there?"

"Yeah, I'm here," she responded, "I'm just trying to figure out all the possibilities."

"Listen," Curtis suggested, "I'm going to the morgue later today to get Dr. Singh's autopsy report. Why don't you meet me there and we can talk?"

Baldoni agreed and Curtis ended the call, then returned to Mr. Martinique's office. Archambault had continued the interview, and without Curtis in the room, had managed to get Martinique to open up regarding Kyle Wilson's business activities.

"The only bad mark on Kyle's record," Martinique was saying, "was one incident more than ten years ago when he aggressively promoted a certain segregated fund to a number of clients. The fund went under and a lot of people lost a lot of money."

"But," he insisted, "those types of funds are always a gamble. You never know for certain how they are going to work, so if you don't want to lose your money then you only invest what you can afford."

"Were there any threats made at that time?"

"Sorry, but I don't know. He was working at a private financial institution back then."

"Can you provide us with any contact information from that private firm?"

"Yes, it is on his resume. I'll have someone retrieve the contact info and provide it for you. Is there anything else gentlemen?" Martinique asked, specifically looking at Curtis.

"Over the course of the next few weeks, we'll probably be back a number of times." Curtis responded in a softer manner, "We'll need to interview the employees who worked closely with Kyle, so we'll need you to provide us with a list of their names and personal contact information. We'll also need the business records of what Kyle was working on over the past year."

"Those financial records are confidential information with our clients." Martinique began to protest but held any more words when he realized that Curtis was going to once more present the law as an over-riding factor. "Can I be assured that they will be treated as confidential unless required as evidence?"

"That's the way it always works." Archambault took the liberty of answering.

****

Curtis arrived at the morgue to find Baldoni already waiting with Singh, who was just completing the autopsy on the body of Kyle Wilson. Curtis motioned for Baldoni to come over to the hallway where they could talk freely.

Outside of the examination room, Curtis gave her a brief description of the crime scene from the previous night and then explained the conversation he had with Mei Liu regarding the similarities FIS had found between this murder and that of Ivan Malinkov.

"I know the Malinkov case has gone cold but give it to me with a bit more detail." Curtis asked hurriedly.

"It's basically a dead stop. We had re-interviewed every single witness, re-examined all the evidence from the crime scene several times, checked every business and personal financial transactions of everyone concerned, all electronic and mobile communications, everything. The case is so cold that it makes the artic feel like summer."

"The implications of these similarities are disturbing," Curtis said and then asked. "When is Boyle back from vacation?"

"He's supposed to arrive either today or tomorrow."

"I think we may need to get both teams in on this." Curtis spoke with a sense of urgency. "I'm going to speak with Stanforth and let him know we might have a potential serial on our hands. We're meeting in the Argo tomorrow morning. I want you there to sit in on the discussions." Baldoni agreed and they both went back into the examination room to consult with Singh.

Dr. Singh was speaking into the overhead microphone, the body on the metalized autopsy table with a downdraft ventilation unit that pulls most fumes away from the working space. He looked up at Curtis and Baldoni and asked, "You two working together?"

"I've asked Baldoni to be here because Mei Liu has found similarities between this murder and the killing of Ivan Malinkov." Curtis replied to Singh. "If this was done by the same killer, then I want to get Boyle's team involved right away."

"I see." Singh's voice sounded troubled. "Well, let me focus on this report first and then we can compare to the other case." He then went into the full autopsy report of Kyle Wilson.

"The left knee was severely damaged. I would say the killer used great force in swinging the crowbar. The iron bar hit directly on the Patella and split it in two. The blow ruptured the Articular Cartilage and displaced both the Medial and Lateral meniscus. Ligament damage is extreme, and the bottom of the Femur is deeply bruised."

"There is a bruise on the right elbow and on the right side of the victim's head, both probably caused when the victim fell after the blow on his knee. This would indicate that the body was most likely lying on its right side. The killer would have had to manipulate the body in order to perform the stab to the right side of the throat. This could easily have been done by grabbing the victim's head and turning it over."

"The killer then stabbed the throat with a deep thrust that cut the Carotid artery and the Jugular vein. The killer did not directly pull the knife out, but instead pulled it across the throat so that it severed the Trachea. Blood flow to and from the brain was immediately stopped and the victim would have died between 30 seconds to a minute later. He was probably unconscious within five to 10 seconds of the initial stab wound to the throat."

"As you saw in the FIS report, the blood sprayed from the stab wound on the right side of the neck toward the outer part of the sidewalk. The blood continued to flow from the slash across the neck and pooled all around the victim's body."

"Any opinions you would like to make?" Curtis asked.

Singh responded after thinking a moment, "I would say the person who committed this knew what they were doing. Not a professional, but someone that studied and planned their actions."

"What makes you say that Surat?" Baldoni asked.

"I don't believe a professional would try to slash someone's throat, especially at this time of year. They wouldn't take that chance, because most people are wearing scarfs and heavy coats that could prevent a clean stab or cut. Personally, I think this was committed by an amateur who thinks they are a professional. If it's the same killer as in the Malinkov case, then it would fit the MO."

"Thanks," Curtis said as he turned to leave.

"Oh, and one more thing," Singh quickly added, "the victim is probably either a homosexual or bi-sexual."

Curtis spun around with an inquiring look while Baldoni stood passively by and asked, "Damage in the rectum?"

"Yes, there is evidence that he was having anal sex. There are some older scar tissues so I would guess that he had been experiencing this lifestyle for some time."

Chapter Thirty-Three

Baldoni left the morgue and met Detective Archambault in the hospital parking lot. She got into his car and asked, "Hi Pierre, how's your leg?"

"A lot better than it was 10 months ago."

Detective Pierre Archambault was originally from Quebec City. To the objections of his parents, he had come to Toronto to attend York University, where he met his future wife. Her father was a retired policeman from the Toronto Police force, and he and Pierre had become more than just father and son-in-law, they became good friends as well. Pierre and his father-in-law spent many family dinners talking about police work, and through his father-in-law's guidance, Pierre eventually joined the force.

He had a solid, six-foot tall body with shaggy, toffee brown hair. His rounded face had a boyish appeal with full lips that seemed to be in a perpetual grin. Though he claimed to be a happily married man, he and Baldoni had developed a flirtatious friendship with each other.

"Is your wife insisting on less dangerous activities from now on?" she joked with him.

"Well, I always thought you were pretty safe." He said with a coy tease.

"Ha!" she retorted, "you wouldn't be able to handle it."

"Probably not," he smiled, "the wolf runner has far too many mysteries for me."

"Who told you about that?" she asked, wanting to know.

"Everyone knows about your sojourns at the zoo, Gina. Don't know who first reported it, maybe even the zoo security staff. A couple of those guys are pretty hot for you."

"Oh please, I'm nothing special." She glanced with an open gaze in his direction meeting his eyes and expecting a playful reply.

"Gina, don't you know," he adjusted his posture, angling his body toward her, "half the men in this city are smitten with you, the other half just haven't met you yet."

Her face brightened at this mockery of a compliment and she wondered if his playfulness was more than just flirtation, if there was any serious intent on his part, and she wondered if she also had any intent, "You want to come and run the wolves with me one day?" she shyly asked him.

Archambault raised a finger to his lips as if scratching an itch. He looked at her with eyes that smoldered with intensity. His hand slowly reached up and touched her hair, moved his fingers to softly caress the back of her ear, and then toward the back of her neck. She leaned forward, moving her body closer to his, letting him know she was willing, and wanting.

He slowly moved forward until the sound of her breathing became a roaring torrent in his brain and was right in front of him like a tornado. He kissed her gently on the lips and then raised his other hand, and as he touched her breast, a startled sigh came from deep within her. A sigh that comes from one whose anticipation of a touch builds to the point of heat, and when that touch finally happens, the heat is released like the ignition of a blowtorch.

She opened her lips slightly and her tongue gently emerged to taste his lips. He responded with his hand starting to caress her breast, probing under her opened coat for the buttons on her blouse and the edges of her bra. She raised her hand to hold his, to momentarily stop his passion and then she leaned back to stare into his eyes.

"So, are we going to interview the sister or are we going to a motel?" her question was almost a dare, but one in which she wanted all the implications to be answered.

A rogue voice inside his brain wanted to say yes, the possibilities laid between them like an open chasm that had no bottom, but then a saner voice of reason, or maybe the voice of guilt, demanded that he take a step back from the precipice of carnal realization, "If my wife ever found out, she would make the motorcycle accident seem like a minor injury. I think Boyle would probably break my neck as well."

They both looked at each other, and each of their eyes warned the other to back down from this threshold of potential, deadly sensations.

"I think I'm more afraid of what your wife would do to me." She gave a little laugh, one more of relief than humor. She liked Archambault, but they both knew that romances within the division, even only short trysts, sometimes ended with someone's resignation or someone's divorce.

He smiled at the knowledge of possibility, then leaned back in the driver's seat and put the car in gear. Without another word between them, they drove to the home of Rebecca Pinson, Kyle Wilson's only sibling.

****

Rebecca Pinson was in her late thirties and her body showed that she had definitely experienced motherhood and didn't lose the weight she had gained during her two pregnancies. She had long, dark, auburn hair that came down to the middle of her back and was un-kept since she had received the news of her brother's death. She was dressed in sweatpants and sweat top and had been grieving so much, her face was tear stained and pale. A policeman had come to inform her early in the morning and she had been crying most of the day. She was still quite distraught.

"Kyle was a wonderful man," she mumbled through her tears, "I was always able to count on him for anything. He was always there for me whenever I needed him. He even lent us the money to put a down payment on our home."

She broke down into big sobs and Archambault offered her a tissue box that was on the coffee table. She picked out four and brought them to her face. After more tears and a few deep breaths, she spoke about her brother again. "Kyle and my husband Joe play in the same hockey league together. Kyle belongs to a few leagues. He seemed to always be either working or playing hockey."

"He was a wonderful uncle, and he loved my children. He loved to take them on day trips to the zoo or the new aquarium and he always took them to the Exhibition in August." Rebecca's eyes welled up again and she broke into another series of heavy sobs and spoke between the tears, "Why? Why would someone do this?"

"Where is your husband Mrs. Pinson?" Archambault asked gently.

"He's in Kingston on a job. I think someone from the police has contacted him and he is supposed to be on his way home." She mumbled and then got excited, "Oh God, I hope he drives safely, he gets so anxious."

"Can I make you anything for you," Baldoni offered, "a cup of coffee or a tea. Maybe you would like a drink?"

"Joe and I don't have alcohol in the house," she spoke as if confessing. "We're not against it, we just don't want it in the house with the kids."

They waited as she slowly regained a small measure of composure, offering her tissues which built up into a little mountain on the sofa beside her. Neither Archambault nor Baldoni had brought out their digital recorder in respect for the grieving sister.

"Mrs. Pinson, I know that this is very difficult for you, but we need to ask you some questions." Archambault tried to be as delicate as possible.

She looked up with misty eyes and said, "I know, I'm so sorry, I'll try." And then she broke into a new cascade of weeping. Neither of the detectives said anything and could only try and sympathize with her pain. Both had numerous experiences dealing with people trying to cope with their grief. It was the bane of all police personnel to deliver bad news, and then try to comfort the despondent spouse or family while trying to also remain professional and distant.

As they sat and offered tissue after tissue, the front door to the house opened and in walked a burly man wearing construction overalls. Rebecca quickly stood and ran to him crying, "Oh Joe, why would someone do this to Kyle," and then she began to weep once more.

"Are you the detectives from the police force?" he asked them as he held his wife in his arms.

"Yes, I'm Detective Archambault and this is Detective Baldoni. We are very sorry for your loss."

"Listen, I'm going to take my wife upstairs and spend some time with her. You can wait if you like or you can come back a little later on. She and her brother were quite close, and we are going to need some private time for a bit. Would you mind?"

"No, of course," Baldoni agreed. "If I leave you my card, would you call us as soon as you can. We are going to need some information, and I know this will be difficult, but the sooner the better."

****

Baldoni and Archambault went out to the car and sat in an uncomfortable silence. Their flirtatious patter from earlier in the evening didn't seem appropriate after witnessing the amount of grief they had seen with Kyle's sister.

"I'd probably feel the same if it was one of my brothers," Baldoni quietly said after a while.

"You very close to them?" Archambault asked.

"Yeah, we're a very close family." Baldoni talked as she stared out the window, "We've had our problems, I guess all families do, and my brother Joseph was against my joining the police force, but he supported me none the less. How about you, any brothers or sisters?"

"Two sisters," Archambault replied, "but we're not very close. My family was against me coming to Toronto for school. They wanted me to go to Laval University in Quebec City or at least to McGill in Montreal, but neither had all the courses I wanted to take, so I came to Toronto and went to York. Met my wife and stayed here ever since."

"How did they feel about you becoming a cop?"

"They all hated it, especially being a Toronto cop. My father passed away three years ago, and my mother died six months later. I was the baby of the family and they were both in their late thirties when I was born. Both of my sisters are married to dedicated separatists and their husband's politics exclude anyone from outside of Quebec, especially authoritarian English police."

He then turned to look at her and asked her if she wanted to grab something to eat while they waited. They drove to a local dinner chatted about the case. Baldoni explained the autopsy report and didn't notice when two other dinners moved to a table on the other side of the restaurant. Archambault laughed and said, "Gina, keep your voice down."

"Ooops," she smiled, "I guess we should be using our bedroom voices."

He gave her a look that indicated his approval the flirtations were once again part of their banter. They talked for about an hour when Baldoni's phone rang. It was Joe Pinson suggesting that they should come back for the interview.

****

In the living room of the Pinson home, Joe and Rebecca sat on the sofa. "My kids are at my sister's place and they're going to stay there for the night." Joe told the detectives. "Please direct most of your questions to me and Rebecca will answer when she can. I'm sorry, but this is very upsetting for both of us, especially for her."

"Would you mind if we recorded the conversation," Archambault asked.

"Yeah, sure," Joe said.

Baldoni pulled out her digital recorder and began with the standard preliminary instructions. She then asked the basic questions about Kyle's family, their relationship with Kyle, their parents and any other relatives. What emerged was a description of a typical middle-class family, the parent's divorced, the two children staying with the mother, and a bond that grew between brother and sister. Archambault asked about Kyle's professional career, his social life, hobbies and other interests.

"Kyle was a regular guy, a good guy," Joe said, "he liked to travel, but the thing he liked to do most was play hockey. When he was younger, he belonged to three or four different leagues at the same time and there were occasions when he would play two games a night. As he got older, he had to cut down the amount of playing time and focus more on his career, but he still played in one league, the one that I'm in."

Archambault asked about the issue with the investment fund, "We were told by his current boss there was a segregated market fund through an investment company that went bust back in 2008. A lot of people apparently lost money."

"Oh man," Joe said with a grunt, "Kyle took a beating on that."

"He lost money?" Baldoni asked.

"No, he made a lot of money on commissions," Joe replied, "but he took it personally when the company went under and many of the clients he advised lost their savings. He was quite downhearted and felt responsible. He would have given all those people their money back out of his own pocket if he could have. He left the personal finance industry and came to work with me in construction for about a year, but construction really wasn't his thing. I think he just did it as some sort of penance. After a year, he applied with the Queen's Bank and has been there ever since."

"This problem with the investment company fund," Archambault queried, "was there ever any problems, confrontations, threats, anything that you might be aware of."

"Sure, there was." Joe said, "Some people lost their life savings. There were lots of problems, people tied their money up on one fund and then had nothing. And many of them blamed it on Kyle like it was his fault. A bunch of idiots some of them."

"We're there any confrontations or threats made?" Archambault asked again.

"I believe there were some, but Kyle wouldn't tell us about them." Rebecca spoke up this time, "Do you think one of those people did this?"

"We don't know, but this will be one of the lines of inquiry in our investigation." Archambault answered. "It was over ten years ago, so if anyone wanted revenge, they waited a long time. We'll be looking into the financial records of the transactions for that fund and make inquiries. Do you know if Kyle kept any records, journals, notes from that period?"

"You will have to check his apartment for those things." Joe said.

"There's one more thing I would like to ask you. It may be a delicate subject, so I want to take this slowly. Can we talk about your brother's sexual orientation?"

Rebecca looked up surprised, "How did you find out?" she asked.

"There was evidence when the autopsy was done." Baldoni answered.

Joe held on to Rebecca's hand and she sighed deeply, "My brother was bisexual, but for the past few years he's been in a relationship with someone."

"What was his partner's name?" Baldoni asked.

"His name is David."

"Your brother intended to hide this from his friends and work. Did he not want to come out?"

"We knew, Joe and I, but we're probably the only ones he confided in." She stopped as if trying the gather the right words to say, "Kyle loved hockey. He loved to play hockey. It was a passion for him. If he had come out as being gay, things would have changed, there would have been whispers behind his back in the dressing room, other players would move away from where he sat, even treat him differently on the ice. Kyle didn't want that, he didn't want people treating him differently, he just wanted to be one of the guys. It was pretty much the same at work, he wanted to be part of the 'old boys' network."

"He knew the way people treated him would change," Joe stepped in at this point, "both at work and on the hockey rink, and amongst friends. He just wanted to be himself without any preconceived attitudes about what or who he was. He kept quiet about it, and sometimes he would ask a woman out to a company party, and sometimes he even hired escorts just so he could keep up the ruse of being one of the guys."

"So, Kyle kept this secret from almost everyone he knew." Archambault wanted to clarify as he knew this could be a crucial point in the investigation.

"My brother was a wonderful person," Rebecca insisted, "however, no matter how much we claim to have an open society, there are still a lot of closed minds out there."

"Do you have David's contact information?" Baldoni asked.

Joe went to the small table in the hallway that held a landline phone. He opened a drawer and pulled out a little brown telephone book. "David Ouspeski," he said, and gave them the telephone number. "He lives in Kensington Market, the second floor of a house, I think. Never been there myself. I don't really go downtown much anymore."

Archambault and Baldoni thanked Joe and Rebecca for their cooperation and explained that they would be back with more questions in the next few days. They went back to the car and before opening the doors, looked across the roof of the car to each other. They stood there wondering what awaited them in the car, each of their eyes transfixed on the other. Archambault looked down and Baldoni knew the moment had passed, that there would only be playful, flirtatious talk between them.

Chapter Thirty-Four

The Wheat Sheaf Tavern, on the southwest corner of King Street West and Bathurst Street, was one of the oldest taverns in Toronto. It opened in 1849 and was the main gathering spot for British soldiers who resided in Fort York, about 500 yards to the south. Its most striking feature is the Mansard roof, which was a popular architectural style of the British Empire in the nineteenth century.

Although the interior had been often renovated to accommodate changes in social and technological advancement throughout its long history, the original brick exterior and chimney provided a glimpse into the early days of the city.

The outdoor patio had been closed for the season and the row of windows on the east side of the building facing Bathurst Street do not have a clear view of the alleyway on the east side of the Sly Fox pub. The windows on the second floor belonged to offices that would have been empty when the murder occurred, and the windows of the third-floor rented rooms have their blinds almost permanently drawn. Curtis did not expect to find any witness that would have seen the crime take place.

The Wheat Sheaf was well known as a hub for sports fans, and anyone in the bar that night was probably watching the Toronto-Edmonton hockey game which didn't start until after nine as the game was played in Edmonton. However, what interested Curtis was the 360-degree panoramic viewing camera that had been installed above the front door by the new owners of the tavern.

The Wheat Sheaf camera was the latest technology in video surveillance, not because it could capture a 360-degree view, but on account of it possessing the 'de-warping algorithm' that would correct the distortion produced by the over-lapping, high density, multiple lenses and output a high resolution flat image in which you could zoom in and view the detail of any specific direction.

Amal Mirwani, the civilian researcher on Curtis' homicide team, had called the Wheat Sheaf immediately following the meeting in the Argo. After a brief conversation, he learned the management at the Wheat Sheaf did not use a private company to manage the recordings. Everything was digitally recorded and stored on a computer in a second-floor office. The manager agreed to transfer all the recordings for the entire week to a USB stick and would have it ready for pick up within the hour.

Curtis entered the Wheat Sheaf just after six o'clock in the evening. He came straight from the morgue and wanted to pick up the USB stick and go home. As he entered the bar, he noticed the plethora of TVs on every wall, varying in size and all showing sporting events; hockey, basketball, football, golf, tennis, whatever was in action.

He went to the stand-up bar and was greeted by a middle aged, gruffy looking man with a horseshoe moustache. "I'm looking for Mr. Walton," he said as he showed his police credentials.

"He's upstairs in the office. I'll ring him for you," the bartender picked up an old rotary style phone and dialed the number zero. Curtis was amused at the reclamation of older technology and transformed for the simple action of an intercom devise. "Are you the guy that is coming for the video surveillance file?" the bartender asked him.

"Yes, that's what I'm here for."

"Go through that door," the bartender instructed Curtis, "there's a stairway on your left and the first door to the right at the top of the stairs is the main office. Bruce is in there."

"Thank you." Curtis turned to go.

"Can I get you anything?" the bartender asked. "Always happy to take care of someone on the finest force on the planet."

"Thank you, no." Curtis replied and wondered if the man truly meant what he said or whether he was just trying to gain favor. There had been numerous times where people showed an obvious distaste for the police in Curtis' presence, and he had learned to steel his emotions like unbendable iron bars.

Many people disliked the police because the only things they ever heard in the media was the violence, or the mistakes, and the only time most of the general population had to deal with the police was when they were being given a ticket.

However, there were the odd times when someone would walk up to him at a coffee shop and request that they buy his coffee, or when someone would greet him on the street and wish him a 'Good morning officer', and once in a while, like this bartender, let him know the police were appreciated for the job they do.

At the top of the stairs, he turned right and into the open door of the office. Bruce Walton wheeled his chair around and stood up, "Detective Curtis I presume," he said as if his jest was something original, and he extended his hand to Curtis.

"Sergeant Detective." Curtis corrected him, "And you presumed right."

"Ah, yes." Walton contrived to retreat from his attempt at familiarity. "I have the USB stick here in my desk," and then he thought to add, "would you like to see how our system works?"

"I only have a few moments," Curtis explained, "there is a murder case that needs to be investigated."

"It will only take a few moments." Walton seemed enthusiastic about his equipment and he offered Curtis a chair. He explained why the owners had decided to get the latest in security technology and how the camera system worked. He told Curtis that there were four cameras in total, one at the front door, two in the bar itself and one at the backdoor. He showed how all four cameras could be displayed on screen simultaneously and synchronized to the exact time. In this way, he could see everything that was happening inside or outside the bar in real time. He then started to show Curtis how the replay functions could be set to specific times by entering the required time stamp into a particular data window, and the many features for zoom and navigation of the 360-degree recordings.

Curtis cut him off before Walton could go any further and excused himself by saying it was necessary for him to get back to headquarters with the USB stick.

"Yes, of course," Walton apologized, "I kinda get carried away with my toys."

"No problem, however, I would like one of my team members to come here and sit with you tomorrow. You can show them all the tools this program has to offer and perhaps you could let them view the surveillance recordings. You spoke with him on the phone earlier, Mr. Mirwani."

"Sure," Walton said, "be happy to. I'm usually here by ten, does he want to come earlier?"

"Is eight too early for you? It's a murder investigation so we'll need the information as soon as possible."

"No problem. Does he drink coffee?" Walton asked.

"Not sure," Curtis replied, "but he'll bring whatever he needs. Appreciate your cooperation Mr. Walton."

"The cops have always done good by me," Walton stated, "in this business, there's always the potential for trouble, either drunks, fights, internal theft, and sometimes dealers using the bar for business. I've had to call the cops on a number of occasions. They've always been quick, respectful and forthright. As far as I'm concerned, the police force is tax money well spent."

"Thank you," Curtis replied with genuine sincerity.

Early the next morning, Amal Mirwani arrived at the Wheat Sheaf and found Bruce Walton waiting for him at the front door. "The bar doesn't open until eleven o'clock," he told Mirwani, "so I figured I'd wait for you here."

He led him upstairs to the office where he had a selection of croissants and muffins, coffee and tea in portable containers sitting on the desk. "Help yourself," he told him.

They reviewed the security video from front doorway camera for Tuesday evening. The 360-camera clearly showed the Sly Fox on the opposite corner of the intersection and the alleyway beside the pub. Just after midnight, the video showed Kyle Wilson emerging from the pub and walking east along King Street. He walked close to the wall of the building and held his hand out a few times to steady himself. He stopped just as he passed the corner of the building, where the entrance to the alley was, and they saw him look into the alleyway. A figure stepped forward from the shadows and they watched as the killer swung the crowbar and hit Kyle on his left knee. Kyle fell sideways to the sidewalk and then the killer got down on one knee beside him, turned his head and stabbed him in the throat. The killer immediately got up and turned down into the alleyway. A few seconds later, they could see the killer come out of the back alleyway on Bathurst and turn north.

"Jesus," Walton said with a heavy sigh.

"Can you show me some of the zoom and orientation directional tools?" Mirwani asked. "I would also like to spend a few hours in private if you don't mind. Lastly, I have to insist that you to keep all of this confidential. Don't reveal any of the details to your staff or anyone else. We may need to question people and keeping the details out of the public realm allows us to verify if they are telling the truth."

Walton agreed and began to show Mirwani the various tools within the program for manipulating the video. When Mirwani was confident he had mastered the program tools, he thanked Walton who then left the office. Mirwani went to work, reviewing the video over and over, zooming in at certain spots, changing the orientation of the view at other times and recording all of his inspection with the software's internal recording system.

He watched as a number of people started milling about Kyle, one man bending down to see if he was okay and then going into the alley. Another man picked up the crowbar, looked at it and passed it to another man who also inspected it. Mirwani took note that the second man was not wearing gloves so his fingerprints would be on the crowbar. He knew FIS would have to identify that person to eliminate their prints, so he changed the orientation of the video to the point where the man came out of the pub and zoomed in to clearly see his face. He took a screen capture of the man's face and saved it in the files he was creating.

It was mid-afternoon by the time Mirwani finished his examination of the video, downloaded all of his files onto another USB stick, and thanked Mr. Walton for his time. He reminded Walton once more that he will need to keep this surveillance file available for the police and that everything he had seen was confidential. He left knowing that Archambault will want to review his files with him well into the evening.

Chapter Thirty-Five

Boyle got off the plane at Toronto's Pearson International airport in the late afternoon and took a cab all the way home. It had been an eleven-hour flight from Greece with a stopover in Lisbon, and he was tired. He dropped his bags onto his living room floor and thought about taking a shower right away, but hesitated and decided to call Baldoni first.

"Hey Boss, how was Greece?" the pleasure of his return was obvious in her voice.

"It was wonderful," he said as the tiredness began to truly sink in, "it is always wonderful when you visit your homeland. The sun, the food, the wine, all fantastic."

"How's Theo?"

"We had a wonderful time together. I think this trip bonded us even closer than before."

"Did you bring anything back for Orestes?"

"I brought him some authentic Greek olive oil. He'll appreciate that."

"Are you coming back into the office tomorrow?" Baldoni inquired.

"Maybe. Anything I need to know about?"

"We might have a new development in the Malinkov investigation." She told him, and after a moment of silence from his end, she went on to explain the murder of Kyle Wilson and the similarities FIS found between the crime scenes of the two cases. "Curtis is calling for his team to meet in the Argo tomorrow morning and wants me to attend."

"I'll be there too." Boyle said grimly, "I also want Donna Chang in the meeting as well."

Baldoni said, "I'll call Curtis to let him know that your back in town and that you also want Donna in the meeting."

****

Theo had moved into his father's home after he had finished the semester at school. Boyle had convinced him to complete the last two months in order to get the university credits that could be used another time. All that summer Theo had been working at the Parthenon, but he was still in a quandary about what he wanted to do with his life.

Boyle had taken Theo to Greece for a vacation at the end of October and stretched it into November, but Theo was determined to stay longer, and to travel through Europe. Boyle thought about the times he had spent travelling as a youth and he wished he could have joined his son on this quest. He pictured his son as Odysseus, roaming the Adriatic, experiencing adventures and facing perils.

Throughout the whole summer, Theo's mother was supportive of her son's needs, but in private she berated Boyle for putting silly thoughts into his head. Boyle took the mauling from his ex-wife knowing that as long as his son was fine, then any castigation from her was a nuisance to be temporarily endured.

The same night Boyle arrived back in Toronto, the Teacher met Christine at the Tulip Restaurant.

****

The Tulip was a well-known secret within the Beaches community. A diner style restaurant with deep red cushioned booths, and 1950s' style Formica tables that were probably installed when Buddy Holly and Elvis were in their heyday.

The Teacher and Christine had dinner and walked to the Beach Cinemas for the latest 'Galaxy Battle' movie. He had parked his car in the cinema parking lot earlier on and had paid with cash. Later that night, he would take the parking ticket and throw it in the garbage so there would be no physical evidence that he had attended the movies on Wednesday night.

He purchased two tickets and paid cash once more. There would be no record of their attendance at the theatre. He believed the police would never suspect him for they would find no evidence that would point in his direction. If they did inquire, it would probably be many months later and he would have the parking ticket and the ticket stubs showing they had attended the later show on the Tuesday evening. He could confidently state he was at the movies on the night of the murder, and if they ever needed to question Christine, she would assume that they went to the movie on the Tuesday night, believing the proof of his tickets.

He had taken Christine to the movies almost every week, and always on different nights of the week. He did this purposely so that months later, she would be unable to remember what day they actually went.

The Teacher had planned his hunt with meticulous care. He developed the hunting blind that would serve as his alibi; stalked his prey to its home range; contrived his method to trap and kill his prey; prepared his weapons; and then patiently waited for the right moment.

His only regret was the inability to hang any mementos on his walls for display or exhibition. His trophy would be confined to his own conscious will, one that he could recall at any time to drive his passions, to validate his dominance and to prove his superiority.

Chapter Thirty-Six

The next morning, the Argo was filled to capacity with most of Curtis' team, Mie Liu from FIS, Dr. Singh, plus Boyle and Donna Chang. Boyle was sitting beside Curtis and being briefed on the murder of Kyle Wilson when Baldoni walked into the Argo. Boyle looked at her with a startled surprise, "What did you do!"

Gina had gotten a short, Pixie style hair cut while Boyle was on vacation in Greece. Everyone at headquarters had seen it, made their comments and moved on, but this was the first time Boyle had seen her since he had left a month ago.

"It was getting in the way when I was pumping weights and doing my cardio," Baldoni said, "it was Orestes who suggested I get it done like this."

Boyle looked at her with wonderment, "You went to the Parthenon to get Orestes' opinion?"

"Nope, I was there for dinner and we got into talking. He suggested a Pixie cut and showed me a picture of Athena from a modern book of Greek mythology."

Still wide-eyed Boyle said. "You went to the Parthenon without me?"

She answered sarcastically, "You were in Greece. What'd you expect me to do, call for permission to have dinner with your drinking buddy."

Boyle laughed out loud and then spoke as he chuckled. "I think it looks great, but I'm going to talk with Orestes about cavorting with my detectives behind my back."

Curtis waited for Archambault to arrive and then asked everyone to settle down. He explained that Amal would not be attending this meeting as he was at the Wheat Sheaf Tavern using their security software to review the video of their cameras. He stated that Boyle, Baldoni and Donna Chang were attending the meeting, as he wanted them involved in the investigation since it was noted that there was a possible forensic link between the Kyle Wilson murder and the Ivan Malinkov investigation. He then asked Archambault to begin with a review of what was known about the murder victim.

Archambault opened his laptop and took control of the viewing screen. He projected a photograph of Kyle Wilson that his sister Rebecca had provided. "The victim, Kyle Wilson, was a financial analyst and advisor at the King Street branch of the Queen's Bank of Canada. The offices for this branch are two blocks east of the Sly Fox pub. Kyle had been with the bank for a little over eleven years: four and a half years at the King Street branch, five years at the branch in the Beaches, one year at the Yonge Street branch and his first year at the branch on St. Clair Avenue. He had spent one year working in construction with his brother-in-law and the previous four years at the Progressive Investment Corporation."

"According to his sister and brother-in-law, he was passionate about hockey, played in a number of leagues when he was younger and was quite competitive. His boss, stated he was just as competitive in business."

"It was reported by Dr. Singh that he may have been homosexual or had bi-sexual relationships, and this was confirmed by his sister. However, this was a well-kept secret from his friends and his business associates. He even went so far as to hire escorts for public events to keep up the appearance that he was a heterosexual male."

"Could be a blackmail situation, or maybe even a star-crossed lover." Boyle suggested.

"His sister stated he was in a relationship for the past four years with a man named David Ouspeski," Baldoni answered. "She seemed to think it was a solid relationship and that Kyle didn't play the field as he wanted to keep his gay side secret."

"Still, we'll need to check out that angle." Curtis said, "Anything else Pierre?"

"Yes, he was working for the Progressive Investment Corporation during the financial crash back in 2008. The funds he was actively promoting collapsed during that crash. Apparently, some of his clients lost a lot of money. Someone could have blamed their misfortunes on him and wanted revenge." Archambault concluded his report.

Curtis looked up at the group. "Ari, can we have Donna start checking his bank records. Amal can help her out when he's finished with the Wheat Sheaf security tapes. I want to start off with the usual stuff; find out if he was a gambler, whether he was a recreational drug user, if he had any vices that would cause him to be a target."

"Blackmail is a possibility, especially if he was working hard to keep his sexuality a secret. The financial fund is also a possibility. When Amal comes back, I'm going to have him search for the names of the people who lost money." He turned to his constables, "Katherine and Owen, I want to start interviewing them right away."

Boyle chimed in and told Curtis, "I would like Donna to check if there are any other connections between the two cases." He then turned to Donna Chang, "I also want you to start looking back on other cold cases that we have on file. Check to see if any part of the MO from these cases show up anywhere else."

"You think we have a serial?" Curtis asked him surreptitiously.

"Don't want to suggest that yet, but the forensics have come up with similarities in the way the weapons were cleaned before the murders took place. However, I would also like to offer another fact for consideration, both murders were very brutal. They weren't simple shoot and run killings. They don't seem to be domestic or family related, or murders of passion or anger. There were no witnesses at either crime scene, and they both seemed to have been intricately planned. There are too many coincidences for me to call them un-related. I want to go back into the cold cases and see if there are any other coincidences."

Boyle then continued, "Check his bank records and financial investments for any unusual deposits or withdrawals. Especially check into the gambling aspect. Malinkov gambled periodically and had a number of business deals that may not have been completely ethical. I want to see any type of business activity which might have linked him with Malinkov, or with any other persons of interest in the Malinkov case."

Curtis then asked Dr. Singh to deliver the results of the autopsy. Singh took over the viewing screen with his laptop and projected a line drawing image of a male. He went on to explain the injuries to the body. He started with the injury to the knee and explained that the injury was so severe that it would have incapacitated the victim and sent him into immediate shock. He then pointed to the areas of bruising on the right elbow and right side of the head, which occurred when the victim fell to the sidewalk. The last thing he described was the stab wound to the right side of the throat and the slash across the front of the throat.

"What did you find in the toxicology analysis?" Curtis asked.

"He had a blood alcohol content reading of zero point sixteen." Singh projected an examiner's form with facts and figures, "This was enough to have dulled his senses so that he may have staggered a little as he walked. His reaction time to any attack would have been greatly affected."

"We also found a significant level of caffeine, sugar and Taurine in his system. This would indicate that he drank a lot of those energy drinks. If he played as much hockey as you state, then he probably used the energy drinks to keep him going."

"There was no indication of any recent drug use in his system. Lastly, as Detective Archambault has stated, the victim was either homosexual or at least he was bi-sexual. The wear and tear to the rectum indicates that there was a regular amount of anal sex performed."

Owen Garrison scrunched up his face and said, "I hate it when you use terms like 'wear and tear' when talking about the rectum. It makes me squirm in my seat."

Constable Evanko chuckled slightly at the comment but everyone else had no reaction. They had all become inured to the descriptions of injuries and found no humor in Garrison's attempt at a joke.

Ignoring the comment, Curtis asked Singh if he had anything further to report.

"Just one thing," Singh spoke up, "the contents of his stomach were consistent with the food served at the Sly Fox pub. It had been mostly digested so I would guess he had dinner in the pub right after work and was killed about four or five hours later. That's a long time to spend in a pub. There must have been many witnesses who would have seen him there."

"Thank you, Dr. Singh, he was probably watching the hockey game." Curtis said, and then addressed the group, "If you have any questions, save them for later. I want to get through all of this as quickly as possible." He then called upon Mei Liu to present the forensics report.

Mei Liu took over the main viewing screen with her laptop. She pulled up a drawing of the crime scene, showing the intersection of King and Bathurst Street. The Sly Fox pub was indicated as a square box on the northeast corner. The alleyway on the east side of the pub that joined to the alleyway on the north side of pub were shaded to highlight them.

There was a silhouette outline of a person on the sidewalk in front of the alleyway on the east side of the pub, showing its left arm outstretched and its right arm by its side. Most of the crime scene drawing was in black and white, but the blood was drawn in red to indicate its location. There was a circular portion of red around the head and shoulders, and a projection of red that started from the right side of the neck and reached across the sidewalk to the curb of the street.

"The victim was attacked at the corner of the pub in front of the alleyway. From the position of the body, we believe the killer came from the alleyway and struck the victim on the knee, then dropped the crowbar, bent down and stabbed him in the neck. The killer then ran northward along the alleyway, turned at the corner where the one alleyway meets the other, and went westward along the back alleyway to Bathurst Street."

"We found the murder weapon, a knife, beside one of the pub's waste bins. The knife itself was a thick handled steak knife that you could find in any of the better steak house restaurants. It once had a serrated blade but it had been grinded down so that the serrated edges had been smoothed into a straight edged blade."

"I spoke to Dr. Singh about this aspect and we agreed that to perform a killing in this manner, you needed a sharpened straight edge blade, first to penetrate the neck cleanly and deeply to ensure you have cut the main arteries, and then to be able to pull the knife across the neck. If the knife had serrated edges, it would have been difficult to cut across the neck and would have caused severe ripping of skin and tissue. The result would cause the killer to stop, pull, stop, pull and probably cause the spay of blood to go in all directions, potentially covering the killer in blood."

"Why would they go to this extent to sharpen a steak knife? Why not simply buy one that already had a straight edge?" Baldoni asked.

"To obtain a heavy, straight edge blade that was short enough to cut and slice," Mie Liu replied, "you would most likely have to select it from a limited number of hunting knifes. A regular kitchen knife would be too long to use, a smaller kitchen knife would be short enough, but the blade would need to be sharpened and end up too thin. Therefore, the hunting knife would be the best option. There are a limited number of stores that sell this type of product. If the killer wanted to ensure the knife could not be traced back to them, they

232

could purchase or steal the appropriate-sized steak knife and fashion it to their needs."

"The knife was found in the back alleyway," Boyle remarked, "did we check the security camera system of the pub? Do they have cameras in the alleyways?"

Archambault spoke up to answer Boyle's question. "We've obtained all the security video from the pub. The cameras are strictly internal, covering the bar, cash register and doorway. I asked them about cameras in the alleyway and the manager stated they didn't bother to install any back there. To paraphrase what he said, 'What would they record, how many rats are eating our garbage. Who's going to waste money on a security system for that?'"

"What else do you have Mie Liu?" Curtis interjected to keep the meeting moving forward.

"The blood on the knife matched the blood of the victim. We examined both the knife and the crowbar and discovered traces of both ammonia and Pine Sol. These traces were found in the handle of the knife where the blade is inserted into the shaft, and a small trace in the crook between the prongs of the crowbar. When we discovered these solvents, I immediately called Curtis to inform him of the similarities with the Malinkov case."

"There were no fingerprints on the knife, but the crowbar does have one full set of prints, however there is nothing in our database that matches them."

Archambault spoke up at this last comment, "There were a number of people milling around the body when the police arrived on the scene. Any one of those people could have handled the crowbar. I'll need to check the list of people interviewed and then have their fingerprints taken to see if we have a match with one of them."

"I want that done right away," Curtis said with immediacy. "Anything else Mei Liu?"

"We found footsteps in the alleyway, quite a few of them. There are a number of different shoe sizes and boot treads. However, there were only two sets of footprints that lead from the entrance on King Street and exited on Bathurst Street. We have complete statistics on these footprints and we're in the process of identifying the maker of the boots. There was also a splash of vomit just a few feet down the alleyway. I believe Archambault has identified one of the witnesses who admitted vomiting after checking the body."

"Okay people, good meeting. Have you got anything to add Ari?" Curtis asked him.

"I don't have anything at the moment. I'll want to review the forensics with Mei Liu later on and talk to Dr. Singh as well. However, I think we need to obtain whatever security footage we can get from the surrounding businesses. You mentioned that Amal was at the Wheat Sheaf going over their videos. There are stores across the street from the Sly Fox and on Bathurst Street across from the alleyway on the north side. I'd like to get on that right away."

"You and I can start on that after the meeting." Curtis began listing the priorities for everyone, "First I'll have to go see Margaret Hinds and discuss the press release. While I'm with her, you can stay here and meet with Mei Liu and Dr. Singh."

He turned to Archambault, "Pierre, you and Katherine need to go back to the Queen's Bank branch on King Street and start the interview process of the victim's business associates. Mr. Martinique is supposed to set up a room for you to use. Also, you need to do a search of Kyle's office. You do the interviews while Katherine goes through the paperwork of the business transactions."

Curtis then turned to face Baldoni, "Gina, Amal has arranged for some of Kyle's friends to come to the 52 Division station. We retrieved names and phone numbers from his cell phone. You and Owen can start the interviewing process. Donna, before you start the research into other cold cases for Boyle, I'd like you to call the rest of names on the list that Amal prepared. He's marked off whom he has contacted already. Have the rest of them come to the 52 Division station and impress upon them that they need to be there today."

"Ari, once we've gone to the businesses in the immediate area, I want you and I to go visit this David Ouspeski. He's Kyle's boyfriend. The others are all going to be busy and I want your help in this interview. I'm guessing that it's going to be interesting."

****

When the meeting ended, Curtis first went to Inspector Dylan Stanforth's office. He told him the details of the murder scene and then explained the discovery by FIS of the similarities between this murder and the Ivan Malinkov case.

Stanforth began to look pensive and spoke in a somber voice, "If this turns out to be a serial, then I want as many resources on it as possible. I don't like the fact that Boyle hasn't solved the Malinkov investigation yet, which is now designated cold. I don't think we'll ever be able to solve it unless we get a deathbed confession. But if this is a serial, then the brutality of the crimes will be a media sensation. I don't want that to happen again, we've been put through the blender by the media enough in the past few years."

"There isn't much to go on so far," Curtis admitted, "if it's the same killer then they don't leave much, if anything behind, and that includes witnesses. We're going to see what we can find from the surveillance cameras of all the nearby stores and we're starting the interview process with his friends and business associates…and his boyfriend."

Stanforth looked up at the ceiling as if he could see through it to the sky, "As of now, both of your teams are assigned to this case. Solve this Curtis. You and Boyle solve this before we all get roasted by the fucking media."

"And because we don't want any more killings," Curtis added to the reasons.

****

Margaret Hinds was sitting in her office when Curtis walked in. He liked her office with its strategically placed green plants, framed front-page headlines whenever a policeman was accommodated for bravery or saved a life, and the coffee machine which always had a freshly brewed pot. Curtis knew she had more visitors to her office than the Mayor of Toronto.

"I read the e-mail about the Wilson case," she started right away. She knew Curtis well and knew his penchant for directness and alacrity. "A banker knocked off on King Street. The press is already going hog wild on this one."

"Yeah, I've seen the morning papers." Curtis sighed heavily, "There isn't going to be any quick arrests from what we've investigated so far."

"Am I going to have as many problems with this as I had with the Malinkov case last year?" she asked with a true sense of concern in her voice.

Curtis didn't say anything at first. His head leaned forward until his chin rested on his chest and he closed his eyes while he tried to decide what he should tell her. After a moment, he came to the decision that she could help with the investigation through the media, if it was done properly.

Before he spoke, she asked, "What is it you're going to tell me?"

"We think there's a connection between the Malinkov murder and this one. It might even be the same killer."

"Oh Christ!" she swore, "has any of this gotten out yet?"

"No, and we want to keep it that way for now. The killer thinks they got away cleanly, so they might not be afraid of any investigation. If they know we are linking the two cases, they will probably go under and take any leads with them."

"Okay, how are we going to handle this?" she asked.

"I want to treat it like we do any other murder. State the facts but leave out the small details that link the two cases together. I also want to get public assistance as soon as possible. We want to ask for anyone to come forward that may have been driving in that area at the time of the murder and especially if they had a dashboard camera. We also want to know if anyone noticed anything from the condo across the street. I've got Stanforth's assurance that I can have any resources I need and I'm going to start with a canvas of every apartment in the condo, but it would help if we were forewarning them that we need their assistance through the media."

"I've got a press conference set for one o'clock. I'll have a statement written up for you," she said.

"Can you make it for two o'clock?" Curtis requested, "Boyle and I are going down to King and Bathurst to check for security camera videos from the local businesses. I'll be back here for the press conference and then I'm off to interview some people that Kyle was involved with."

Chapter Thirty-Seven

Before he left the Queen's Bank offices the previous day, Detective Archambault had insisted Mr. Martinique ensure Kyle Wilson's office was locked and that no one was allowed entry. He reminded Martinique that this was a murder investigation and Kyle's office would need to be searched for any clues that might point to potential suspects. When Martinique had locked the door, Archambault had placed a red tape seal over the handle and lock. He told Martinique that if anyone entered the office without prior approval from the police, there could be potential charges for tampering of evidence.

When he and Constable Evanko arrived on Thursday after the meeting in the Argo, the Queen's Bank financial division offices had been decorated with memorial flowers and the doorframe of Kyle's office was covered with cards and letters addressed to Kyle. Someone had also placed a hockey stick in front of the door as a tribute.

Archambault removed the tape and Martinique unlocked the door. Archambault then told him he and Constable Evanko would go through Kyle's office and prepare a list of anything that was required to be removed for evidence, a copy of which would be given to Martinique after their search. He invited Martinique to stay and watch if he so wished, but Martinique politely thanked him and said he had other business to attend.

The office was typical of what you would find in most modern financial institutions. It was the first in a series of offices with glass walls that were frosted halfway up from the floor. They began their search by going through the two drawers of Kyle's desk. The top drawer contained the usual assortment of office supplies; pens, a stapler, post-it notes, paper clips and other sundries.

The larger bottom drawer contained a variety of papers, mostly outdated blank forms that were now computerized. They found a box of tissue paper and a laminated calendar which listed the schedule of all Toronto Maple Leafs hockey games for the current season. There were also two used, decorated notebooks, evidenced by the creased side bindings and the elephant eared corners of some pages. The notebooks were full of handwriting which Archambault presumed was Kyle's. Both of these notebooks were placed in an evidence bag. His laptop computer would also be taken and listed in the evidence log.

A small bookshelf on the wall behind the desk contained a number of books about financial planning and advisories, a volume of the policies and procedures for the Queen's Bank of Canada, two books on business psychology and one large tome on the history of the National Hockey League. This appeared to be the most well used book on the shelf. On the top shelf of the bookcase stood a family photo of Kyle's sister Rebecca, her husband Joe and his niece and nephew. There were also individual photos of the two children.

When they completed the search of the office, Archambault informed Mr. Martinique that he would begin interviews of the office staff in the boardroom at the end of the hall, while Constable Evanko would stay in Kyle's office and begin to review the files on his computer and whatever files Martinique had retrieved for them to inspect.

As the interviews of Kyle's co-workers progressed, it became very clear to Archambault that Kyle was well liked and held in high regard by those who had worked closely with him. They told stories about Kyle's involvement in office social events, his enduring enthusiasm for the Maple Leafs hockey team, his devotion to playing the game as often as he could, his infectious high spirits, his good sense of humor, and his general harmonious temperament.

Archambault was dubious of all the accolades and believed that in some instances, it was a case of not wanting to speak ill of the dead. However, the sincerity of some of those interviewed, and the pure sadness that showed on some of their faces, painted a picture of a man that was very well liked, if not loved.

Justin Morgan was an associate of Kyle's and he assisted Constable Evanko, explaining the processes of setting up financial accounts for clients and the different types of investment options that were offered. Justin showed Evanko a series of charts that would be used to advise a client based on their personal preferences for either conservative investments, balanced or high growth.

As they discussed the type of work Kyle did, Evanko noted a sense of something that could be described as 'veneration' when Justin spoke about Kyle's abilities to achieve the highest ratings in customer service. When she asked how Kyle managed to be so successful, Justin angled his body closer to her in an obvious gesture that wanted to ensure no one else could hear.

"Kyle had this way about him," Justin spoke with a tone of admiration, "people trusted him, usually right from the first meeting. He was very amiable, always had a smile that seemed to encompass his whole face. When he looked at you, it was as if you were looking into the eyes of your most trusted friend, or your beloved father. Hard to really describe, but he wasn't disingenuous. He honestly wanted to do what was right for his clients."

"You make it sound like he was Saint Kyle of the markets," Evanko said with comedic irony.

Justin was taken aback by this remark, and it was clear from the look on his face that he found the remark offensive.

"Sorry," Evanko said with a sense of apprehension, "I didn't mean to be so callous or insensitive."

Justin looked away toward the other offices and then asked with indifference, "Would you like a coffee or a tea? I'm going to get one for myself."

She accepted the offer and hoped her remark would be forgiven and that Justin continued with his guidance in the paperwork that needed to be reviewed. When he returned with two cups and sat down once more, she turned to him and said, "I apologize for my attempt at humor. Was Kyle a friend as well as an associate?"

"Yes," Justin blinked away the mist in his eyes, "we often went to the Sly Fox together after work, with a couple of others. I was at the Sly Fox with him on Tuesday night. I was probably the last person he knew to see him alive." Justin reached for a tissue and turned away from Evanko to blow his nose. "Excuse me," he apologized, "it still hasn't sunk in that he won't be back in the office tomorrow, or ever. Kyle was one of those people you just felt good to be with. He seemed to have a positivity about him that made you want to be his friend."

With the ice broken, they continued to review the history of investments Kyle had set up for his clients. As the review progressed, Evanko was impressed that each client seemed to have made the right decision based on

Kyle's advice. She had the wistful feeling that wished she had also come to him for advice for her own money.

****

The 52 Division station was located near the heart of the city on Dundas Street near University Avenue. It was one of the older stations of the Police Force and had a public parking facility on the street to the west of the station. This made it an ideal spot for interviews during investigations because of its locality to the subway on University and because it was central to the downtown core of businesses and residences. The station was also near the core of Toronto's major medical district located on University Avenue; which included Toronto General Hospital, Mount Sinai hospital, the Princess Margaret Cancer Centre, and the world-renowned Hospital for Sick Children.

Detective Baldoni and Constable Garrison had set up in two interview rooms on the first floor of the station, just inside the main reception area. There were several people to be interviewed. Only one of them was female and her name had been provided by Kyle's brother-in-law, Joe Pinson.

Five of Kyle's friends were teammates he played hockey with and one was a friend he had stayed in touch with from high school. Peter McDougal was one of Kyle's teammates. A short, robust man with slick backed black hair. He had known Kyle for twelve years and had played with him in different leagues, including the expensive summer leagues that maintained the arenas all year long. They had become friends because both were highly competitive, talented players. They both also worked in the financial industry, Peter with a competitive bank.

Baldoni started the interview asking the basic questions of how Peter had met Kyle, how often they played games, when they were played and where. Peter explained that the league played games in the evenings and on weekends as most members of the league worked day jobs. There were occasional games in the very early mornings prior to work, but these were usually only pick-up games not affiliated with any league.

"Can you give me a description of what Kyle was like?" Baldoni asked.

"He was ruthless," Peter stated with a sense of caution. "He put his heart into every game. You'd think he was born with skates on the way he took it so

240

seriously. He wanted to win every shift he was on the ice. He skated hard and he would pulverize anyone who tried to get past him with the puck."

"Do you think there could have been animosity from the other players, a grudge someone might have?"

"Oh no, he played hard, but he was fair. He didn't play dirty, didn't slash or trip, kept his elbows down. All his hits were clean. He didn't want to hurt anybody, he just played for the enjoyment of the game. Everyone wanted him on their teams because he made it fun. His enthusiasm was infectious, and he was always encouraging his teammates to try harder and enjoy themselves."

"Were there ever any fights or injuries that could have been attributed to his play?"

"Well, he played in more leagues than I did, so I can't say if nothing ever happened 'cause I wasn't there for all the games. However, I'd be surprised if there was. His sportsmanship was always first rate. He would be the first to congratulate another team if they won, and he would gladly help someone out with their stick work or skating if they asked. He played so much hockey in so many leagues that the members of opposing teams were probably teammates with him at one point or another."

"Outside of hockey, did he socialize with you and other players?"

"Oh sure, we often hung around the dressing room after the games, especially the late-night games. Someone would bring a case of beer and we'd talk about all sorts of stuff. Sometimes he would even give financial advice with a beer in one hand and still wearing his shoulder pads and shin guards."

"Did you ever socialize away from the rink?"

"Yeah, we'd go to a bar to watch the Leaf games when he didn't have tickets. In the off season, we would catch a Blue Jays game now and then."

"Did you ever socialize with him when there weren't any sports involved?"

"Yeah, once, he came to my wedding." Peter smirked.

"Okay, we know he loved hockey and that he played all the time, but what can you tell me about the man outside of hockey? What was he like as a person?" Baldoni wanted to get away from the sports that seemed to be the only thing people wanted to talk about.

"He was a good guy," Peter said, "always had a joke. He was very personable, quick witted. We'd often go for a drink after the game, and he knew a lot about hockey, tell you any statistic for the Maple Leafs off the top of his head going back for years."

"Was he open about his sexual activities?" she asked, still wanting to get off the topic of hockey.

"He didn't talk much about it, but I think that was because he didn't like to brag. He was an honorable gentleman. He wouldn't talk about his women out of respect." Peter's mouth curved into a smile.

"Did he ever mention anything about his bi-sexual activities?" Baldoni said flatly.

"What!" Peter exclaimed with shock, "Get outta here!"

"Yes, we had reasons to believe that he was bi-sexual or even strictly homosexual." Baldoni said in a tone that sounded flat.

"No way, not Kyle!" Peter almost yelled with incredulity, "the guy was a chick magnet. We'd go to a bar and he would go over and be chatting up chicks and would score with them as often as he scored on net. I mean, the rest of us were jealous of the way he could just pick 'em up."

"Sorry to disappoint you," this time it was Baldoni that smirked, "I guess you really didn't know Kyle that well after all."

****

Brenda Lewis was an attractive thirty-something woman with shoulder length butterscotch hair.

She was of average height with a slender curvy body, smooth alabaster skin, a cat-like face with big round eyes of hazel green. Garrison gave a faint whistle when she walked into the room and his faced turned red when he noticed the hard stare Baldoni was giving him. She asked Brenda to sit down in the chair opposite the desk.

Brenda sat and crossed her right leg over the left, in such a way that her tight black leather skirt distinctly outlined the sensual shape of her thighs. She knew the effect it would have on Garrison as she had also heard the soft whistle when she entered, but her pose also wanted to draw a reaction from Baldoni. When none was forthcoming from the female detective, she relaxed her body and settled into the hard, un-cushioned chair.

Baldoni briefed her about the digital recorder and then started the interview. "What was your relationship with Kyle?"

"He was a friend." Brenda said casually.

"Where did you and Kyle meet?"

242

"It was through and on-line dating service."

"Which one?" Baldoni asked.

Brenda looked down at the digital recorder and didn't say anything. Baldoni took note of this action and took it as a confirmation of her suspicions about Brenda's relationship with Kyle.

"How long have you been acting as his escort?" Baldoni candidly asked.

Brenda looked at Baldoni with a playful pout on her lips. "I'll be glad to talk about Kyle, but I'm not going to say anything into that recorder that could be used against me at some point in time."

Baldoni reached over and turned the recorder off. "Alright then," she said and then made a statement that sounded like a question, "off the record?"

Brenda leaned forward putting her elbows on the desk and her hands under her chin. She looked directly at Baldoni, her eyes conveying a mischievous sense of playfulness. "I like your hair," Brenda told her in a seductive voice.

Baldoni sat back and returned Brenda's gaze with a look of indifference. She had spent half of her life dealing with flirtations, come-ons and direct advances. She watched as Brenda moved her head to the side so that she could see her profile and then move her face forward once more with an open gaze that looked directly into Baldoni's eyes. Her lips parted slightly, and her tongue licked the bottom lip in a slow, caressing manner.

"You're good." Baldoni said in a soft voice. "Too bad I'm not a homosexual banker that needs a mirage to keep the closet door shut."

The smile left Brenda's face and she sat back in the chair, her body posture perceptively changed. She uncrossed her legs and then re-crossed them with the left leg over the right, restricting any previous view of her thighs. She folded her arms across her chest and her face went blank of any expression.

"How long had you and Kyle been…umm," Baldoni paused for a moment to think of the right word, "how long have you been dating?"

"We started dating," Brenda put an emphasis on the word 'dating', "about two years ago."

"Was it strictly as an escort or was there any intimacy involved?"

"It was mostly for show, but yeah, we fucked once in a while." Brenda's voice was now cold and unemotional. "He needed to show people that he was straight, and he wanted a beautiful woman to make his friends and colleagues envious. I understood what he needed and was happy to play the part."

"How often did you see him?"

"Every couple of months, usually for a company function or a social gathering of the hockey teams he played for."

Baldoni parted her lips and licked the bottom one, mimicking Brenda's earlier attempt at mockery, "Were you jealous of his real lover, his male lover?"

Brenda's eyes narrowed and she pressed her lips together in a hard line. Her cheeks flushed with a touch of anger. "Kyle was a good man. We had fun whenever we were together. It was an honest arrangement, and I knew what he wanted of me. There were no strings and no expectations other than the charade he wanted me to play. He was honest, which is something that I respect in a client...I mean friend. He even let his family know about me so that they weren't surprised if we ever met."

Baldoni leaned back in her chair and gave Brenda an easy smile. The competition between the two distinct female egos was finished and they could now speak openly about Kyle. She asked Brenda to give examples of the 'dates' she and Kyle had. Brenda talked about attending a party thrown by the Queen's Bank at the Royal York hotel. She had met Kyle's associates and at Kyle's direction, she had even made a slightly flirtatious move toward Mr. Martinique, Kyle's boss.

"Why did he want you to do that?" Baldoni asked.

"We had a room booked in the hotel and I asked him about it later that night. He said his boss was a snobby, misogynist jerk that believes he's the privileged upper class. He wanted his boss to be turned on by me, to think there was a chance. It worked, because Martinique started to return the flirtations, touching my arm, telling me how beautiful I looked, and making suggestive comments. Then, without making it too obvious, but ensuring that Martinique got the message, Kyle suggested it was time we went upstairs to the hotel room. I remember the way he described the look on Martinique's face when he realized that his hard-on had been conjured by a deception."

"You really liked Kyle, didn't you?"

"I try not to get personal with my, friends." Brenda said, her lower lip quivered as she fought to maintain composure. "But yeah, I liked him. He was fun to be with because he was always honest and open with me. There were never any false pretentions about who he was or what he wanted. Every time he asked me to accompany him, we would talk about it and make a game of it, make it interesting, like the thing we did with his boss."

Baldoni's voiced now turned serious, "Do you think Mr. Martinique or any of the others might have taken affront to these games, feel like they had been insulted and wanted to do something about it?"

Brenda's eyes widened and the color drained from her face when she began to comprehend the purpose of the interview. Then she winced, "No, it couldn't have been anything like that. Nobody would want to kill Kyle for such a stupid reason as that!"

"Probably not," Baldoni said, "but over the past few years, I've seen people killed for reasons that were even more stupid. I'll need you to recall all the times you and Kyle played 'games' with other people. We need to look into every possibility as to why someone would want to kill him."

They sat in the interview room for another two hours. Baldoni informed Brenda they were now back on record and that Detective Garrison would take notes while they talked. Brenda told about the times when she and Kyle acted out scenarios for his hockey team. During those instances, Kyle never wanted to single-out any one person. He just wanted to put on a show for the whole team in which Brenda would hang off his arm and suggest what a virile man he was.

It was only at social occasions within the financial industry that Kyle would want to make a display with a particular individual in mind. It was usually with people who thought they were better than others, like Martinique. She didn't know who most of them were or where they worked. She usually didn't even know what the social function was all about. It might have been a fund-raiser, someone's retirement or an awards ceremony. It didn't matter to her, she was there to accompany Kyle, that's all.

****

Curtis and Boyle spent the later part of the morning visiting the local businesses and condos around the King and Bathurst Streets area. At each location, they checked for the positioning of security surveillance cameras and spoke with the management of each business or residence, requesting the security footage for the time period just before and during the crime scene.

Some stores and restaurants did not have any security cameras and the ones that did had cameras near the cash registrars or near the front doors, but only showed the entrances and the sidewalks directly in front of the businesses.

Both men felt the only hope of having any clear image of the crime scene would probably have to come from the surveillance camera on the exterior of the front doors of the Wheat Sheaf Tavern.

Curtis made a note to call Amal Mirwani.

****

Curtis and Boyle left the King-Bathurst area and drove east to Spadina Avenue then turned north until they reached Baldwin Street. They turned west and into the heart of Kensington Market, one of the older neighborhoods of Toronto and one of the most well-known. It is a multi-ethnic area that was full of eclectic shops, fish mongers, vegetable and fruit stalls, bakers, discount clothing stores and a milieu of cafes and restaurants.

David Ouspeski lived in the second-floor apartment on Wales Avenue in the heart of the market.

It was one of the old Victorian style homes that had been built during the period when the market was predominantly Scottish and Irish.

David met the detectives at the front door and asked them to come up to his apartment. Before heading up the stairs, he suggested that if they wanted something to drink, like coffee or tea, there were a couple of good cafes just around the corner on Augusta Avenue. If they wanted water, all he could offer was tap water from the kitchen.

David was always leery when in the presence of the police. He was an openly gay man, and his experiences with the police department had not always been friendly or even sympathetic. He had twice made complaints of being assaulted on the street and each time little or nothing had been done. He even saw one of the assailants on the street two weeks later, followed him home and then reported where he lived to the police. The officer at the front desk of the 14th Division station took down his information and promptly filed it. The whole time he spoke with the officer he felt this sense of abasement and bias to his complaints.

Neither Boyle nor Curtis accepted the offer for anything to drink. They sat down in David's sparse living room, one purple divan and two red modern wingback chairs. The detectives chose the wingback chairs while David sat on the divan. Curtis placed the digital recorder on the ornate Indian coffee table in which each leg was a carving of one of the Hindu Gods. Boyle was impressed by the table and asked David where he had purchased it.

"There used to be a store on Baldwin that sold all sorts of exotic small furniture," he told him, "I found this piece one day and emptied my bank account to get it."

"It's beautiful," Boyle said, "I like the depiction of the Hindu deities."

Curtis was not a patient man. He was the type of person who always wanted to get straight to the point. He liked Boyle but found his attitude toward investigations a bit too friendly. Curtis' method was to be direct, ask the question you needed to ask, and if the person was hesitant or seemed like they might be lying, he would repeat the question and inform them that this was a serious matter with consequences. Curtis believed a little fear always worked as a prompt to cooperate. A little fear also seemed to make any deception unravel as the person kept talking.

He wasn't an obtuse man, and there were times when he was quite sensitive, depending on the situation, but even to himself he admitted that he was often hard. This discussion over the coffee table seemed unnecessary to him and he went straight into a question for David.

"Where did you first meet Kyle?" he asked.

"Kyle came to one of our coexisDance events. He came with a female associate of his from the bank. Her sister was one of the members of our troupe and I guess she persuaded him that it would be something he would enjoy."

"Coexistence? What is that, like a spiritual meeting?" Boyle asked.

"No, it's coexisDance, with a 'D'. It's a group of musicians and dancers who gather to do experimental performance collaborations. It was started by Colin Anthony a number of years ago. He was a musician, dancer and writer and he wanted to put together a community of performers that would improvise explorations in artistically different forms."

"So, you were introduced to him at this event." Curtis stated.

"I wasn't ever formally introduced. Like I said, he was with this woman, a sister of one of the other dancers, but I immediately knew he was gay, just the way he looked at me. When the performances were over, people would mill around afterward and chat. I went up to him and told him my name. He told me that he loved my dancing, the way I moved. We talked for a bit and when his, well I guess you would call her his date, wanted to leave, he gave me his business card and asked me to call him. I knew exactly where this was going to go. He was quite good looking and seemed like a nice guy as well."

"How often did you see him?" Boyle asked.

"Depended on what season it was. I hardly ever saw him during the winter. He was always either playing or watching hockey. The man was a fanatic about the sport. However, he always made up for it as he would take me on his Caribbean vacations. Those were fun and he paid for everything. We always went to a resort, and always on a different island than before. Once in a while in Mexico."

"How did you feel about his wanting to keep the relationship with you secret?" Curtis asked.

"Where did you hear that from?" David seemed suspicious.

"His sister, Rebecca. Apparently, he confided everything in her. We had a long conversation with her and her husband Joe." Curtis said.

"Joe's a good guy." David said mildly, "He called me yesterday to let me know. He said Rebecca was taking it very hard. I hope she's okay, Kyle loved his family very much."

"How did you feel about Kyle keeping his relationship with you secret?" Curtis repeated the question.

"I understood. I've been through a lot of shit myself over the years. I came out when I was a teenager, but I had a large artistic community around me, and they're much more supportive than the rest of the world."

"But how did it make you feel?" Curtis persisted.

"When we were in the Caribbean together, it was wonderful because there was no hiding. I think that's when his real side came out, and I don't mean his gay side, I mean his relaxed side. He was free to be himself and not worry about who saw him. It seemed to be the only time he was totally relaxed, no stress."

"Did you see other people?" Boyle asked this time.

"Occasionally."

"How did they feel about your relationship with Kyle?" Boyle asked.

David looked at Boyle then over at Curtis. "Are you trying to suggest that someone may have been jealous?"

"We have to investigate every possible angle," replied Curtis.

"Well, I'm pretty sure that angle isn't going to go anywhere."

"What makes you think that?" Boyle asked.

David sat back on the divan and took a moment to think. "Kyle was a man that was easy to love. He was sincere when he spoke. He didn't hide his fears or his paranoia from me. We talked about it, wanting to keep his homosexuality secret. He was an honest individual. And I don't just mean honest in a vaguely moral sense, his honesty seemed to come from his core. He knew what he loved, and he would indulge in his passions. I could never understand his devotion for hockey, but it was complete."

"Kyle had his own life," he continued, "and he liked his life. He spent time with me because we were attracted to each other. I wasn't enamored by some of the things he did, like hiring that escort girl. He couldn't fool me, I know he was having sex with her once in a while, but he never tried to deny or lie about it. He always admitted whenever I asked him."

"I'd like to ask you a personal question." Boyle interposed, "Perhaps it hasn't affected you yet, but you don't seem to be grieving over your lover's death."

David was startled by the question and he had to calm his nerves for a second before he answered. "Yes, I'm sad that he's dead. I'm sad for anybody that gets killed un-naturally, but you have to appreciate that we had an understanding. He used me for his pleasure, just like he played hockey, or just like he sometimes used that woman for his pleasure."

He breathed a little as if he was trying to understand his own feelings, "So am I full of grief…no, I'm not. You may think badly of me, but he made it perfectly clear, it was strictly pleasure. He wasn't going to make any commitment, and as far as I know, he had no intention of ever coming out of the closet."

"There was no real commitment between you then?" Boyle pointed out.

"There's nothing wrong with that, it's just not what most other people would expect from a relationship. We were together because we liked each other, and we had fun together. He had his life and I had mine, and we enjoyed our time together. That's about it."

"You didn't want any more?" Boyle felt that David was not completely forthcoming and tried to dig out the truth.

"Listen," David said with the hardest voice the detectives had heard so far, "when there was a Maple Leafs hockey game on, I would always be his second choice. When he had a social function at work, I was never going to be the one that accompanied him. I was always in the background. I was always the secret.

He made his choice. I had to make my choice. I chose to accept him as he was. It also meant that there was very little love between us, so yes, I have grief, but it's minimal. There was no jealousy on my part and probably not on anyone else's part. As far as I know, there wasn't any other men, and I probably wouldn't care if there was. The woman he sometimes was with was an escort, a pro, so I don't see her being jealous in any way. I think you guys are looking in the wrong place."

Chapter Thirty-Eight

Curtis asked for everyone from both homicide teams to convene early on Friday morning in the Argo. Curtis started the meeting as soon as everyone arrived with their coffees, teas and other morning beverages. "We're going to start with the security surveillance video from the Wheat Sheaf. Amal, did you and Pierre review it in full last night?"

"Yes, Mie Liu also viewed it with us. We went over it a number of times, edited it down to the crime scene and made short clips of different sections we thought were pertinent."

"Alright, take us through it." Curtis said.

Archambault connected his laptop to the view screen and opened the server partition called 'Kyle Wilson', then went to a folder entitled 'Wheat Sheaf Videos'. He selected the first video file and before he clicked the arrow icon to start the play mode, he provided an explanation of the content.

"What you are going to see is a section of the full 360-degree view of the camera. It provides high-definition quality of the complete panoramic view. The camera has multiple lenses, so Amal was able to select a separate view from any of the lenses, and since it's high definition, we can zoom in and out without losing quality. There is a de-warping mechanism that corrects the distortion of any view."

"This first file is the view of the northeast corner where the Sly Fox pub is located," and before he pushed the play arrow, he warned the group, "it's very graphic and unsettling."

Both teams watched as the video showed the Sly Fox pub, with only a couple of cars passing through the intersection. There were no pedestrians on the street until two people emerged from the Sly Fox and turned north on Bathurst Street. A few minutes later, they saw the lone figure of Kyle Wilson emerge from the front doors. He stopped for a moment just outside the door, then turned and began to walk eastward along the sidewalk on the north side of King Street.

His walk had an unsteady sway and he walked close to the side of the Sly Fox building, holding out a hand a couple of times as if to steady himself. His walked appeared to show that he was inebriated as reported by the alcohol level in his blood stream. He continued his slow walk until he reached the corner of the building, then he stopped and looked into the alleyway, as if someone may have had called to him.

A figure quickly emerged from the alleyway. They watched as the figure swung their arm, holding the crowbar and aiming at Kyle's knee. Kyle bent forward on impact and fell to his right side. The killer dropped the crowbar, then bent down to one knee and reached out with their right hand to Kyle's forehead. The killer turned Kyle's head up and toward them, exposing the right side of Kyle's neck. They watched as the left hand was raised, holding the knife, and was brought down swiftly, stabbing the neck. They could not see the slashing motion across the neck, but the killer immediately rose and turned into the alleyway.

The only motion of Kyle's body from the moment the knife was thrust into his neck, was his left arm rising for a brief second and then falling to the sidewalk. There was no other motion of the body, just as Singh had explained the previous day, unconsciousness would occur within a few seconds.

The Argo was deathly quiet. Donna Chang rose from her seat and excused herself from the room.

Constable Singleton swore under his breath, "Fucking hell." Constable Davis, Evanko and Garrison looked over to Archambault, as if he was to blame for the intensity.

Curtis spoke abruptly to alter the harsh gravity in the room. "Okay people, this is a powerful video, and it gives us a great deal to go on. One thing we can now say for certain is that this wasn't a random killing, someone passing another person on the sidewalk. The killer hid in the alleyway waiting for their victim to walk by. We cannot say for certain the killer was waiting for Kyle, but the killer was definitely waiting in the shadows. Pierre, I understand you and Amal have edited a variety of views."

"Yes, we have a few clips we want to present." Archambault opened another video file, "This video is just a few minutes after the murder." He hit the play icon and then narrated the action on the screen. "There is a small group

252

of four men exiting the Sly Fox. At first, they don't notice anything until someone sees Kyle lying on the street. They casually walk over to him and then look down at the body. One man squats down to check the condition of the person, and you can see by the action of his body movement when the realization of what he's seeing affects him. The man stands and enters the alleyway, presumably to vomit."

"We interviewed the man later that night," Archambault continued, "and he confirmed that their first impression was that someone was drunk and passed out. When he was checking on his condition, he noticed the blood all over the sidewalk and the gash across the victim's neck. He was immediately nauseated and went into the alley."

"The other three men stood motionless while their friend was vomiting. Then one man picked up the crowbar from the sidewalk and inspected it. This man is wearing gloves. Another man held out his hand asking to see it. The crowbar was passed over to the third man who was not wearing gloves. After a minute when they realize the significance of the crime scene, the third man placed the crowbar back on the sidewalk in the approximate place where the other man had picked it up. A fifth man, who had come from the Wheat Sheaf tavern, joined the group after crossing King Street."

"Have we checked the fingerprints yet?" Boyle asked.

"I have the names and contact info for all four men," Archambault replied. "During the interviews at the scene, none of them had stated that any of them had touched the crowbar. We'll be getting back to all four this afternoon and taking their fingerprints to see if they match the ones that FIS found."

Archambault closed the video file and opened a third one simply called 'Exit'. From the view of the Wheat Sheaf security camera, the entrance/exit of the back alleyway behind the pub was visible. "This takes place fourteen seconds after the killer enters the alleyway on the east side of the pub, right after the murder."

They watched as a figure dressed in black and wearing a full ski mask walked out of the alleyway and turned north on the Bathurst Street sidewalk. They saw the figure walking quickly for about ten steps before the view is cut off by the eastbound King Streetcar as it stopped at the intersection.

"This an important part of video." Mei Lui now spoke boldly. "By the gait and physical structure of the figure, we are certain that the killer is a male under the age of fifty."

"How can you tell he is under fifty?" Boyle asked.

"If he was over the age of fifty, then he would have to be in excellent condition to commit the murder and make it down the alleyway and out the other side in fourteen seconds. Plus, you can see the way he walks, his bearing. He's not a teenager, but he's also not an older man."

"Are we absolutely sure about this?" Curtis asked.

"No, but it is an educated guess by me and Aaron Silverstein. We reviewed this video this morning and we think that his bearing, the way he walks, fully upright, almost pride-full, suggests more maturity than a younger man, and physically more able than an older one. We also discussed that if this was the same killer as the Malinkov case, then the physicality of that murder would also suggest a middle-aged male committed both crimes."

After Archambault shared the connection of the screen with her laptop, Mei Lui used the screen pointer on the still picture where Archambault had paused the video, "The clothes he is wearing are very nondescript. A cheap black coat, dark sweatpants and heavy walking boots, plus the ski mask. However, when you look at this view of him walking (Archambault began the video once more in slow motion), it looks rather bulky. I think he was wearing a set of clothes underneath these garments. Probably to do a quick change in case these clothes were blood stained."

"The boots he is wearing are a common, inexpensive, hiking boots that many men in urban cities wear during the winter and are consistent with the type of tread marks we found in the alleyway." Mei Lui opened another file to create a split screen effect and showed a picture of the tread marks they had photographed, another picture of the tread marks outlined in black and white, and then a third picture of the tread marks of a boot from one of the discount stores. All three pictures matched. Archambault then zoomed in on the feet of the man and the boots were identical to the picture of a brand of boots found at the discount Shoe Warehouse.

"Based on the evidence we have," Mei Liu continued, "he is about six foot tall, and weighs about one hundred and seventy pounds. We are unable to determine his ethnicity because of the close-fitting ski mask. Also, the video was taken from over two hundred feet away and just after midnight."

"Great work Mei Liu!" Boyle's enthusiastic response caught Curtis by surprise. Boyle turned toward Curtis and saw his startled expression, "This is the first indication to any possible identity we have had of the Malinkov killer.

We assumed it might have been a male, but there was not a shred of evidence to indicate any gender. Even the bicyclist that was spotted on the street was wearing bulky, gender neutral clothing."

"Yeah, I see your point. Good work Mei Liu." Curtis repeated the platitude. Then he addressed the whole group once more. "These videos are on the server system for anyone to review. I think the security video for the entire 24 hours before the crime scene is also available. Is that correct Pierre?"

"Yes, that's right. Amal will be reviewing the whole sequence and isolating clips that may be of relevance."

****

"Okay, let's carry on." Curtis said, "Since you have the floor Pierre, give us a brief about the interviews with Kyle's business associates."

Archambault briefly spoke about the genuine respect and fondness his co-workers seemed to have for Kyle. Some of his associates also socialized with Kyle after work, usually at the Sly Fox, but there were also a few who would support him and attended the hockey games when his team was playing for a championship. He went on to state that he did not believe most of his co-workers were simply being polite. He believed what he was hearing was true affection and friendship with Kyle.

Constable Evanko supported Archambault's view by recounting her discussion with Justin Morgan and how he seemed deeply caring about Kyle. Evanko then gave an account of the review of the financial documents. She conveyed the opinion that Kyle had done well by his clients, proposing financial plans that seemed to fit their needs. The profiles he had developed were done with depth, and based on the notes he had taken, she felt Kyle was a conscientious individual that actually did try to do his best for his clients.

"The guy sounds like a saint." Boyle said smugly.

"You know, that's what I said," replied Evanko, "and my remark was taken as a slight by Morgan, so much so that it almost brought him to tears."

"The opposite of Malinkov," Boyle offered. "In his case, everyone we spoke with either hated the man or detested him because of his treatment toward them, especially the women. This Kyle character seems to have been respected by everyone. Hell, we even call him by his first name which shows some sort of desire toward familiarity."

"Did the two of them ever meet?" Curtis pondered aloud.

Donna Chang had returned to the room after she had collected herself and she spoke up at this point, "There is some connection between the two cases in that Kyle Wilson worked at the Beaches branch of the Queen's Bank. He worked with a number of the agents from Beaches Realtor, including Malinkov. He helped set up mortgages and other financing for the real estate clients. There's no way of telling how closely he worked with Malinkov, but perhaps we could speak with Mr. Wicker once more."

"The love fest for Kyle extends to his friends as well." Baldoni declared to the group. "Garrison and I met with a number of his hockey chums. They all had platitudes and admiration for him, his abilities on the ice, and his abilities in a bar. They all pictured him as a real ladies' man who could, and I quote one of them, 'score with a woman as easily as he scored goals.'"

"However," she quickly added, "none of them had the slightest clue Kyle was bi-sexual. Some of them even refused to believe it after we mentioned it to them. The only one we interviewed who knew of his sexuality was the escort, Brenda Lewis, whom he used as his 'girlfriend' at most company functions and other social activities. And yet, I think she also had a deep affection for Kyle. Their relationship was professional, but from the way she spoke, it seemed she truly enjoyed the time she spent with him, and there was a sexual element to it as well."

When Baldoni finished, Curtis related his and Boyle's unsuccessful attempts to find more video footage. He then asked Boyle to brief the group on the interview with David Ouspeski, Kyle's male lover.

"David and Kyle met about four years ago at a musical dance event." Boyle began, "Their relationship was primarily sexual in nature. David was fully aware of Kyle's desire to keep their relationship secret. David was also aware of the escort, Brenda Lewis. He seemed very indifferent to Kyle's professional relationship with her. He was aware that Kyle occasionally had sexual encounters with her. David also knew of Kyle's close relationship with his sister's family, so it seems Kyle was mostly honest and forthcoming with David."

"Overall," Boyle postulated, "I think Kyle Wilson was a strong, independent person who lived his life on his own terms. He was deliberate in having his own way but generally without deceit or dishonesty. He wanted his sexuality to be kept secret, which he had every right to keep private. However, he honestly revealed this desire to those in his private life. Neither David nor Brenda seemed to feel cheated. By my reckoning, it was a very civilized arrangement Kyle had crafted."

"Apart from the deception of his sexuality," Boyle continued, "Kyle was well liked by his co-workers and his friends, which were mostly hockey teammates and a few others. And, according to Constable Evanko, he also seemed to be honest and forthright in his business practices."

"So, the question is why?" Boyle concluded, "Why would someone want to kill Kyle Wilson? The guy seemed like a wonderful person to all around him, whereas in the Malinkov case, it seemed like everyone had a motive to kill him."

Curtis intervened at this point, "I think we need to dig deeper into this 'secret' that he kept. Were there other male or female lovers we don't know of. We also need to go back to the financial collapse of the fund from his previous employ, what was it called again, PIC something or other? Are there people who were still feeling animosity toward him for their financial troubles."

"The company was called 'Progressive Investment Corporation' or PIC for short." Evanko stated. "It went out of business shortly after the collapse."

"Then we need to get in contact with the owners or directors of the company. We will need their list of clients and who was affected by the fund collapse." Curtis said. "Owen, you and Pierre get on it this afternoon. Donna Chang might be able to help you with that."

He then listed the priorities for each individual, "Baldoni, you and Boyle perform the search of Kyle's apartment. Amal will continue to review the Wheat Sheaf video. Katherine, please continue to go through all of the paperwork for the transactions at the Queen's Bank. Remember, this guy was good at keeping secrets, so keep that in mind, and search for anything that might be unusual. Singleton and Garrison will continue interviewing the friends and teammates that we haven't got around to yet. Constable Davis, I want you to get in touch with Beach Realty and interview anyone who had any dealings with Kyle."

"I'm also going to visit Mr. Wicker of Beach Realty once more," Boyle pronounced, "see what kind of dealings he had with Kyle. We know that his dealings with Malinkov were suspect, so there may be an angle there. What about you?"

"I'm going to visit Mr. Martinique once more." Curtis replied with a sly smile, "He seemed to be protective of Kyle when we first spoke with him. I'm wondering how protective he will be when he finds out the truth about him and his escort."

Chapter Thirty-Nine

Kyle Wilson purchased his condo on the Toronto waterfront near Queens Quay and Spadina because it was located just over a mile from where he worked, but more importantly, it was near the arena that was home to both the Toronto Maple Leafs hockey team and the Toronto Raptors basketball franchise. Just northwest of his condo was the baseball stadium that was home to the Toronto Blue Jays baseball team. It was also just a short cab ride from the stadium where the Toronto FC soccer team played their home games.

The condo security team had been alerted about Kyle's death the morning after the murder. They had been told to ensure Kyle's unit was locked and no one was allowed entry without expressed permission of the Toronto Police Department. Boyle and Baldoni retrieved the keys to the unit from security and proceeded up to the eleventh floor.

When they opened the door, they were met by a distinct, unpleasant odor, and a cat darted around the apartment like a feral predator.

"Watch your step," Baldoni said, "there's some cat shit on the carpet and probably other places as well. I'll check the bathroom for the kitty litter box. He'll probably need feeding as well."

Baldoni found a small litter box in the bathroom and litter sprayed all over the bathroom floor. She looked under the sink, and then in the bathroom closet and found a small pail of fresh litter. She replaced the litter and then went into the kitchen where she opened a couple of cabinet doors until she found the cat food. She rinsed the bowl that was on the floor and filled it with food and replenished the water tray.

The whole time she was doing this, Boyle was squatting on the living room rug trying to coax the cat out from under the sofa, but when the cat heard the 'pop' of the tab on the cat food tin, it darted into the kitchen and straight to the area where its food was usually placed. The cat pounced on the bowl that Baldoni placed on the mat in the corner of the kitchen.

"Poor little thing probably hasn't eaten for three or four days," she said coming out of the kitchen. "Beautiful little Himalayan with those misty blue eyes. I wonder why no one has been up to take care of him."

"Maybe nobody knows about him." Boyle responded. "When you were in the bathroom, did you check the medicine cabinet?"

"I'm going to find a broom first. The bathroom floor is a mess, and I don't want to be dragging that stuff all over the apartment." She found a broom and dustpan set in the hall closet and did a quick sweep of the bathroom. "We're probably going to have to call animal services," she said with a note of concern on her voice. "Poor little guy. I wonder if his sister will adopt him."

"Give her a call," Boyle suggested.

Baldoni retreated back into the bathroom and searched the cabinet while Boyle went into the bedroom. Kyle had a double bed, a large dresser and closet. Both the dresser and closet were overfilled with clothing. The top shelf of the closet contained two boxes of new ice skates, one box with new shin guards and a fourth box that contained photos, papers and various other memorabilia. There was only one framed picture and Boyle smiled at the signatures of the Toronto Maple Leafs from the 1976 season.

It reminded him of when he was a teenager and would watch hockey games with his father on Saturday nights. Orestes was often there as well when he wasn't working in his parent's tavern. Boyle's father would let them drink a bottle of beer 'as long as he didn't tell his mother'.

Baldoni walked into the bedroom and asked, "Found anything?"

"Hockey," Boyle said, "a lot of hockey and some memories."

"The bathroom only has the basics," Baldoni went on without catching the comment Boyle made about memories, "toothbrush, soap, shampoo and the rest of men's preening procedures."

Boyle turned with a bemused look, "Men's preening procedures?" he said with a sardonic query.

"Yeah, you know, all the gigolo stuff. Electric manscaping razor, hair mousse, nose hair trimmer, skin cream, body wax, etcetera."

"Nope, sorry Gina, but I don't know. However, I'm glad that you're completely enlightened with this knowledge. By the way, how's the bartender at the Lion on the Beach?"

"One and done," she said bluntly.

Boyle shook his head and breathed out a small sigh that ended up in an even smaller laugh. "Sometimes you kill me, and sometimes I wish I was as young as you again. Manscaping? One and done? What's next?"

"Don't worry Boss. As long as you got me around, you'll always be up to date with the latest trends and requirements for the modern world."

"Thanks," he grunted, "let's go over the kitchen and the hallway closets."

They started with the main hallway closet and found three leather coats of varying thickness, a trench coat, and a fashionable windbreaker. The shoe rack contained a variety of foot ware for business, all types of weather, and sports. They also found more hockey equipment.

The equipment bag contained his current uniform with skates and pads, plus there was a dozen hockey sticks leaning up on the inner wall, and another pair of skates hanging over the rod of the coat rack.

"He's got two more boxes of ice skates in his bedroom closet as well." Boyle mentioned, "I would have expected two pairs of skates, one as a backup, but four?"

"Maybe he got them on sale," Baldoni replied.

They checked the second hall closet and found the usual pile of towels, toilet paper, boxes of tissue paper and bedding. They also found about a dozen hockey sweaters. Half were Maple Leaf sweaters, and the rest were league sweaters of the teams he played on.

Baldoni was squatting down, looking toward the back of the closet when she suddenly jumped in the air and cried, "Holy fuck!"

"What is it!" Boyle said surprised by her sudden reaction.

"Fucking cat crawled between my legs into the closet. Scared the shit out of me."

Boyle burst out laughing, "Not so cute now, is he?" and he laughed so hard that tears came to his eyes. He doubled over as the laughter overtook him, but he managed to squeeze out some words, "Him-a-layin' in the closet now."

Baldoni released a small chortle, which dissolved into a roar. The two of them held their sides as the waves of laughter washed over them. Each time one of them looked at the other, a new round of laughter would grip them. After a few more minutes, Boyle managed to gain a measure of composure. "C'mon he said, let's call the sister about the cat and then I'll buy you dinner at the Parthenon."

****

Sergeant Detective Randal Curtis walked into the front doors of the Queen's Bank of Canada and headed toward the reception desk. The receptionist saw him enter and the expression on her face immediately went from a generic smile to a serious dour frown. She immediately pushed the console phone button for Mr. Martinique's office.

As Curtis approached the reception desk, the receptionist held up one finger, said yes into the small microphone of her phone headset and then looked up at Curtis and told him that Mr. Martinique is on his way to the front lobby. Curtis smiled and said thank you.

In less than a minute, Martinique walked around the corner and into the lobby, holding out his hand and saying, "Good afternoon Detective Curtis. What can we do for you today?"

Curtis shook his hand this time and Martinique felt more comfortable. "We have learned quite a bit of information in the past couple of days about Kyle Wilson and his affairs and I wanted to get some clarification from you."

"Would you like to come into my office?" Martinique offered, "Perhaps a coffee or a cup of tea?"

"I'll take some water if you have a bottle." Curtis expressed more to the receptionist than to Martinique.

"I'll get one from the kitchen," she immediately replied and rose to retrieve one.

They walked through the corridor of glassed walls to Martinique's office. Martinique sat behind the large glass edifice that served as his desk. Curtis took the chair in front of the desk and retrieved his digital recorder, which he placed on the desk with a heavy clink. As he was recording the requisite information, the receptionist knocked gently on the door, opened it, and brought in a bottle of water. It was one of the cheaper brands that were kept in the kitchen for the staff to use and not one of the more expensive designer brands that are given to clients, of which Martinique had an open one on his desk.

Martinique watched with a sense of superiority as Curtis opened the cheaper bottle and drank several large gulps. Martinique picked up his more expensive brand and took a small sip, then smiled at Curtis and placed the bottle on the glass desk once more.

"Tell me detective, what is it that you want me to clarify?"

Curtis, who was always economical in his direct approach of speaking, came straight to the point. "There was a social function about a year ago, I believe it was someone's retirement party, Kyle came to the party with a woman, her name is Brenda Lewis, mid-thirties, long light brown hair."

"Yes, that was his latest girlfriend." Martinique said flippantly, "very nice girl, quite pretty, seemed quite friendly. He brought her to a number of different office parties and events."

Curtis waited a moment and then spoke in a solemn tone, "She told us that Kyle liked to have fun at the expense of other people and often included her in his antics. She related an experience where at Kyle's behest, she started a flirtation with you, one that you reciprocated, and then later on in the evening, Kyle made a show of taking her up to the hotel room where it was obvious that they were going to have sex."

The thin superficial smile on Martinique's lips slowly turned into a serious line. "I don't recall," he coldly responded.

"She stated that Kyle wanted this done as a personal affront toward you."

"Like I said, I don't recall," his voice now taking on a caustic tone.

The tone of Curtis' voice now became distinctly boorish, "Brenda Lewis is a professional escort. Kyle hired her to accompany him on social business functions at the Queen's Bank."

"Why would he do that?" Martinique seemed mildly interested.

"Kyle wanted to mask his homosexuality from his business associates."

Martinique sat stupefied behind his desk, silent, a look of incredulousness upon his face. He was speechless, as if somebody had sucker punched him. He opened his mouth twice as if to speak but was nonplused with amazement until he finally spoke, "I had no idea. He was such a hockey enthusiast."

"Are you saying that you don't believe a gay man can be a hockey enthusiast?"

"No, no, of course," Martinique tried to recover, "it's just that, well, I'm just shocked, that's all."

Curtis waited for a minute in order to allow the weight of his next comment to have sufficient bearing, "And now the inevitable question; Where were on Tuesday night, just after midnight?"

Martinique's eyes slowly narrowed and his answer disdainful, "I was at home," and then his voice became hard and belligerent, "I was at home, with my wife." His brow began to furrow, and his eyes narrowed even further. "Are you trying to insinuate anything detective?"

"I don't make insinuations," Curtis said contemptuously, "I search for facts. I listen to testimony, and then I put answers together after I've gotten all the information I need." He watched Martinique fume as he sat there, his arrogance crumbling, subjected to the governance of a cop, a black cop, "what time did you go to bed?"

"Just after eleven-thirty," his reply obsequious, "when I have finished watching the world news."

"I'm going to need a sample of your DNA and your fingerprints." Curtis said in a patronizing manner. "Anytime this afternoon. Make your way to the Police headquarters on College Street. Go to the Duty desk and somebody there will take care of everything. I'll let them know you're coming."

The seething fire in Martinique's eyes was barely kept under control, like a coal burning stove that had been filled to its limit. Curtis was fully aware of the effect he had generated. A sense of righteous elation filled him as he rose out of his seat. "Have a good weekend," he said and walked out of the office of this privileged white bigot.

Chapter Forty

It was Monday morning, but it didn't feel like the start of a new week. For most members of the two homicide teams, it felt like the extension of a working weekend. The Argo looked like a war situation room on the eve of battle. Empty coffee cups, an empty box of donuts except for two half-eaten ones, sandwich wrappers, crumpled papers littered around a full garbage bin, the cork-board west wall covered with papers, photos, hand-drawn diagrams and post-it notes. A row of laptops lined both sides of the boardroom table with a row of bodies, some bent, some slouched over the keyboards. The tap of the keyboards created a synthetic rhythm as fingers tried to enter information, complete reports and send messages.

Boyle looked around the room and commented to Curtis, "Looks like a group of Trojan warriors returning from battle and preparing for the next assault."

Curtis sipped from his second cup of coffee and without looking responded, "It all boils down to Greek mythology to you Boyle. The Iliad, the Odyssey, Olympians," and then he grinned slyly as he turned, "and all mixed up into one big fucking moussaka." Boyle looked puzzled for a second and then returned a broad smile to Curtis' attempt at humor.

"Alright everyone," Curtis spoke to the entire room, "I know that it's been a hard weekend. I appreciate everyone's time, so let's start sharing what we've each found out about our assignments. Donna, I understand that you've researched a bunch of info about the company Kyle used to work for prior to 2008. Bring us up to date please."

Donna Chang looked up from her laptop, which had only been closed for a few hours all weekend. "The company was called 'Progressive Investments Corporation' or PIC for short. It was incorporated in 1996 as a financial investment and advisory business. They acted both as advisors for their clients and as an investment company that held shares in other portfolios."

She stopped to take a sip of her Green Tea and as she reached for her cup, she let out a wide, involuntary yawn. Realizing everyone was watching, she flushed and quickly apologized, "Sorry about that, didn't get too much sleep last night. Where was I?"

"You just started describing PIC," Boyle told her, "and by the way, you work too much, but that's why we all like and respect you."

Donna Chang's face flushed at Boyle's comment then continued, "The company invested heavily in the mortgage-based investment trusts, also known as MBIT's, in the late nineties and the early part of this century. They were quite profitable until the mortgage investment crisis in the United States started in 2007. When the crisis hit its peak in 2008, the bottom fell out of the real estate market and the MBIT's dropped drastically in value. This led to a crash of many funds as people started panicking and taking their money out, some at great losses."

"The value of the PIC investments fell far below what the original investors had contributed, and this caused a number of lawsuits, because PIC was selling some of their investments as 'guaranteed'.

The investors who had purchased the higher priced guaranteed shares managed to get some of their money back when the remaining monies in the fund were distributed, but the greater majority of shareholders lost almost all of their investments."

"Can you explain what the MBIT's are?" Baldoni asked, "this investment stuff does my head in sometimes, like trying to learn a new language."

"Yeah, me too." Archambault concurred.

Donna Chang took another sip of her tea, paused and then took another sip before continuing, "A mortgage-based investment trust is like a portfolio of companies that deal in the buying and selling of real estate and the buying and selling of mortgages. An investor buys into the MBIT in the same way they would buy into mutual funds, or stocks of a company. No investor actually owns any of the property with the mortgages, just shares of the fund. The MBIT makes gains based on the performance of the companies contained within the fund, the actual companies that are buying and selling property, and from the cash flows of the mortgage debts."

"So please explain what happened in 2008 that caused these MBITs to crash." Curtis requested.

"Well in 2008," Donna Chang explained, "there was the sub-prime mortgage crises, south of the border. Banks were giving out mortgages to people who really couldn't afford them. People working part time jobs or people working for minimum wage in some service industries. The housing market peaked around 2004, but then the market took a sharp dive. Housing prices began to fall significantly and speculators who bought homes to flip, soon found their mortgages on the speculative properties became much greater than the actual price of the property. Many of these people found it cheaper to simply default on the mortgage and lose the property than to keep paying the mortgage."

"This caused a spiral affect," she tried to suppress a small yawn and her face scrunched up in the process, "sorry, please do me a favor and poke me if I fall asleep," and then she continued with the explanation. "The defaulting mortgages added to the increasing number of properties for sale on the market, and this caused the housing prices to fall even further. By mid-2008, the country went into a deep depression and many of those employees who worked part-time or for minimum wage, lost their jobs."

"Many of these newly unemployed people also had mortgages that were often worth more than twice the value of their property. This caused the spiral effect to get even worse, or faster, or whatever spirals do. Basically, imagine an unemployed person with a mortgage of one-hundred thousand dollars on a house that was now only worth fifty-thousand dollars. They can't afford to pay the mortgage and they can't afford to sell the house because after selling the house, they would still owe some mortgage on it. Many of those people defaulted on their mortgages as well, which caused more houses to be on the market, and on and on."

She stopped to take a short breath and another sip of her tea, which had now gone cold. She looked around the room and saw the dull, glazed-over, tired eyes of people who had worked too many hours now trying to comprehend the monotone lecture of finance. "Sorry if this is boring, but I got a lot of this info from the Financial Crimes Unit and I've tried to pare it down to something less than a major essay."

"Actually Donna, you did very well, thank you." Boyle said, "Do we know how many people lost their money by investing in PIC?"

"That information will have to come from the former company executives, or from the company that supervised the bankruptcy." Donna Chang sipped her cold tea and tried to smile through her half-opened eyes. "There were two directors of the company, one was Lawrence Greenbaum, who is now retired, and the second director was Cyril Mahoney who recently passed away."

Donna Chang then raised her shoulders and sat erect in her chair. A glint of a twinkle flickered in her eyes as she gazed around the room for dramatic effect. Her gaze stopped at Boyle and she lifted a tired smile, because she wanted to watch his reaction, "There was also a third partner in the company, a silent partner. Brian Wicker of Beach Realty."

****

Boyle's eyes instantly turned from sleepy exhaustion into wild-eyed adrenaline. "Brian Wicker!" he said loudly, and then more softly and ponderously, "Brian Wicker." He turned toward Curtis who was also aware of what this meant. "We now have a direct connection between the Ivan Malinkov murder and the Kyle Wilson murder."

"I spoke with Brian Wicker yesterday," Constable Davis spoke up surprised. "He did not mention anything about knowing Kyle Wilson prior to his time at the Queen's Bank in the Beaches."

The entire room picked up on the vibration of this revelation and Boyle's enthusiasm. They began to discuss the implications of Brian Wicker being involved with PIC and whether he would have any direct dealings with Kyle Wilson at that time. A silent partner would probably not have had any involvement with the day to day running of the company, but the coincidence of Kyle Wilson working at PIC and then at the Beaches branch of the Queen's Bank was bandied around the room like a pinata.

Curtis sat back and listened, letting the energy of the conversation awaken the buoyancy and verve of his tired co-workers. He was about shout for order when Boyle put his hand on Curtis' arm and gave him a glance that said, "Not yet, let 'em go for a bit, let them talk it out." Curtis nodded and then rose from his chair and looked down at Boyle. "I need another coffee, you want one?"

Boyle shook his head but also rose, "You get a coffee and I'll use the facilities. When we get back, we'll resume the meeting." Ten minutes later, Curtis and Boyle quieted the group and requested reports for the rest of the weekend activities.

Donna Chang and Amal Mirwani reported they had checked into possible connections between the two cases. Donna Chang stated she could not find any connection with Anton Malinkov, or any of Anton's extended family. Amal Mirwani reported there was nothing in any of Kyle's electronic notes, address books, phone book and mobile phone pertaining to any of the people interviewed in the Malinkov case except for one file.

Amal then shared his laptop so that it projected on the screen. He opened an Excel file that dated back three years and was entitled 'Contact List'. "Kyle had this file on his computer, and I am assuming that it goes back to the days when he was at the Beaches branch of the Queen's Bank. It's a listing of real estate agents he worked with including those at Beach Realty. Many of the agents listed in the Malinkov case files are also in this contact list. This is the only other connection we have between the two cases so far."

Curtis asked Constables Singleton and Garrison to report on the additional interviews with Kyle's friends. Garrison commented that what they heard began to sound like a broken record, Kyle was a great guy, loved hockey, and was fun to be with.

"What records did he break?" Donna Chang asked innocently. "Something to do with hockey?"

The laughter started slowly, after a moment of silence, but the weariness and stress of the long working weekend began to dissipate and unhinged itself into a ridiculous sense of relief.

"Donna," Baldoni started to explain as the laughter subsided into weary giggles, "a broken record. A vinyl record album. When it has a break or other damage, then it skips and plays the same few seconds over and over again. It's a simile, a way of describing something that keeps repeating."

Even though she was the one who had originated the outbreak of laughter, it had become infectious and had engulfed her as well. She wiped away a tear from her cheek and replied to Baldoni, "Oh, I've never seen a record album."

Even the always stoic Randal Curtis had let out a few guffaws. He waited until the noise fell back toward a saner altitude, then asked Baldoni to describe the search of Kyle Wilson's condo.

"Well, we found a lot of hockey gear," she started, "I think that's all he lived for. Multiple sets of some equipment, plus a number of Maple Leaf jerseys with some of the players from the seventies and eighties. There was also a framed poster with signatures from the seventies' era. It's probably worth some money to some people." Then she paused and looked directly at Boyle, "Oh, and he had a cat."

Boyle was drinking from a water bottle when she made that last comment and he had to cover his face as his reflex to laugh prevented him from being able to swallow.

"You okay Boyle?" Curtis asked.

"Yeah, but I think we're having too much fun this morning." Boyle coughed out an answer, "We all need a to take a turn in the Rest Room. Why don't we break so that everyone can get some rest, some food and some renewed intelligence?"

****

An hour later, Boyle went up to the Rest Room and woke Archambault and Mirwani who were both sound asleep. Baldoni was already awake but still lying down when Boyle came into the room. "I missed the wolves this morning," she said.

"They probably missed you too," he replied, "you've become their Artemis, the goddess of the hunt. However, now I need you to come down and hunt for the killer." As he said this he stopped, and his mind turned on the phrase. "A hunter," he said partly to himself and partly aloud, his thoughts turning on the idea of hunting and making offerings to the Gods.

"Yes, Boss, we're coming," Baldoni thought he was still quoting Greek mythology.

After another twenty minutes, everyone was back in the Argo. Constable Evanko reported she had reviewed the history of the financial files Kyle prepared for his clients and she couldn't find anything that might even hint at being unethical.

Over the weekend, Archambault had contacted each of the four men who had been present on the scene of the murder. Each one responded that they were friends who were at the Sly Fox, they all decided to leave at the same time, one of them noticed a person lying on the sidewalk and they went over to see if he was okay. One man, Willy Hepler, had bent down to check on him and was the first to notice the blood. He was the man who went into the alleyway to vomit. A second man, Lawrence Walker absent-mindedly picked up the crowbar and then passed it to the third man, Mark Moore.

When questioned, Mark Moore admitted he held the crowbar and that he was not wearing gloves. He timidly apologized, thinking he may have messed up the evidence. Archambault assured him that he wasn't in any trouble as these things often happen. At a crime scene, people usually go into a 'mindless realm' and they often become like zombies for a temporary period of time.

Constable Davis had fingerprinted all four men, and the fingerprints of Mark Moore matched the prints that had been found on the crowbar.

Curtis related his meeting with Mr. Martinique of the Queen's Bank. Even though he tried, he was unable to mask the contempt he held for the man. Archambault was in agreement with Curtis' assessment of Martinique and stated, "The man is pure WASP, and I would even go so far as calling him a closeted white supremacist."

Donna Chang leaned over and whispered in Baldoni's ear, "What's a WASP?"

Baldoni gave a half-suppressed chuckle, knowing that Donna did not want to cause another round of laughter at her expense. Baldoni whispered back, "It's an acronym for the term 'White Anglo-Saxon Protestant'. Toronto was first settled by immigrants from England and Scotland who were primarily Protestant and they dominated the colonial governments."

"Okay everyone," Curtis spoke amidst a yawn of his own. "Pierre and I are going to visit Mr. Greenbaum of PIC this afternoon. Gina, I believe Detective Boyle is going to want your company when he meets with Brian Wicker this afternoon. The rest of you go home and get some sleep. We're going to meet again in the morning, so be here bright and early."

****

After the meeting was adjourned, Constable Singleton stopped Boyle in the hallway. "Can I ask your advice about something Ari?"

Boyle knew that 'something' meant more than a question about police procedures or even about the cases they were working on. Singleton never called him by his first name unless it was a personal matter. "Why don't we go for a drink after work," Boyle suggested, "unless it is something pressing?"

Singleton liked the idea of meeting away from Police headquarters where he thought he could probably speak more freely. "Yeah, that would be great, where?"

"I always go to the Parthenon up on Danforth, near Chester. A friend of mine owns the place and we'll get a table that's secluded. How does seven o'clock sound? That will give me time to meet with Wicker and then head up there."

"Great, thanks." Singleton sounded relieved.

"What's it about Bill?"

"Well, I'm not exactly sure how to put this. I've heard around the station that when you got divorced from your wife, that you came out the winner. Beth and I are getting divorced and I wanted to know if you could give me some advice on how to win it."

Boyle looked quizzically at Singleton when he made that last remark, but they agreed to meet at the Parthenon later and Singleton left headquarters for home. Boyle called Baldoni on her cellphone and told her she needed to take her own car to the Beaches for the meeting with Wicker. He would need to drive somewhere for another meeting later on.

He went to the underground parking lot and thought about what Singleton had said to him, that people around the department gossiped about how he had 'won' during his divorce. Now Singleton wanted his advice on how to win. 'What does he want me to tell him?' the questions came to Boyle's thoughts, 'What the hell can I tell him?'

'Winning?' he tried to conceptualize the idea of winning as being a good thing, but he could only contemplate the idea of winning a battle, in which one side loses less soldiers than the other, but both sides are still faced with death and sorrow.

Then Boyle thought of an answer. Tell him the truth. Tell him there are no winners. Everyone loses one way or another.

Chapter Forty-One

The Greenbaum residence was a modest, split level brown bricked home of Lawrence Greenbaum, the managing director of PIC. The moderately sized front lawn had a brick wall on the southern border that matched the inlaid brick of the driveway. A mature Red Oak tree dominated the front lawn and would have covered the view of the house when the leaves came back in the spring.

"Looks like a place where someone with money was able to retire." Curtis remarked as he and Archambault got out of the car and walked toward the front door. They rang the doorbell and could hear the distinct sound of gentle chimes in the interior of the home.

Mrs. Greenbaum was a petit, seventyish woman with grey hair that was tinted brown. She opened the front door with a courteous greeting and asked if they were the policemen who were scheduled to meet with her husband. The detectives showed their credentials and Mrs. Greenbaum provided each of them with a pair of disposable slippers after they had removed their shoes. "You can never be too prepared in this weather," she said with a polite smile.

She escorted them into the spacious living room where Lawrence Greenbaum was waiting. She asked if they would like anything to eat or drink. She offered a selection of beverages and both Curtis and Archambault settled for iced tea.

Lawrence Greenbaum had a distinguished look about him. His thinning gray hair was cut short and the deep wrinkles in his forehead gave him the appearance of a wise old sage. He wore wire-framed glasses on a Romanesque nose surrounded by leathery dimpled cheeks. His narrow lips sat above a rounded chin.

He sat in a leather armchair at the edge of a small fireplace that crackled with burning wood.

There were two more chairs in a semi-circle around the fireplace and he offered them to the detectives. As Curtis sat down, he had the feeling that this gathering around the fireplace was Greenbaum's preferred method of having business meetings or other formal assemblies. It was meant to keep everyone friendly, but with the distinct air that you were merely a guest, and not the CEO. There was a round pavilion coffee table finished with a deep mahogany stain, which sat on an exquisitely patterned Persian carpet. Curtis looked around the room and reckoned there was a lot of money here for someone who had declared bankruptcy a decade before.

"I guess you're here concerning the murder of Kyle Wilson," Greenbaum remarked.

"Would you mind if we recorded this conversation?" Archambault asked.

"Not at all. A lot less bother than writing all those notes on a pad of paper, I would presume." Greenbaum offered. "Was Kyle's death an unpleasant one? I hope not. He was such a fine young man when I knew him."

Greenbaum had a pleasantness about him, a sense of civility that translated into cordiality, so when Curtis spoke, he did so with considerate respect. "I'm sorry to inform you, but Kyle's death was quite brutal."

"Oh dear," Greenbaum sighed, "it's a shame that someone with his exuberance and joyful perspective on life should suffer a malevolent end. I always feared that there could be repercussions to the collapse of our company, but as time wore on, I had hoped any thought of vengeance had faded."

"You think his murder was the result of someone wanting revenge for the collapse of the PIC funds?" Archambault raised the question.

"What else could it be?" Greenbaum enjoined, "Kyle was a good man. I don't believe he could have had any enemies. Mind you, it's been a few years since we've spoken, but unless he changed his temperament dramatically, then I don't think anyone could have disliked him."

Archambault was about to ask a question when Greenbaum put up his finger to indicate an interruption, "No wait," he said, "the last time I saw Kyle was three years ago at Cyril's funeral. Oh, that was Cyril Mahoney by the way, he was the co-director of the PIC corporation. Kyle was genuinely sad at Cyril's passing and he was a great comfort to Isabel, Cyril's wife. She's gone now too, passed a year after Cyril."

He reached down to the coffee table and picked up the glass of iced tea Mrs. Greenbaum had brought for all of them, placed on expensive coasters to protect an expensive table. He picked it up as if it was a delicate, fragile eggshell. He took a sip of the iced tea and then continued to ramble on,

"Sometimes that happens when a couple are together for a long time. One passes and the other one doesn't know what to do without their spouse in their life anymore. They simply fade out of existence as well."

"Mr. Greenbaum," Curtis calmly interjected, wanting to start the real process of the interview, "you stated that you think Kyle's death was the result of someone wanting revenge. We need to discuss this in much greater detail. I want to understand how the whole financial process worked, what was Kyle's involvement and some information about the clients who lost money."

"Alright, how deep do you want me to delve into it? I could talk about it for hours upon end."

"Why don't we start with the basics," Curtis suggested, "we may need to return a few times when we start interviewing your clients and other interested parties, like Brian Wicker of Beach Realty."

"Oh, him." Greenbaum said with antipathy, "He was a friend of Cyril's. '*A rather vulgar man,*' I thought. Not vulgar in his use of language, but more in his attitudes and the way he did business. I fancy that owning a real estate company best suited him. Doing business with deceit and deception."

"How did he get involved with PIC?" Archambault asked.

"He had money." Greenbaum said plainly, "Cyril brought him in to bolster our start-up funds. He had no part in our business except for being an investor. He participated in a few of our origination meetings, but I could barely tolerate his presence. I expressed my distaste for the man to Cyril. I told him that I would probably feel unwell if we had to deal with him on a regular basis. Cyril understood and let him know that his input was not required, only his money."

"When Kyle Wilson ended up working for the Queen's Bank in the Beaches, was Wicker involved in any way with him getting the position?" Archambault looked for a trail to find any connections between the murder victim and the real estate company owner.

"No, I imagine that was pure chance." Greenbaum speculated, "Kyle was quite devastated when PIC went under. He felt terrible that so many people had lost their money. It wasn't his fault, of course, that's just what happens with investments sometimes. A Great Depression hits the economy, a government falls to a revolution, a natural disaster wipes out industry, any catastrophe of great magnitude can cause an immediate collapse to someone's investment."

"Kyle was young, and he took it personally, because he believed what he was doing was providing his clients with a safe, secure and profitable future. After the disintegration of the funds and PIC, he was morose and despondent. He told me that he never wanted to work in finance again. He went to work with his brother-in-law in construction, but I knew that sort of manual labor would not suit him. It wouldn't allow him the freedom to pursue his desires. When a position with the Queen's Bank came up, both Cyril and I gave him glowing references. He got the position and worked his way up. The Beaches branch of the Queen's Bank was always one of the more prestigious positions because of its location in that egocentric neighborhood."

"So, it was a coincidence that they both worked in the Beaches and had a number of financial dealings with each other." Archambault offered.

"Yes, I would say that is probably the right word for it, coincidence. I don't think Wicker ever met Kyle when PIC was in business." Greenbaum went on to explain, "Cyril had convinced Wicker of his non-participation in the company before Kyle had joined us. We never held any social functions so I cannot fathom any circumstance where they could have met previously. However, that's simply my perspective."

Curtis finished his iced tea and set the glass down on the coaster. Greenbaum called out to his wife and asked her to bring a fresh pitcher to re-fill the glasses. Archambault asked if he could use the facilities and Mrs. Greenbaum led him to the stairway and indicated which door to use at the top of the wooden spiral staircase.

"It's a very nice house you have," Curtis said to Mrs. Greenbaum.

"Thank you," she replied, "Lawrence and I have lived here for over forty years. Our children are long gone so we've been able to cultivate the surroundings to our own tastes."

"When PIC went bankrupt, did it cause any severe financial crisis within your household?" Curtis asked as he attempted to puncture the veneer of the Mrs. Greenbaum's self-effacing refinement.

The expression on Mrs. Greenbaum's face turned into perplexed confusion. She looked toward her husband who was the one who dealt with all frictions or confrontations.

"Detective Curtis," Greenbaum spoke candidly, "PIC was an incorporated company. When the corporation dissolved, only the assets of the corporation were affected. My personal finances and those of my wife were not an issue and were not liable to the claims on the corporation."

"I was not trying to imply anything." Curtis said bluntly, "I must remind you that this is a murder investigation. Some of our questions may be unpleasant, and some will be disagreeable, but they all have to be asked at some point. We are searching for a person who inflicted a brutal, monstrous atrocity on another human being. Sometimes, politeness must be damned."

****

Archambault came down the stairs and noticed the distinct change in atmosphere. He made the assumption that Randal had returned to his bellicose way of interrogation. Brusque and straight forward. He was unlike Detective Boyle, who had a way of cajoling people into open discussion, Curtis almost always used an uncomplicated directness, asking a question, re-asking and then rephrasing the question until the answers were eventually given to his satisfaction.

"I understand your point Detective Curtis," Greenbaum's address became formal, defensive, "but what I don't understand is what you are trying to derive from this line of inquiry."

"Perhaps we should start with the situation behind the collapse." Archambault suggested, "That may lead us toward an understanding of the financial circumstances of your clients, and possibly even lead us toward potential suspects."

Curtis liked having Pierre Archambault on his team. He respected the man's judgment and his keen ability to bridge situations that have come to an impasse. "Thank you Pierre, I think that is a good suggestion."

Archambault began to change the line of questioning, "Mr. Greenbaum, can you explain what caused the collapse of PIC? We have already garnered much information relating to the sub-prime mortgage crisis in the United States and any public information regarding PIC."

"Your research is accurate," Greenbaum plainly stated, "it was the mortgage crisis that directly caused the whole problem. When the real estate market crashed, all mortgage-based funds forfeited their validity and decreased in value at alarming rates. Our company was heavily invested in mortgage-based investment trusts, something we call MBIT's for short. The PIC funds lost close to seventy-five percent in value in a few short months. Everyone lost money," and then turning to face Curtis, "including myself."

"Was this something that you could foresee or even insure against?" Archambault asked.

"Hindsight is a wonderful thing detective. If we could make our investments based on hindsight as opposed to foresight, then we'd all be very rich."

"How aggressive were you in selling the MBIT's?" Archambault continued while Curtis listened, waiting for anything that might present an opening.

"We were very aggressive in recommending this type of investment to our clients." Greenbaum stated honestly, "We pushed the MBIT's because the management fees were high, and the commissions were excellent for us. As for our clients, if you look at the five-year period before the crisis, the PIC fund was rising, soaring even, and our clients profited greatly. The ones who were smart, or lucky enough, to redeem their shares prior to the crises often received amounts that doubled their original investments."

"And those who weren't lucky enough?" Curtis asked.

Greenbaum had spent the past decade trying to explain what happened. He had explained it to the Business Network branch of the government, to the representatives of PIC's bank, to hundreds of PIC clients, to his friends, and to the Financial Crimes Unit of the Police Force.

He sighed at having to repeat the answers once more, "Detective, nobody knew so many people south of the border were getting mortgages that they couldn't afford to keep, and then literally having to walk away from their properties because their mortgage was worth more than the property itself. That became the cascading trend, and housing prices fell, and fell and fell. Mortgages didn't correspond with those falling prices, so people were cash strapped and they stopped paying their debts. Mortgage based funds became almost worthless at one point."

"In America," he continued heavily, "some of the big investment firms and banks were bailed out by the government, some went under. We were a small Canadian firm, so we were not lucky enough to get a bail out."

"Some of your clients had guaranteed investment shares. How did they fare?" Archambault asked to get clarification.

"Those with guaranteed shares received whatever money was accumulated from the selling of the company's holdings in MBIT's and other stocks or funds. None of them received their full investment back, but they did receive a percentage based on the amount of shares they owned."

"And what of the people who didn't own guaranteed shares?" Curtis' voice sounded critical.

There seemed to be a genuine sadness in Greenbaum's voice when he answered the question. "Some of our clients had to declare personal bankruptcy. Those that put all, or most of their investments into the funds. This is not something we recommended they do. We always suggested they diversify their investments. However, the ultimate decision is always with the person making the investment. The fund was doing so well prior to the crash, some people got greedy and invested solely in the MBIT funds."

"For my part," Greenbaum said with a touch of melancholy, "I wish it had never happened. Like when you wish a loved one wasn't sick, or when your community is devastated by a disaster, because you have no control over the situation. I wish I was able to forecast the crisis of 2008, and that I could have gotten all my clients out of the market. That would be my wish detective. God didn't grant me that wish, and to this day I have to live with the knowledge of my failure. Yes, my failure, to all those people who put their trust in me."

Curtis felt a sudden sympathy toward the man. He could discern his integrity, and how it had been vanquished in one crushing blow. Behind the veneer, he could see an honest businessman, one who truly cared about his work and the people who invested their lives in his dream. Albeit a dream of monetary structure, but one man's dream none the less.

"We are going to need a list of all your clientele who had investments in PIC, especially the ones that Kyle Wilson managed." Archambault asked mildly.

"Detective, you're talking over a hundred clients." Greenbaum responded with reserve.

"I understand sir, however, as you pointed out earlier, this seems to be the most likely motive."

"Well then, I will have to make inquiries with the former company treasurer to see what information he has maintained. However, you might be able to obtain a list from the company that supervised the bankruptcy."

****

Boyle and Baldoni went to 55 Division station, where Brian Wicker had been summoned to meet them. Boyle introduced Detective Baldoni as she set up the digital recorder and completed the preliminaries to the interview.

"Mr. Wicker," Boyle started, "we are investigating the murder of Kyle Wilson. I understand that you and a number of agents at Beach Realty dealt with Kyle with regards to financing real estate properties."

"Yes, Kyle was the financial advisor to a number of our clients, however, I told all of this to your Constable Davis yesterday."

Boyle took a slow moment to allow Wicker's brain to wonder and then proceeded, "Kyle Wilson worked at the Progressive Investment Corporation. Don't you think you should have disclosed that you were a partner in that company?"

"I didn't have any dealings with Kyle back then." Wicker replied with a skittish voice, "I never met the man. I was a silent partner and didn't have any dealings in running the business. I was just an investor. Cyril and Lawrence took care of managing the affairs of the company."

"The company went bankrupt and we believe that might be a prime motive behind Kyle's death." Boyle said forcefully, "This is another murder investigation in which someone you dealt with, and in which there are financial implications, was brutally murdered."

"That was completely coincidental," Wicker's voice rose in anger. "I invested money in PIC because my friend Cyril Mahoney suggested it would be a good investment. For ten years before the mortgage crisis, I made a lot of money, and then in 2008 I lost money just like everybody else. I didn't personally know any of the employees at PIC, only Cyril and Lawrence. I was strictly a silent partner."

"When did you find out Kyle had worked at PIC?" Baldoni threw in a question.

"The first time I met Kyle was when he worked at the Beaches branch of the Queen's Bank." Wicker seemed highly strung and apprehensive, "We did business based on real estate mortgages and other financial planning for my clients. Kyle was excellent in his job and it was well over a year before I learned that he had worked at PIC. We were casually talking about past experiences and he mentioned he had worked with Lawrence and Cyril. I told him that I knew Cyril quite well and that I was an investor in the company. Hell, we both attended Cyril's funeral."

"What else haven't you disclosed about Kyle Wilson or Ivan Malinkov?" Boyle's anger showed in his glaring eyes.

"I had never even met Kyle back then. I had nothing to do with what happened at PIC. It was a complete coincidence that he worked at both places. As for Ivan, you already know everything concerning his financial misgivings. I run a real estate business, but the agents run their own affairs. Honestly Detective Boyle, I'm starting to feel persecuted here."

Boyle stared at Wicker and then coldly stated, "Persecution is the forbearer of prosecution, and that only happens when you are formally charged," he paused and then added, "alright, get out of here."

Wicker scurried out of the room. Baldoni watched as Boyle paced around the interview room, thinking to himself, *'I don't like that man Gina,'* he confessed, "I have always felt negative about real estate agents. They only seem to want one thing, to make a sale, and they seem to lie and cajole without any personal integrity or honor. That's been my experiences with them."

"Some might be honest and upright." Baldoni said thinking back on her interview with Awesome Gandhi.

"One or two, maybe." Boyle grinned as his anger began to subside, "Wicker has his fingers in a lot of spun webs. I want to take a deeper look into his affairs."

"Okay Boss, first thing in the morning after the meeting in the Argo."

"What time is it?" Boyle took out his cell phone and looked at the time. "I've got to go meet someone. I'll see you in the morning."

"Did Bill ask to speak with you?" Baldoni asked him.

"Yes, how did you know?"

"I kinda told him to go to you for advice."

"Why did you tell him to talk to me?" Boyle asked quizzically.

"He told me that he was splitting with Beth. He wanted to talk to me, but I told him that you're the one he should speak with. You always seem to know everything Boss. You're Aristotle," she said with an impish smile.

****

Boyle arrived at the Parthenon at ten minutes to seven. Singleton was already there, and Orestes pointed to a booth in the far corner, away from any other customers. A bottle of wine was on the table and Singleton poured a glass for Boyle as he sat across from him.

"Thanks Bill," he started the conversation, "I'm sorry to hear about you and Beth," he offered, "but what is it that you want to know?"

"She's a bitch," Singleton blurted out. "She wants everything."

This wasn't going to be easy Boyle thought. "What do you mean everything?" he asked.

"Everything, I mean she wants everything. She wants custody of the children, she wants the house, she wants all of my paycheck, she wants our savings…everything."

"Bill," Boyle tried to calm him, "I'm guessing this is a recent thing. People get mad and become irrational, both of you, and people say and demand things that are unreasonable. Have you got a lawyer yet?"

"I'm going to see one later in the week. They were recommended by the employee assistance program through our HR department."

Boyle took a sip of his wine and calmly told him, "That's where you have to start. It's a process, and you have to go through this process until the court decides what's right, or unless you and Beth can agree on the separation of everything yourselves."

"Yeah, I know, but what I want to know is, what do I do while all this shit is going on. How can I best make sure my kids are going to be alright, that she's not going to try and turn them against me, that I still have some money left over and that the lawyers don't take everything."

Boyle put down his glass and cast his eyes on Singleton, knowing his next question would be the most personal one. After a pause, he asked, "Did you hit her?"

Singleton looked up surprised and annoyed. "Fuck no!" he almost shouted, "I'd never do anything like that. Jesus Ari, what do you take me for?"

"Sorry Bill, I had to ask."

Singleton drained his wine glass and poured another. He drank it down in three gulps and then poured one more. "Well, it wasn't anything like that. It's just all went shitty, that's all."

"Tell me about it, maybe that'll be a release for you and give me some perspective. I mean, if you want my advice, I have to know what I'm advising on. However, let's order some food. The way you're pounding back those glasses of wine I'll have to prevent you from driving home tonight."

Singleton sat back in his chair and looked up. There was now a puppy dog quality to his face, something that expressed the need to talk and be listened to. Boyle called Orestes over and placed an order for Greek salad and chicken souvlaki with rice and potatoes. Nothing fancy, just some good protein and carbohydrates to line the stomach in preparation for a long night of conversation, confession and the cleansing of one's soul.

Singleton sighed and nibbled on the Greek salad when it came. He put an olive into his mouth, chewed on the black skin and pulp, then took the pit in his finders and examined it. "The first hint was when she started needing 'her space'," he opened up, "she used to complain that we never spent enough time together, that my schedule was an obstruction to our relationship, and that I needed to dedicate more time to her."

"Now she needed 'her space'," he said using his fingers to identify quotation marks, "without me, without any explanation as to what 'her space' was," without any answers to, "what did you do last night?"

Orestes brought a large tray containing a row of chicken souvlaki skewers and a plate with roasted potatoes on one side and a mound of rice on the other. Boyle and Singleton heaped a quantity of both on their plates and scooped spoonfuls of Tzatziki sauce onto the souvlaki.

Singleton ate quietly for a time and then felt comfortable enough to continue. "The second clue that it was coming to an end, was her newly found indifference to me. She used to always want to know where I was and what happened on the job. Now she couldn't care less, even when I want to tell her everything, she no longer wants to know nothing."

He drank down another glass of wine and Boyle knew the extra bedroom in Orestes' apartment upstairs was going to be occupied once more.

"She used to smile whenever she saw me. Then one day that smile turned into a look of annoyance. She used to like it when I caressed her, and then just like that, she started avoiding my touch." Singleton's voice started to become melancholy, "You know, she used to striptease in front of me. In the end, she would change in another room."

"Maybe I just wasn't reading the signs. Maybe I could have done something about it." Singleton was now rambling, and Boyle let him go on.

He knew it was something Bill needed to do, something Boyle remembered doing himself while he sat in the same seat with Orestes listening.

"It used to be fun to be together," Singleton was starting to slur his words, "it used to be an adventure with each opportunity for us to be alone. Now being alone was something that felt like work, and I don't like work, not when I'm with her. So where did it go wrong or was it just inevitable. When did the spark dwindle into a smoldering ash? I wasn't always expecting fireworks and comets, but then I wasn't expecting the dull throb of a migraine either."

Boyle called Orestes over and whispered in his ear, asking him if the room upstairs was free.

Orestes smiled and nodded, "The couch in the office is free as well," he whispered back to Boyle, indicating that he expected his friend was in for a long night.

"When did the quiet moments where we laid in bed and felt each other's essence turn into long periods of solitude side by side?" Singleton asked nobody, or maybe asking himself, "When did the trust that opened our feelings and emotions turn into shallow excuses and secrets."

He looked up at Boyle, bleary-eyed and sullen, "She used to tell me her dreams, now all I ever hear is her complaints. She used to share her burdens with me, now she just unloads them." Singleton slumped over his folded arms on the table. Boyle could hear the soft tears flowing as he wept into his folded arms.

Boyle sat silently, sipped his wine and reflected on the thoughts he had earlier in the day, his thoughts about the idea of winning, his thoughts about the truth and the agony of emotions everyone faces.

"Listen Bill, I don't know if you are sober enough to hear me, but this is my advice," he said in a low, tranquil voice, "there is no winning in hatred or anger, there is only redemption if you can somehow manage to survive without destroying the lives of others. There is freedom and clarity if you are able to live through this with your heart and mind intact. There will eventually be liberation if you can endure this hell of a self-inflicted contest of animosity."

He stopped for a minute to collect the rest of his thoughts, "But to win?" he began again, "if you can walk away with your self-respect, if you can walk away without a prolonged sense of hate and bitterness, then you've won. If you can leave with a complete set of intangibles; the love and care for your children, your integrity and your honor, then you've won. If you can walk away and still be able to live with yourself, then you've won."

"Other than that, nobody wins." He said with empathy, "C'mon Bill, Orestes has a nice bed upstairs. In the morning, he'll make us the best espresso you've ever had."

Chapter Forty-Two

It was mid-morning on Tuesday and both homicide teams were absent from the Argo. Detective Curtis wasn't too perturbed as he himself had only arrived at nine-thirty. Lateness was not uncommon when working for a homicide team. One person could go days with little sleep, and then spend twenty-fours in bed to catch up.

He took a sip of his coffee and surveyed the room. The Argo was home to a constant flow of homicide meetings and had been refurbished numerous times over the years. He remembered his first meeting in the Argo when he was a junior constable, a room full of cigarette smoke, the old pinewood table covered with overflowing ashtrays and note pads. It wasn't called the 'Argo' back then, but it was the same room used by homicide detectives for over thirty years.

The last change in décor was the inclusion of two HD screen monitors, side by side on the south wall and a customized conference table that included a central trough with electrical outlets to plug in laptops and cabling connections for sharing the screen displays. Seated on either side of the table and staring at their laptops were Donna Chang and Amal Mirwani. Curtis watched the two of them at work, focused on their laptop screens, and thought to himself, '*How important these two researchers were.*' They were expected to have instant answers to impossible questions, and they usually did.

He thought back to the other day when Boyle was thanking Donna for her work, and how he thought that it sounded like superficial platitudes, but he knew Boyle wasn't a superficial type of person and could be quite forceful when required. Boyle showed genuine appreciation to those with whom he worked, and they seemed to appreciate his compliments by their dedicated loyalty.

He put down his coffee cup and folded his hands on the table in front of him, "Amal, you and Donna have done a wonderful job on these cases. I just wanted you both to know that."

Donna Chang glanced sideways at Amal with a look of mild astonishment. Amal looked at Curtis with a mildly befuddled bewilderment. "Thanks detective," he said hesitantly. Donna also thanked Curtis with an uncomfortable reply and then turned back to her laptop.

"You're welcome," Curtis said as he rose to leave the room. He felt a touch embarrassed at the reaction of the two researchers. "Well, I tried," he mumbled to himself as he left the room.

"What was that all about?" Donna Chang asked Mirwani when Curtis was gone.

"I don't know," Mirwani replied, "maybe he's just over-tired."

****

An hour later, all members of the homicide teams were present except for Constable Singleton. When asked, Boyle stated that Singleton would not be present for a couple of days to deal with personal matters. Baldoni looked over at Boyle with a questioning look and Boyle just shook his head to mean 'let it go'.

Curtis started the meeting by asking Archambault to relate the interview with Lawrence Greenbaum. Archambault related the specifics of the interview but added, "The interesting part was when I asked him if he thought the motive for Kyle's death was revenge and he stated, 'What else could it be?'"

"We will obtain a list of all investors in the fund and then we will start assigning names for interviewing." Curtis explained, "However, before we start the interview process, I want to go through the list with Mr. Greenbaum and ask him to identify names we should start the investigation with. We'll go through all of them one by one. It's going to be a long process and I expect everyone's cooperation."

"Randal," Donna Chang looked up from her laptop, "I've already received the full list of clients from the Financial Crimes Unit as they had investigated the affair back in 2009 to ensure there were no irregularities. The records were kept with the licensed Insolvency Trustee firm of Goodman and Partners. Amal and I have already started to sort and weed out names."

Curtis gave his head a little shake, as if he was re-setting his brain into working mode, "Do you remember what I said earlier to both of you?" Donna Chang nodded meekly, and Amal Mirwani just stared back at Curtis. "Well, you just proved me right. Good job, both of you."

There was an uneasy silence that settled in the room. Curtis scanned the faces that seemed puzzled by his remarks, "C'mon," he finally said, "I'm not that bad, am I?"

"Randal," Boyle broke the silence, "you have been known to be quite…uh quite…uh how shall I put this…quite undeviating in your no-nonsense, frank demands for the expectations of your team. Personally, I like the honest and plain-spoken directness of your approach to the job."

A degree of tension filled the room like a large balloon that was about to burst. Curtis turned to Boyle with a big smile, "Are you trying to say that I'm a hard-driving, son of a fucking bitch?"

"No," Boyle smiled back, "I try to never use the word 'fucking'."

The tension in the air peaked for a second and then was released like a long sigh. Curtis laughed, and the rest of the room felt partly exuberant at having witnessed the formidable Detective Randal Curtis laughing two days in a row.

****

Curtis allowed the brevity to continue for a few minutes longer, and then decided that it was time to get down to some real work. "Amal, can you and Donna show us what you have regarding the clients of PIC."

Mirwani pulled the file up on one of the two main viewing screens. "We exported the database of the names into an Excel file," he explained, "the list in column A were the 296 investors in the MBIT's that the company offered at the time of the collapse. We added additional information in the columns to the right of the main list including contact information in column B, investment amount in column C and current status of the investor in column D. The status column is incomplete as some investors were from other provinces and some from the United States. Also, we'll need to search the public records to determine if anyone on the list is deceased. Lastly, in column E, we listed the investors who had purchased the guaranteed investment funds. These people didn't lose as much money and are probably less likely to want revenge."

Donna Chang took up the explanation at this point, "We exported the information into an Excel spreadsheet in order to utilize the sorting function of the software. The names in column A can be sorted in alphabetical order, however, we can sort column C to determine the investors who lost the most money."

"I like your idea of sorting the list by total financial investment." Boyle said, "We can use that to start interviewing the most likely candidates, and then work our way down from there."

"Add another column that states who we have interviewed and who we have ruled out as potential suspects?" Curtis ordered.

Mirwani answered, "We can add as many columns as we want, including a column that states which constable or detective is assigned to interview each investor. We can color code the names to show which investors have been interviewed, plus we can add color codes to indicate the investors we suspect are capable of committing the crime."

"Okay, this is good. Our task somehow seems a bit easier for documenting the interviews, but we still have to do the footwork and actually talk to people." Curtis said.

"I'm planning to import the database from the provincial death records and then run a comparison simulation between the two lists." Donna Chang stated. "That will give us a head start on who we won't have to interview."

Boyle was sitting back and thinking about the implications of having a list of investors. He made a point to the group, "We may need to interview more than the investors themselves," he stated, "there could be many potential situations. For example, an investor may have been someone who lost all their money and committed suicide. The children of that person may have blamed Kyle for the death and wanted revenge. We need to identify which investors Kyle dealt with directly and then sort that particular list by dollar amount. This will probably be the list that has the greatest number of people with motivation."

"I'll get a list from the corporate treasurer to determine which clients were managed by Kyle." Amal stated.

"Amal," Curtis spoke up, "you and Donna start tracking that info from the treasurer. Pierre has the phone number and e-mail address. I want those Excel files kept on the server system so we can all access them. Editing privileges are to be restricted to you two. Boyle and I will start assigning names for people

289

to interview once the columns have been sorted. Anybody have any questions or anything to add?" When no one responded he turned to Boyle, "Tell me about Mr. Brian Wicker," he asked, "can we arrest him and close off both cases."

"I wish," Boyle replied. "Whenever I talk to that man, I feel like I've been caressed by a snake."

Baldoni giggled at the remark, "It's true. I've only met the man once, but he feels like the type who can wiggle out of anything that might make him look bad. He insisted that he had never met Kyle when he worked for PIC, even though Wicker was a major investor. He would only admit to having business relations with Kyle when he was working at the Beaches branch of the Queen's Bank. You should have seen him run out of the room when the Boss put the death stare on him."

"Death stare?" Boyle looked quizzically at Baldoni.

"You're the pseudo psychologist," Curtis said, "and a good one at that. I guess your parents picked the right name for you, Aristotle."

Chapter Forty-Three

All members of both teams met in the Argo Friday afternoon to plan their strategy for interviewing the long list of PIC clients. The waste bins were full of empty coffee cups and tin cans of energy drinks. Amal Mirwani had dark circles under his eyes and his unshaven cheeks and rumpled clothing were signs that the Rest Room had been used often during the past three days.

Donna Chang had spent the same amount of time working with Amal, but she was impeccable in her appearance. Like a dowager princess, her prideful self-will always insisted on her being presentable. Only when exhaustion overtook her like a crumbling wall did she ever let her guarded poise down. This was not one of those times. She sat erect and prepared, her laptop open, waiting to present or manipulate her files.

Curtis scrutinized the two researchers and asked Donna Chang to brief the group on what they had accomplished to this point. Amal yawned and seemed pleased that he didn't need to speak. Donna Chang opened the first Excel file and explained their findings.

"There were 296 investors in the PIC funds at the time of the financial collapse," Donna Chang read the numbers directly off the screen, "we have determined that 39 of these investors have died in the past ten years, but as Detective Boyle pointed out earlier, the families of the deceased could still be suspect and blame PIC for their deaths."

"A total of 87 investors had bought the 'guaranteed funds' and some of them were paid in full when they cashed in their funds. The standard penalties were deducted for early withdrawals, but basically, they did not lose any substantial amounts. When the company filed for bankruptcy, the rest of the investors who held 'guaranteed funds' were the first to be compensated with the remaining assets. There were losses, but nothing significant enough to warrant a murder for revenge. I think we could probably leave those interviews until the end, if needed at all."

"Now the more poignant facts," she declared to the group. "The amount of people who declared bankruptcy when the fund collapsed was eighteen. I thought that was rather high, but I discovered that in most of these cases, personal bankruptcy was declared and most of them had transferred their actual properties, like their homes, monies in their bank accounts, and other retirement funds to their spouses or families prior to their filing."

"Of those that declared bankruptcy, ten are now deceased. The total number of clients that Kyle Wilson dealt with was 78. There were 21 who had purchased guaranteed funds and there were six of Kyle's clients who declared bankruptcy, two of which are now deceased."

Curtis and Boyle stared at the screen for a few moments and then Curtis spoke, "Did any of Kyle's clients with guaranteed funds declare bankruptcy?"

"No sir," Donna Chang responded, "none of the 87 investors with guaranteed funds declared bankruptcy."

"So then, according to your figures, Kyle had 57 clients who lost money and whom we may need to interview." Curtis made the statement with a heavy breath, "This is going to take a long, long time."

"Not if we go by monetary losses," Donna Chang chimed in once more, "of the investors who were managed by Kyle, there were four that lost over five hundred thousand dollars and only two of them declared bankruptcy. I believe we can start with those four and then go to the other four who declared bankruptcy but lost significantly less money."

"'Significantly less money' may be a mathematical equation but could mean just as much or more to the people who lost it," Boyle calmly said.

"There were five investors that lost more than two-hundred and fifty thousand dollars." Donna Chang continued, "In this group, there were three that declared personal bankruptcy. Also, there were ten who lost over one-hundred thousand dollars and one of them declared bankruptcy. In total, there were nineteen clients of Kyle Wilson that lost more than one-hundred thousand dollars, so I believe it's a less daunting task than it first seemed like."

Boyle leaned over to Curtis and whispered in his ear, "Remember, she's on my team. Mine, not yours," he said with a taunting jibe.

Curtis shook his head at Boyle's droll sense of humor and then returned to Donna Chang, "Okay Donna, can you make a list of the nineteen investors we're going to start with and then start adding my name, Boyle's, Pierre's and

Gina's beside the nine biggest losers on the list. We'll start the interview process with them."

"I want the other constables to start on the investors that lost between fifty and one-hundred thousand. There appears to be twelve on the list."

Boyle cut in before Curtis had the opportunity to speak again, "I know they are not the major losers, but it's still a lot of money. I want to weed down that list as fast as possible so that we can concentrate on the people whom we feel are potential suspects."

"Okay," Curtis said, "let's discuss how we should do these interviews." Just as he said this, the main phone on the table began to ring. Curtis picked up the receiver, "This is Curtis," he listened to the person at the other end without saying anything and then he simply stated, "Okay, thanks," and hung up.

He turned and looked around the room with eyes that appeared to take on a somber aspect to them. "That was Mei Liu," he said, "they discovered something in the paperwork we retrieved from Kyle Wilson's condo. There was a letter in an envelope posted to Kyle. It simply said, 'You're dead asshole'."

****

Boyle stood up and walked over to the viewing screen. With his finger, he pointed to the Excel file that showed all the statistics of the PIC investors. "One of these people probably wrote that letter," he said, "one of these people lost their money. Maybe they also lost their home, their life savings, their futures. Maybe they lost a loved one. That's what we want to find out when we do the interviews. With that letter, the evidence now points to someone on these lists. Someone that probably has a connection with both Kyle Wilson and Ivan Malinkov."

"What other information do we have on the letter?" Archambault asked.

"Mie Liu said there are no fingerprints on letter. There are fingerprints on the envelope but we're going to assume those prints are from the post office sorters and mail carriers. Obviously, we'll check it out, but with what we know of the killer so far, I'm pretty sure he's not going to slip up with prints on an envelope. He's proven to be too methodical for that type of mistake."

"The stamp was one of the self-adhesive ones. They haven't done a DNA test on the glue flap yet, but she will call me as soon as it's complete. The postmark indicates the letter was sent about two years ago, which would put the date a year before the Malinkov murder."

"This would mean that he was planning both murders at the same time." Baldoni observed.

Boyle thought out loud, "Like Randal said, he's meticulous in his planning. He probably planned the Malinkov murder for a year or two before he actually committed it. If he intended to murder Kyle Wilson when he sent the letter, then you're right, he was planning both murders at the same time."

"My fear is if he had planned these murders for a couple of years," and then he paused, "what else does he have planned?"

Then that word all police departments fear sat like a huge unwanted dragon in the room, "Serial." The press would tear them apart if it continued. The public would be outraged if they could not catch him. The ego of the killer would taunt them in their sleep, and their self-confidence would nag at them every day he remained at large.

Curtis now became the expert at breaking silence. If he was going to be known as a hard-driving son-of-a-bitch, then he was going to use his reputation to his advantage, "Listen up," he said in a loud, demanding voice, "we're looking for a male, probably between the age of thirty and fifty, six-foot tall and weighing about 170 pounds."

"We'll start with those four investors who lost over five-hundred grand, especially the two who declared bankruptcy. I want to know if any of them fit the description of the killer. I want to know if any of their children fit the description of the killer."

"I want to start the interviews immediately. Amal and Donna, I want you two to put everything else aside and start getting the background information on those investors. I want their contact info and I want interviews arranged ASAP!"

"If this a Serial, then he might not wait another year, especially if he believes we're the bumbling fools that he thinks we are. He was confident when he killed Malinkov. That confidence led him to believe that he could kill someone out in the open," and now Curtis got angry and slapped his hand on the table, "on a public street for God's sake, and get away with it."

Curtis took a deep breath and composed his nerves, stood up from his chair and looked around the room. "Well, he's not going to get away. We're going to make sure of it."

****

The cell phone in the breast pocket of George Martinique's dark gray Brioni suit began to vibrate.

He was sitting in his office at the Queen's Bank of Canada, researching golf courses in Bermuda. He reached into his pocket and looked at the call display and gave a small frown when he saw the name of the caller.

"Hello Brian, what do you want?" he could barely hide the displeasure in his voice.

On the other end of the line, Brian Wicker paused for a moment then spoke, "Hello George, I just wanted to call and catch up on some personal business."

"What kind of business." Martinique asked, more like a statement than a question.

"I was just wondering if you remember our conversation from a couple of years ago down at the Hunt Club when we played that round of golf."

"Which conversation are you referring to?" Martinique asked carefully.

"I think we were on the eighth hole at the time and we both expressed the idea of how nice it would be to get rid of the 'pains-in-the-asses' we both had to deal with on a regular basis."

"I not sure if I remember that conversation very clearly." Martinique replied, "Why are you calling?"

"Sometimes people wish for things, and sometimes they come true." Wicker coyly replied, "Was this a wish that you expressed to someone other than me?"

"My recollection was that you had this same wish."

"I was wondering if our conversation was something that you took to heart." Wicker said in a conservative manner.

Martinique paused and then replied, "I was kind of wondering the same thing about you," and then a slight grin started to show on his face.

Chapter Forty-Four

The snow fell like translucent feathers on the first Monday of the new year and a blanket of snow had covered southern Ontario from the city of Windsor in the west, all the way east to the border of Quebec. The snowdrifts in Toronto were piled high on the front lawns where homeowners had deposited their shoveled driveways. Four lane streets had been reduced to two and sidewalks were narrow pathways amidst the shoveled snow.

Aristotle Boyle and his friend Orestes Panikos sauntered eastbound along Danforth Avenue, walking at a slow even pace and talking about Boyle and Theo's journey to Greece and Orestes complaining about the usual problems at the Parthenon; finding good help, rising prices and the many other aspects all small business owners face.

"Slow down Ari," said Orestes, "I need to rest for a bit."

"Are you alright?" Boyle asked with concern as he saw the wearied look in his friend's eyes.

"Yes, yes, I just need to rest a little bit. I just get tired more quickly these days, especially after being in the restaurant all day and then walking in the evenings with you." Orestes said as they sat on the public bench in front of the ornate building of the Holy Mary Catholic Church.

"You know you're supposed to relax," Boyle reproached, "the doctor told you to take time off from the restaurant. If you can't stay away for full day, then only go in the afternoons for a few hours and only look at the books."

"I know what the doctor told me," Orestes growled, "but I have a business to run."

"Why don't you let someone help you with it. Hire a business manager to run the restaurant and you start taking it easy. The doctor says your blood pressure is high and told you to slow down, so maybe you should start."

"Ari," Orestes said as he looked heavenward, "I have worked in that restaurant my whole life. I grew up there, worked with my father and mother.

That restaurant is my life. I can't just turn away from life, even for a short while."

Boyle replied sympathetically, "Orestes, you're not the man who took over the business from his parents twenty years ago. If you don't take care, you'll work yourself to death and then I won't have anyone to drink with. Isn't there someone who can take over, even a short while?"

"Who?" Orestes says, his forehead furrowed with consternation, "Kostas? He would probably forget to total the daily receipts and he doesn't know how to really treat customers. He's too abrupt and doesn't realize that you need people to come back in order to stay in business."

"What about Maria?" Boyle asked.

"If I put Maria in charge, then I would be under more stress than I am now." Orestes said with a scowled expression on his face.

They sat in silence for a while, their minds stewing on thoughts of the Parthenon. Orestes looked over at Boyle and motioned that he felt better and was ready to continue their walk. They got up from the bench and headed back toward the Parthenon when Boyle suddenly stopped, his eyes widened with inspiration.

"What?" Orestes asked at the expression on his friend's face.

"What about Theo?" Boyle said.

Orestes' eyes grew watery with the thought of Theo working in the restaurant again, maybe one day even taking over the business. He rubbed his hand across his face and then with a weak voice said, "Do you think he would do it?"

"I don't know," Boyle answered, "he is still on his quest to search for a purpose in life. Last week he was in Rome and then he was going to Venice. I think he will then head back to Greece to stay with my cousin Nicolas. I'll call him and ask. This would give him an opportunity to work, to really work, and hopefully figure out what he truly wants."

"I would be honored to have your son with me," Orestes spoke as the mist shone in his eyes, "you know I would my friend." Then he put his arms around Boyle and bear hugged him with deep affection.

****

The next morning, Detective Randal Curtis sat alone in the Argo, his laptop opened in front of him, reviewing the interview reports of the PIC clients prepared by Donna Chang and Amal Mirwani. Of the six clients who declared bankruptcy and were associated with Kyle Wilson, two were now deceased. None of the seven children of those two fit the physical profile of the killer. All had been interviewed and none of them were in any financial predicament, so the motive for murder was unlikely.

Curtis had decided to focus on the remaining group of four who had declared bankruptcy. There were three males and one female. One male was in his eighties and living in a retirement home. The two other males had been interviewed but their alibis had not yet been verified, and this is where Curtis wanted to start the meeting.

****

"Of the deceased clients, did any of them commit suicide?" Curtis asked as the recap of the interviews continued once the two teams were present.

"Yes, one of them." Archambault stated, "He was a senior who was living in Sudbury and he had lost over five-hundred thousand. He was a widower and living with his son's family. He had two sons and the second son was killed in Afghanistan while serving with the Canadian forces. Reports state he was depressed after the collapse of the fund, but that he became more despondent over the death of his son."

"There was also a second man who attempted suicide who was forty-two at the time of the collapse. He was heavily in debt with a huge mortgage and credit card balances. The bankruptcy caused a permanent rift in his marriage and his wife and children moved back to her hometown, Calgary. His failed suicide attempt was an overdose of antidepressants and sleeping pills, which left him in a coma, which he is still in. His wife and teenaged children still live in Calgary."

"And the other deceased client?" Boyle asked.

"He was ninety-one and lived in a retirement home, died peacefully in his sleep. He died eight months ago, after the Malinkov murder," Archambault replied.

"Any connection between him and Malinkov?" Curtis questioned, "any children that might be holding a grudge?"

"We couldn't find any information that would have connected him to Malinkov. He had worked in factories all his life, owned a home up in North York for over 45 years. He had four children, all daughters, all married with families of their own, and all in good financial standing."

"Okay, what about the other two people that lost big?" Curtis continued to question.

"One woman is now in her sixties and lives in a condo in the Yonge and Eglinton area, very near to where Barbara Booth lives." Baldoni stated after taking over the reporting, "Her husband had died prior to the collapse of the fund, but both of her sons are doctors who live in the United States. The condo is owned by one of her sons and both contribute to the financial care of their mother."

"The last investor to lose five-hundred grand is a dentist in his late fifties. He has a full-time practice in Bermuda and was in Bermuda at the time of both murders. He has numerous other investments, mostly in his wife's name. They still own a home in Toronto and a cottage in the Muskoka area. They only return to Canada for the summer season or for special family affairs. They do not have any children together, but she had one child from a previous marriage, a daughter who lives in Vancouver."

"This is taking us nowhere in a real hurry." Boyle complained.

"We're eliminating possible suspects." Curtis said unconcerned, "The less we need to focus on, the more productive we can be."

"I know, you're right," Boyle reflected. "I'm just feeling distracted this morning, like the unease of a pending doom or calamity."

Curtis looked twice at Boyle, and then went straight back to business. He continued by directing another question to the two detectives, "That leaves us with three other investors who declared bankruptcy. What about them?"

Baldoni responded that one of the bankrupt investors was a 'numbered corporation'. When they investigated further, the owner of the corporation was a famous retired hockey player. The lawyer representing the hockey player stated his investments are commonly made through numbered corporations in order to keep the former player's name out of the public eye.

"The fifth bankruptcy was a man in his late-forties and currently lives in St. John's, Newfoundland. However, the man is a professional musician with a successful east-coast musical group. As part of the bankruptcy, he relinquished his share of the royalties to the bands previous recordings and this satisfied the creditors, so he was discharged from the bankruptcy within a year. Nevertheless, in the past ten years, the band's popularity has grown internationally, and he was once again in good financial standing. At the time of Wilson's murder, his band was on tour in Japan, Australia and New Zealand."

Baldoni paused at this time and after a few moments Curtis asked, "What about the last bankruptcy. Do we have any information on this one?"

"Yeah, but it's a bit weird."

"What do you mean by weird?" Boyle asked.

"Well, the investor and the bankruptcy were registered to a five-year old child at the time of the fund's collapse."

"A five-year old child?" Boyle asked, "What did the investigation by the Financial Crimes unit say?"

"I couldn't find any reports from them on this," Baldoni stated, "they completed a general investigation when the fund collapsed, but they didn't find any irregularities or cause for further investigations. The bankruptcy was declared because of all the other debts the five-year old had."

"The five-year old kid had other debts?" Boyle's voice sounded amazed.

"I can only imagine the financial transactions taking place in this scenario," Baldoni continued, "but it appears the parents found a loop-hole in the system with regards to inheritances. By the time the child reaches the age of twenty, all of the bankruptcy requirements will have been cleared. I don't know the legalities behind this, but it's now been over ten years and the statute of limitations for debt collections is two years in Ontario. Somehow, the parents got away with it."

Everyone in the room looked around at each other, some grinning, some befuddled, and some thinking about their own situations and debts. Mirwani inadvertently spoke his thoughts aloud, "Makes a person think about having children just for the sake of debt relief."

Boyle chuckled at the comment, "I wouldn't advise that as a financial plan Amal."

Curtis grunted in what could only be called a surly mood. The inability to find any true leads had also left him with an inner frustration about the whole investigation. He stood up from his chair and spoke to the detectives in a gruff, almost angry tone, "I want to re-focus our concentration on this group of six who declared bankruptcy. We are going to re-interview all of them and I want full details about their children or spouses. The constables are to continue with the list on the Excel file and start crossing them off one by one until we get to the end."

"However, I also want Pierre to go back and re-interview the sister and brother in-law and I want Gina to re-interview the escort, I think her name was Brenda, and the gay lover, David. I want you to bring a copy of the letter threatening Kyle's life. I want to know if any of them had any knowledge of this letter. Did Kyle express any fear, or if he may have mentioned any names that could have been associated with the letter. I want this done fast. Do you have anything to add Boyle?"

Boyle also stood up to talk. He had been taking a back seat on the investigation because the murder of Kyle Wilson had been assigned to Curtis' team. He respected and liked Curtis, and didn't mind his command of the investigation, but he felt lessened by not leading himself.

"Donna, have you completed checking all the cold cases to see if there are any similarities to these two murders?"

"Yes Boss," she replied, "I checked the data to all the cold cases dating back to 2000. The majority of those cases are believed to be gang related so I concentrated on the cases that were unresolved murders. I couldn't find anything that would relate to either of these two murders."

Everyone in the room remained silent until Baldoni spoke up and asked, "Did you just call him Boss?"

Donna Chang blushed and hid her eyes as she responded, "Yes, I'm sorry, was that inappropriate?"

Curtis simply grinned and Boyle started to chuckle to himself and said, "It's okay Donna, that's Gina's nickname for me. You can use it too if it makes you feel more comfortable." He then turned to Davis and Singleton, "No way, not you two. Next thing you know they'll start using it down at the Duty Desk, and then I'll have Stanforth on my ass for more than just investigations."

Curtis leaned toward Boyle and smiled, "Hey, can I also call you Boss?"

Boyle started to laugh as the cell phone in his pocket began to ring the generic tone he kept for calls that were not from his family, friends or the department. "This is Boyle," he answered. He listened and didn't say anything. Gina watched his face turn to an ashy, pale gray and the muscles in his face become rigid. He closed his eyes and took a deep breath, "Yes, I'll be there as soon as I can."

"What is it?" Baldoni asked with trepidation.

"Orestes is in the hospital," he said in a hushed tone, "he's had a heart attack. Curtis, I need to take care of this, can you carry on without me for now? I need to go over to the hospital right away."

"Yeah, go." Curtis said, "I'll take care of everything."

"Sorry people, but I have to go." Boyle said as he walked quickly to the door, "Gina, can you take over the other investigations for now?"

"Yeah, yeah, I will. Go!" she stated with a sense of urgency. Just before he closed the door to the Argo she called out, "Hey Boss, call me...let me know, please."

Chapter Forty-Five

Boyle sat pensively in the chair beside his friend who lay asleep. He could hear the rhythmic beat of the heart sensor and various other beeps and whirs chime their sounds in the stillness of a hospital room. He continued to read aloud from a book of Greek Mythology, but in a soft voice so as not to disturb the hushed silence in the room. Although his friend was in a drug induced sleep, Boyle read to him with the understanding that even the sleeping mind could hear words of solace.

At seven-fifteen in the evening, Gina Baldoni walked through the doorway and could hear Boyle's soft words through the curtain around Orestes' bed. She quietly sat down in the armchair beside an unoccupied bed and listened to Boyle as he read the story of Pandora's Jar from Hesiod's Theogony. As she listened, she wondered why the story seemed so different from the one she heard, or at least thought she had heard. As Boyle continued, she realized that she had never heard the actual story before, only references made to it in different books and movies.

When he finished the story, she rose from the chair and gently drew back the curtain. Boyle looked up at her and smiled. "Did you bring any wine?" he asked playfully.

Baldoni smiled back and then her expression changed to one of concern, "How is he?"

"He had a mild heart attack," Boyle spoke in a subdued tone. "They inserted some cardiac stents, but the prognosis is good. He should be up and about in a few days."

She reached down and took the book from his hands and started leafing through some of the pages. "Good stories, but do you really believe in the Greek Gods that meander through these stories? They all seem like whimsical fairy tales."

Boyle's smile faded into the expression of patience, which his experience had taught him was needed when explaining mythology. "You have to remember these stories are meant for education. They are meant to teach different values."

"And you believe this stuff?"

"The concept of believing in the Gods is fallacious. The Gods are meant to represent certain manifestations of reality, like Death. You wouldn't ask someone if they believed in Death, but you could ask what they thought about death. The stories focus on the various aspects of life and the world around us. They represent the divine presence in everything, including our emotions, our actions and our knowledge."

"But you treat it so seriously," she professed, "it's like learning how to live by reading Dr. Seuss, or Mother Goose."

"And don't we?" he replied, "doesn't Dr. Seuss profess love and friendship, loyalty, compassion and perseverance."

Baldoni looked quizzically at Boyle. He saw the expression on her face and thought to himself, *'How often will I have to explain what people should already know.'* And then he had to catch himself once again, his own sin of egotism. He sighed a deep breath and forced his mind to accept that he was just as fallible as Zeus, as mistake prone as the children of Olympus, and in great need of self-discipline by the Hera within him.

"In Greek, there is a word 'philosophia'," he said with tender resignation, "it means the 'love of wisdom'. It's where we derive the word philosophy. Do you remember that painting by Raphael, 'The School of Athens' in the Vatican?"

"Yeah, I saw pictures of it during art class in high school." Baldoni answered.

"To me, it is the most beautiful painting because it represents an age when people thought about what life meant, what the world around us meant, and what the soul within us meant. The painting shows many of the Greek scholars meeting in a great hall that has statues of the Gods all around them. Those scholars were taught the same stories that I am now reading to Orestes and they shaped the philosophy, mathematics, science and societal structures that we live by today."

"But aren't those stories, and the stories from other ancient religions outdated. How can they still have relevance with the knowledge we have today?"

"Why wouldn't they?" Boyle calmly asked, "The old testament of the Bible has the same wondrous stories that you find in the mythology of the Hindus, ancient Egypt and in the Zoroastrian traditions. They all have the same direct interaction with God."

"The stories describe the world around us and how everything came to be. The Hindus and the Navahos have wondrous tales of Goddess mother giving birth to the world, or maybe a better way of putting it, giving birth to our reality."

"Listen Boss, I know my history and about religious beliefs throughout the ages. I just don't perceive the relationship between the ancient stories of Mount Olympus and the modern world."

"When you look at the philosophers and academics of that age," Boyle went on, "they learned to use their minds through the stories of the Gods. Ptolemy is a good example. He was the first to determine the earth was a sphere and not flat. He would watch ships sail away in the sea, and they looked like they were slowly sinking, but in reality, they were sailing beyond the curved horizon. As a child he learned that Helios drove his chariot, rising from the east and dragging the sun behind him, navigating the sky until he dived under the earth in the west. Ptolemy developed a complete cosmos with the earth at the center and the sun and stars revolving around it."

"The ancient stories are beautiful reminders of the beginning of thought and imagination. When you teach a child mathematics, you don't start with Calculus, you start with simple addition, one plus one."

Orestes opened his eyes ever so slightly and Baldoni's face brightened. Boyle saw her expression and turned to his friend. Orestes opened his lips slightly and weakly said, "I've been listening to you two," and he looked at Baldoni, "my Gods talk to me, every day. They speak in the silence and in the storm."

****

The next afternoon, Boyle was back at the hospital with Orestes, now awake but still in a weakened state. The stents that had been inserted were proving to be effective and the doctors stated the prognosis appeared good. However, the damage caused by the myocardial infarction had left him with a weakened heart.

"I think Persephone wants me." Orestes whispered in a weak voice. "I could hear her calling me in my dreams."

Boyle looked at his friend, eyes half-shut, lying on his back with an oxygen tube affixed to his nose, an intravenous tube in his left arm and heart monitors taped to his chest. He tried not to think about what his own life would be like without Orestes. Who would he confide in? Who would he feel safe with when he wanted to drink too much? Who would he depend upon to be his moral compass and his guide?

Boyle sat beside the bed for a long time and watched his friend fall asleep, wake, fall back asleep.

When he awoke once more, Orestes looked over but did not say anything. The look in his eye was one that conveyed sadness, a look which asked what the future would hold.

Boyle looked into his friend's eyes and told him softly, "I spoke with Theo earlier today. He sends his wishes for you to get better. He said he is coming back from Europe."

Orestes looked over at Boyle with questions in his eyes, "He's had enough travels?"

Boyle smiled weakly and said, "No, not really, but he wants to come back."

Orestes lifted his chin slightly and looked at Boyle as if to ask why. Boyle spoke with a voice that cracked with emotion, "He said he wants to come back and help you at the Parthenon."

Orestes' eyes began to mist, and a tear trickled down his left cheek. He reached for Boyle's hand. Boyle saw the motion and reached with his own. Orestes weakly clasped Boyle's fingers and managed a faint smile on his face. No more words were exchanged, but the gestures and touch told of a bond between the two men. A bond that is full of sentiment and memories, of respect and honor, but mostly a bond of love.

****

"I spoke with Theo again this morning," Boyle said the following day.

Orestes showed a marked improvement and there seemed to be a brightness that shone from his face. "He hasn't changed his mind, has he?" he said playfully.

Boyle's grin turned into a sly smile as he said, "No, he hasn't changed his mind. However, he said he would only do it under one condition."

A quizzically look came over Orestes' faced as he asked, "What condition?"

Boyle's turned his sly smile toward Orestes and said, "He said he would only do it as long as you banned me from the bar."

Orestes looked confused for a second, and then his face began to sparkle with laughter, a hearty laughter that came from deep in his belly and worked its way up and filled his eyes with joyful tears. He looked at Boyle and said between the laughter and tears, "Tell him, whatever he wants. So mote it be."

Boyle had started to laugh when Orestes first began his contagious outbreak of joy and his laugh increased as he heard the response from his friend.

Baldoni entered into the room with a small bouquet of fresh cut flowers. "I could hear the two of you from all the way down the other end of the hall."

"Look, Ari, look," Orestes said between the laughs, "it's a beautiful angel, sent from heaven for me, or it is the Goddess Athena that has come through the veil into this world to visit this humbled Greek warrior."

Baldoni blushed and smiled. Orestes looked over to Boyle and said, "Ari, I must be feeling better, I think I've got a hard-on."

Boyle burst into a new spasm of merriment while Baldoni blushed a deep crimson and then walked over to the bed, bent down and kissed Orestes on the cheek. "You lecherous Greek bastard," she said with a laugh.

Orestes turned toward Boyle again, "You see, I told you she loves me."

"Settle down Orestes," Boyle said while still smiling, "you're supposed to stay calm and rest. You'll have another attack if we keep this up."

"Ari, how can a man rest when there is a Goddess to be worshipped."

A nurse walked into the room and began to mildly reprimand Boyle and Baldoni, asking them to reduce the levity as the patient needed to remain calm in order to properly recover. Orestes waved her away saying, "Relax yourself my darling nightingale, the strength that my friends bring me is a better medicine than any you could provide."

"There are some things your friends cannot provide," she extolled.

Orestes turned toward the nurse and said with sincerity, "My dear, if I have learned anything in this life it is this: If you don't have friends that you can depend on, then you don't have friends."

****

Later that evening, Boyle and Baldoni returned to Orestes' room after having dinner in the hospital cafeteria. They talked about the progression of the cases, interviews with the former PIC clients and Baldoni brought Boyle up to date on the homicide of a wife by her husband. The man had come home one evening and walked into the kitchen, picked up a knife and repeatedly stabbed his wife a total of 46 times. He was present when the police arrived and the husband babbled on about the changing shape of the moon, the whispers of the blades of grass, and the constant yapping of her little dog, which the police could not find and of which the neighbor had never seen.

Back in the hospital room, they found Orestes was out of his bed and sitting in a chair. "Did they say that it was okay for you to get out of bed?" Boyle asked.

Orestes ignored Boyle's comment and held out his hand to Baldoni as if pleading, "Gina, my sweet lovely, do me a big favor. The next time you come, can you stop in at the Parthenon and bring me a nice salmon plate, with rice and potatoes and a little Tzatziki on the side. This bastard here," he said pointing at Boyle with his thumb, "some friend he is, he won't bring me anything, not even a canter of wine."

Boyle rolled his eyes and said, "We we're discussing some cases downstairs in the cafeteria. We have other concerns to take care of, murders that need to be solved, evil people that have to be arrested."

"Evil," Orestes mused, "that's just a word, an imaginary concept, something that doesn't really exist."

"I have seen some of the evil that people commit on other people." Baldoni mildly protested.

"There is stupidity," Orestes began to list, "there is ignorance. There is irrationality. There is cruelty. There is a wide variety of psychoses, depressions, depravities, but pure evil? No, it is not something that is inherent in the world. It is only something humans generate within their minds."

"You're partially right," Boyle said to Orestes, "There are liars. There is greed, and there is addiction. There is power, and there is addiction to power. There is jealousy and selfish expectations, and it is from these frailties where evil comes."

Orestes turned to Boyle, "Ari, we've discussed this many times. You make it sound as if evil was a quantifiable reason for people committing horrendous acts, as if they couldn't help themselves. When you turn evil into an outside force, then you take away the responsibility for people to be accountable for their own actions. You give them a reason to blame something else, like the devil, instead of owning up to their own fallibilities."

"There is no devil in Greek mythology because the myths emphasize humans have free will and must deal with the challenges life presents. An exterior force like a devil would eliminate the ability for someone to choose the path they should take."

"So that would mean you also don't believe in fate." Baldoni pointed out.

"One of the things that makes me cringe is when I hear someone tell me that things happen for a reason." Orestes said, "Why? Why do people believe that there is a reason for the good or bad things that happen to them? Someone's mother dies and they say that God decided it was time for her to join him. Someone wins a lottery, and they say that it was through God's blessing. An earthquake kills thousands of people and someone says it was all part of God's plan. What a lode of nonsense."

"Perhaps people need to believe there is something else really going on when they experience bad times." Boyle offered, "Perhaps it's a way for people to cope with problems they are facing. Maybe things happen because they just do. Maybe things happen because we simply just screwed up. But people need a relief from the grief and anxiety they experience."

"Sometimes we get hit in the head by a rock that fell from the sky." Orestes answered, "Sometimes we are the ones throwing the rocks."

****

It was two o'clock in the afternoon on Thursday and Boyle was in the hospital lounge waiting for Orestes to finish his meeting with the doctor. Orestes was being released and Boyle had spent the night on the phone with members of the Greek Cultural Association to set up care for his friend. Phedra and a number of other women had all agreed to spend time in Orestes' apartment above the Parthenon. They would make him his meals as prescribed by the hospital. Boyle was worried Orestes would simply call downstairs and have them bring up foods he should not be eating, and wine or Ouzo.

When Orestes emerged from the doctor's office in a wheelchair, he was as grumpy as Boyle had ever seen him. "Do you want to see the diet they have given me. I'd rather be with Persephone in the Underworld than to eat the crap they want me to have."

"I've been eating a Mediterranean diet my whole life. Maybe a little too much wine, but it's the diet of my ancestors. It's the food of both our ancestors."

Boyle said nothing and picked up the travelling bag with clothes and other personal items he had brought for Orestes. He followed the nurse toward the elevators that lead down to the main reception. He told Orestes to remain seated until he brought the car from the parking lot.

"I'm not a cripple." Orestes growled.

Boyle still said nothing and let his friend vent his frustrations and fears. He knew Orestes was worried about the change this would cause in his life. He knew his friend was anxious about the future and the weight of the responsibilities he carried with him. The restaurant had been his life and it had been the life of his parents and the life for many of the people who had worked with him.

The mood in the car was somber and Boyle wanted to cheer his friend, so he turned to Orestes and said, "One day, I was on a field trip with Theo's class, back when he was in grade five. He must have been about nine or ten years old. The teacher asked for parent volunteers to come on the trip to the historical Sainte Marie among the Hurons Jesuit village on the shores of Georgian Bay. The school bus arrived first thing in the morning and I knew the long bus ride loaded with kids was going to be an experience."

"At one point, we were driving along Route 9 and we passed a farm that had cows wandering in the pasture, very near the side of the road. All the animals were grazing except two. There was a bull that had mounted one of the cows. He was in full sexual throttle."

"Can you imagine a busload of ten-year old kids screaming with delight. They knew what was happening and it was as if we had shown them a comical porn movie. I looked at the teacher who was sitting across the aisle from me and she gave me a grin like a Cheshire cat."

"It's a field trip," she said. "We learn a lot on field trips."

"Thank you," Orestes said, "you're a true friend Ari, and you are right. The bull was probably Zeus, and the Gods have sent me a challenge. No one knows what the future will hold, but I know the quality of my past. Thank you."

Chapter Forty-Six

Throughout the months of January and February, both homicide teams staggered through a number of violent deaths. Working overtime had become the natural state of affairs and everyone was on edge.

The recent legalization of marijuana had street gangs looking for new business markets in harder drugs and illegal weapons, which resulted in stiffer competition and retribution. Curtis' team worked with the Integrated Gun and Gang Task Force on two gang related deaths. Boyle's team was investigating a domestic homicide in which a jealous wife had poisoned her husband, and the multiple murder of a married couple in a home invasion.

The interviews with former PIC clients were progressing slowly and both Boyle and Curtis had been called in by Stanforth who impressed upon them the need to wrap these cases up as quickly as possible. "The potential of another serial killer is not what this police department, nor the city of Toronto needs." Stanforth had yelled at them.

The next day, a joint meeting of the two teams was held in the Argo. The volume of work required for the PIC interviews, combined with the other cases, felt like the gloomy drudgery of extended exertion and was wearing on the fiber of their confidence.

****

Archambault began with a report on two other investors who had lost over two-hundred and fifty thousand dollars but hadn't declared bankruptcy.

One of them was another numbered corporation and the owner of the corporation was the wife of Lawrence Greenbaum. When questioned, Mr. Greenbaum stated they had created the numbered corporation because they didn't want their names listed as one of the investing clients. There were no illegalities involved, they just wanted to avoid any need for explanations.

The other investor who had lost over two-hundred and fifty thousand dollars was a former member of the Toronto Police Services Board, Dominic Corrado.

Boyles ears perked up, "Wasn't he the one who wanted to severely cut our budget?"

"That's him," Curtis said. "Corrado thought the police force was too privileged and expensive, and that it needed trimming as part of the former Mayor's promise to reduce the overall city budget."

"I once heard that he was the king of corporate anal sniffing." Boyle snickered, "Always wedging his way into parties and events that featured notable business tycoons and trying to claim friendship with the 'who's who' of Toronto's celebrities."

"Well, I didn't quite hear it the same way that you put it, but your description suits the character."

Archambault looked across the table and asked quizzically, "The king of corporate anal sniffing?"

"Like a dog," said Boyle, "you search for friends by the scent of their anus, or in his case, social class. Dogs mark their territory, and he wants to be included in their domain."

****

Baldoni continued with a report on the investors who lost over one-hundred thousand.

"Three were listed as males over the age of seventy. They were all financially well off and living in various locations outside of Toronto. One was a woman who is married to the owner and CEO of a chain of furniture stores across Ontario. Another woman was currently in care at the Centre for Addition and Mental Health. She is in her early fifties, separated from her lesbian wife and is childless. She entered the CAMH facility and has been diagnosed as schizophrenic and manically depressed."

"There were two cases of seniors who are now living in retirement homes. One is a woman who suffers from Alzheimer's. The woman's sister, a nun of the Carmelite Sisters of the Divine Heart of Jesus, has power of attorney over her sister's finances. The other senior also suffers from Dementia. His daughter lives in Italy and manages her father's expenses from there."

Curtis sat back and looked downcast at the screen which displayed the Excel file of the interviews and results. "So, we've basically eliminated all of the potential suspects who lost over one-hundred thousand dollars?"

"Actually," Archambault responded with a bit of trepidation, "we've already eliminated about half of the investors who lost under one-hundred thousand dollars as well. None of the ones we interviewed fall into the category of potential suspects."

"Explain." Curtis stated roughly.

"There were forty-four in total and six were guaranteed investors, which left thirty-eight potential suspects." Archambault continued, "None of this group declared bankruptcy. Five of them are now deceased as they were quite elderly, all over the age of eighty. Three of the five were living in government sponsored retirement homes. We haven't been in contact with the children of those cases yet. The other two were living with their families when they died."

"We have interviewed eighteen of the others and in almost all cases, very few of them fit the profile of the killer. The ones who did fit the profile were either living out of the province or were financially stable."

****

"Somewhere in this list of people is the killer." Curtis called out to the group. "Let's keep eliminating the obvious names so we can re-focus on the ones that are left." He paused for a few moments in order to ensure his next words were clearly heard by all. "However, first let me state what a great job you have all done. We've had other casework that needed to be worked on, but we've still managed to get through a good portion of the PIC list. I'm proud of you."

Curtis had always been known for his hard expectations and his cold admonitions when you failed to accomplish your tasks. He looked into the faces of his team around the room and saw a sense of befuddlement, and he knew they were trying to decide if this was a trick of flattery or whether he truly meant what he said.

"This isn't fake plaudits," he grumbled loudly, "I truly mean it, you've all done a good job during a busy, stressful time."

Boyle sat back in his chair and faintly smiled to himself. Over the course of the past few months, he had noticed a distinct change in Curtis. He always liked the man because he was dedicated and honest in his methods, even if his way of leading differed from his own.

"I agree with Randal," Boyle remarked, "Gina, Pierre, what's next on our list?"

The atmosphere around the room seemed lighter and the tension within everyone's hunched shoulders dropped into more relaxed postures. Archambault spoke up, "We'll need input from the constables on how their interviews progressed."

Constable Evanko took the lead in reporting as agreed by the other constables prior to the meeting. "As Pierre said earlier, there are thirty-eight potential suspects and five are deceased. Jasmine and Bill managed to interview ten of them and Owen and myself have interviewed eight. The investors were a variety of ages and genders. None seemed to be exceptionally well-off or decidedly poor. No one stood out as a potential suspect, but most of them had lost very little money in comparison to the big losers. We could not determine if any of them would want revenge on Kyle Wilson or would have even been involved with Ivan Malinkov."

"Thanks Katherine," Curtis' gratitude seemed warm, "however, as Ari stated in previous meetings, what may seem like a little bit of money to some, may be a lot to others." He then asked Donna Chang and Mirwani if they were able to find any connections between the two cases. Mirwani stated they had found a number of links, most of them being the real estate agents who worked for Beach Realty and other real estate companies located in the Beaches.

"However," he continued, "we also found two of Malinkov's clients that had invested in PIC. One didn't lose anything as they had purchased guaranteed funds. The other lost under fifty thousand."

"That investor has just moved to the top of our priority list!" Curtis mildly exclaimed, "get all the information on this person. We want to interview them ASAP."

"There was one more interesting connection that showed up through a chance search I did on the internet." Mirwani spoke with a tone that seemed playful, almost teasing. "It turns out that both Brian Wicker and George Martinique are members of the Hunt Club, the one down on Kingston Road."

"Isn't the Hunt an exclusive golf club for the uppity-ups?" Boyle asked.

"Yes, that's the one. They have both been members for a number of years."

"Interesting," Curtis said, "however, it could just be coincidence."

"I don't like coincidences, especially in a murder investigation." Boyle stated.

"It's definitely something to question the next time either one of them are interviewed." Curtis mentioned.

"Yes," said Boyle, "another little fire I can start under Wicker's house of cards."

****

Boyle turned to Curtis and stated he wanted to discuss some other issues he had thought about.

"Were these thoughts during a cigar meditation?" Curtis joked.

Boyle smiled and responded. "I've been thinking about the motive. We seem to have the motive for the Wilson murder, a motive of revenge for the loss of money, however, other than the two cases where the investors were also clients of Ivan Malinkov, there doesn't seem to be any other connection, apart from Brian Wicker."

"Wicker is deeply involved in both cases, and the man seems to have questionable business ethics, but I don't see any motive for him wanting to kill either man. He definitely doesn't fit the profile of the killer and I can find no reason why he would hire someone to do the killings."

"What are you getting at?" Curtis asked.

"Perhaps we are looking at the wrong motive." Boyle suggested, "We assume the motive is revenge. However, what if the motive was something else. What if the connection between the two killings was actually the way in which the killer chose his victims? Revenge might have been an influence in his choice, but the main motive could have been something else altogether."

"If we are talking about someone who wanted to kill more than one person, then we'd have to look at motives of a sociopathic nature. Deviant desires in which someone kills for pleasure, or to increase their power, or in the belief they are acting out God's will. These could even have been professional hits that were made to look like they were done by a psycho."

"There's no further evidence that this is a Serial," Curtis said, "and I don't think a professional killer would go to the trouble of committing the murders in such a brutal and risky manner. I think we should continue with what we've got and move forward with the rest of the interviews."

Chapter Forty-Seven

Tuesday morning in the middle of April, and the rain poured down in Toronto, turning the city streets into small rivers and causing the residents of Toronto's Island community to evacuate their homes once again. The Argo was situated in the middle of the seventh floor with no windows. The teams were oblivious to the weather and were often surprised when they left and passed a window to see the rain falling like a biblical cloudburst.

Both teams had spent the past few weeks interviewing the PIC investors in between other casework. In the Argo, Curtis asked for the latest reports on the interviews.

Archambault immediately turned to his laptop and began speaking, "Of the remaining investors who lost more than fifty thousand, it was determined there were no cases that stood out as being potential suspects. In most cases, it was accepted the investment was a 'gamble' and no one was to blame for the losses."

"We also interviewed the children of the elderly investors who passed away and most of them did not fit the profile of the killer, or they were simply not concerned about the loss of money."

"However, there were three children who did fit the profile. One man was living in Exeter, England. A second man was the owner of seven fast food franchises and the third man had been in and out of CAMH for a number of years and was currently of no fixed address. It was determined he probably would not have the means or the abilities to plan and execute both of these murders. In all three cases, the investigations turned up no connections with Ivan Malinkov."

"We also re-interviewed the lover, the escort and the family." Baldoni took over the review, "We showed them the death-threat letter that Kyle had received, and no one expressed any knowledge of its existence. Apparently,

Kyle either didn't take it seriously, believing it was a joke of some sort, or just didn't want to share with the persons who were closest to him."

"The list of suspects just keeps getting smaller." Boyle commented. "Hopefully, the list will eventually shrink down to just a few individuals we can focus on."

"What about those who lost under fifty thousand?" Curtis directed the question toward the constables.

Constable Davis stated, "All of the remaining investors fell into the same categories Pierre mentioned, either not fitting the profile of the killer or just simply not concerned about the loss of money."

"However, there are two notable exceptions. One was a man, early thirties and he lost just over twenty-five thousand. It was part of an inheritance he received from his grandparents. He had bought property in Oakville with the rest of his inheritance, so even though he lost money, he still had means to live the lifestyle he wanted."

"The second exception was another hockey player. The investment was in his name and he lost just over forty thousand. We haven't had a chance to interview him yet because he is now a sports analyst on one of the networks, He travels extensively with many of the teams, both in hockey and soccer. His name is Nicholas Talbet."

"Can you put him on my list to interview?" Baldoni asked, "My brother would give his left arm for an autograph."

"This isn't a fan club Gina." Curtis said.

"I know, but he's a famous star, and he's still kinda cute, even at his age."

"Even at his age? What does that imply about me and Curtis?" Boyle asked.

"Sorry Boss, but like I said, he's still kinda cute."

A short silence followed her last remark until Constable Davis dryly said, "Queen of the Cool."

Archambault followed with, "The Princess of Poise."

"Ha, ha, not funny," Baldoni snarked annoyed.

"The Glacier Goddess," Evanko laughed.

"Hey Gina, does any of your brothers have children?" Mirwani asked smiling.

"Yeah, what of it?" she said with greater annoyance.

"Then that would make you the aunt of the Arctic."

"Oh, for fuck's sake, will you guys stop this!" Baldoni's irritation rose with each new jest.

"Okay everybody, settle down," Boyle said to the room, and then added, "besides, that should be Aunt of the Arctic Wolves."

"Oh fuck, thanks Boss." Baldoni's face reddened as the room erupted in laughter.

****

When the joviality started to subside, Curtis impatiently brought the tone back and brusquely asked, "What about the two investors that had a connection with Malinkov?"

"As we had found out previously," Baldoni spoke while still red in the face, "one had purchased guaranteed funds and didn't lose any real money. The other had lost less than fifty thousand and does not fit the profile. She is a woman executive for the Ontario Hydro corporation and only knew Malinkov as the sales agent when she purchased a home in the Beaches eleven years ago. She insisted there were no other dealings with Malinkov since. She claims her involvement with PIC is coincidental."

"Dammit!" Curtis said to no one in particular, "this is worse than the proverbial needle in a haystack. We're picking through straws that have the ability to lie and deceive in order to not be found."

Boyle spoke up once more, "The note that Mie Liu found among Kyle's possessions," he wondered aloud, "it might not have anything to do with the PIC investors. It could have been from one of his lovers, or even from one of the hockey players he competed with over the years. Hell, it could even have been a joke someone played, and he decided to keep the note as a memento."

"We are only looking for someone who wanted revenge, someone who had lost money in the PIC funds and potentially someone who also had a gripe with Malinkov, possibly over a real estate deal or perhaps Malinkov made advances toward their partner."

"For the past month, I've had Donna punching in all the names of the people involved in the Kyle Wilson investigation, including all the PIC investors, the names of their children and so forth. She's been researching if any of them, from either list, had criminal records that might lead toward identifying an ulterior motive to the murder of both men. Donna, can you show us what you found?"

Donna Chang sat straight in her chair. Her laptop prepared, files opened, and the windows reduced so she could quickly move from one file to another. She had prepared Jpeg images of people she wanted to highlight, and they were contained in one folder with the last names in alphabetical order. Donna Chang was always prepared.

"I've researched all the people who were associated with Kyle Wilson and all of the investors in the PIC corporation, including the children we identified that could potentially fit the profile of the killer. Approximately seventy-five percent had received traffic tickets, and if that was their only infraction, I eliminated them from the list. I also deleted the ones who are now deceased."

She opened another Excel file on her computer and said, "On screen two is the file I want to review. In column A, there is a list of all the people who have a criminal offense record. Under column B is a listing of their relationship, whether they were an investor or related to one of the investors."

Column C is the criminal offense they were found guilty of. Columns D, E, F are the additional offenses attributed to the same person.

"Through the sorting function," Donna Chang continued, "I can sort the columns so we can group each of the offenses, or group the people with more than one offense. I can also select particular offenses and hide the others in the background."

"Is this file on our server?" Curtis asked.

"Yes, I loaded it up last night after getting the last set of names from Katherine and Jasmine."

Boyle felt the need to provide an explanation, "I asked Donna to put this together because I don't think the information obtained from the initial interviews will be sufficient to point us in the direction of the killer. However, this list could give us an insight into the type of person they might be and whether they would be liable to commit murder."

"Thank you, Ari, but you should have consulted with me first." Curtis said sternly, "If we're going to coordinate the investigations of the two murders then I think any intensive plans, or change in the course of the investigations, should be a shared communication."

Boyle had been put in his place, and he knew it. He was always preaching about full disclosure of all work and information to his team so that anyone could develop an insight, spot an inconsistency, or maybe even a lie.

"You're right Randal." Boyle admitted meekly, "I had a hunch, and I should have let you know what Donna was doing for me. I guess I should learn to follow my own advice."

Curtis smiled at Boyle's show of humility. "We're all cops with egos. Let's look at this list and see what we can find."

They reviewed the full list of people one by one. Archambault suggested that Donna start eliminating names in which the criminal offense didn't provide any reason to suspect a person for two murders, and to delete names of people who do not fit the profile of the killer.

****

There was a total of forty-seven names on the list.

The first deletions were twenty-one people who did not fit the profile. They also decided to delete the eight people who only had a criminal record for drug possession. Most of these were for the possession of marijuana and most of them were prior to the year 2000.

They eliminated the names of three sexual offenders but both Baldoni and Archambault argued one should be kept on the list. He had been convicted of possessing child pornography and the two detectives felt this could potentially lead to a blackmail motive.

Next, they eliminated one conviction of disorderly conduct, which had additional crimes listed for disobeying a court order and failure to appear in court. They also eliminated two cases of impaired driving, of which one also included convictions for bodily harm or death while impaired.

This left a total of seven people remaining on the list.

****

The two homicide teams stopped for a break. Archambault and Garrison went to the Rest Room as both of them had young children and experienced sleep interruptions during the night. Donna Chang and Amal Mirwani headed to their respective desks to start compiling information on the remaining seven people on the list.

Boyle and Curtis went down to the main lobby and out the front doors. They walked mostly in silence until they reached the Prana Coffee shop. "What makes you think there is an ulterior motive?" Curtis asked when they sat down at one of the tables.

Boyle took a sip from his espresso and said, "Each of the murders have two things in common, apart from the cleaning solvents. One is that there is no evidence that could lead to a suspect. That's the most significant commonality."

He continued, "You and I have been in this racket long enough to know that there is always some sort of evidence left behind, and as experienced professionals, we have to deduce how this murderer managed to leave absolutely no evidence. This can only mean careful, deliberate planning, for both murders."

"The second commonality was that they were both viciously brutal. They weren't shootings and they weren't crimes of passion. They were planned and committed with the intent of causing as much pain as possible before the actual demise of the victim."

"You think this is the beginning or part of a Serial." Curtis surmised.

"Two does not make a serial, but it could be the start," Boyle suggested, "the killer may have done something in the past, something less than murder, and was never caught. Now he's learned, and he's getting better at it. Ivan's killing seemed to be pretty safe for him because the victim was alone in a sound proofed house and no witnesses. Kyle's murder was more brazen, out in the open, with a greater sense of risk. That meant something more to him, a sense of uncertainty that provided him with pleasure, power or some other delusional motive. I'm also still not convinced these weren't professional hits, made to look like they weren't."

"You think we're going to find something in that Excel chart?"

"I don't know, but I know we're not getting anywhere, and we're speeding to get there."

"Yeah, I agree," Curtis said. "You work a lot on intuition Boyle. I'm more pragmatic, I need to see the angles, the evidence and the motive."

****

322

Two hours later, the teams were once more in the Argo. Donna Chang and Amal Mirwani had split the list of seven names and researched information on their criminal records.

The first person was a former gang member with the Streetriders Motorcycle Club.

"I thought the Streetriders had gone by the wayside, most of their territory and business taken over by the Angels." Singleton stated.

Mirwani confirmed, "All the charges against this person were at least twenty-five years ago. The man barely fits the profile as he is now in his late sixties. My guess is he needed to invest his drug money. However, there were numerous charges of assault, weapons related, drug trafficking and one aggravated sexual assault."

"Put him down as a positive potential." Curtis instructed.

Mirwani continued, "There was another investor who had been convicted of drug trafficking, but it was noted he did not have an affiliation with any of the known gangs. He had also been convicted for carrying concealed weapons and had one charge for assault that was overturned."

"We never found any traces of drugs within either of the victim's systems, but I don't want to rule this character out of the picture." Boyle stated, "Malinkov had numerous shady business deals and he may have even purchased drugs for someone else."

"I wouldn't have put it past him to include an ounce of coke with the purchase of a home as part of his sales pitch." Baldoni said sardonically.

"Good point. Keep 'em on the list." Curtis said.

Mirwani continued the review of potential suspects, "There were two people who had been convicted of attempted murder. One had tried to kill his wife for her alleged affairs, and a second who had tried to kill his boss when he was being fired from his job."

"The man who tried to kill his wife had strangled her into unconsciousness and stabbed her three times, then went to a bar. A sister found the wife, called the police and an ambulance crew managed to resuscitate the woman. The husband was picked up outside of the bar and confessed to the crime."

"The second man literally jumped across a boardroom table and attacked his supervisor and the human resource person informing him of his dismissal. He used the boardroom phone to strike the supervisor into unconsciousness and then proceeded to choke him. The human resource person ran from the room and summoned help. He was still holding the supervisor around the neck when he was pulled off by a number of other employees."

"Even though the incident could have been deemed as assault causing bodily harm, the lawyers for the corporation aggressively pushed for an attempted murder conviction, wanting to set a precedent for future cases of such nature. The lawyers were successful, and he was convicted. When he was released from prison, he moved in with his sister who had held his bank accounts for him."

Boyle and Curtis both agreed these two men should be kept on the list because of the time spent in prison. They wanted the backgrounds of both men looked into and whether they had any connection with Malinkov as well as being PIC clients.

At this point, Donna Chang reported on the three investors she had researched.

"The first person on my list also had a homicide conviction. He was charged with murder but was only convicted of manslaughter and spent fifteen years in prison. He killed another man whom he claimed had molested his twelve-year old daughter. There was never any proof of the molestation apart from what the daughter reported, but there were accusations and a fight. His wife had made investments in PIC while he was in prison, and they were quite profitable until the crash. She managed to pull some of their money out prior to the fund going under."

"He's also at the top end of the profile, age fifty-seven, but he is in good condition according to his parole officer and has not had any parole violations. He was released early from his sentence for good behavior."

"I want to keep this man on the list." Curtis said. "His crime may have been one of passion, but I've always found that people learn a lot in prison. A lot of bad things, and with a lot of time to think about it."

"Agreed," said Boyle. "Please continue Donna."

"There was one investor who was convicted of arson which included fraud charges and attempted homicide. It was a case in which the man's business was set on fire for the insurance claims, however, there was a homeless vagrant in the business at the time it was burned down. The homeless man was rescued by the fireman on the scene and only suffered smoke inhalation."

"Did this man have any dealings with Ivan Malinkov?" Boyle asked.

"I couldn't find any connection."

"I think it would be safe to say this man probably isn't a suspect in the murders." Curtis said as he turned to face Boyle.

"Agreed." Boyle said again. "Who's the last person on your list Donna."

"The last person on the list was convicted for Trafficking in Persons. The man had been luring young women from southeast Asia with promises of a new life in Canada, and wonderful job opportunities. When the women arrived, they were placed in massage parlors where they worked as prostitutes. There were a few other charges, but most had been dropped. His investments in PIC were just over one hundred thousand, and they fluctuated monthly with the selling of shares and purchasing of new ones. It appeared to be his way of laundering money."

"Malinkov may have been one of his customers at the massage parlor." Singleton piped in. "He was a known womanizer and an unscrupulous one at that."

"Kyle was gay," Baldoni added, "but he did use escorts."

"Kyle could have used more than one escort over the years," Curtis said. "I want this man kept on the list as there may have been an obscure connection with both victims."

"That gives us six people who may be potential suspects." Boyle said, "Let's get them all back for interviews, and this time I want the interviews to be hard. If the killer is in this group, their background might just make them slip up."

Chapter Forty-Eight

It was the first week in May and Boyle had come to the Parthenon after another day of murder, meetings and interviews. He needed the comfort of familiar surroundings, his friend and his son. He needed a meal and a few glasses of wine to wash away the tedium of investigations that had turned up nothing but frustration. He watched with pride as his son seemed happy with his new endeavors, and he also reminded Theo to make sure Orestes was not overworking himself.

He had two glasses of wine with dinner and a few glasses of Ouzo with Orestes later on. His mood was light, and for this one night, he felt genuinely happy.

The evening was cool and the air crisp as he stepped onto the sidewalk outside of the Parthenon. He took a deep breath and could sense the Gods of Olympus hinting at the fates, so he turned east and walked the north side of Danforth. His sobriety slowly came back to him as he passed Pape Avenue and he turned to hail a taxi.

"Where to?" said the Sikh driver with a turban headdress.

"There's an all-night coffee shop just past Woodbine," said Boyle.

"The Coffee Express?" asked the driver.

"Yeah, that's the one."

****

The neon sign flashed 'open' in the window of the Happy Sushi diner, even though it was past eleven. Night doesn't seem to fall in the east end of the city, it creeps in like a burglar, and then settles like a stale donut.

A streetlight flickered on and off, pulsating with the need for a new bulb. It illuminated the prostitute that materialized from out of a darkened doorway.

She stood in front of Happy Sushi, hip cocked to one side, short skirt, fishnet stockings. The flashing neon sign seemed appropriate for her stance.

Boyle inhabited the north window of the all-night coffee shop across the street. He listened to the dope deals happening in the back corner with amusement. Three teenage girls in the next booth looked rough and ragged and he could hear them chatter about their lives. '*They might be homeless,*' he thought, '*or wanting to be homeless, maybe destined to end up across the street in a couple of years.*'

He was fully awake, knowing sleep would not come this night, and he thought about the murder cases he had dealt with for the past few months. A mild melancholy settled into his psyche, and he wondered if anything he had accomplished would ever prevent any more crimes from happening? He thought about Theo and envied his son, working with Orestes these past couple of months. His son was both Icarus and Jason, living adventures and finding ways to fly.

He thought about his own life, how the days fell like dominoes, one moment crashing into another while he waited for the last door to be closed. He used to wonder what the meaning was, the purpose, and now he just wondered why he even bothered at all.

"What can one really do?" he spoke softly to himself as he watched the hooker bend down to speak with someone through the passenger window of a car. "What can any one person do to change the world, to fix what we all know is wrong. What could I do that would make any difference?"

He looked down into his half-empty coffee cup and confirmed his belief. "Nothing," he mumbled softly, but his voice was just loud enough for the teenage girls to hear, "there's nothing we can do, so why bother?"

The girls giggled and one arose from the booth where they were sitting and sat beside Boyle. She sat close to him, her thighs touching his leg and asked him if he was lonely and wanted company. He looked at her and said, "The only thing we can ever hope to accomplish is to survive and try to improve ourselves. There's nothing else we can do, because we really don't want to."

The girl pushed herself closer to him and put her hand on his knee. "My name is Calypso," she said, "we could spend one night in eternity if you'd like."

Boyle reached down and put his hand on top of hers, preventing her from moving it any higher.

He wanted somebody to listen, but he didn't want to feed her habit. He spoke directly to her, "You read about the carnage around the world, the horrific slaughter of innocent people, the starving refugee children, and you are disgusted by what goes on. You sit back and disdainfully watch as political leaders lie and cheat and follow their corporate religion of corruption. You are repulsed by the knowledge that our environment is slowly changing from something we once called 'nature' into something that we now call natural."

The girl tried to remove her hand, but Boyle gripped it tightly, letting her know that he wanted her to stay with him, "You can see and feel all of this happening around you, but you are complacent to survive in this secure, consolidated existence that you have fallen into."

"You cannot effect change because you truly don't want it. You do not want to give up this life, which you placidly endure because you are not willing to make the sacrifice necessary for change. Your interests lie in the minimal comforts of your own existence, the one that was handed to you by the very people you revile."

"Let me go," she said and pulled her hand away from him. She got up hurriedly and moved back to her friends and then through a bundle of whispers, they quickly left.

Boyle looked out the window and watched the teenagers walk out onto Danforth. As they passed the window where he was sitting, the girl who had sat beside him made a gesture, giving him the middle finger.

"You've made a sacrifice, haven't you?" Boyle whispered to himself and to the vision of the killer sitting across from him. "You decided to do something, to change your own world. You have created a power…a God unto yourself, one that can kill, again and again. Your motive isn't revenge. It's one of fulfillment. The fulfillment of your supremacy over the world."

Boyle sat back and grinned. He looked over at the dealers and the junkies and smiled at them. A smile that Boyle made for himself, a smile that said he knew what the soul of the killer was. A smile of satisfaction in which he now knew how to pursue a killer.

****

Spring had arrived early, and the air was warm. It was the time of year when homicide teams cleared up old paperwork, prepared files and evidence for prosecutors to use in forthcoming trials. The FIS team cleaned and re-calibrated their instruments, did inventory and re-stocked supplies.

The spring interval seemed to be a time when no one in Toronto wanted to kill anyone else. It was a respite from the hectic winter of murder. Boyle wondered if climate change had any effect, if the mild winter weather caused attitudes and tempers to shift. Did the subconscious mind of ordinary people rebel against the warmer climes when they had expected cold.

Winter meant hockey and travelling to southern resorts. Summer meant baseball and outdoor festivals. The lines between had always been clear, you lived in expectation of the change, even looked forward to what made life in Toronto something to be proud of. Did this blurring of the seasons affect the tempers of its people?

He puffed on his Cuban Cohiba as he sat on a Queen's Park bench facing the statue of King Edward VII. His plan to investigate the people who had previous convictions had utterly failed. None of the main potential suspects had any connection with Malinkov and all had perfectly acceptable alibis for the time of Kyle Wilson's murder. It seemed that there were more avenues closed on these cases than there were roadwork closures in the city.

Nonetheless, one of Boyle's best qualities was his persistence and his slight obsessive-compulsive nature. He knew there was always an answer to any question, always one piece in any puzzle that would lead to a cascade of solutions.

He puffed on his Cuban and let his ruminations flow through his mind like jazz music, one idea blaring a long solo like a Charlie Parker saxophone, the other ideas playing backup. Then another idea would come forth and layer its theme through his brain like a Dave Brubeck piano while the first idea retreated to join the backup band. He continued to puff on his cigar as he sat on the Queen's Park bench.

His contemplation shifted and fell onto the statue of King Edward VII. He had read the plaque at the base of the statue, which stated that it had originally been erected in Edward Park in Delhi, India and had been re-located to Toronto in 1969. He looked up into Edward's stoic face.

'The fashionable playboy, waiting forever to rule the world.' Boyle thought to himself. *'Waiting for your mother to finish her long, long life so that you could be king.'*

He smoked his cigar and watched students from the university carrying their satchels and heads bent to their cell phones. The park was located just north of the provincial government Parliament buildings and was surrounded by the building complexes of the University of Toronto. He watched the roaming students and thought about Theo and the journey that had brought him to the Parthenon.

"Edward," he said aloud to the statue, "you were king for nine years," and then the thought revisited him, '*And once you're the king, then no one but death could take that from you.*'

His eyes suddenly turned into a hard glare as the jazz music abruptly stopped and one clear thought emerged like a distant bright star. He spoke aloud to the statue once more, "The killer also thinks he's a king, and he thinks that he's going to be a king forever. But what he doesn't know is that I'm going to de-throne him."

He picked up his cell phone and pushed the automatic dial for Baldoni's number. "Hey Boss, what's up?" she answered.

"Gina, where are you right now." Boyle asked.

"I'm at the front desk, I was just about to sign out."

"Listen, I want to discuss something with you. Can you meet me in front of the King Edward statue over by Queen's Park? Bring a couple of coffees with you. I want to talk about the cases, the Serial, but I want to talk about it outside of work."

At first, Baldoni didn't say anything. It was the first time she had heard Boyle use the word 'Serial' and she didn't like the way he made it sound. "Okay, I'll be right there," she responded and headed down to the underground parking lot.

****

He remained at the statue smoking his Cohiba when he saw Baldoni walking up from the parking lot of the Parliament buildings.

Every so often Boyle would meet with Gina or other officers in this park, which was only a few blocks away from Police headquarters. He sometimes needed to get away from the constant pressure of the homicide office and into the fresh air, surrounded by trees. He came here when he wanted to think, or when he wanted to talk to someone privately, and what was more private than a public park.

Gina sat down on the bench beside him and handed him his coffee, "Double cream, no sugar."

"Thanks," he said and took a long puff of the Cuban panatela.

She sat and sipped her own coffee, waiting for him to speak. She sat there beside him and knew his thoughts were being organized inside his head and that they would come out when he was ready to verbalize them.

"We've been looking for the killer of Ivan Malinkov and Kyle Wilson," he finally said, "and we're never going to find him."

She disliked the sound of that statement even more than his use of the word 'Serial'. She remained silent, knowing he was just beginning to reveal his thoughts, one at a time.

"He's planned these murders so well, leaving nothing but ammonia and Pine Sol as clues. We've been seeking for someone based on the motive of revenge. However, I believe the motive is one in which a person seeks some type of illusionary power, a chance to be a king in his own mind."

"If this was the same killer in both the Malinkov and Wilson cases, then I'm positive there had to have been an accomplice. I can't believe the killer would have known the victim was alone and vulnerable. It cannot have been a coincidence both times. It must have been planned with somebody's help."

"Serials usually work alone," Baldoni pointed out.

"Yes, but the key word in your statement is 'usually'. That doesn't mean always. How did the killer know Ivan was home and alone, and how did the killer know when Kyle was leaving the pub, and leaving on his own? There had to have been someone else, an accomplice in both cases."

The thoughts in her mind began to form her own cacophony of jazz. "A woman?"

"Ivan Malinkov must have been waiting for somebody, probably a woman. With Kyle, somebody must have been in the pub and seen him leaving and called the killer." He quickly reached for his phone before Baldoni had any time to respond.

The phone rang in the pocket of a well-dressed, tall police detective who was sitting in his office at police headquarters, "Hello, this is Curtis."

"Curtis, it's Boyle. Allow me the honor of buying you a beer."

"What's the occasion?"

"I want to go down to the Wheat Sheaf, and I want to discuss something with you. Gina is with me right now and we'll meet you there if you're not too busy. Please ask Pierre to come along as well. I think we have a new angle for the Wilson case."

Chapter Forty-Nine

They arrived at the Wheat Sheaf just after six and took seats on the patio facing the intersection of King and Bathurst streets. Boyle ordered two pints of locally brewed beer and they talked privately about Gina's family, friends and her lovers and losers while they waited for the other two detectives to arrive. They talked about Theo and Orestes and how life seemed to have drawn the two of them together like Socrates and his students.

When Boyle saw Curtis and Archambault walking up Bathurst Street, he stood and motioned for them to come to the patio. As they sat, the waitress arrived to take their orders. Curtis ordered a mineral water and Archambault joined Boyle and Baldoni with a pint of beer.

The drinks were brought to their table by the bar manager Bruce Walton. "Good to see you again Detective Curtis. I hope the video surveillance helped in your investigation. By the way, this tab is on me."

Curtis made to protest but Walton cut him off before he could say a word. "I know what you're going to say, but I don't care, this is my bar, and I can run it anyway I want to," and with a big grin on his face said, "You're either going to allow me to take care of the tab or I'm going to have to throw you out."

Curtis rolled his eyes and chuckled, "Alright then. This time."

The four detectives sat back with their drinks amid a good-humored sense of appreciation, something that rarely happened toward the police. Curtis broke the momentary silence and turned to Boyle, "Thank you for the offer to socialize Boyle, but I don't think the weather or sports was what you had in mind."

"Very perceptive Randal," Boyle said grinning, "take a look around, tell me what you see?"

"Okay Boyle, forget the quiz games and get to the point." Curtis requested.

"Alright then, I'll tell you what I see." Boyle said. "Look at this intersection, it's a very public place. I see many cars passing through. I see a lot of people on the sidewalks, in all directions, people going in and out of this bar on the southwest corner and from the Sly Fox on the northeast corner. I see streetcars going east and west, north and south. I see a lot of human movement."

After a pause, he continued, "Why would anyone pick a spot like this to commit a murder? There's far too much to be left to chance; somebody walking on the sidewalk, a car driving by and stopping, streetcars going in both directions, security cameras in the stores and pubs. Why would he pick a place like this to commit Kyle's murder? Why not in the parking lot after one of his late-night hockey games? Why not almost anywhere else? Why here?"

He stopped for a moment to collect his thoughts and then continued, "You don't plan for a murder in an area like this, unless you plan it with complete accuracy in every aspect and plan it for a specific reason to be done here. You would have to know the Sly Fox was the pub that Kyle regularly went to," as he pointed toward the Sly Fox. "That is the first thing you have to do, find out where the victim would be most vulnerable. And once you know where he's going to be, then you have to pick the most opportune moment, the day of the year, the best time of day, the weather, the method. You would develop the plan by knowing how often the streetcars run; and you would calculate how many people would be on the street by staking out the area night after night."

"You would have had to research the area in great detail. Pick your spot," he continued, "prepare your weapons, stalk your prey, and then wait for that perfect moment when the stars align, and all the factors are in your favor. Both murders, Ivan's and Kyle's were planned like this to the smallest detail."

He stopped to let this insight become perceptible in their minds, "It wasn't by chance that there wasn't anyone on the sidewalks. It wasn't by chance that the streetcars weren't passing by at that point in time. It wasn't by chance that there were very few cars on the street. The killer waited for his time. He waited for the time to be perfect."

He paused once more for effect, "This killer is a hunter. An intelligent, meticulous hunter."

Curtis sipped his mineral water and then said, "I've been thinking somewhat along the same line of reasoning myself. However, it's quite extravagant planning to get revenge."

"I've talked about this before and I don't believe revenge is the main motive." Boyle answered, "I believe revenge was used for the way in which the victims were chosen. The main motive is something else. Whether it was for some sort of perverse pleasure, a thrill of excitement, or some sort of psychosis like the fairies talking to him in his sleep."

He stopped once more and looked around the table to ensure he had their full attention, "It's the planning, that's where the killer gets most of his joy. If you plan it properly, then it's for the sheer excitement. It's for the exhilaration of being so perfect that you're not going to be caught. It's for that thrilling stimulation it's going to give you, not just at the time of the killing, but every night afterward. It's to prove that you are better. No, it's to prove that you are superior to everyone else."

"The killer committed the act here, in a public place, to increase the intensity of his aspirations to god-like domination. He started with Malinkov, knowing the privacy of the scene. Then he gained confidence with our failure to find him. With Kyle's murder, he's becoming more confident, and he's going to believe he is invulnerable, almost god-like."

"You think this is a Serial, and it's going to continue." Archambault voiced what they were all thinking.

"Yes." Boyle said resolutely. "However, there's one more thing," he stopped and looked around the table once more at his three fellow officers for dramatic effect, "what does a hunter often use?" and he kept the dramatic effect lingering before he answered his own question, "A well trained and obedient hunting dog to spot the prey."

****

"An accomplice?" Archambault asked, "You think there's more than one person who acted in these murders?"

"Most definitely. Think about it for a moment, the killer had to know when Ivan was going to be home and that he was going to be alone. The killer had to know nobody was going to hear anything from inside Ivan's home because of the sound-proofing insulation and that the security system had no cameras. The killer had to know exactly when Kyle was leaving the pub, and that he left on his own, and how susceptible he would be by the amount of alcohol he had consumed. He had to know which direction Kyle was going to walk."

"We've been looking for the killer. We should be looking for the accomplice." Boyle said as he sipped his beer.

Curtis, Baldoni and Archambault sat quietly, looking at Boyle, the air between them heavy with their thoughts. Curtis took a breath and then spoke, "Insightful. One of your cigar meditations I presume," he took another long intake of breath and then let it out slowly while his own mind contemplated the theory. "Alright, say your correct in all this. How do we investigate the link between the two murders and come up with one killer, or should I say one killer and his partner?"

The calm, tranquil look of someone who is holding a royal flush in a poker game came over Boyle's face. "There's a connection between these two cases in which the accomplice plays an important part. Wicker is one connection but he's not a hunter. I don't think he has the wits about him to plan something like this. There is another connection somewhere and that's where the accomplice fits in, and what we have to find."

"Where do you want to start?" Curtis asked.

The look on Boyle's face remained the same, knowing Curtis also thought him to be right. "I want to re-review all the security film that we managed to gather on the Wilson murder. I want to review the video from the Wheat Sheaf, all of it, for the whole of that day. I also want the security camera video from the Sly Fox. I want to identify any customers that might have been on the phone when Kyle left."

"I also want Donna and Amal to start a comparative analysis of both cases. I want everything we've got on both murders, all information, the interviews, names of associates, friends, family members, everything we know about both murders. I want this entered into the computer system and I want a systematic comparison of both. I want to know what commonalities there are, what names show up in both cases, what business deals coincide, what clubs or associations are the same, whose having sex with who, whose gambling at the same casino, and so on."

"That's a lot of input." Archambault stated, "Amal is working on a couple of other projects, how much time is this going to take?"

"They're both computer experts." Boyle extolled, "Most of the info is already on file and they've got programs that will do comparative analysis. I don't know how much time it's going to take, but I hope they're done before our killer is ready for this coming November."

"Why November?" Curtis asked.

"For whatever reason, that seems to be when he works." Boyle answered, "That's when he can wear enough clothing to disguise himself but still have freedom of movement. That's when most people who could be witnesses are inside, hunkered down in their homes, waiting for the winter. That's his hunting season."

Chapter Fifty

The killer was a hunter, and now Boyle was zeroing in on his prey. He started the meeting in the Argo very early the next morning. "We are going to take a new approach to these two cases," he began, "we are no longer looking for the killer. He's too smart, too precise, he's covered his tracks and has left no spoors behind. We could interview PIC investors until we are blue in the face and still not have a suspect. However, when you look at the evidence from a different viewpoint, it shows us that he had an accomplice."

"How can you be so sure Boss?" Donna Chang asked.

Boyle turned toward Donna and saw the serious intent on her face. He looked down and shook his head amused, *'Looks like I'm going to get stuck with that nickname,'* he thought to himself.

"There are too many things the killer had to know in order to successfully commit both murders," he answered, "in Ivan's case, the killer had to be totally sure Ivan was alone in the home because he attacked him as soon as he opened the door. The killer had to be aware the house was sound proofed."

The killer knew there was a landline phone in the kitchen and a second cradle with a phone upstairs in the bedroom, and he had to be pretty confident there would be no one walking the street when he left. Most importantly, he knew that Ivan probably wouldn't have any callers for most of the weekend.

"In Kyle's murder, he was waiting in the shadows of the alleyway, and had been there for some time. He had to know exactly when Kyle left the bar and that he had left on his own. Someone must have informed him, probably by phone that Kyle was on his way."

"So now we're going look at everything from a different perspective, and I want to approach this in two ways. First, I want Amal to prepare all of the security footage we have on the Kyle Wilson murder. We're going to sit in this room and review all of it, but instead of looking at the actual murder scene, I want to look at the peripheral action from the Wheat Sheaf footage and the security footage from inside the Sly Fox."

He looked directly at Donna Chang knowing that what he was about to ask would mean tired eyes, black coffee and power drinks, "Donna, I want something special from you."

Donna Chang smiled inwardly to herself, not letting her pride show to the others, keeping it solely for her own gratification, "Name it, Boss."

Boyle slowed his pace as he wanted to make sure the instructions were clear, "I know that we have everything in the computers, all the names and associations for both cases, all the forensic information, all of the families, all the associates, and all the relatives of all the families. I want everything that had even the slightest, remotest, potential connection with each case. I want you to do a comparison between to the two case files, and I want to see what connections come up."

"We already did that a couple of months ago." Baldoni said.

"I know, but I want to do it again, but remember, we are looking for an accomplice, not for the murderer. I want every single bit of information compared, including the names of the companies that Malinkov did business with, like that sound proofing company, and any other businesses. I want all of the clients he worked with put into the data. I want everything."

"That's going to take me a bit of time to prepare." Donna warned.

"Donna, you're the best computer expert I've ever known, and your research abilities never cease to amaze me. I have every confidence that you will perform this duty faster than I would expect, and with as much diligence as anyone could possess."

This time the smile of pride on Donna Chang's face was visible for everyone to see.

****

Amal Mirwani had the video files of all the security cameras on two folders on the server. One folder was named 'Original_Files' and the second folder was called 'Condensed_Files'. It was the second folder that had been scrutinized during the initial investigation, but now Boyle wanted to review the original files, which included hours before the actual murder.

However, they first watched the zoomed in footage of the murder from the Wheat Sheaf camera. They watched for the hundredth time as Kyle Wilson walked unsteadily along the sidewalk, stopped and looked in at the alleyway, and then the killer spring out from the shadows and strike with the crowbar.

Boyle then requested the original files in which the entire camera view of the northeast corner was visible. He asked Mirwani if he was able to zoom in at any point from these original files. Mirwani stated the hi-definition of this digital software had zooming features, change of angle and slow motion.

"Good," Boyle said, "I want to see who emerges from the Sly Fox after the murder, the people standing around Kyle's body and those who leave the scene."

Mirwani fast-forwarded the video and stopped on the frame where Kyle exits the front door of the pub. He then copied and saved the next thirty minutes of footage into a separate file so that it could be re-reviewed from start to end without going through the many hours of previous footage.

They watched the video after Kyle's murder. Four men left the pub and stood on the sidewalk.

They seemed to be talking when one of the men noticed someone lying on the sidewalk. He pointed and the other men do not seem concerned, until they casually started to walk over to the body.

They watched as another two men exited the pub and turned west on King Street, crossing the lights and not noticing the other group around the body. Of the first four men, one man knelt down by the body and sees the pool of dark blood, almost black in color. He quickly stood and went into the alleyway to vomit. The other three men stood around the body, one picked up the crowbar, passed it to another, who then dropped it on the sidewalk.

A fifth man joined the group after crossing King Street. This was the man that came from the Wheat Sheaf tavern, and after a few moments, reaches into his pocket for his cell phone and calls 911.

Another two men and a woman emerge from the Sly Fox and notice the scene. One man motioned for the woman to stay behind and then he also moved down the sidewalk toward the body. The woman and the second man beside her, slowly moved toward the scene as if drawn by a magnet.

The woman stops as she sees the reality of the dead body, turns and runs back inside the pub.

After a moment, three more people emerged and headed toward the small but slowly growing crowd.

Another man exited the pub and stood by the front doors, looking down the sidewalk, afraid to move closer. Archambault says to no one in particular, "That's Justin Morgan, one of Kyle's associates at the Queen's Bank. He stated during our interview that he was there with Kyle that night."

They continued watching the video as more people come out of the pub and other curious onlookers from around the area. Some cars have stopped, and people have gotten out to either offer help or to gawk.

Boyle suddenly tells Mirwani to stop the tape and rewind for about a minute. "Do you see that woman coming out with the big floppy hat. That's a strange hat to be wearing on a cold November evening. She's also wearing sunglasses after midnight. Who does she think she is? Corey Hart?" She stops and looks at the crowd, but she doesn't go over to look at what everyone one else is staring at. She simply stops outside the front door, looks and then brusquely turns and heads north up Bathurst Street.

"I want to re-examine the security tapes from inside the pub. I want to see what we can see about her actions in the pub."

****

Amal Mirwani opened the security video from inside the Sly Fox. He fast-forwarded the video to the point where Kyle Wilson and Justin Morgan are at the bar, conversing and drinking from shot glasses. At ten past midnight, Kyle Wilson requested his bill, paid with his credit card, put on his coat, said goodnight to Justin, waved another goodnight to the bartender.

They checked the different cameras and synchronized the time to when Kyle left the pub. They spotted four people using their cell phones when Kyle Wilson was paying his bill and putting on his coat. Three of the people on the phone were men, and the fourth was the woman in the floppy hat.

Boyle spoke directly to Mirwani, "Amal, I want you to follow this footage through and find out how each of those people paid their bills. If they used a credit or debit card, then we can identify them. If not, we can use the facial recognition software to match against driver's licenses and health card photos."

"Detective Boyle," Curtis announced dourly. "What is in those cigars that you smoke?"

Boyle looked at Curtis and grinned, "Cuban tobacco, delicately rolled by hand with knowledge and experience. Smoked in contemplation of the consequences of life, love and catching criminals."

****

The next day, Mirwani reported that two of the men had paid by card and the third man and the woman paid with cash. The security cameras were able to capture full facial pictures of all three men and he ran the pictures through the facial recognition software and was able to identify each of them, matching photos to their driver's licenses.

With this information, Curtis and Archambault went back to the Sly Fox and requested the credit and debit transactions for the day of the murder. The identity of the two men were verified and the third man had his identity confirmed by the pub staff as he was a regular customer and a boyfriend of one of the waitresses.

Mirwani was unable to identify the woman due to the limitations of the software. The face of the woman was never fully exposed as she constantly wore the floppy hat down low and never took off her sunglasses.

A search warrant was requested for the phone records of the three men for the specific time and day of the murder. Boyle and Baldoni interviewed the man who paid cash. He was texting a friend about a meeting the next day. The friend was interviewed, and the meeting information was verified because the topic of the murder was almost the only thing they discussed at the meeting.

Curtis and Archambault interviewed the other two men. The phone records showed one man had phoned home and had spoken to his wife. Neither could remember the actual conversation, but the records did prove that he had called home. The second man had called his brother's phone asking him to come and pick him up as he was too drunk to drive. The brother who received the call remembered it because they had an argument about his brother's alcohol problem.

That left the woman with the floppy hat.

****

Boyle and Baldoni met with Donna Chang in the Argo. She had spent close to a week entering and preparing all of the information into the data banks of the two cases. This included all of the investors of the PIC fund, plus all of their families. It also included all the people that Ivan Malinkov had dealt with as a real estate agent, plus all of the businesses he had associations with.

She had to prepare the information in a specific manner in order for the comparison software to examine both sets of files and identify any commonalities, including names, financial transactions, relationships to the two deceased men, and social functions.

When she was ready, she launched the software to perform the file comparison. It took only a matter of seconds for the computer to complete the search. She watched the results appear as flashing elements on the screen, and an electronic report detailed the similarities.

'The Boss called me the best,' she thought to herself, but as she ran the program another thought began to come forth, and it concerned her, *'but how long before even the best is replaced by automation.'* She dismissed the thought and told Boyle she would have a full report by that afternoon.

****

There were twenty names that appeared in the results. Fourteen of them were real estate agents who had dealt with Kyle when he was at the Beaches branch of the Queen's Bank of Canada. There were the two real estate clients of Ivan's who had also invested in PIC. Another name was Lawrence Greenbaum and Brian Wicker who were associated with PIC.

There was one name that surprised them, Brenda Lewis.

"How is she associated with Ivan Malinkov?" Boyle asked.

Donna Chang pulled up the data files for the Malinkov case and did a search for the name Brenda Lewis. "She was listed in one of Ivan's business contact lists." Donna Chang said.

"She's the escort Kyle would hire whenever he attended a company function or some affair with the hockey association." Baldoni said aloud to no one in particular, "Was she also an escort for Ivan?"

"Why did this not come up in previous searches?" Boyle asked.

"The previous searches only had specific information that was entered." Donna Chang replied. "The software will only make comparisons against the data that is input. This is the first time that we literally input everything."

"Why didn't we interview her when we investigated all the women Ivan dated?" Boyle asked.

"Her name is included under one of the businesses Ivan dealt with. We only interviewed the head of that company."

"We need to inform Randal and Pierre about this." Boyle said, "In the meantime Gina, bring Brenda Lewis in for questioning again."

****

Brenda Lewis sat in Interview room, her head lay upon her arms on the interview room table, and Baldoni could hear the heaving breathing of a person in an uncomfortable slumber.

Baldoni and Singleton had arrived at her apartment at six-thirty in the morning, and under protest she accompanied them to the station. She was a woman who lived a nocturnal lifestyle, which meant that early morning was usually the time she went to sleep.

Brenda had demanded her lawyer be present for the interview and Boyle went out for coffee and croissants while they waited. By the time he returned, Brenda was fully asleep, and he found Baldoni sitting slouched in the chair opposite, heavy eyelids and head drooping.

He tapped Baldoni on the shoulder and she jolted awake. "Sorry Boss, watching her just made me tired as well."

He handed her the coffee and left one for Brenda on the table. The box of croissants was opened and Baldoni picked out a chocolate filled one.

"I thought you were going to eat healthy so that you didn't end up looking like Stanforth," she said with her tongue firmly planted her cheek.

Boyle grinned and after a bite of his croissant he asked her, "When did the lawyer say he would be here?"

"He stated he would come first thing, whatever that meant."

Almost as if on cue, the door to the interview room opened and in walked Mr. Thomas Montgomery, LLB, BCL.

He was of average height, slightly pudgy wearing an elegant suit. He had a high forehead with a salt and pepper hairline that was emphasized by the thick, black-rimmed glasses. His clean shaven, oval face showed that 'first thing' meant after he had showered, shaved and made himself impeccably presentable.

He pulled the chair out beside Brenda and placed a hand gently on her shoulder to awaken her. She shuddered slightly and turned to open her eyes and looked at him. "Good morning Tom," she said in a voice that would make you think she was greeting her lover.

"Brace up Brenda," he said in a formal, authoritative manner.

"Hello Tom." Boyle said as well, "Been a while since we last talked."

"I'm sorry Detective Boyle, but I am here in a professional capacity, so can we please dismiss with any social niceties."

"As you wish." Boyle replied.

Montgomery asked for a brief recess before the start of the interview so that he could speak privately with his client. Boyle agreed and he and Baldoni left the room. They stood in the hallway until Montgomery opened the door and stated they were ready.

"I understand that you have already interviewed my client more than once with regards to the murder of Kyle Wilson," he crisply stated. "Unless you have a specific line of inquiry, I don't believe she has anything more to say on the subject."

"This interview is not about the Kyle Wilson murder." Baldoni stated roughly.

"Then why have you brought her in for questioning? Is she required for another investigation? Why didn't you inform her when you brought her in?"

Boyle looked over at Baldoni with a questioning look.

"We informed her when we first arrived at her condominium. Her protestations were very raucous and indignant. However, Constable Singleton and I explained we wanted to speak with her about the Ivan Malinkov investigation."

"Who is Ivan Malinkov?" the lawyer asked.

"He was the real estate agent that was murdered two years ago come this November." Boyle calmly elaborated. "We found her name in one of his phone books."

"And how does this implicate my client?"

"She was also dating Kyle Wilson." Boyle went on, "We have reason to believe it was the same person who committed both murders. She is one of the few people who was connected to both victims. We think she may have some further information for us."

Montgomery leaned over and whispered in his client's ear, holding his hand up to cover his lips to prevent any of the conversation from being heard. She replied back with a whisper in his ear.

"Go ahead, ask your questions," the lawyer succinctly stated.

Baldoni turned to Brenda and asked her directly, "Did you know Ivan Malinkov?"

Brenda bent toward Montgomery with a questioning look. He nodded his head. "I dated him once or twice," she said.

"Was this a professional date?" Baldoni asked abruptly.

"She will not answer that question Detective Baldoni." Montgomery curtly replied.

"Okay, then can you please explain the nature of these two dates with Malinkov." Baldoni asked with a punchy tone.

"Whom my client has dated is a personal preference, detective. She is not at liberty to describe her emotional or physical attachment to anyone without due cause. If you have specific questions regarding the murder investigation, then please keep the questions to that subject."

Boyle reached over to the digital recorder. He spoke into the machine and stated he was putting it on pause for a recreational break in the proceedings. He then turned to Montgomery and spoke candidly. "Tom, off the record, we're not trying to implicate Brenda in either of the murders. We already know of her involvement with Kyle Wilson, be it professional or otherwise. We need to know her involvement with Malinkov. If this was the same murderer in both cases, we fear the killer may continue. We need Brenda's cooperation."

Montgomery looked hard at Boyle, the implications of what he said going through his mind, and how those implications would affect his client, and potentially even himself. He told Boyle that since the recording device was already off, he asked for another recess to talk to his client. Boyle agreed and both he and Baldoni left the room once more, but first asking if the lawyer or Brenda would like fresh coffee.

Montgomery took note of Boyle's offer and understood that it was a sign they were not looking to ensnare Brenda in either case, or to even compromise her professional services. Boyle had made it clear that they needed her help.

****

Boyle and Baldoni returned thirty minutes later with fresh coffees and muffins. Brenda had freshened up and applied some make up. She seemed better composed and less tense. Montgomery took his coffee and thanked Boyle for the refreshments, which was his way of saying his client had a better understanding of what the detectives were looking for.

"May I suggest we keep this off the record so that my client will feel more congenial toward cooperation." Montgomery started the conversation.

Baldoni glanced over to Boyle who nodded. She turned on the digital recorder and stated the interview had concluded. When the lawyer was sure the unit had been shut off, he turned to his client and told her that it was okay to speak with the police, but not to answer if he interrupted her.

"How did you know Ivan Malinkov?" Boyle asked softly.

She turned to Montgomery who nodded to her. "He was a client for a short while," she responded.

"How long ago?"

"Four or five years I think."

"You still remembered him?" Boyle's question held a note of curiosity.

"Yeah, I remembered him. He was on my list of unwanted money."

"What do you mean by unwanted money?"

She turned to her lawyer once again looking for his advice. He asked Boyle if this was positively off the record, and when Boyle agreed he nodded once again.

"It basically means that I don't care how much money is offered, the person is not worth my time or my attention." Brenda calmly stated.

"We've heard a number of reports about Ivan, from his family, his colleagues and his ex-girlfriends. He was somewhat nefarious in his treatment of women." Boyle commented, "In your opinion, do you think his attitude or actions would cause someone to murder him?"

"I only met him a couple of times," she replied, "he was callous and indignant when I didn't measure up to his expectations of me. I left after getting paid and didn't return any of his phone calls."

"Where did you go on these dates?"

"Dinner, then back to his place."

"Was he ever violent?"

She did not answer but looked down into her coffee cup. Her eyes glistened with moisture and Boyle wasn't sure if it was because she was tired or if she remembered something. Her voice was subdued when she answered, "I don't remember."

"That would be something that I would remember." Baldoni said with a huff.

Brenda sat up straight with determination in her eye, "Look, the guy had my name in his telephone book. My name is probably in many other telephone books as well. I dated him, but I'm not going to incriminate myself with how I go about dating men, or women for that matter. I saw him a couple of times. I didn't like him, but I saw him because that is what I do."

"Did you ever speak to Kyle about him?" Boyle took a softer tone again.

"I don't speak to anyone about other people I date," she said bitterly, "I know you want to find the person who killed Kyle, and I hope you do, because Kyle was a decent man. If you catch the person who killed Ivan, tell them they have my thanks for removing a scumbag from the world."

Montgomery was concise, "I think that we are finished here detective. My client has answered your questions and I feel it is pointless to continue. If you feel the need to question her again, I will request that you provide a court order."

Montgomery stood from the table and took Brenda by the elbow, almost physically lifting her out of her chair. She followed him obediently out of the door.

Boyle and Baldoni sat back in their chairs, both heavy with the knowledge that another door had been closed on both cases.

"I kind of agree with her." Boyle finally spoke up after a while.

"What do you mean Boss?"

"Whomever killed Ivan Malinkov might have done the world a favor."

"Is that what you're going to tell Curtis?"

"No. But we need to find the woman with the floppy hat. That's it, that's all we have."

****

"I want to review those files again and again and again if we have to." Boyle almost shouted to Amal Mirwani and the other three detectives in the room. "We need to be able to identify her."

"I'm sorry, Detective Boyle, but like I told you before, the software needs more features if it's going to do a facial match with anyone." Mirwani pleaded. "That big floppy hat and those sunglasses pretty much covers up most of her face."

"When did she arrive at the Sly Fox?" Curtis asked, sensing Boyle's frustration. Curtis understood Boyle's irritability because he also knew they had reached the end, that this was probably the last lead they would be able to investigate before both cases were put on hold.

"She arrived about eight-o'clock in the evening, just about a half-hour after Kyle." Mirwani said.

"Then we go through all four hours of footage from all three cameras until we find enough of her face that we can use." Boyle insisted.

"Are we able to piece together a face from different shots?" Baldoni asked.

"That will be difficult," Mirwani said, "the cameras are at different angles so if we did that, the face will be distorted, and the software may choose someone totally not compatible because the nose is at a different angle, or the cheekbone seems higher, and so on."

"Then we start looking at four hours of three different cameras." Boyle sighed. "I suggest we split this up into groups. Donna Chang with Pierre and Gina, Amal with me and Randal."

They loaded up their laptops, with the required files. Boyle, Curtis and Amal Mirwani went to one of the interview rooms after first stopping off at the cafeteria to load up with coffee and sandwiches. Donna Chang, Archambault and Baldoni stayed in the Argo and ordered pizza, power drinks and water to be picked up at the front desk.

The hours ticked by while both groups reviewed the videos. The woman in the floppy hat was careful, very careful, as if she had been given instructions on how to hide her face. She spent most of her time looking down at her phone and only looking up furtively to look around the bar, then bent her head down once more to her cellphone.

"Why did you start calling him Boss?" Baldoni asked Donna Chang as she yawned and stretched her arms up in the air.

"I noticed how he usually smiled when you called him Boss," she replied with a contagious yawn in response to Gina's. "I thought that maybe he liked it. I also find it easier to use. Using their first names seem too informal, and Detective Boyle seems too impersonal. I think it just fits."

"I know what you mean." Baldoni twisted her head from side to side to ease the tension of her muscles from constantly looking up at the big screen and studying the footage.

"Wait! Stop!" Archambault cried, "look at that view."

The woman with the floppy hat had looked up from her phone and checked the bar once as she had done every few minutes. However, this time a waitress had come up from the other side of her to ask if she wanted anything else. This must have startled her momentarily and she lifted her head to reply to the waitress. In that moment, she looked directly into the camera, just enough to capture the entire lower portion of her face, from her cheeks down to her chin.

Baldoni called Boyle on his cellphone and told him to get back into the Argo right away. In the meantime, Donna Chang blew up the picture as much as she could without losing resolution, and then made a still shot of it.

As the other three came rushing back into the room, they could see the still shot up on the screen.

Boyle looked at the screen and smiled, "Gotcha."

****

"Okay, so explain to me once more how this facial recognition software works." Boyle calmly asked Mirwani.

"It takes one picture of a face and analyzes the facial features: the shape of the face, the position of the eyes, the forehead, the lips, the nose, the cheek bones, shape of the chin, and so forth. It then does a comparison search to other faces in the database for the same features. It identifies aspects of the face that are common or similar. However, the most common feature it works best on is the eyes, because the eyes can be measured for size, shape, distance apart, heavy or light eyelids and the distance from the brows. The woman with the floppy hat never takes off her sunglasses, so the main featured used is not available to us."

"Also, with the hat on, the software can't use the shape of her face as a distinctive feature either. All we've got is the nose, lips, cheek and chin. If we do a comparative search with only those features, we'll end up with half the women in Canada coming in as a positive match."

"What if I could greatly reduce the size of the database you would need to compare these facial features to?" Boyle said playfully.

"That would narrow down the field considerably and would work a lot quicker."

Boyle's confidence now came to his voice, "I want that picture put through the facial recognition software and only compared to every single woman in the Ivan Malinkov case."

"Why just the women on the Malinkov case?" Archambault asked.

"We know this woman is involved with the Kyle Wilson murder. She was at the pub and she was making the phone call when Kyle left. If the limited facial features we have for her match up with any of the women in the Malinkov case, then we might have our connection, our accomplice."

****

Detective Sergeant Curtis and Detective Pierre Archambault opened the doors to the Queen's Bank of Canada branch on King Street West. They walked down the marble hallway to the financial management offices and opened the familiar heavy glass door. The receptionist immediately dialed George Martinique to inform him the detectives were back once again.

As Curtis and Archambault approached the reception desk, the receptionist told them Mr. Martinique was on his way to the reception area to greet them.

Curtis smiled, and his eyes gave her an expression that communicated his pleasure the bank employees had learned to treat the police with respect and courtesy.

As George Martinique turned the corner leading to reception, he announced so all could hear in an obviously pseudo friendly tone, "Detective Curtis, to what do we owe this pleasure of another visit?"

"We have a couple of more questions for you." Archambault replied for Curtis.

"Do we need to go to my office, or can we use the small boardroom just over there?" Martinique answered the question looking directly at Curtis.

"The boardroom will be fine." Archambault said in a hard tone, letting Martinique know he did not like being ignored or being used as a pawn in this game of wills.

Martinique led the way into the small boardroom that had a round table and four chairs. He closed the door behind them and then sat in one of the chairs, motioning for the detectives to take a seat themselves.

Neither detective sat down, Archambault standing in front of the door and Curtis standing across the table from where Martinique sat. Curtis did not waste any time and went directly into the interview as soon as Archambault had completed the information for the digital recording.

"How well do you know Brian Wicker?" Curtis asked.

"Brian Wicker?" Martinique questioned. "I know that he's a member of the Hunt Club where I go golfing from time to time."

"But how well do you know him?"

"I've played a little golf with him over the years. Members are always looking for a foursome when you get there. So yeah, I've played a few rounds with him but that's about it."

"Have you spoken with him recently?"

Martinique's composure started to wane. He couldn't be sure if they had spoken to Wicker before coming to see him, so he could not know if Wicker had mentioned the phone conversation. He quickly analyzed the situation in his mind and decided it was best to admit to the conversation, and only reveal as much as needed to alleviate the suspicions of the detectives.

"As a matter of fact, I had a phone conversation with him a few months ago. He was asking about a golf trip somewhere down in the Caribbean, the Bahamas, I think. He wanted to know if I was interested."

"Were you?" Curtis looked down on him.

"I politely told him that I wasn't, made up an excuse of some sort. I don't particularly like the man. Not the kind of person I associate with." Martinique said with a touch of droll.

"Just a salesman." Curtis said with his own touch of sarcasm. "Money, but no class." Martinique's expression did not reveal any hint of the barb that was delivered in Curtis' comment. He simply sat there and waited for any more questions to be asked. However, Curtis could not conceal the contempt he had for this privileged banker.

"That's all for now," he said. "We'll let you know if we have any more questions once we've spoken to Mr. Wicker."

Again, Martinique's expression did not reveal any sense of the anxiety that was building within his inner being. He just smiled and escorted the detectives to the glass door. "If there is anything else you need to know for your investigation, please come see me."

As he walked back to his office, his mind raced through a number of thoughts. Was this a ruse? Had the police already spoken to Brian Wicker, or were they off to see him now? How did they know he knew Brian, even if only as a fellow member of a golf club? Were they suspecting him of any involvement in Kyle's death?

When he got back to his office, he removed a bottle of vintage port from his cabinet. It was only just before noon, but he felt that he needed a little stimulation to settle his nerves.

Chapter Fifty-One

It was Friday morning at Malvern Collegiate Institute and the windows of the history class looked out on the cenotaph statue of a sword-bearing young man facing west toward the sunset. It had been erected in 1922 to honor the Malvern students and graduates who had fallen during the First World War.

"Today we're going to talk about the differences between societal and personal history," the Teacher spoke once everyone had taken their seats. "Does anyone remember the murder that happened in the Beaches a year and a half ago? Was that an historical event for the Beaches community, or maybe it was an event that affected you on a personal level."

"Sir, isn't it true that history is dictated by the victors?"

"Thank you, Thomas, that's an old axiom, but does have some merit for this discussion. If we use the Crusades as an example, history can be dictated and compromised in some sense the by the historian who records it."

"The scribe or scholars during the third crusade kept detailed records of the events. However, the historian who was a subject of King Richard the Lionheart would record how Richard was brave, courageous and how all his men loved him. He recorded that he was a superior tactician and general, and how he led the charge into battle and single-handedly defeated the Saracens. This same scribe would describe King Philip of France as cowardly, incompetent and self-serving, only interested in the riches and power of the conquest."

"However, the monk who served under Philip would describe Richard as cruel, egotistical and mistaken in his use of the divine right bestowed upon him. He would describe Philip as lordly, compassionate, and a true Christian wanting to protect the Holy Sepulcher from the enemy."

"Now, does the same happen with our own personal histories? Do we dilute the truth based on what we see and feel, on what we think happened?"

"That murder happened just down the street from me." Daniella said loudly to the class, as if her locality to the incident raised the importance of her opinion.

"What do you remember of it?" asked the Teacher.

"The cops had our street blocked off the whole day. Nobody knew what was going on, and the cops came to our house several times to ask questions."

"Did they find the killer at your house?" the Teacher asked.

Daniella looked puzzled, "Uh, no, we didn't do it." The rest of the class began to laugh and snicker at Daniella's discomfiture.

"Of course, and I'm sorry Daniella, I didn't mean to be disrespectful, I just wanted to use the example of how history affects everyone."

"Did they ever catch the killer?" Georgina asked.

"Not that I've heard of," replied the Teacher. "There haven't been any news reports about it for quite some time now. However, as we've just seen, Daniella was affected by the simple fact that she lived a few houses away. That is now a part of her personal history. Was anyone else affected by the murder?"

"My parents knew him." Joel stated, "He was the agent they used when we bought our house. I remember them talking about him when he was killed."

"What did they have to say?"

"They said he was a jerk. He pretended to be friendly, but as soon as the sale was finalized, he acted like an asshole."

"Language," the Teacher remonstrated.

"Sorry," Joel said, "I was making a direct quote."

"Sir!"

"Yes Jamal."

"My dad said he knew the real estate agent and that he was a really good guy. He said he did a great job for us when we bought our house, and then did a great job for my uncle as well."

"So, your family has a different opinion about the victim than Joel's family," said the Teacher, "are there other opinions to be presented?"

A girl in the corner of the classroom timidly raised her hand. She looked shyly down at her desk over her thin wire-framed glasses.

"Yes, Constance, do you want to add something to the discussion?"

"My mother said he was an evil man." As soon as she spoke, she felt as if the entire classroom had turned to look directly at her. Her sheepish nature shrank even further with the attention.

"It's okay Constance, thank you for sharing. Can you to tell us why your mother thinks that man was evil."

Constance tried her best to hide inside herself. She looked harder at her desk, hoping it would swallow her up and take her away from the stares of the others.

"It's alright Constance, you don't have to say anything more if you don't want to."

"He tried to rape her," she blurted out in a loud guarded voice. The whole class fell silent, and their stares became unconscious penetrations into the fragile ego of the shy girl.

"That's a very strong accusation," the Teacher said, "and against a man who cannot defend himself."

"He did!" Constance yelled, "my mother used to work at the realty company as a secretary. At one of the parties, he took her into a back room and told her he wanted to talk to her about a promotion or something. Then he made a pass at her and she said no. Then he grabbed her, but my mom hit him and got out of the room."

"How do you know all this?" the Teacher asked.

"I overheard her telling my dad. I was sitting at the top of the stairs and they didn't know I could hear. My dad said he was going to punch him out, but my mom made him promise not to do anything. She didn't want him to get arrested for assault. She said the agent wasn't worth the trouble that my dad would get into."

"Thank you, Constance. I know this must have been difficult for you to relate," the Teacher's voice held genuine sympathy for the girl. "This incident is recorded in history as an unsolved murder, and yet we have three different accounts of how it has affected us."

"Tomorrow we are going to start watching a movie called 'Rashomon' by the Japanese director Akira Kurosawa. It is a story about a crime that happens, a robbery and a rape in medieval Japan. It is told through the perspective of four different people; the bandit, the samurai husband, the wife and a woodcutter who witnessed the crime. Each tells a different story about the incident through their own subjective and contradictory views."

"Later we are going to discuss the murder of the real estate agent. We are going to discuss if we can apply the same parameters that was used in the

Kurosawa movie and see how the personal histories of different people might differ."

"Your homework for this weekend is to research the real estate agent's murder. His name was Ivan Malinkov. See how much information there is on the internet, if there are any different stories or perspectives, maybe even ask your parents what they remember."

Chapter Fifty-Two

Michael punched the access code to the Umbergo retirement home and entered the drab, sterile environment of the lobby. The reddish-brown, ceramic floor tiles gave the entrance and the hallways the ambience of a kitchen. A dark gray loop carpet covered the lounge area and was meant to allow wheelchairs and walkers easy access, but also meant to hide the dust and dirt that would travel with these mobility aids for the elderly.

Michael glanced at a family gathered in the lounge, an ancient grandmother sitting in a wheelchair, her black shawl covering her head. Her daughter holding her hand and leaning forward to speak to the almost deaf ears. The husband sitting uncomfortably on the faux-leather lounge chair, wondering how many times the chair had been cleaned due to leaky adult diapers. Their teenage daughter looking down into her cell phone.

Michael walked to the elevator and went through the process of entering the security code twice more before he was able to visit his uncle. He passed the gauntlet of wheelchairs in the hallway where vacant minds were left to sit as part of the 'daily activity' that was mandated in the terms of care for the Alzheimer's and Dementia residents.

As he passed the room beside his uncle's, he noticed an old woman lying silently in the bed. He felt a tinge of sorrow for the old man who used to shout for Tony and Rita and wondered if either of them had ever come, or if they had just come for his funeral. He couldn't hear any singing from across the hall and wondered if she had also passed or whether her mind had depleted so much that even a trip to her childhood had been abandoned. Michael thought to himself, '*How this floor was once a Fellini film festival but had slowly dissipated into a silent limbo.*'

He walked into Uncle Pino's room, which was dimly lit with the curtains drawn, and he closed the door behind him. He greeted his uncle in his traditional way, bending to give him a kiss on the forehead. "It's dark in here

Uncle Pino," he said as he drew the curtains open. He unlocked the bottom drawer of the cabinet and retrieved the little boombox. He reached into the drawer and pulled out the five CDs he had collected over the past few months.

He put on the Buster Hawkins CD and the lyrics of the first song reminded him of how a lot of country music could be used as theme songs for the entire seventh floor of the retirement home.

"Alone on the prairie, Miles from my home, Dark skies are my friends, Where the doggies roam."

He sat in the chair beside his uncle, wondering if the spot on the wall where Pino constantly stared had any significance in another worldly dimension. He sat for ten more minutes in silence, listening to the music, collecting his own thoughts, waiting for his uncle to start the conversation, to ask the questions about the promise Michael had pledged to fulfill.

"Yup, I know what you mean," Michael said aloud, "those old country crooners really knew what they were talking about."

He waited a while longer until the CD finished playing and then he leaned over to his uncle, "Why do we have to go over this again and again? Yes, I did it just the way you told me too. Planned it all out and did it without leaving a trace. He has done penance for his sins."

After another moment of silence, he said with apprehension, "The gloves? There at the bottom of the Don River, weighted down with rocks."

He sat and listened to his uncle's response. "I know, I should have burned them too. I'm not sure how to put this, but those gloves represent a glimmer of excitement, an ascendancy to the celestial self. Just the fact that they remain somewhere sends chills up my spine. It's like a child stealing cookies, knowing if they were caught would mean trouble. That's what those gloves do for me, keeps that sense of adventure alive."

He watched his uncle and winced as if he was being admonished. "No, no, don't worry. Even if by some miracle they were found, they wouldn't be able to get anything from them. I wore those blue medical examination gloves underneath them, so there wouldn't be any hairs or sweat or anything they could use. Besides, after all this time in the river, they've been washed clean."

He sat quietly once more as if he was listening, and then smiled with affection, "You would have been proud of me Uncle, he's not going to be doing that kind of crap with anyone anymore."

The room was filled with a hollow silence while Michael put on another CD. He leaned back in the chair and stared at the ceiling. "What do you see?" he asked his uncle, "Is there an answer to what your life meant, an answer to wherever you go when the lights are turned off? Do you think that banker has gone to the same place?"

"I planned it perfectly. After I hit him with the crowbar, he went straight to the ground. I could see the bewilderment in his eyes, wondering what was going on and trying to scream at the same time. I added to the confusion in his head when he saw the knife in my hand. I'm sure shock had him in a deep state of paralysis and I don't know if he was able to understand the reality of what was happening when I thrust the knife in and pulled the edge of steel across his throat."

"And that was it, he was gone." Michael began to muse. "He was nothing more than the blood that poured onto the sidewalk. His existence would only be remembered until the chalk outline was washed away. His petty aspirations and insignificant desires brought to a climax in that moment when the crowbar swung toward his knee and the steel blade opened the veins in his neck. I wonder if he even realized the complete waste of his life as it flashed before his mind."

Michael listened to the music and felt a sense of pride. He had sought revenge for this man who raised him when his parents had died. He sought solace for the uncle who had taught him how to fish and hunt, who told him all about women and how they should be treated, who sent him to university and told him to become somebody.

He turned his head toward his uncle once more. "Yeah, I know, but he deserved it. Like you always told me, is there anything more useless than a banker? The only way they can make money is by taking yours. So, they scheme, and they plan, and they smile as they lie. And then they wonder why people despise them."

After another moment, he replied, "Yeah, you're right, it's all the simple manipulation of numbers, the basic principles of the universe devoid of all human senses. To them, we are nothing more than a few megabytes of data, a combination of zero's and one's. Zero for you, and one for them."

The music continued to play to the unreceptive audience, and Michael didn't move as he listened to the long ramble of his uncle's words. "Yes Uncle, you're right, where is the heart and soul of the human when they cannot see beyond the numbers, or feel beyond the ledger, or hear beyond the tap of the keyboard. Can they feel the void that is their lives and smell the fear that this may be their numeric karma?"

Michael felt tension in his shoulders. He wasn't expecting his uncle to question his actions or the reasons for them one more time. He didn't feel he needed to constantly justify what he did, and that his uncle should have been more supportive. He listened to the music and began to tap his feet to the honky-tonk rhythm of 'The Sky Up Above' as he looked around the room.

'It's depressing,' he thought to himself. This sterile, artless environment. A prison for the thoughtless continuation of nothing. He looked over at his uncle and wondered about the repercussions of humane euthanasia. He knew that if his uncle ever had one brief moment of clarity, he would look over at Michael and ask him, "Why are you leaving me like this? I don't want this. Put the pillow over my head and end this!" At that thought Michael shook with a nervous twitch, retreating from the reverie he feared.

He leaned toward his uncle and nodded a few times, answering invisible questions. "The alibi? Don't worry, it is virtually foolproof. I went to the late movie at the Beach Cinemas and bought two tickets with my credit card. That way there's a record of me being at the theatre on that night, supposedly with someone."

"The next night, I took Christine to the same movie but paid with cash. If for any reason they were to suspect me, I would have the credit card record for the movie and Christine wouldn't remember which night it was we went. I made sure to take her to the movies every week, at different times during the week."

He sat and listened to his uncle once more.

"If the police investigate or ask questions at the theatre, the kids working there don't know anything. A bunch of teenagers working part time jobs."

After another pause, "I checked. The video surveillance records are kept for three months. They are backed up to a tape and the tapes are sent for storage. They don't have permanent archives because the security surveillance is only for when something happens at the theatre. If nothing happens at the theatre, then the tapes are re-used."

He sat and listened to his uncle's criticism, then replied with vigor, "I'm a professional, I don't leave anything to chance. I went to the pub three or four times per week and at different hours of the evening. Sometimes I had dinner and sometimes I just stayed for a couple of drinks."

"I always had a notebook, and nobody could see what I was writing. If a waitress asked, I would just tell her that I was writing poetry or entries for my journal."

"Yes, my notes were thorough, just like you taught me. I knew how many drinks the prey usually had, what he was wearing, how long it took him to pay the bill. I always stayed near the corners, but I could see the prey whenever he was in the pub. I always paid cash for each drink, and I would leave at different times, sometimes before the prey and sometimes afterward."

Michael listened solemnly and then responded. "I did it this way to prevent any sort of pattern developing so no one would notice when I came and went."

He listened to his uncle once more and answered, "They were 'burner phones' and I paid with cash. They ended up in the river as well, and before you ask, yes, they were cleaned, not a trace left on them. The water will take care of everything else about them."

Michael sat back and listened to the music while he tried not to listen to his uncle's reprimands. "It was all his fault," Michael raised his voice. "He suggested you purchase those bonds or stocks or whatever they were. He told you they would take care of your future. It was because of him that caused the rift within the family. After those fucking things collapsed, you and Zia fought so much that she went back to Rome with Maria. And when Zia died, you were too sick to even go to the funeral. And what happened to that bastard? He walked away and went to work for another bank while all those people who lost money suffered."

Michael got up and started to pace the room, turning toward his uncle every few moments. The anger inside of him seethed for the banker.

"Yeah, I killed him. I brought him Karma with pain."

He stopped pacing and turned toward his uncle. His expression of anger slowly turned to a resignation of bitter truth as he responded to his uncle. "The only people who can understand hell," he said, "are the ones who have been there. And I've sent him there."

Chapter Fifty-Three

Michael arrived at his home on Crown Park Road and parked his car in the small driveway. He loved living in the Beaches and could hear the rat-a-tat-tat of a woodpecker in the park to the west of his home. He casually walked the twenty-odd yards to the park and stood looking into the Glen Manor ravine. He breathed in the crispness of the early evening.

The trees were fully covered in leaves and the birds began their ritual song and dance in worship of the setting sun. They flew one full circle in the sky, hundreds of them, and then settled into two trees that were side by side. They sang to the sunset, just before the sun dipped below the horizon, when the last shards of light were still illuminating their avian world.

Michael stood at the edge of the park and listened to their song, like a frantic prayer to the fading light, and then they zoomed once more into the sky. They soared, circling and then came back to the highest tree branches where the last remnants of light still shone.

He watched the sun fall under the buildings on the other side of the ravine. The birdsong ended and after several minutes of contemplation, he turned and walked back toward the house, a small smile of gratification on his lips. A confident smile in which he knew his life was good and would continue to be good. His thoughts were clear, without anxiety, and he walked up the stone walkway to his front door.

He didn't use his key because he was confident she would be there, patiently awaiting the arrival of her master. He turned the knob and felt the unlocked door give way, and this knowledge of his surety gave him a feeling of comfort, and a feeling of supremacy.

He found her kneeling in the middle of the living room on the Persian carpet, her back straight, head up and hands folded on her lap, wearing only the black leather basque around her torso.

"Good evening Sir," she said in a calm, modest, respectful tone.

"Good evening my Jewel," he replied and removed his shoes. He stood tall and took a deep breath, feeling a sense of empowerment, but the smile quickly turned away from his face. He looked over to his Jewel, "That is not the incense I told you to use for my arrival."

She bent her head down and gazed at the floor, "I am sorry Sir."

He slowly walked over to her and reached out his hand, stroking through her blonde hair, then he walked over to the high back, velvet accent chair which almost looked like a throne, and spoke as he sat down. "Were you not listening when I gave your instructions?"

"I'm sorry Sir," she repeated with a tremble in her voice.

With his left hand, he motioned for her to come and lay face down across his lap. Bending over, she crawled on her hands and knees until she was on the floor beside him. She rose and laid her body across his lap, her hands and feet on the floor to either side of him. He commenced to spank her with light taps that slowly grew in intensity until the smacks were loud and hard.

She did not cry out, and there was no hint of complaint. She accepted her punishment until she could bear it no more, and she began to whimper. After another minute, small tears began to appear on her cheek. That's when he decided to stop, for he knew that her tears were not because of the pain, she cried because she had disappointed him.

He motioned for her to remove herself from his lap. She lifted her arms and slid down to the floor by his side. Once sitting, she lifted her right arm over his lap and placed her head upon his thigh, her traditional pose of respect and worship.

Michael began to stroke her hair in a sedate manner and then spoke to her, "I listened to the ritual of the birds again and it left me breathless. I'm often amazed that so many people pass by without any notice of this mystical spectacle that happens above their heads."

"Wonderful Sir," she purred a reply, "perhaps the birds recognize the power that stands before them. Was it a beautiful end to your day?"

"Yes, today was good day. In one class, we had a discussion that you would have taken great joy in participating. We discussed the differences between societal history and personal history. At one point, I reflected on the death of Ivan and how it may have personally affected people who lived in the Beaches community. I asked the class to tell me about their own personal experiences of the murder."

"That would have been most interesting to hear, Sir. I can almost see you standing in front of the class, listening to them repeat the gossip and news articles, but if they could only see behind your eyes the knowledge of the truth. It must have elevated your sense of power to stand before them and listen."

"It was a most exquisite feeling," Michael admitted, "the discussion was exceptional. To listen to all the stories and rumors that these kids had heard, it glorified our joining. I found it difficult to keep the discussion as a class lesson and to remain outside the actual events. I was almost tempted to reveal something about the murder."

She looked up into his face with an expression of alarm in her eyes. Michael looked down and smiled, "Don't worry my Jewel, I would never threaten our union on a whim."

She lowered her head on his lap once more, "Sir, may I ask a question?"

"Yes, my Jewel, you may."

She began to speak with a touch of trepidation in her voice, "I was wondering Sir, if you will be required to date any other women in the future?"

"That would depend upon the need," he responded warmly, "for now we are going to lay low and not draw any attention to ourselves. Perhaps, at some point, we may feel the need to raise ourselves to that special intensity once more. Our anniversary is only a few months away and I may want to give you another gift."

"Do you have plans for anyone in mind Sir?"

"There is one person that I have been contemplating," he said with an eyebrow lifted, "but we will have to discuss this at a much deeper level and determine if she meets all the criteria before we begin planning."

"The people we have brought to our dominion both deserved to die." Michael said as if giving a lesson in philosophy, "When we look at the aspects that define the quality of life, we can define it with certain principles; there is love, there is also creativity, compassion; intellect; education; honor and respect. And lastly, there is a sense social morality."

"When I contemplate those aspects in determining the quality of anyone's life, I would have to conclude that both Ivan and Kyle had very little, if any quality. When we evaluate those two individuals, most of their actions would classify them as inferior."

"Thank you, Sir, your perspective is always concise and accurate. What they did to other people was a complete lack of respect for the ideals of life itself."

The two sat quietly while Michael continued to stroke her hair. They often discussed the intensity of the pleasure they felt. The union of their secrecy had created a bond between them, a bond that went very deep into their psyche and resulted in the ultimate connection between two people in their conspiracy for murder.

It wasn't something they had originally planned for and didn't know they would achieve that coalesced fusion of two people, but once the bond was formed, it became an unbreakable intimacy. Their secret was their proof, and it provided the power to electrify their sensations and intensify the ecstasy of both their physical pain and pleasure.

"May I ask another question, Sir?"

"Yes."

"When you talked about having someone else in mind, you said it was a 'she'. May I ask whom you intend to elevate to our dominion?"

"I was thinking about a certain police detective, a woman. The one who interviewed me for Ivan's murder. She believes she is a dominant because of her police training, but it is not a power that comes to her naturally, so we may want to show her who she really is."

"I have given it great thought and I believe it would be best if we approached her in a bar, and we would have to figure out a way to slip her drink with a roofie and then bring her home. We have a lot of details to work out, but the basement is almost ready with the modifications I have made."

"Do you mean we are going to keep her in my dungeon Sir?"

"It is Our dungeon Jewel," he corrected her, "and when she is here, we will have a new playmate for a short while. I want her to see who I truly am, see what you truly are, feel what true domination is. I want her to see what real power can be and I want her submission."

"This would be a special anniversary present for you, one in which you could partake in the pleasures of her submission. Probably not this November, but perhaps the next."

****

They continued to sit in the living room for a short while and then Michael moved her head aside and rose. He went to the liquor cabinet and poured himself a glass of Tullamore Dew Irish whiskey. He did not offer any to his Jewel, for he would never 'offer' her anything. He would always tell her what she wanted, and she would accept whatever he chose.

He sat back in his chair and she resumed her position by his side, "Sir, can we talk about the banker?"

"Yes, of course."

"I was so afraid when I was in that bar, wearing that black wig and floppy hat. When I called you, I was terrified, the phone was shaking in my hand. When I left the pub and I looked down the street and saw everybody crowding around the body, a part of me felt like running, but then another part of me wanted to move toward the crowd, to see what we had done. It took a few moments to remember what you told me to do."

"You did very well Jewel." Michael said as he lovingly stroked her hair, "You turned the corner and walked up Bathurst just as we discussed, and nobody noticed you. Anything that might have been caught on camera would have showed a woman with long black hair, a floppy hat and a long dark coat that will never be found. If anyone had been looking out the window of the condo across the street, they would have been watching the crowd around the body. Even if they did see you, no one would be able to identify you at that distance."

"I felt…I felt so alive Sir. I felt so terrified and so excited at the same time. And later, when I dropped the phone into the river off the Arch bridge, well…no one will ever know what we did."

Michael now spoke with warmness in his voice. "You are my Jewel, my exhilaration, my source of rhapsody. You are my secret treasure. I love you more than anything else."

"When I think about that night," she continued excitedly, "coming out of the pub and seeing Kyle's body lying there on the sidewalk, the chill started in my brain and began tingling at the base of my neck. Then it went straight down my spine and right into my vagina. I got so wet thinking about you, thinking about what you did…for us. Whenever I think about it, I get so wet, and then an insatiable desire for you to fuck me just overtakes me. I want you so much Sir, I want you so deep inside of me."

Michael grabbed his Jewel by the hair, pulling it back hard and exposing her neck. He sank to his knees beside her, biting into the skin of her neck, pulling her hair and making her squirm. He pulled her body down to the rug and quickly removed his pants. He moved his body down and took her breast into his mouth. He bit hard on her nipple until she whimpered at the dual sensations of pain and pleasure. He moved over top of her and entered her with all the force of his power.

They made love on the living room floor, a fierce, exited, rough sex that was empowered by the raw feelings of their crimes. He exploded inside of her and when both were spent with exhaustion, they showered together, washed each other's body and made love one more time under the steaming hot water.

Later, they both slipped into bed, under the covers, wrapped in each other's arms. They held on as if they were protecting each other, as if the entire world outside of their bedroom was nothing more than memory.

"May I speak, Sir?" Jewel whispered.

"Yes." Michael whispered back.

"May I honor you Sir and use your name?"

He lifted his head and looked directly into her eyes and gave a slight nod. She bent her neck up and kissed his lips. "Goodnight Michael, I love you."

He kissed the top of her head, "Goodnight Laura."

****

The next morning, Michael rose from the bed, put on jeans and a T-shirt. He went into the kitchen, unscrewed the large espresso pot and carefully measured the imported Italian coffee into the small cylindrical basket. He put the pot onto the stove and turned the heat up high. As the pot began to steam and percolate, Laura came into the kitchen wearing a thin, short bathrobe that Michael had bought for her.

"Good morning Sir," she said, "the coffee smells wonderful."

Michael walked over to her and slowly opened the front of her robe, cupping her left breast in his right hand. "Good morning Jewel, are you ready for another busy day at the office?"

She felt the warmth of his hand as he fondled her breast, her mind wandering to the different scenes in their relationship he had created specifically for her. He removed his hand and poured two cups of coffee, handing one to her.

At that moment, the doorbell rang, and Michael went to the living room. He took a quick look at the front window and wondered who would be calling at this hour in the morning. He called out as he approached the door, "Who is it?"

"Good morning Mr. Barratino, it is Sergeant Detective Boyle. I spoke with you last year about the Ivan Malinkov murder case, which I am still investigating. I have a number of questions I need to ask you."

"I'm not dressed right now," he lied, "can you wait a few minutes."

"No Mr. Barratino, we cannot. We need for you to open the door right now." Boyle insisted.

Michael quickly stepped back into the kitchen and put his finger to his lips in a motion for Laura to keep quiet. He went up to her and whispered in her ear, indicating she should go into the bedroom and wait out of sight, away from the windows.

"Mr. Barratino," Boyle called out once more, "open the door immediately or we will have to use force to gain entry."

Michael opened the door and saw Boyle, Sergeant Detective Curtis, Constables Singleton and Garrison standing on his doorstep, "What's this all about officer. I thought you were finished with that case last year."

"We have developed a new line of inquiry," Boyle said as he was about to step into the door. "We have a warrant for you to come in for questioning."

Michael tried to close the door, but the heavy booted foot of Constable Garrison blocked the threshold of the doorway. Garrison then used his body as leverage and with the help of Singleton they forced the door inward knocking Michael back into the living room. Singleton and Garrison quickly went inside and grabbed Michael by the arms. Detective Curtis followed them in and slapped a handcuff on Michael's wrist, then twisted his arm behind his back. Garrison forced the other arm behind the back and Curtis snapped on the other half of the handcuff.

"Mr. Michael Barratino," Curtis stated with authority, "we are arresting you for the murders of Ivan Malinkov and Kyle Wilson. You have the right to retain counsel immediately. You can call any lawyer you want, or you can be provided with a legal aid duty lawyer. Do you understand?"

"On what basis are you making these charges? What evidence do you have?" Michael yelled back at Curtis.

Boyle stared directly at Michael, catching his eye and holding him in place with his glare, "We've been monitoring the movements of Laura Cahill for the past week. This has led us to you."

Boyle then turned to Detective Baldoni who had now walked into the living room, "Gina, please take your team and find Ms. Cahill."

Baldoni, Evanko and Davis moved through the house, checking each room until they came to the master bedroom. They found Laura standing still, petrified. Laura offered no resistance while Evanko took one arm and fastened a handcuff on her wrist. Davis placed Laura's other arm behind her back and Evanko handcuffed that wrist as well. Baldoni then stated the charges and while she was explaining her rights to her, Laura's eyes rolled up into her head and fell faint to the floor.

Chapter Fifty-Four

Boyle and Baldoni sat pensively in the interview room at 55 Division station. Michael Barratino sat across from them, handcuffs attached to a steel ring near the edge of the table. His lawyer sat beside him, scribbling fast on a notepad to incorporate as much information as he could gather on his client's behalf.

"Detective Boyle," the lawyer stated, "I cannot see any evidence that suggests my client has anything to do with either of the murders. He has a proven alibi for both nights the murders were committed; you have no physical evidence that incriminates him, and you have no witnesses that can identify him at the scene of either crime. You don't even have any evidence that could be considered circumstantial."

Baldoni opened her laptop and turned it so both Michael and the lawyer could see the screen. She played the video footage from the Wheat Sheaf security camera that displayed the killing of Kyle. The lawyer objected, stating it was irrelevant to Michael's arrest. The killer in the video could have been anybody, male or female. Michael watched the video with no visible reaction. Baldoni then played the video when the woman with the floppy hat left the Sly Fox. She then switched to the footage of the security camera within the pub, and the one frame where Laura turned her head, and the lower part of her face was clearly visible under the dark glasses and hat.

She opened a picture of Laura from her driver's license and placed them side-by-side. The facial recognition software took a split second to analyze both pictures, survey the bone structure of the chin, nose and cheeks, and concluded they were a match.

Michael said coldly, "That doesn't prove anything about me, and it also doesn't prove she had anything to do with it. If you ran that software through the health card registrations photos, there would probably be thousands of matches."

Boyle sat back calmly and asked Baldoni to play the final video. "This is from the Wheat Sheaf Tavern security camera once again." Boyle stated, "It was recorded about three hours before the crime was committed."

She stopped the video and froze on a car travelling north on Bathurst, toward Adelaide.

"You drive the same model and color of car Michael." Boyle slowly unwound his conversation, "Now, we know it's not the exact same license plate number, however, a little white tape can alter the eight into a three, the 'E' into an 'F' and a 'O' into an 'C'. We believe this is what you did and that this was your car. So, if your car was there, you couldn't have been at the theatre."

"That evidence is circumspect," the lawyer plainly stated, "you can wish the license plate number was Michael's, but it's not. Also, there is no evidence that my client was anywhere near the Malinkov murder scene."

Boyle remained icily calm and continued to stare at Michael, "Laura knew all about the security system Ivan had in the house, how he turned it off when he was home."

Boyle kept any excitement in check and wanted to only show restraint in his manner of speech.

He wanted Michael to feel secure in his knowledge they didn't have anything, so he calmly went on, "She also knew about the sound-proofing insulation that had been installed. She even recommended the same company to some of her clients. You both knew Ivan was going to be there alone, because Ivan was waiting for her."

"This is all theoretical detective," the lawyer interjected, "you still haven't shown me anything that validates my client being arrested at all."

"We found ammonia and Pine Sol in the laundry room of your client's house." Boyle stated, not looking at the lawyer.

"And how does that implicate my client?"

"The weapons used in both murders were intricately cleaned with those chemicals."

"Those solvents can be found in thousands of homes across Toronto. This evidence is also improbable and highly circumstantial."

"I don't know exactly how you did it," Boyle spoke directly to Michael, ignoring the lawyer's comments, "between the gags, blindfolds and that sensory deprivation mask we found in your bedroom closet, I imagine there was some sort of ruse to make Linda believe you were with her the whole time. I can only imagine what her reaction will be when we suggest you may have brought in other men as substitutes during your play."

"Still speculative," the lawyer insisted. "Linda Santiago has already stated Michael was with her the whole night. Unless you can present any shred of evidence that my client was anywhere near either of the murder scenes, then I must insist these charges are expeditious."

Boyle leaned forward and put his elbows on the table and cupped his hands in front of him. He did this while looking directly into Michael's eyes. "Laura has been identified as being in the Sly Fox on the night of Kyle Wilson's murder. She was captured on the security video footage making a phone call just as Kyle was leaving the pub. She left a short while afterward and went straight north to her car."

"The only thing that proves is someone who looks partially like Ms. Cahill was in the Sly Fox on the night Kyle Wilson was murdered. That still does not prove anything about my client," the lawyer stated emphatically.

"We'll see what Laura has to say in her interview." Boyle confidently said while still staring in Michael's eyes.

"Detective Boyle," the lawyer began to insist, "my client has an air-tight alibi for both evenings when the murders took place. There's no real proof he was at either scene. You also have admitted that Ms. Cahill wasn't actually at either of the murder scenes. My client has an alibi for both evenings and has people who will testify that Michael was with them the whole evening and night. Anything Ms. Cahill may tell you would simply make it his word against hers, but his alibis still hold the greater weight."

"We'll see," said Boyle, "we'll see," but Boyle knew they didn't have enough to keep Michael Barratino in custody, and that he would probably get bail at the arraignment. Boyle had nothing else to use, and he was quickly running out of tactics to utilize. Michael's lawyer was good, and their positioned seemed legally judicious.

It was already past five o'clock, and Boyle was tired. He didn't know where to take the interview without simply repeating everything the lawyer had already answered, and he desperately needed something, anything to keep Michael Barratino under custody. He sat back thinking, trying to seem confident while he stared at Michael.

"Detective Boyle, if there isn't anything else—" the lawyer began to say but was interrupted by a loud knock on the interview room door. Pierre Archambault opened the door and without entering summoned Boyle to come out for a moment. Boyle went into the hallway and the two detectives spoke for a minute. When Boyle re-entered the room, he sat once more at the table, facing Michael. He sat calmly and stared into Michael's eyes. Michael's demeanor remained imperturbable and he simply looked back at Boyle with a confidence.

Then a small smile broke upon Boyle's face. Michael saw the smile and his brain started working quickly, but before he could come to any conclusions, Boyle broke the silence and spoke with a cold, deliberate voice, "She gave you up."

****

Later that evening, the sun was slowly setting over the houses to the west of Boyle's front porch. Glimmers of light siphoned through the leaves of the neighboring trees. Boyle puffed on his Cubano, then blew the smoke out in a slow, lazy exhalation that created a long drift of whitish fumes. He reached down for his glass of brandy, took a long sip, then turned to speak.

"How do you like that Monte Cristo?"

"Smooth," said Curtis, "this is something I could get used to. Sitting here in contemplation, with a cigar and a brandy. Reminds me of those crime novels by Raymond Chandler, the ones with Philip Marlowe sitting at his kitchen table with a pot of coffee and a pack of cigarettes."

Boyle smiled at the analogy he had often considered. It had been a long day and he felt comfortable being with a person who understood how he felt, who appreciated the need for release from obligations, and for de-stressing. It had been a full day of questioning. Michael Barratino was intelligent and confident, and Boyle knew that unless he could get something from him, the prosecutor would not have much except for Laura's testimony.

However, a psychological assessment of Laura could provide the defense with enough doubt to put the case against Michael in jeopardy.

"Tell me, Randal," Boyle asked calmly, "how did you get Laura to talk so quickly?"

Curtis took a long puff from his own cigar and contemplated his words. He exhaled slowly and then spoke frankly, "I knew we didn't have much, only the possibility that she was in the bar. I knew that if she kept quiet and didn't answer any questions, our case would fold like an accordion."

"However, I also knew she was a complicit part of the things Michael did. She had to be more than just his submissive in a BDSM relationship. She would have been a willing, brainwashed slave, susceptible to any suggestion Michael gave her. I researched some interesting facts about mind control and the power dynamic it entails. Michael pushed that power to the extreme. He may have even used hypnotic suggestions to manipulate her. I reasoned that I needed to break that power Michael had on her and to prove to her that I was in power."

"Brilliant," Boyle said honestly, "but how did you manage that in one day of interviewing?"

Curtis took another puff of his cigar, "I knew she was afraid, probably terrified, and I decided to tap into that fear. I started with the silent treatment, just starring at her with a look of pure domination. She kept looking down and then would briefly look up to glance at me and then look down again. Every time she looked up my stare grew harder. I knew her mind had been subjugated for at least a couple of years and that Michael's power over her was absolute. I had to give her time to think, and time to feel the presence of another power."

"I kept up the silent treatment for over an hour. Her lawyer kept objecting, but then she started crying and I knew she was becoming susceptible. Her fear was mixed with confusion, because she no longer had Michael to direct her thoughts and actions. I started by giving her small commands as sublimely as I could. First, I told her to sit up straight, then to put her hands on the table. Whenever she looked at me, I could sense the confusion and fear. I could also sense she knew I was acting as her dominator because her willingness to obey my suggestions was like a reflex she couldn't stop."

"I continued with the small commands and then asked her what her name was. When she didn't respond right away, I asked once more with a louder, heavier tone. She glanced up, and in a whisper said Laura. I pounded the table once and it made her jump, and in a forceful voice I told her to call me Sir whenever she replied."

"The lawyer tried to protest but I kept looking directly at her and told the lawyer that my rank of Sergeant Detective deserved respect. When the lawyer continued to protest, I continued to stare at her and announced that I have decided to stop for a break, and I instructed Pierre to handcuff her to the table."

"She looked up at me and the glint in my eyes made it clear that this was her punishment for disobeying. Just before I left the room, I turned and stared hard at her, then said what I hoped would be the beginning of her break from the grip of Michael."

"What did you say?" Boyle asked.

"I told her that she will never see Michael again, that he no longer owned her, and right now in this moment, I own you. Then I stared at her for a while to let that thought sink in, then left. When I returned, I instructed Pierre to remove the handcuffs, and in this way, she knew that I controlled the scene. I told her once more to sit up straight, then I again asked her to tell me her name. She meekly said her name but didn't use the proper honorific of Sir. I glared down at her and said we would take another break. I instructed Pierre to handcuffed her to the table once more. I continued this treatment for as long as it took."

"The lawyer protested, but there wasn't anything that was inappropriate. Everything was within the confines of standard procedure and there was nothing he could really argue against. However, Laura got the message and after the fourth or fifth time I re-entered the room, she immediately sat up straight. When I asked her name, she squirmed a little and replied, 'Laura, Sir'."

"I had Pierre remove the cuffs, but I noticed a peculiar look on her face, almost like a look of disappointment. I saw that this could be my opportunity to gain her confidence, or her submissive confidence, or whatever that state of mind is." So, I gently asked her, "Do you like wearing the handcuffs?"

She hesitated for a moment, and then replied, "Yes."

I gently asked, "Yes, what?"

She looked up at me and I could see that look of resignation. It was a strange look, like the act of relinquishing your will. And she responded, "Yes, Sir."

I asked her if she would feel better with the handcuffs on, and once again she responded, "Yes, Sir."

"I instructed Pierre to put the cuffs on her again and I noticed a sense of calm, or relief come over her, then I told her to give me her full name. She calmly replied, 'Laura Elizabeth Cahill' after a second of silence I slapped the table hard. She jumped in her chair and then replied with the honorific 'Sir'. That's when I knew she was beginning the ritual of submissiveness, that she was gradually accepting me as her dominant. In the world of BDSM, this is part of the training for a submissive."

"How do you know all this?" Boyle questioned.

"Hell, Ari, you can find out anything you want on the internet these days. I found a ton of information on protocols, training and procedure. They were even some blogs written by Dominatrix's on how to make your submissive obey."

"We knew that we didn't have enough evidence to bring them to trial, so the only option was to secure a confession. Laura was probably the most susceptible to confessing, but I knew that I would have to re-condition her mind from the control Michael exerted over her."

"Once I had her in the state where she accepted me as a Dom by showing the signs of respect like automatically using the proper honorific, I progressed slowly and drew more of her submission out of her."

"I told her to take a deep breath in a calm but insisting voice. She was so afraid that she just fell into being a submissive, probably because that is what was natural to her. I would almost say it seemed more comfortable for her. As we began to talk, I would constantly give her commands to follow. When she slouched, I would tell her to sit up straight. I would tell her to put her hands on the table and I would tell her to take a drink of water. When she responded to all of my commands with 'Sir', that's when I knew that she was going to be receptive to any question I asked."

"I don't know if the lawyer ever figured out what I was trying to do, but when he saw the reactions of his client to everything I asked or commanded, I think he was a little fascinated by it, and if it wasn't a sense of fascination, then it was definitely a sense of doubt about his client's mental state."

"I'm surprised her lawyer didn't have any stronger objections." Boyle said.

"Honestly, there wasn't anything for him to object to. The interview was conducted strictly within the letter of the law. I'm sure he noticed that I was being harsh with her, but he had probably seen much more intense interviews in the past. Nevertheless, there was no severe yelling or threats, just simple commands."

"I admit that I might have been approaching the boundaries of impropriety, but I never stepped over the line, so there's nothing they could claim as being improper. If anyone questions why I kept handcuffing her when I left the room, I can honestly claim that I was concerned about her potentially trying to injure herself."

"As we continued with the questioning, it became obvious that she was accustomed to being controlled, so I continued to give her small commands throughout. I told her to look me in the eyes, take more deep breaths, take a sip of water. When I saw that she was immediately following the commands, and always responding with 'Yes, Sir', that's when I took it a little deeper."

"It almost seemed too simple, but the fear and anxiety she must have felt was probably overwhelming her. She even began to gently stroke the handcuffs, as if she was rubbing a lucky charm. I guess she was so used to obeying orders from her dominant that a void was created within her mind when she realized Michael would no longer be directing her life. She needed that sense of control, of being commanded and being told what to do."

"That's when I started to question her in earnest, or should I say, subtly commanded her to tell me what she and Michael had done. At first, she hesitated, and she tried to avoid eye contact, so I went back to commanding her to sit up straight, take a breath, drink some water, but now I began to use a softer voice with a little edge. I kept reinforcing this perception of control. This went on for a couple of hours; question, command and compliance, until one point when she looked up at me and I saw that blank stare of someone who had surrendered."

"I decide this was the time to begin maneuvering toward a real confession. I gave her some more simple commands, then I asked her about her relationship with Ivan, about what she had told Gina in her interview a couple of years ago. I asked her to repeat what she had said about Ivan abusing her. She started telling the story, but I interrupted her and pointed out how he cheated her. She looked up at me a little surprised and replied, 'Yes, Sir, you're right'. Then she continued with the story and I interrupted her once more and pointed out how he had duped her into having sex with him. She seemed to appreciate the validation I was giving her, and her sense of shame mixed with anger came forth as she continued to relate her story."

"Did you hate him for what he did to you?"

"Yes," she replied, "Sir."

That's when I asked the question, "Was he expecting you that night?"

She bowed her head and in a small, tiny voice said, "Yes, Sir."

That was it, her confession, her surrender. Then I quickly asked, "You were not part of the murders, were you? You just followed your commands and helped in the planning."

In a soft, acquiescent voice she replied, "Yes, Sir." She bowed her head into her hands and started to sob. I let her cry until she regained her composure. From that point on, I commanded her to slowly tell me the whole story. And it all came out."

"And the lawyer?" Boyle asked.

"When we showed the security video footage of her at the Sly Fox after she made the initial confession, I could see he was starting to think about an insanity plea. You know, brainwashed captive, Stockholm syndrome, something like that."

"Brilliant," Boyle repeated, "how and when did you decide to use this Dominant/Submissive technique. I don't know if I would have figured out doing the interview in this way."

"Well, to be honest," said Curtis, "I thought about it the night of the arrest. Laura's reaction to being arrested, fainting and then acting like small frightened rabbit. I decided to research the mind control aspect, how it could affect her emotionally. I went online to research BDSM after we found the leather and fetish gear at Michael's place and especially that dungeon scenario we discovered in his basement. We knew what Michael was capable of and how meticulous he was in planning and executing his crimes. I felt he had probably planned her control just as much as he planned everything else."

"Full control," Boyle said more to himself than to Curtis. He took another long puff from his cigar and then turned to Curtis, "Michael controlled everything. He orchestrated both murders to the finest details, including having a partner he could control, one that he could manipulate and use as another tool in his crimes. He used her to get exact information about Ivan's home, and he used her to set up the situation with Ivan being alone. He used her to be the advanced scout, so he knew exactly when Kyle was leaving the bar and if he was alone. It was complete control of everything."

Curtis took a long drink from his glass, tilting it high so that he drained it in one large gulp. Boyle reached for the bottle and offered to refill but Curtis put his hand over the glass.

"There's something else," Curtis spoke in the same tone members of the police force use to tell someone of a death in their family. Boyle looked over, his eyes making direct contact, and waited for whatever it was Curtis wanted to tell him.

"There's something else that you should know, and I wanted you to hear it from me. They, or should I say Michael, had started planning another murder."

Boyle didn't say anything and waited until Curtis was ready to continue. Throughout his career, Boyle had learned the value of silence, and the patience of waiting until someone was ready to divulge whatever news was forthcoming.

Curtis exhaled a deep breath, "I haven't put it in the report yet, but I thought you should know. Laura confessed that Michael was planning something special for Gina."

In an instant, Boyle's mind envisioned thousands of scenarios that could have happened. He slowly turned his head and with a serious, angered look said. "I'm interviewing him again in the morning, I'm going to reveal to him that the control of his submissive was not as intense as he believed it would be. And then I'm going to break him."

Curtis looked over, "I'll take that refill now if you don't mind."

Boyle poured the brandy into Curtis' goblet. The two detectives looked into each other's eyes. It was a look that only people who fully understand the emotions, frustrations and anger of criminal investigations could share.

Chapter Fifty-Five

The next morning, Boyle sat in the interview room with Baldoni to his right, Michael and his lawyer across from him at the table. Michael was handcuffed to the heavy ring and the lawyer requested these be removed as his client did not present a threat to anyone in the room.

Boyle smiled and looked at Michael as he said, "A professional hit-man is always a threat."

The lawyer looked stunned by this comment and spoke with dismayed appall, "Detective Boyle, are you seriously suggesting that my client is some sort of professional killer for hire?"

"No, of course not," Boyle said, still smiling. "However, according to Laura, he seems to think he is."

"I repeat my statements from yesterday," the lawyer went on, "unless you have some substantial physical evidence to hold my client in custody, we will be seeking bail and immediate release this afternoon."

"We have a full confession from his lover, Laura Cahill, and we will be objecting to any bail agreements as we feel he is a potential risk to society and that he may try to flee. The judge will agree, and he will remain in custody until I'm finished with him."

"Detective Boyle, once again I have to state my client has valid alibis for the evenings of both murders, and you still have no evidence that places him anywhere near the murder scenes. You may have secured a questionable confession from his lover, but we will argue that she confessed under duress and fear and maybe even jealousy as it was revealed that Michael had been with other women."

Boyle ignored the lawyer's comments and just kept smiling while looking at Michael, "You chose a wonderful submissive in Laura. She seemed to fulfill all of your needs. However, your one mistake was that you failed to realize how highly submissive she is to all Dominants," and then he slowly enunciated each of the following words, "and there is no one more dominant than Sergeant Detective Randal Curtis."

Michael didn't say anything but looked over to the mirror on the far wall. As he stared at the reflection of his image, the idea slowly germinated in his brain and the realization of his loss of power. He turned toward Boyle and they stared at each other across the table, like hunter and prey.

Boyle slowly repeated his last statement from yesterday, "She gave you up," he said, "she gave you up, completely."

Michael starred hard at Boyle and then spoke, "You've got nothing."

Boyle sat back in his chair and decided to slowly begin the revelations, "Detective Baldoni is an attractive woman, but she is extremely physically fit. She could probably break you in half." He sat forward once more, leaning on the table, the smile gone from his face, "What did you have planned for her?"

Michael glanced in Gina's direction and saw the intensity of her anger. His brain started to cipher through all the different things Laura could possibly have told them.

Boyle saw Michael's demeanor change slightly and quickly struck another psychological blow, "Maybe we could speak with your uncle, Giuseppe Garabaldi, or Uncle Pino as you call him. I'm sure he will have a lot to tell us. Laura says he is your personal confidant, that you discuss everything with him."

"Leave him alone." Michael spoke with a strong voice, "He's a sick man and doesn't need to be bothered by you."

"Laura says that you tell him everything." Boyle poked harder.

This time it was Michael who smiled, "Ask him, see what he has to tells you."

"I won't need to." Boyle kept his calmness, "Laura has already told us everything. She has given us details of every plan, including the bonfires up north to destroy evidence. We have some officers on the way there to see if there is anything they can find in the ashes."

"Laura has been very cooperative." Boyle continued, "She is no longer your slave, but most of all, she knows that you no longer have power over her."

Michael pulled at the handcuffs on the table with a sudden jolt and said with a confident, hard equal tone, "She is my treasure. That will never change."

"She belongs to Detective Curtis now." Boyle spoke with a determined sarcasm.

Michael kept his voice even but strong, "She is mine. I trained her. She does what I tell her to do."

"What is the point of these questions, or allegations Detective Boyle?" the lawyer tried to intercede to keep his client calm and then advised him, "Michael, only answer questions directly related to the accusations they have made against you."

"Did you tell her to call you when Kyle left the bar?" Boyle asked quickly.

As if he hadn't heard his lawyer's advice Michael responded, "She does everything I tell her. She is my slave. She is mine."

"Not any longer." Boyle leaned forward to look deeper into Michael's eyes. "She belongs to Detective Curtis and she is going to do and say whatever Detective Curtis wants."

The anger within Michael started to rise, "No! She's mine."

"Stop this!" the lawyer interjected.

"Did Uncle Pino tell you to kill Kyle Wilson or did Laura tell you to do it?" Boyle quickly asked to keep the momentum of anger.

Michael's misguided pride caused his anger to rise, "No, she does exactly what I tell her to do."

"Did she manipulate you into killing Ivan?" Boyle continued taunting him.

"No!" Michael shouted, "I'm the Master, I'm the one in control."

"Did she sleep with Ivan? Was that something you wanted her to do or was that something she wanted to do. Did she sleep with Kyle Wilson?" Boyle used as much sarcasm as he could.

"She's my treasure and she does what I say." Michael said as if he was trying to convince himself.

"She wanted revenge on Ivan for what he did to her. She convinced you to kill him," the intensity in Boyle's voice became thick with his own anger.

"No!" Michael pulled on his handcuffs.

"She was the master planner of these murders, wasn't she Michael." Boyle mocked him, "Laura was the one in control."

Michael yelled as he stood to his feet, "I'm the one in control."

"You're not in control. She's the one who manipulated you. You're a pathetic dominant that has control over no one."

"I said stop this!" the lawyer tried to intervene once more.

"Laura convinced you to kill Ivan, and then she commanded you to continue her wishes and kill Kyle." Boyle's anger seethed through his teeth.

Michael remained standing, looking down at Boyle, hovering over him, "I'm in control. I am the Master. I tell my treasure what to do and she obeys only me."

"If you're the one in control, then why was she in the Sly Fox that night? Why was she the one controlling the scene and telling you what to do?"

"She was instructed to call me when he left." Michael said in defiance.

An astonished silence filled the atmosphere of the room. Boyle sat back in his chair, knowing that the hunter had now trapped his prey. Michael fell back into his chair, the shocked looked of disbelief covered his face. The lawyer had a dumfounded look, his mouth slightly agape.

Boyle's anger quickly dissipated, and he spoke in a calm finality, "Yes Michael, you were in control. You were in control."

Michael sat in a morose silence, and then he slowly lowered his head and placed it in his arms on the table. He began to softly cry and murmured some words through his tears, "Don't tell Uncle Pino, please don't tell Uncle Pino."

Boyle turned to the lawyer, "I think we have enough to prevent your client from ever being released on bail. He will be held in custody as we continue our investigation," then he turned to Michael and said, "those handcuffs will stay on until I say for them to be removed. In this place, I'm in control."

Boyle turned to the lawyer once more, "We're going to need some psychological assessments. I suggest you get your own people to do the same."

He stood up from the table and took one last look at the man whimpering before him. He felt empty of thought, empty of purpose, empty of any emotion. He turned and opened the door, then turned back toward Baldoni, "Gina, I need to have a cigar and a walk in the park. Want to have a coffee with me and King Edward?"

"Sure Boss," she replied, "double cream, no sugar."